ROGUE

James Swallow is the *New York Times*, *Sunday Times* and Amazon bestselling author of the Marc Dane novels *Nomad*, *Exile*, *Ghost* and *Shadow*. He is a BAFTA-nominated scriptwriter, a former journalist and the award-winning writer of over fifty books and numerous scripts for radio, television and interactive media. He lives in London, and is currently working on his next novel. Find him online (along with more about the Marc Dane series and free downloadable fiction) at www.jswallow.com.

Also by James Swallow

Nomad
Exile
Ghost
Shadow

ROGUE

JAMES SWALLOW

ZAFFRE

First published in the UK in 2020
This edition pubblished in 2021 by
ZAFFRE
An imprint of Bonnier Books UK
80–81 Wimpole St, London W1G 9RE
Owned by Bonnier Books
Sveavägen 56, Stockholm, Sweden

A CIP catalogue record for this book is
available from the British Library.

Paperback ISBN: 978–1–83877–057–0
Hardback ISBN: 978–1–83877–055–6
Trade Paperback ISBN: 978–1–83877–056–3

Also available as an ebook

1 3 5 7 9 10 8 6 4 2

Typeset by IDSUK (Data Connection) Ltd
Printed and bound in Great Britain by Clays Ltd, Elcograf S.p.A.

MIX
Paper from
responsible sources
FSC
www.fsc.org   FSC® C018072

Zaffre is an imprint of Bonnier Books UK
www.bonnierbooks.co.uk

For those who weather the storms

ONE

The wipers chased each other across the windscreen of the decrepit Volvo, and from inside the trail car, it was hard to keep a clear line of sight on the target.

The downpour turned the asphalt into shimmering metallic sheets, falling in hard surges pressed northwards by the wind. Heavy clouds darkened the late day into a pre-emptive twilight, bleeding colour from the buildings, the people, the trams and cars.

Anyone who didn't have a good reason to be outside retreated into doorways to find shelter. Some stoic locals clung to umbrellas as if their lives depended on it, but the torrent was coming in almost horizontally, soaking through coats and into clothes beneath.

All week long, Oslo had been threatened by a turbulent cold front over the Skagerrak, and today it had finally come inland, sweeping rapidly up the fjords and over the city, releasing a month's worth of rainstorm in a matter of hours.

The dark-skinned man in the Volvo's passenger seat was lean and tense in that way only ex-soldiers could be, his lanky form swamped by a blue parka big enough to conceal the Maxim 9 pistol holstered under his armpit. He leaned forward, eyes set, determined not to lose their quarry.

The driver deliberately kept the speed down, her long-fingered hands gripping the steering wheel. Light where he was dark, she wore a coat with a fake-fur collar that pooled around her neck. With the sharp features of her face, it gave her the look of a carrion bird spying for prey.

The target was moving at a steady pace, betraying no awareness of the trackers. The hunter team had not been given her identity, only a coded designation. They knew the nameless woman as Echo-One, and for the past six days they had been stalking her through the backstreets of the Norwegian capital.

Piece by piece, the trackers assembled a model of Echo-One's movements, looking for places where she intersected with persons of interest. The target was slim-built, of average height beneath a long, dark storm jacket with the collar turned up. A baseball cap covered a face turned pink by the chill. Her hands were buried in the jacket's deep pockets up to the elbows, and she moved purposefully, hunched forward against the inclement weather.

So far, Echo-One had given them nothing of value to report, and there was a tension building among the members of the team. Soon a decision was going to be made by someone higher up the chain of command, and then the target's fate would be sealed.

The man and the woman in the car had communication beads in their ears, connecting them to the team's encrypted radio network. There were three more operatives out there; one on foot on the same side of the street as the target, another on the opposite, and the last sitting in a cafe a few blocks west, monitoring the operation via a laptop computer. Chatter was minimal, cut down to terse reports on Echo-One's movements and little else.

In the back of the Volvo was a gear bag with everything in it they would need to take the woman alive; duct tape, cable ties, a stun gun, a clamshell case containing two injector pens loaded with a pentobarbital derivative. The bag also held the items required for disposal of a corpse, if it went that way. Everyone in the team had memorised the locations where they would take Echo-One for detainment or dumping, depending on how it played out. The former was a vacant house in the Old Town, and for the latter, an isolated deep-water spot along the dockside at Bekkelaget.

They had handled operations like this one before, renditions both legal and prohibited. The trackers worked as a well-oiled unit, enough that one single target was unlikely to stand a chance against them. This was a confidence born not of complacency, but from experience.

The thin briefing from their superiors suggested that Echo-One was former armed forces, but she had no network, no backup, and no organisation behind her. Echo-One was alone and out in the cold, in both the figurative and literal senses.

What this woman had done to deserve such scrutiny had not been made clear, but there was the usual amount of supposition and rumour. Echo-One was most likely someone who had gone off-book and earned the displeasure of her former masters. Perhaps she knew too much, perhaps she had exposed the wrong secret. Whatever the reason, this isolated, rain-soaked figure was being stalked like an animal, and her life hung in the balance.

Her booted feet making splashes, she jogged over a pedestrian crossing where two four-lane streets intersected. The hunters in the car saw another of their team move to follow, the third man staying far enough back that the target wouldn't make him. A radio call from the other hunter on foot warned that Echo-One was picking up the pace, turning into a side street that led north through the top end of the Majorstuen district, in the direction of more sparsely populated streets. If she continued that way, off the main drag and in this filthy weather, the few pedestrians around would make the trackers stand out.

The driver exchanged a wary look with the dark-skinned man, who returned a nod. The Volvo moved off, crawling around a tram and shifting into the slow lane. Both of them knew that they were on the cusp of a go or no-go choice. If they maintained the follow, the chances of Echo-One spotting them rose significantly. If they broke off, they might not be able to reacquire the target at the hostel she was staying in or the bars she frequented.

Then the target made the decision for them.

The dark-skinned man saw it first and called out a warning. Echo-One abruptly broke her pattern and ran diagonally across the street, towards a shelter concealing a set of turnstiles. Over the shelter, the sign of a blue 'T' inside a circle indicated the entrance to the *T-banen*, the local metro system that crisscrossed the city. Majorstuen station was an interchange that spanned five of the metro's lines, and if Echo-One escaped her hunters there, she would be able to resurface anywhere in Oslo.

The Volvo jolted to a halt, and the dark-skinned man was already out of the car, quickly slipping over a low gate to get onto the platform ahead of the target. Through the windscreen, the driver watched the other two hunters follow Echo-One through the ticket barriers. Then all of them were lost to sight and she called in a message to the man in the cafe with the laptop. He was already at work, bringing up a timetable for the trains passing through Majorstuen and their destinations.

The driver opened her coat and checked her gun as she listened to him speak. Like all of the hunters, she carried the same nose-heavy Maxim semi-automatic. The blocky front end of the weapon concealed an integral sound suppressor, reducing the noise of the pistol's discharge to a heavy metallic clatter. But if the guns came out, it would not take long for the Norwegian police to arrive on the scene. They needed to deal with this quietly and quickly, without drawing the attention of the *politi*.

The driver scowled and told the man in the cafe to call up the chain with the new development.

The doors of the train in the station slammed shut as the target reached for them, and the dark-skinned man watched her flinch, as if shocked back by the realisation that her hasty escape was cut off.

Echo-One looked up and down the platform, and he could sense her trying to pick out her pursuers. He gambled that she hadn't seen him in the Volvo, and affected a bored look, standing in plain sight as he pretended to study a route map. In the reflection of the panel, he took in the layout of Majorstuen station with a practised eye. It was open to the air, a cutting through the middle of the district with tracks that threaded back underground at one end, vanishing into narrow concrete tunnels. There was precious little cover, and few routes in or out. They could take the target here, he decided, if they moved fast.

From the corner of his eye, he saw her gaze slip over him and pass on. Someone else in the team must have spooked her, most likely the man pacing her from behind.

As that thought crossed his mind, the target caught sight of the other two trackers and she reacted, turning away to move down the platform.

The situation wasn't ideal. It would have been best to catch her between them, but they would work with what they had. The woman walked as quickly as she could without showing outward panic, but her movements were jerky and fearful. The exit at the southern end of the platform was closed, the barred metal gate chained shut. As he started walking after her, the dark-skinned man saw Echo-One shoot a desperate look across the train tracks.

An express metro rumbled past at fast clip, wheels keening over the glistening rails, and the woman turned away. He could almost read the pattern of thoughts on her face. Crossing the tracks would cause a scene and it meant braving not only any oncoming trains but also avoiding the live electric rails that fed them power. Would she take the risk?

One of the other men subvocalised a radio reply, catching on to the same conclusion. He turned right and jogged up a footbridge, crossing to the far platform in case she did make a run for it.

Echo-One saw her two pursuers split, and her face fell. She had nowhere to go now, and she knew it. The handful of other travellers on the platform thinned out around her as she reached the southern end of the station, her pace slowing.

Her body language changed, her shoulders dropping, her posture telegraphing the sense of defeat that had to be coursing through her mind. She came to a halt and drew her arms tight. Rain ran off the bill of her cap in streams as she stared bleakly into the tunnel beyond the platform's edge.

Flickering lights danced in the blackness down there, and an automated announcement gave a warning to stand back from the platform edge as another train approached. The dark-skinned man kept up his careful, casual pace, drawing closer to the woman with each footstep. His hand slipped under his parka to rest on the grip of his pistol.

A chattering line of white and grey carriages rolled out of the gloom and sped past, the empty train heading back to the depot, and the sound and motion of it was a trigger.

Echo-One exploded into motion, sprinting towards the tunnel at the end of the platform even as the train was still emerging from it. The dark-skinned man heard the snarl of annoyance from his teammate a few steps behind, and for a split second he hesitated.

As the last carriage of the empty train passed out of the tunnel, the target vaulted off the platform and landed square-footed on the trackbed, scattering gravel as she lost no pace and fled into the poorly lit subway.

He broke into a run, calling out to the other hunters. They had to contain this situation. If Echo-One was operating out of blind panic, there was a good chance she might injure herself dashing through the darkness, or worse, get hit by another fast-moving train. They had to secure her before that could happen.

The other passengers on the platform were slow to react, still caught by surprise, and no one stopped the dark-skinned man and his colleague as they dropped over the edge and went after the woman in the cap. The third hunter on the far platform followed suit, moving behind them to come up a parallel tunnel.

Once they were in the shadows, the dark-skinned man drew his gun and held it close to his chest. His boots crunched on the stone chippings between the rails, and he moved as quietly as he could, straining to listen.

In his ear-bead, the voice of the agent in the cafe made him wince as he shot through a string of rapid-fire chatter. According to the man on the laptop, the next station was a long way off, but that didn't rule out maintenance tunnels or other access routes that could lead back up to street level.

The dark-skinned man demanded radio silence as he spotted movement ahead, the flicker of a storm coat caught in the yellow burn of service lamps bolted to the concrete walls. More light spilled into the tunnel from that direction, as the narrow channel opened out into a wider, cavern-like space.

The second hunter, his gun hanging at the end of one arm, came over and offered the dark-skinned man something he had found on the tracks. It was the soaked-through baseball cap Echo-One had been wearing.

The two of them moved cautiously into the area ahead and found themselves looking at a set of abandoned platforms on either side of the parallel rail lines. They had emerged in a ghost station, a gutted space that had been abandoned in favour of the bigger terminus.

A low, curved ceiling and denuded grey walls extended towards sets of stairs and a shared balcony bridge. Dust-caked graffiti covered the walls and the cold air smelled of rainwater and rat piss. At the opposite end of the platforms, the far tunnel was lit up by more yellow lamps, and there was nowhere to hide. Echo-One was in here, somewhere.

Closer to the hunters, other safety lights cast pools of weak illumination, but the platforms were deep with shadows. Cable reels and piles of debris from unfinished works lined the bare spaces, and the hunter picked out a cracked plastic sign that gave the ghost station's name: *Valkyrie Plass*.

He radioed that detail back to the man in the cafe, but the signal was heavy with static, the thick walls playing havoc with the transmission. He gestured to his team. The third hunter had arrived, and in silence, they split up to comb the abandoned station for the target.

Capture, hold, and determine. Those were the next steps. It would be up to others to decide if Echo-One was to be taken from here alive and whole, or terminated on sight. If it came to it, the team could drop the body on the tracks and make it look like an accidental death.

The dark-skinned man moved down the narrow median strip between the sets of metro rails, and the other hunters each took a platform. As they swept forward, he tried to sift through the sounds in the tunnel, listening for a human noise.

Distantly, something scraped on stone. It came from the direction of the balcony bridge over the rail lines, and he waved his men towards it.

The hunter on the right reached the base of the stairs first, the other man still picking his way through heaps of debris. As the first man began to climb, a plug of warm, oily air left the tunnel ahead – the metro exhaling ahead of an oncoming train. The dark-skinned man dropped down into a crouch and concealed himself behind a signal panel as the noise grew louder. White light flooded over him as a train rolled past, wheels spitting sparks a few centimetres from his face.

Mingled with the racket of the passing carriages, he heard someone cry out in pain and then a rough metallic sound he didn't recognise.

The first hunter was almost at the top of the stairs when his boot snagged on the fishing line tripwire hidden in the shadows.

The line pulled tight and released a jury-rigged trap. It was a clever improvised thing, made from cheap household items.

Bungee cords wound around eye-bolts snapped back, driving a pair of duct-taped kitchen knives into the hunter's leg. The knives and the trap mechanism had been sprayed black with car paint to make them blend in. The blades buried themselves deep in the muscle and he cried out in shock, collapsing against the wall. The sound was swallowed by the noise of the passing train, and the hunter tried to shift his weight, distracted by the sight of the blood gushing from his wounds.

Something moved up on the middle of the bridge, someone breaking concealment from beneath a paint-spattered tarpaulin. He saw Echo-One emerge and caught a glimpse of her face. Short dark hair, ruddy skin and healed burn scars over her right cheek. She had a stub-barrelled pump-action shotgun in her hands, the muzzle hidden behind an improvised silencer made from a spray can. Before the hunter could bring his own pistol to bear, she fired into his head, a burst of heavy-gauge buckshot turning his face into wet red pulp.

The second hunter was at the base of the stairs on the opposite platform when he heard his comrade choke out a scream. As the roar of the train rolled away towards the next station, he surged forward, over a mess of broken planks and building debris.

His boot came down on a thin piece of wood, beneath which two shotgun cartridges had been fixed upright with a plug of epoxy glue. His weight compressed the shells into pipe caps fitted across their bases, each one threaded with a thick screw, the tips of which rested against the faces of the shell's primers.

Both rounds discharged with a crash, blasting through the wood and the sole of his boot. Skin, muscle and bone were shredded instantly, and he fell backwards, down to the platform.

Jagged streams of agony tore through his nerves, catching his breath, making him gag. He heard his teammate calling out as the woman they had been chasing hove into view at the top of the staircase, and he tried to wave him back.

The dark-skinned man heard the improvised trap go off and saw the other hunter collapse, his face sweaty and pale, and his leg a bloody mess from the ankle down. He scrambled up onto the platform and called out a warning, but the comm network spat back static instead of voices.

On the stairs, Echo-One was out of cover, leading with a short shotgun. She fired twice, filling the air with buckshot, and he felt hot pellets rake his face as they passed. The woman dropped back behind the low wall and he heard the oiled metal noise of rounds being loaded.

Ignoring the pain and the stinging wetness across his cheek, he grabbed the injured man and hauled him away, looking for some kind of cover and finding little fit for purpose. Behind him, boots scraped on stone and he knew she was coming after them. The dark-skinned man let his colleague drop with an agonised moan, turning with the Maxim pistol in his hand. He fired back at the staircase, cracking off four rounds to discourage any immediate pursuit.

His mind raced. *This is a set-up.* Echo-One had deliberately drawn them to the ghost station, a location she had prepared in advance with traps and a stashed weapon. Those actions spoke to a mindset beyond that of some ordinary ex-soldier. That performance out on the street, on the metro platform, it had been an act designed to make them lower their guard. He spared a curse for his commanders, for keeping the hunter team in the dark, and for all their need-to-know bullshit.

He scanned the space for the other hunter and his gut twisted as he found the other man on the far platform, slumped against a wall painted with fresh crimson.

Another rushing roar of air came sweeping through the chamber as a train raced by in the opposite direction. He saw glimpses of commuters in the windows of the carriages as they hurtled past, most of them not even seeing the two men with guns and the blood on them, and those that did barely able to register the sight before it was gone.

The last carriage flashed by and revealed the woman on the far platform, her shotgun aimed directly at him. He vaulted away as she fired, and the echoing report of the gun told him Echo-One had switched from shot to heavy, man-stopping slug rounds. She leapt down and crossed the gap between the platforms, racking and firing again. The next slug smacked into the wall near his head and the dark-skinned man returned fire with the Maxim, hating himself for leaving his fallen teammate behind.

But she gave him no time to dwell on that. The shotgun's third round skipped off the platform in a sparking ricochet and hit him in the gut. The blow burned red-hot, it was hammer-hard and it sent him sprawling. He tasted blood in his mouth and suddenly it was hard to breathe.

He heard her reloading again. The *snick-clack* of shells going into the feed, and the slide ratcheting one into the chamber.

She walked over to his teammate and took her time about aiming for the shot that killed him.

The empty Maxim fell from his hand as the dark-skinned man lurched up and bolted towards the woman, dragging up his last reserves of strength. He felt the wind at his back, pushing him forward, the tunnel's greasy metallic odour filling his nostrils.

Echo-One saw him coming and yellow light flashed off a black-painted blade in her hand. She was faster than he expected, going low to cut him across the chest. The cut was deep and filled with fire, and it robbed him of his momentum.

He tried to grab at her, and she kicked out, collapsing his knee. As he fell to the platform, it seemed to take forever – but even then, she wouldn't let him go down on his own terms. She could have finished him with the gun, but she was taking her time, making a meal of it. The woman kicked him again and he tumbled over the edge, landing across one of the rails.

White fire washed over him as the trackbed started to shake. A huge shadowed shape behind the light was bearing down on him, and he couldn't move, couldn't get away.

He shouted out for it to stop, but his cry was lost in the squealing of iron wheels on steel.

The Volvo's driver knew something was wrong when the train halted short of the platform, half of it still inside the tunnel, half of it out in the rain.

Commuters came out through the turnstiles with ashen faces and hands covering their mouths. Emergency lights were flashing, and the patient, motherly voice of the automated announcer kept repeating something in Norwegian that she couldn't understand.

None of the men who had gone after the quarry were answering their comms. Then the howl of an ambulance siren reached her and her blood chilled. She leaned down to put the Volvo in gear, and missed the figure exiting the station.

The driver saw a shadow at the window and turned, her heart leaping in her chest as the maw of a makeshift silencer pressed against the glass, protruding from the folds of a dark storm coat. The shotgun discharged with a heavy chug flattened by the hissing downpour, shattering the window and painting the Volvo's interior with fluid and brain matter.

The woman discarded the shotgun, tossing it through the broken window and into the murdered driver's lap. As an afterthought, she grabbed the dead hunter's bag and walked away with it, holding it close as she rooted through the contents.

An ambulance skidded to a halt across the street with a police car close behind, but she was already at the intersection, lost in the confusion.

There was a radio handset in the bag and she tapped the push-to-talk button experimentally. After a moment, a man's voice issued out, asking for a comm check. He sounded young and worried.

The woman found a sheltered alleyway behind an apartment block, out of sight from the street, and took a moment to school her voice. To make it sound thick with pain and fear, almost plaintive. Then she toggled the radio, playing with the settings to mess up the reception.

She improvised the sketch of a story, a lie about how she was hurt and the others were dead, about how she couldn't make it back to the exfil site. She kept her accent toneless and vague, letting the worried young man fill in the gaps.

He said he was close. It wouldn't take him long to get to her. She still had the knife she'd used back in the ghost station, and cleaned it off as she listened. He would be there soon, he said.

The skies overhead grew darker as she settled in to wait.

TWO

'What is her name?'

The old man looked up at him from beneath the bill of a grimy cap, squinting into the bright sunshine and smiling as he crossed the garage's forecourt.

'The car?'

Marc Dane watched the old man insert a pump nozzle into the fuel tank of the steel-blue Audi R8 Spyder, and set to work.

The pump chirped as petrol flowed, the cost climbing on the meter. Marc would have been happy to fill her up himself, but the elderly gent minding the combination gas station–cafe wouldn't hear of it. He insisted on doing the job, first attempting to engage the Englishman in a discussion about football and, when that didn't take, switching to talk of the weather and the road ahead.

'Not the car,' corrected the old man. His accent was thick, but his English was good. 'The *woman*.' His grin widened. 'You're not here for the golfing. You are out here to see someone.'

Marc couldn't help but smile a little, confirming what the old fellow surmised.

'It's not what you think.'

He put a hand on his chest and made a mock-pious face.

'I do not judge.'

'I'm just calling in on a friend.'

'Oh.' The old man nodded in the direction of the hills. 'Up in *la clínica*, yes?' He gave the pump trigger an extra squeeze, finishing off the top-up. 'You should not keep her waiting.'

Marc paid him with a fold of euros and nodded.

'You're right there, mate.'

'*Obridago.*' The old man pocketed the notes and eyed him. 'You one of them?'

'One of who?'

That earned him another smile. 'I've been here many years, my friend. Seen many come and go. People up on the hill, they like to keep their secrets.'

Marc climbed in behind the driver's seat.

'I'm just out for a drive.'

'You picked a fine day,' said the old man.

The Spyder bit into each turn along the highway with perfectly machined ease, and from behind the steering wheel of the humming sports car, it occurred to Marc that operating in the private sector had its benefits.

The wiry ex-MI6 officer had been cut loose from working for Queen and country for a while, but he could never really detach the ghost of that old life from the one he had now. He tried not to dwell on the changes in his circumstances. That felt too much like standing still. But Marc wasn't the same man he had been back then. He carried himself a little more confidently these days, even as the wary edge he'd grown up with stayed as sharp, as present, as ever.

A narrow and wolfish face hid searching eyes behind dark aviator sunglasses, and his deliberately shabby beard matched unkempt dirty-blond hair that badly needed a trim. He had the Spyder's top down, and the breeze played over him along with the throaty rumble of the Audi's V10 engine.

The car was one of a fleet of vehicles made available to high-clearance employees of the pan-global Rubicon Group, and while he could have taken something more conservative as his ride, it was hard to resist the perks.

A crooked smile pulled at the corner of his mouth. Working for one of the wealthiest men in the world came with a lot of strings attached, so why not make the most of it?

Sunshine flashed through trees on his right as Marc made another smooth turn, and the car entered a straight. The Audi climbed gentle switchbacks, past clusters of resort villas and the manicured lawns of golf courses, speeding from the outskirts of Vilamoura and into the shallow hills sloping down on the southerly edge of the Portuguese coastline. The satnav led him through decorative olive groves to an estate behind whitewashed walls, set just off the beaten track.

The Clínica Delphi resembled the home of some moneyed recluse, but it was the property of Rubicon – a satellite facility belonging to MaxaBio, the corporation's biomedical subsidiary. The Delphi clinic did cutting-edge work in organ rejection therapy and artificial bone structures, but it had a secondary, clandestine function.

It was one of the best places in the Western hemisphere for combat trauma recovery, somewhere people could rest and heal after gunshot wounds, blades, burns or any one of a bestiary of critical injuries had taken them to the edge of death. Marc had briefly been a resident himself, in the weeks after a zealous US Secret Service agent had shot him in the chest. Without being aware of it, he reached up with one hand and scratched at the site of the old entry wound on his torso.

He didn't like hospitals. There was something about the smell of disinfectant and the oppressive atmosphere built up from the suffering and pain the buildings contained. It brought back too many unpleasant memories, not just of his own hurts but of loss and fear from sharing the pain of those he cared about. The Delphi clinic worked hard to make itself different from those kind of places, looking more like a day spa than a medical centre. But still it felt unwelcoming to the rail-thin Englishman. He took a breath and banished those thoughts. Today's visit wasn't about him.

The clinic's gates opened as the Audi approached, the smart sensors in the driveway detecting the car's arrival, the discreet cameras in the surrounding trees having already captured and confirmed the driver's identity. Marc slowed as he came to the main building, a low two-storey mansion in a faux-Greek style, surrounded with satellite cottages connected by sunlit colonnades.

At the main entrance, a brass panel by the doors announced the name of the clinic but gave no other details about the facility. If you didn't already know so, there was nothing here to immediately connect Delphi to the Rubicon Group. That kind of engineered discretion, that stealth by wealth, was inherent in everything that Rubicon did. It flowed from the example set by Ekko Solomon, the man in charge, the inscrutable billionaire who had founded the company from humble beginnings in strife-torn East Africa. Solomon was good at staying out of the public eye, and his company mirrored that ethos.

Rubicon's aegis encompassed dozens of subdivisions – MaxaBio and Delphi just two among many – but the part Marc worked for was unique among them. The vaguely named 'Special Conditions Division' was part of Rubicon's private security contracts sector and, like the clinic, its unassuming mantle concealed something more complex. While Rubicon's overt work in security was a matter of public knowledge, providing bodyguards and the like, the SCD had a mission brief that too frequently put its operatives directly in harm's way.

Marc often tried to parse the SCD's remit into a simple, clear statement. *Sentinels, watchmen, guardians* – none of those words really encompassed the whole of what Ekko Solomon's people did out in the world.

We're vigilantes, Marc told himself. *Nothing more, nothing less.*

An attendant met him at the portico to park the Audi, and Marc passed into the cool, air-conditioned interior of the clinic. The first face he saw drew a wary smile from him.

'Benjamin. Hey.'

'*Mon ami.*' Smiling broadly, Benjamin Harun came across the chequerboard tiles of the reception, placing a big, thick-fingered hand on Marc's arm, and he said the same thing he always did when they met. 'How is it going?'

'It's going.' Marc deliberately kept his reply vague.

Harun was as broad as Marc was tall, and burly in the truest sense of the word. The Frenchman was built like an old-time circus strongman, affecting a wax-tipped moustache in the Imperial style. Marc had no doubt that he was capable of bending iron bars in those beefy paws of his, but Harun's calling was aligned more towards the shaping of people than it was to twisting metal. Harun had served long tours with the Foreign Legion, but he had come into Rubicon's orbit because of his training as a therapist and expert in post-traumatic stress. Every six months, active members of the SCD had mandated meetings with the avuncular ex-legionnaire, and Marc's was overdue.

Harun didn't call him on it, though. That wasn't his way.

'You're here to see her,' the Frenchman noted.

Marc gave a nod. 'You two talked?'

'I talk,' Harun corrected. 'Her, not so much. You might have more success.'

'How's she doing?'

'Catching up on her reading. Complaining that Delphi doesn't have a shooting range for her to practise on.' He paused. 'It's not easy for people like us to accept this kind of thing. The Americans trained her to believe she was bulletproof. When it becomes clear one is not, that can be a shock. We're all mortal.'

Marc nodded, momentarily looking inwards to catalogue the many near-hits and lucky breaks that had kept him upright and still breathing.

'She's the most resilient person I've ever met,' he said honestly. 'Tougher than me.'

'She's been asking after you.' Harun eyed him. 'A couple of months since you've been here, Marc.'

He gave a guilty nod. 'It was . . .' Marc fell short of a good explanation, and finally chose a more succinct one. 'Work,' he said.

'Ah.' The Frenchman gave a knowing nod. 'I did hear some talk.'

'It got busy,' Marc replied, and he left it there.

Harun knew well enough not to pry.

'Come see me soon, then.' He smiled and patted Marc on the shoulder as he walked away. 'Stay out of trouble, *rosbif.*'

'Never can tell,' said Marc.

The main building opened into an airy courtyard with a shallow pool and a space for eating and resting in the sunshine. A few of Delphi's patients were taking advantage of the lovely day, but the one Marc Dane had come to see was in the shade of a parasol, pushed up into the frame of a lounger with her head buried in a leather-bound hardcover.

Six months ago, on a canal-side dock in Brussels, Marc's partner Lucy Keyes had taken a lungful of an aerosolised biological agent. An engineered variant of the haemorrhagic Marburg strain, the so-called Shadow virus had almost killed her, and it chilled Marc to think how narrow the survival window had been. If Lucy had made it to the hospital fifteen minutes later, today he would been putting flowers on a grave.

Keyes was ex-US Army – everyone who worked for the Special Conditions Division was ex-*something*, Marc reflected – once a highly trained sniper in a secret all-female unit of Delta Force, but that had been a different life for her. As with Marc and the British secret service, and Benjamin and the *Légion étrangère*, the SCD was populated with people who had left what they once were far behind.

The book in Lucy's hands was a translation of Sun Tzu's *The Art of War*, the pages yellowed and well-thumbed. Marc had read it when he was training for the Royal Navy Fleet Air Arm, but found it slow-going.

'I already read the other books in the library,' she said, without looking up. Her voice still had the scratchy, brittle quality it had taken on after the doctors had given her the all-clear. Although the corrupted Shadow bioweapon had burned out of her system, it had damaged a lot of her on the way, not least her throat and her lungs. 'I read a bunch of those fantasy sagas too.' She made a shape with her free hand to indicate a thick, brick-sized novel.

Marc brought tall glasses of ice water and set one down before her, taking a seat.

'Sorry I haven't been up.'

'Work,' she said, still reading the book as she reached for the glass. 'I know.'

'You look good,' he offered, and that was true. As far as he could tell under the loose tracksuit she wore, Lucy had put back the muscle mass lost in her stay at Rubicon's Zurich medical centre, but that new distance in her eyes had not gone away.

As Benjamin said, it was one thing for a soldier to face off against guns and bombs, quite another to endure the ravages of a germ weapon that could turn your body against you, and consume you from the inside out.

She finally graced him with a glance, her deceptively sleepy gaze coming up sideways from a boyish face the tone of deep burnt ochre.

'How's life on the outside?'

He snorted. 'You're not in prison, Lucy.'

Then he immediately regretted the comment, because she *had* been a convict once, back before Ekko Solomon had recruited her into Rubicon from a military stockade.

'You brought me a cake with a file in it, right?'

He gave a weak smile as she let him off the hook. 'I did. But I ate it.'

'I miss cake,' she said, with feeling. Lucy put down the book, pulling absently at the short braids of her hair, grown longer than her usual military-style buzz cut. 'Sons of bitches here make me eat healthy, can you believe it? I miss red meat even more. Tried to explain to them about my exceptional metabolism, but ... I mean, everyone's nice and all, but I'm starting to climb the walls.'

'I spoke to the doc, he said you're still a few weeks away from—'

'I know I'm not at top kick,' she broke in, the words coming out in a growl. 'Sure, I may sound a little sexier than I did before Belgium, but c'mon, I'm going stale here! They don't sign me back on to operational status soon, I swear I'm going to exfil myself in the dead of night and bust up whoever gets in my way.'

'There's plenty of people who would pay a lot to sit on their arse in a place like this for a couple of months,' Marc countered.

'Would you?' She didn't give him time to answer. 'You and me, we're not *plenty of people*. Jeez, Marc, don't make me break something to prove I'm serious.'

'I have no doubt you are.' He gave a solemn nod. 'It's just . . .'

He paused, thinking on what the doctor had told him. *Scarred lungs. Reduced operational capacity. The possibility of permanent nerve damage.* There were precious few people in the world that Marc trusted, and Lucy was one of them. Marc's gut twisted as he thought about putting his friend and partner back in danger too soon.

She leaned close to him. 'I appreciate what you did for me, I do. But that doesn't mean you get to bench me.' Again, she didn't give him time to frame a counter. 'Solomon wants you to report in when you get back to the Monaco office, right? He did the same with me after you took that hit in Washington. You know how he is, he likes his people to be optimal.'

'True.' Marc nodded again. Whatever he told Solomon about Lucy's condition would carry weight, one way or the other. He didn't have the right to determine her future, not now, not ever. 'I'm just worried about you, yeah?'

'I appreciate that in the manner in which you intend it,' she said, with deliberate over-formality. 'But there will be fire and blood if I don't get outta here real soon, hand to God.'

'I can't be responsible for that,' he said, matching her tone. 'The doc did say I could take you out for a while. You want to grab a pint?'

A sly smirk split her face. 'Oh, hell yeah.'

The old man's big grin returned in full beam when the Audi pulled in at the roadside cafe once again.

'Welcome back,' he said, doffing his cap to Lucy before directing them to a table inside. He threw Marc a knowing look.

They were the only customers, alone aside from a surly calico cat sunning itself on a windowsill. The place was in the sweet spot between rustic and tumbledown, rough uneven floors and old wooden furniture. The old man served up glasses of Sagres, the beer crisp and cold, the perfect thing to cut through the heat of the afternoon.

Lucy went through hers in a few quick pulls and asked for another. Marc paced himself and for a while they talked around things.

There was an odd reticence between them. When the bullets were flying, when the clock was running, the impulsive Londoner and the sardonic New Yorker meshed into an effective pairing, but away from the action the distance between them increased. Marc told himself that they knew each other well enough not to need to spill out every last detail. Or perhaps it was that neither of them really knew how to disengage, to switch off from a constant on-alert mindset.

The conversation drifted back towards the job, like it always did. *The life*, Marc corrected. Calling it just *a job* was a weak definition, barely scratching the surface of what they did. Once you were part of this world, there was no going back. Not after you had seen what Marc and Lucy had seen, the threats and the horrors out there that everyday people never registered.

Marc watched the old man walk away after depositing Lucy's refill.

'Must be nice to be that guy. He's only got this to worry about.' He gestured around at the walls of the cafe. 'I forget what having a smaller world-view was like.'

'What, you wanna retire?' Lucy eyed him. 'Get a little place to put your feet up? Live in the same town for the rest of your days?' She shook her head. 'Not for me.'

'Nah,' Marc admitted. 'I get bored too easy. Always want to see what's over the next hill.'

She chuckled. 'Wow. It's almost like Solomon has the eye for recruiting folks that don't know when to quit, huh?'

'Like knows like,' said Marc.

'I'm not the same as Solomon.' Her reply had more chill in it than he expected. 'The man's a puzzle box, is what he is.'

'And you're such an open book,' Marc deadpanned. 'Heart on your sleeve, so to speak.'

'Fuck you.'

He drowned a laugh with a sip of his own beer. 'And there's my point made – cheers.'

Lucy scowled. 'Okay, maybe you're a little right. But the work does that. You operate on the margins, you learn to play your cards close to your chest or you get dead pretty quick.' She chewed on the thought. 'Solomon, though . . . he's a master. What do we really know about him, aside from the man he is today?'

'African success story,' Marc began. 'Self-made bloke. Pulled himself out of poverty from one of the most war-torn pieces of dirt on the planet. You know this.'

'Former child soldier,' she added. 'Ever wonder what growing up in that would do to a person?'

'We do know, don't we?' Marc gestured with his glass. 'He got rich enough to live a soft and easy life, and chose not to. Decided to use his money and influence for something better.'

That *something* was the Special Conditions Division. Their mandate was to act as a privately funded intelligence-gathering and black ops unit, with no allegiance to any one nation, and a firm ethical code. They were the spear-tip of Ekko Solomon's personal crusade, out in the world looking for terror threats and organised cruelty of every stripe, doing what they could to hold back some of the darkness that lay forever on the horizon.

The thought made Marc shiver and he covered it with another swig of beer, his gaze drifting to the open door across the cafe. The circumstances that had brought him into Rubicon had been out of his control, but what kept him there was an undeniable sense that he was doing the right thing. The needed thing in a dark world desperate for any light it could get.

'Solomon keeps secrets like a collector,' Lucy was saying. 'We do because we have to.'

'I don't,' Marc said, after a moment. 'I'm pretty bad at it, actually. You get what you see with me.'

'I've kept stuff from you,' she admitted. Marc looked up and found Lucy studying him intently. Her voice was husky, and the sound of it made him flash back to a moment months ago in a Reykjavík hotel, when the two of them had almost crossed a line that would have taken them beyond being friends and team-mates to something else entirely. 'Never told you why I was in jail when Solomon brought me in. Not the full story.'

That had been before Marc's time in the SCD, before he had found himself on the run from his own government, before Solomon had offered him another path.

'You don't need to. I don't need to ask.'

She shook her head. 'Don't be so goddamn British about it.' She took a breath. 'I was serving time in a military stockade at Miramar because I assaulted my commanding officer. I threatened him with a loaded weapon, hit him.'

'He must've deserved it.'

'He was an okay C-O but he was a shitty human being,' she explained. 'You know the type. They work okay inside the green machine but they got something missing in the heart. They can't be good people.' Marc said nothing, letting her carry on at her own pace. 'Long story short, we had local confidential informants in-country, people who were feeding us intel on high-value targets. Vulnerable people, a lot of them. Women.' Her expression darkened. 'You consider how a man with power and zero empathy could abuse that relationship, and . . . You get the picture?'

Lucy told him there was a death, a cover-up. And that was when she had enough.

'Next thing I know, he's on the floor of his hooch, pistol-whipped and covered in blood, and I'm being dragged away by the MPs. He was – he still is – connected, so it didn't end well for me.'

Marc looked past Lucy's shoulder. 'No wonder Solomon brought you in.' His attention wandered to the road outside. 'The guy likes your sense of justice . . .' He trailed off.

She frowned. 'Seriously? I'm having a sharing moment here and you're not paying attention.'

'I am,' he insisted. 'But I just noticed that van parked across the street, and it looks a lot like one that was following me on the motorway from Faro.'

'Uh-huh.' Lucy's posture shifted slightly as she picked up on the sudden tension in his expression. 'Now you mention it, the old dude went into the kitchen a while ago and he hasn't come back out.' She leaned in. 'You have a weapon?'

'In the car,' he admitted, taking his time over his beer. 'I could be wrong. It's probably not the same van.' But the battered grey Toyota Hiace looked very similar, and hard-earned experience had taught Marc not to ignore his instincts.

'You think it's nothing?'

He gave a slow shake of the head. It *was* the same vehicle. It had paced him to Vilamoura before it vanished, and he'd thought no more of it. That was looking more and more like a mistake now. His mind had been on seeing Lucy again, and he had allowed his tradecraft to slip.

Lucy palmed one of the knives on the table between them.

'So, we gotta—'

Before she could finish, a fizzing metal cylinder came tumbling in through the street-side door. It landed on the stone floor with a clank loud enough to wake the dozing cat and send it rocketing out of the room. In the next second, jets of white smoke spewed from the canister.

Marc and Lucy bolted from their seats. He was nearest to the door leading into the kitchen and instinctively turned towards it, away from where the van was waiting.

He tasted the acrid chemical smell of the smoke in the back of his throat. It wasn't CS gas, which was a good thing, but it was most certainly the precursor to a room breach. That meant armed assailants already on the move, giving the two operatives a fraction of a second to react before the attack would be upon them.

Marc grabbed the tall beer glass, still half-full with his drink, and spun into a figure coming in from the kitchen. In the haze he had an impression of a man his size, broader of build, wearing a breather mask and leading with a pneumatic dart pistol.

The gun meant that this wasn't an assassination. Whoever was in the grey van wanted them alive, which gave a fractional advantage to the SCD operatives.

Marc smashed the glass across the man's faceplate, sending beer and fragments everywhere. The attacker wasn't ready for it and lost a step. Marc knew he had to keep up the momentum for as long as he could, and he slammed himself into the masked man, forcing the pistol away. The gun discharged with a chug and a thick dart hummed across the room, clattering off the skirting.

Marc heard Lucy coughing from somewhere behind him, but he couldn't disengage. His weight turned the tide against the attacker and they both stumbled into the kitchen, through a dangling bead curtain and down a couple of steps into the back of the cafe.

The old man was in there, trembling on his knees, with a black cloth bag over his head and another masked figure, a woman, holding a gun on him. She reacted and fired at Marc. He tried to pivot and pull his opponent into the path of the shot, but inertia was going the other way.

The dart buried itself in his chest and a jolt of searing heat shocked through him, immediately followed by a flood of icy cold. Marc staggered back through the clattering beads, swatting away the projectile. Numbness raced across his torso, along his arms, up his throat and face. He tried to make his legs work but they were shaking, turning to rubber. Half of his body became slack, as if he were the victim of a stroke.

Whatever drug load had been in the dart's reservoir, enough of it was in him that he would barely be able to make it another few steps. Marc struggled to stay awake, crashing back through the smoke-choked cafe. He wanted to call out a warning but nothing was working.

Everything slowed, became glassy, the air thickening to the consistency of heavy oil. Through the haze he saw Lucy framed by the bright sunshine through the front door. She jammed the table knife into the shoulder of another masked man as he shot her in the gut, and Marc watched her fall into her attacker's arms, her eyes rolling back to show the whites.

This isn't supposed to be happening. The broken, direction-less impression tumbled down and down through Marc's mind. *Who is doing this?*

The last coherent thought he had was a bleak one.

Too many enemies to know for sure.

In the predawn light, the cold black waters of the Baie de Roque-brune pulled on Ekko Solomon's body as he knifed through the shallow waves. The muscles in his arms and legs were starting to burn as the effort grew greater. He had already turned back to the shore as the lights in the houses on Cap Martin came on, the residents waking to begin their lazy days even as he decided to end his exercise early.

This was becoming a regular occurrence. There had been a time when he could defy the currents and swim out to the rocky point of the peninsula, but those days were behind him. For a man of his age, Solomon was fit and strong, but his body was slowing by increments with each passing year, and it grew more difficult to deny it. To accept it.

He had always thought of his body as a machine, something to be sustained with precision care, a synchrony of well-maintained parts that worked as one. The mindset was a holdover from his time in the war, when he imagined himself like the rifle he had carried. A tool that had to be ready at all times, every element functioning perfectly to keep him alive. To be anything less was to risk a critical failure at the worst possible moment. His hard life had taught him that to be found unready was to invite death.

But the fatigue in him was not just from the swim. Like the water dragging on each overhead stroke of his arms, each kick of his legs, other forces were acting on Solomon. He had come so far over the years and faced down one injustice after another – yet still he had only kept the darkness in the world at bay. Not banished it. In truth, barely diminished it.

At this moment, in dozens of places around the world, elements of his company were working to do right. Rubicon sponsored initiatives to cure diseases and improve social conditions, to fight climate change and eradicate poverty, taking the billions of dollars the corporation earned from minerals, technology patents and manufacturing concerns, and pouring some of it back into the world.

He thought of it as balancing the scales, but would it ever be enough? Some issues could not be answered with a vaccine or an aid parcel. Some problems could only be solved by the application of brute force, by a silenced bullet or the destruction of a target. That was the lesson he had learned as a boy, when his childhood was traded away for an AK-47 assault rifle and indenture to a vicious warlord.

That boy was forty years gone, but he lived on in Ekko Solomon, his anger and his fear channelled into something better. At least, that was the hope.

The waves pushed him to the shore, and Solomon found the spot on the Plage du Buse where his morning swim had begun. A lone torch speared in among the white pebbles burned in the chilly air, and he aimed for it. With each stroke, the beach drew closer.

He turned in the water, looking east towards Monte Carlo. He knew where to find the gold silhouette of the Rubicon tower, rising up over the streets of Monaco as a monument to his endeavours. All he had built was reflected in that glass and steel, but it would matter for nothing if he could not see his cause through.

I have so many enemies, he told himself. *I have given myself too many wars to fight.*

It would be easy to let it exhaust him. But not today, he vowed. And not tomorrow. There was still much to be done.

His feet touched the bottom and Solomon stood in the shallows, wading up through the breakers towards the torch. At the foot of it was a folding table and upon that a heavy towelling robe. Water sluiced off his broad, teak-coloured shoulders and he ran a hand over the skin of his shaven head, drawing himself up to his full, imposing height. Other than his black trunks, the only other item on Solomon was a chain around his neck, and hanging from it a piece of curved metal. The trigger from a long-destroyed rifle, the ice-cold steel comma was a piece of his past.

At this time of the morning, the beach should have been empty of all but a lone bodyguard and his adjutant Henri Delancort, but Solomon found a third person standing in the flickering light. The older woman had dark red, shoulder-length hair that fluttered around her pale face in the stiff breeze, and she wore a long coat that gave her a gothic profile in the dawn light.

'She arrived just after you set off,' Delancort began, stepping gingerly over the pebbles and wet sand in his expensive, hand-made shoes. He handed Solomon the robe.

'Swimming, Ekko?' said the woman, as he put on the robe. 'I thought you had a yacht to sail about on.'

'The *Themis* is in dry dock,' said Delancort. 'For maintenance.'

The cold and the effort sent tremors though Solomon's muscles, but he stood his ground, meeting the woman's gaze.

'Esther,' he began, stones crunching beneath his bare feet as he walked up. 'This is an unexpected pleasure.'

'You don't mean that.'

Esther McFarlane's blunt Scottish burr was carried away by the breeze, and he noticed for the first time that the woman was holding something. A file folder.

'I thought you were still in Edinburgh.'

'Came over early,' she explained, 'to get a head start. Check up on operations.' By *operations*, she meant the Special Conditions Division.

'I did suggest Ms McFarlane wait in her car,' offered Delancort. The well-dressed, waspish French-Canadian had never liked

Solomon's early morning jaunts out to the bay, and he was even more terse than usual in the face of this unanticipated visitor. 'She declined,' he added.

While Solomon was at the head of the Rubicon Group's hierarchy, he could not operate the company alone, and among the three board members who worked directly with him, the Scottish oil heiress was the most outspoken.

It was Esther McFarlane who pressured Solomon to rein in his work with Special Conditions, citing the legal grey areas where its people operated and the potential for catastrophic blowback. Months earlier, a critical SCD intervention against a far-right extremist group had almost been derailed by the disunion she fostered in Rubicon's boardroom.

Those terrorists and their plans for a biological attack in Europe had ultimately been foiled, but for McFarlane the end did not justify the means. She continued to push for a full decommissioning of the group, crossing swords with Solomon again and again as she demanded insight into the SCD's activities, even if that put their operations at risk.

'I know you like your privacy,' she said, 'but I thought it better we speak outside the office.'

Solomon pushed away a flash of irritation. He was a man who prided himself on his appearance, taking pains to present his best face to the world. Coming here now, McFarlane was deliberately showing that she didn't care for any of that, literally catching him underdressed. It seemed petty for her, and out of character. In the torchlight he saw the hardening of her jawline and knew something was wrong.

But he was too tired to do anything more than dispense with formalities.

'What is so important that you need to bring it to me out here at sunrise?'

She offered the folder, and Delancort took it, opened it. |Solomon saw pages of redacted files, and blurry scanned images of a swarthy, middle-aged man.

'I'd like to know how much it cost us to buy this crooked bastard,' said McFarlane.

Solomon recognised the man immediately. *Mateo Garza.*

Formerly the chief accountant for a brutal South American criminal cartel called La Noche, Garza had been extracted from Colombia by Rubicon operatives in the previous year, after the money man had gone on the run from his masters. In exchange for a new identity, he had turned over gigabytes of financial data. In turn, the SCD had used that to impede La Noche's ambitions to expand and consolidate their hold on the drug trade.

Much of the vital information had gone into Rubicon's intelligence database – a system Solomon christened the 'Grey Record' – and even now it was still working for them. Garza was a repellent man, but his defection had allowed Rubicon to drag a piece of the criminal dark net into the light.

Solomon gave Delancort a warning look. As far as the rest of the world knew, Mateo Garza had perished in a plane crash. The fact that McFarlane had this file, that she knew something of the man's fate, was a serious problem.

'Where did you get this?'

'You're not going to deny it,' said the woman, ignoring his question. 'Well, at least you're not insulting my intelligence by saying otherwise.'

He took a moment to frame his reply.

'Garza supplied us with a strong intelligence take, which was of great use to our operatives and our contacts in the US Drug Enforcement Agency. Many lives have been saved because of it.'

'The drug war in Colombia. Extremists in Europe. Criminal gangs in South-east Asia. Domestic terrorists in America.' McFarlane ticked them off one by one. 'You're using Rubicon assets to play black ops in flashpoints around the world and you put us in danger every time you do it.' She shook her head. 'How many times do we have to have this conversation, Ekko?' McFarlane pointed at the file. 'You bought a criminal a new life with money from our company coffers. Do you have any idea what would happen if our competitors got hold of that information? Or, God forbid, those animals Garza worked for?'

'It had to be done. The opportunity presented itself. It could not be ignored. And good has come of it.'

'That's debatable. These are not opportunities, they're your addiction.' She came closer, and her tone briefly softened. 'There's so much Rubicon can do that doesn't need us to break the law. I believe in this organisation. I wouldn't be here if I didn't. But your vigilante crusade is going to ruin it.'

'You do not understand,' he told her. 'I built Rubicon for . . . my crusade. It is not some game. It is our *responsibility*.'

'It's really not,' she replied, shaking her head. 'Six months ago you said you would reel this in, but you haven't, have you? The SCD is still operating. You're still intervening in other people's fights.'

'Someone has to. We have the means, we have the clarity.'

'Is that so? Then where does it end?' McFarlane shot back. 'If you decide you don't like the North Koreans playing with nukes, is Rubicon going to invade Pyongyang? What if America's president crosses one line too many on your moral compass – are we going to shoot him?'

'We take what actions we can.' Solomon's irritation flared again. It annoyed him to continually have to justify himself to her. 'Small acts with large consequences.'

'Consequences are right.' McFarlane drew back. 'I brought this to you first so you can think about your next decision, Ekko. I've called a meeting of the board, to review the situation regarding the SCD in the coming days. I wanted to give you time to prepare a full response.' She turned as she walked away. 'Don't waste it.'

Solomon snatched the folder from Delancort's hand and held it to the naked flame flickering at the head of the torch.

'How does she know about Garza?' The folder caught alight and he watched it burn.

'I do not know,' said Delancort. 'Our security is airtight.'

Solomon threw the ashen remnants of the file into the surf.

'It would seem otherwise.' He looked back at the other man and saw a flicker of anxiety in his eyes. 'There is something else,' he surmised.

'I thought it best not to say anything while McFarlane was listening—'

'Tell me,' snapped Solomon.

Delancort frowned. 'Lucy Keyes and Marc Dane are missing.'

THREE

Lucy crawled her way back to consciousness, rising up through foggy layers of awareness until she could open her eyes.

Hard sunlight penetrated the rough cloth bag over her head, enough to give her the vaguest impression of where their abductors had taken them.

The air was still, damp and stiflingly warm. It lay heavy in her lungs and it smelled of earth and rotting vegetation.

Farm, said a voice in the back of her mind, as her combat instincts kicked in and the odours connected with old memories. *You're on a farm.*

That made sense. There were hundreds of olive groves in southern Portugal, places away from the main roads where bad things could happen that no one would know about. If that assumption was on the money, it meant that Lucy hadn't been taken far from where she and Marc had been snatched.

Lucy took stock, mentally checking over her body the same way she would have with a loaded firearm. Inwardly examining herself, she looked for the places where it hurt. Her joints ached, and there were plastic ties around her wrists and ankles. She was secured to a heavy wooden chair that creaked underneath her. *Good.* Wood was better than metal. That was something she could work with.

Her tongue was furred and she felt slow, still gripped by fading effects of the powerful sedative from the tranquiliser dart. *Pentobarbital*, she guessed, by the speed and force of the drug shot. It was tricky, and could kill if not administered in the correct dose.

That gave her another piece of the puzzle. The people who took them had to be professionals, not just hired hands.

This felt like an agency takedown, she decided. The Russians, maybe? They liked chemical interventions. Mossad were another possibility, but she dismissed that quickly. The Israelis wouldn't have stuck around.

She shifted in the chair, feeling it move slightly beneath her. Through the hood she could make out another slumped form close by.

'Marc? That you?'

'This place smells funky. Ugh.' He slurred a few words, then shook it off. 'Shit. Let my bloody guard down and now look at us.' She could see him rolling his head, trying to dislodge his hood. 'How long . . . you think we've been here?'

Lucy felt an IV line taped into the vein in the crook of her arm, and dimly she pulled up recall of darkness, a night's chill, of someone putting the needle in her.

'A day? At least.'

'Yeah.'

Both of them fell silent, listening to the world around them. Faint birdsong and the sound of a jet passing over were the only noises. She cocked her head.

'Not a military plane,' she offered.

'No. Airliner,' confirmed Marc. 'If we're still local, it could be coming from or going to the airport at Faro.'

'Okay.' Having another fragment of information gave Lucy the impetus to strive for the next, to keep building up the jigsaw. 'Sun's not overhead yet, so it's gotta be mid-morning.'

'You get a look at the creeps who grabbed us?'

'That's a negative. They were masked up. Didn't recognise the kit either.'

From somewhere off in the distance, they both heard a door slam.

Marc's next words echoed Lucy's own thoughts. 'If they're pros, they'll know how long the sedatives last. They'll come back.'

'Copy that.' Lucy shifted and pressed her feet into the ground. 'I'm gonna try something.'

She could make out the cannula tube from the IV line hanging near her head, which meant there had to be a stand behind her, out of sight. Lucy rocked forward and back, getting momentum, and sunlight flickered off the dangling pipe as it moved with her.

'What are you doing?'

'Quiet! Need to concentrate.'

Motion overcame gravity and the chair tipped forward. Lucy put her weight in the direction of the tube and landed face down on the earthen floor. The arm of the chair caught the cannula tube against the dirt and held it there, close enough for Lucy to get her fingers to it. Slowly, she wound the thin plastic around them and felt the needle inserted in her arm pull at the skin. Lucy worked at the tube, gathering a loop of it in her palm, gently tugging. It was hard to do face down with her ass in the air, but with a stinging sensation, the IV needle finally popped out.

She smiled. 'Jackpot.'

The needle was thin but strong, and she manipulated it until the tip was in the strap-lock of the closest cable tie.

'I hear someone moving around outside,' whispered Marc.

The needle found the right angle and Lucy used it like a shim, manipulating the locking bar on the tie around her wrist by feel. Her right hand flopped free and she used it to pull the hood off her face.

Earth and stale plant smells assailed her as she rolled onto her side and used the needle on the other ties. The guess about the olive grove was dead on. They were inside a disused growing space, a metal-framed half-cylinder draped with thick polythene sheeting, and through the dirty plastic she could see stands of trees and the side of a low, shabby farmhouse. Plant pots and bags of fertiliser were stacked nearby.

Once she was free, Lucy crouched at Marc's side and got him loose, discarding his hood and using the needle trick on the ties again. He pulled the IV line in his own arm and winced.

'Two ways to play this,' he noted. 'We peg it, get to a road, put as much distance as we can between us and these pricks. Or . . .'

'We fuck with their program.' She found a shovel and weighed it in her hands, considering how much damage she could do with it.

'I thought you might prefer that option.'

Marc stood up unsteadily, then kicked out a leg of the chair he had been sitting on, twisting it off where it broke to create a makeshift side-handle baton.

Lucy heard the scuffing of boots and turned towards it. Through the grimy polythene, she could see two shadows approaching. She threw Marc a warning nod and they both shrank back, out of sight.

There was a sheet-metal door built into the greenhouse's rickety frame, and it slid back on poorly greased runners. A white woman with a bandana holding up a shock of dark hair entered first, a bigger guy with East Asian features coming in right behind. They both wore jeans and sweatshirts of the same deliberately unremarkable style, and the man had a dart gun in his hand.

The woman was two steps into the greenhouse before she saw that the chairs were empty, and jerked to a halt. She paid dearly for her hesitation.

Down low, Lucy swung the heavy shovel out at kneecap level and smacked the woman hard in the backs of the legs with the flat of the blade. She fell down in the dirt with a pained yelp, and at the same time Marc attacked the guy with his chair-leg *tonfa*.

The Brit hit the gunman twice in the head, rolling the other man away in pain and confusion. Marc let his improvised weapon drop and grabbed for the dart gun, trying to wrestle it out of the man's grip.

Meanwhile, Lucy was already on her target, getting a choke-hold around her neck. She pulled it tight and felt the woman claw and kick as the blood flow to her brain was strangled. She tried to choke out something, but Lucy held on, counting off the seconds. Keep the hold going for the right amount and she would put her abductor out for the count. Too long and it would be a death sentence.

Lucy considered it. In the moment what stopped her was that the attackers had used non-lethal weapons against her and Marc, and reluctantly, she decided to return the courtesy. *Hope I won't regret it later*, she thought.

From across the greenhouse, she heard the pneumatic pistol cough and saw that Marc had forced the man to fire a dart into his own thigh. The second assailant exhaled half a swear word and sank into a heap. In a few moments, he was dead to the world.

Marc and Lucy checked the pockets of their abductors, collectively coming up with a few reloads for the trank gun, a walkie-talkie, a pack of Marlboros and a disposable lighter.

'No pocket litter,' Marc noted. 'Nothing to identify who they are or where they're from.' He glanced at the radio. 'This kit is generic.'

Lucy pulled up the woman's sleeves, looking for tattoos or identifying marks, and came up empty.

'Just a pair of nobodies, huh?'

Marc opened the door a crack and peered out.

'I see the van. No sign of the Audi.' He frowned. 'You know if I lose that car, Delancort will never let me forget it.'

'Priorities,' she admonished.

'Yeah, yeah . . .' Marc handed the dart gun to Lucy. 'Here, I'm a decent shot, but you're better.' He picked up the shovel as she looked over his shoulder.

'Don't jinx me,' she told him. Across the way, Lucy saw a single door leading into the farmhouse. 'Okay, dynamic entry right there. I'll shoot anyone who gets creative.'

'Leave one talkative.' Marc's expression hardened. 'We'll have a nice chat.'

'Copy that.'

Lucy eased the sliding door open and gave a count of three, then ducked out, low and fast.

They had ten metres of open ground to cover. The key to turning the tables on their captors would be speed and surprise.

But it went to hell when a third man came around the corner of the farmhouse with a cigarette in his hand, a shotgun hanging off a strap over his shoulder and one arm done up in a makeshift sling. He had to be the one Lucy had introduced to the table knife back in the cafe. The man blinked in shock at the sight of the two escapees and Lucy had the measure of him in an instant – a thickset white guy, short-haired, with the gait of a soldier.

He fumbled at his gun, at the same time shouting '*Oi!*' as loud as he could in a rough British snarl, and that was the end of any kind of sneak attack.

Lucy squeezed the trank gun's trigger, but the weapon was light and it pulled off to the right. The dart whistled through the air and missed.

Marc ran at him, swinging the shovel at his head, and he brought up his other arm to deflect the blow, falling short because of his earlier injury. Lucy ratcheted the dart gun's slide to put another trank in the chamber.

The farmhouse door slammed open and two more figures burst out into the daylight, each armed with the same weapon as Lucy. One was a shorter woman, hard-faced and angry, the other a man in his late forties with the look of a veteran about him. A light went off in her head; she'd seen the older man before, but couldn't place him.

The veteran saw them and immediately held up his gun.

'Stop! *Everyone stop!*' Another Brit by the accent. 'Dane, just *hold it!*'

Marc locked eyes with the older man and he stopped dead.

'What the hell?'

'Put it down, love,' said the angry woman, never taking her gaze off Lucy.

'Blow me,' she retorted, aiming the dart gun at the other woman's chest. She wouldn't miss a second time.

'John?' Marc said the other man's name like he was waking up from a dream. 'What are you doing here?'

'You know these people?' Lucy asked, still glaring at the other woman.

She and the others were British, which likely meant MI6, the UK's external security and intelligence service. Marc Dane's old crew.

'John Farrier,' said Marc, nodding at the veteran. 'Recruited me into K Section at Six, a dog's age ago. And the lady there is Tracey Lane. Don't know the rest of them.'

'Charmed,' sneered Lane. 'Tell your girlfriend to drop the gun, Dane, or I *will* shoot her again.'

'That's Pearce,' said Farrier, nodding at the man with the shotgun. 'Who you stabbed.'

'All right?' said the bigger guy in an agreeable tone.

Farrier went on. 'The other two are Regis and Suresh, and I'm really hoping you haven't done them any serious damage.' He walked forward and put his hand on Lane's gun, forcing her to aim it away. 'Tracey, let's not escalate this.'

Marc still had the shovel in his hands, his knuckles white around the wooden shaft.

'What. The fuck. Is going on?'

'This is OpTeam Paladin,' said Farrier. 'I'm running on-site command and control. You're our target, mate.'

Lucy knew only bits and pieces about the MI6 Tactical Operations Team programme, and most of that had come from Dane. Before joining Rubicon, he'd been a member of a unit like this one, codenamed Nomad.

At that time, he was working as a field technician, the one in the van running comms and tech while operatives with Lucy's skill set did the door-kicking and trigger-pulling. The OpTeams were agile, cellular units deployed by British Intelligence for what spy agencies called 'kinetic actions', a euphemism for counter-terrorist missions, surgical strikes or anything else off the black ops menu.

Not a million miles away from what the Special Conditions Division did, in point of fact. But unlike these folks, the SCD operated outside nations and governments.

Anger and disappointment twisted in Marc's expression. Lucy could see that Farrier meant something to him, immediately getting the sense that the two men had been friends. Then it came back to her in a flash and she remembered where she had first seen the other man's face.

A brief glimpse of Farrier following Marc into a graveyard in East London, after they stopped the terrorist group Al Sayf from triggering a suicide attack in Washington DC.

'I'm here because I wanted to bring you in personally,' Farrier was saying.

'I don't work for Her Majesty's Government any more, John,' Marc broke in. 'Being accused of killing my team, and getting framed by a traitor, was more than enough to make me pack it in.'

'That's a fair point,' the other man allowed, and he gave a weak grin. 'In retrospect, we could have handled this better.'

Marc let the shovel drop, and his hands tightened into fists.

'If you wanted to talk to me, you could have just done it!'

'Not with her around,' snapped Lane, pointing at Lucy. 'She's a criminal, a deserter, a known killer. Standard Operating Procedure is to isolate first, explain later.'

'Aww, you kids are that scared of little old me?' Lucy drew out the words. 'I'm flattered.'

'As far as I'm concerned, you're both trouble,' said Lane.

Marc glanced at Lucy, nodding in Lane's direction. 'Don't mind her, I made her look bad once,' he said, by way of explanation. 'She clearly hasn't forgiven me.'

Farrier held up his hands in what he clearly hoped was a calming fashion, as Pearce moved over to the greenhouse to check on the other agents.

'Look, Marc. Something serious has come up, and like it or not, you're connected. The Head of Operations ordered me to bring you in, and that's why we are here.' He paused. 'I mean . . . You wouldn't have just come if I asked you.'

'Yes I fucking would!' Marc retorted hotly. 'We could have done this without the drugging and the kidnapping, mate!'

'We couldn't take the risk you'd refuse,' Lane said flatly. 'If it was my choice, you two wouldn't have woken up until you were in the basement at Vauxhall Cross.'

'Lane, you're not helping.' Farrier gave his agent a hard look, then turned back to Marc. 'I'm sorry, but this is how it had to be done. Fact is, Rubicon is an unknown quantity and you've been out of the family for a couple of years. We didn't know how you'd react.'

'To what?'

'Tell him,' said Lane. 'You'll have to, sooner or later.'

Farrier gave a sigh. 'Samantha Green.'

'What about her?' snapped Marc.

'She's alive.'

Lucy watched the colour drain from Marc's face.

'No,' he said, after a long moment. 'I was there. She's gone.' The words came out flat and toneless.

This part, Lucy *did* know about. Sam Green had been part of OpTeam Nomad, and one of Marc's former teammates. A victim of an ambush that had killed six intelligence operatives and half a dozen civilians, when a massive bomb destroyed a freighter at the port of Dunkirk.

But Green had meant a lot more to Marc than he was willing to admit. He'd let things slip a few times about how the two of them were closer than regulations allowed. The murder of his team had hit him hard, but Sam's loss was the worst of all.

I watched her die, Marc had once told Lucy, lost in the recall of something terrible. *I watched her fade out and drift into the dark.*

Lucy felt a jolt of empathy for her partner, mingled with an edge of anger that came out of nowhere. It had taken Marc Dane a long time to let go of the responsibility he felt for the deaths of Nomad, to get past the compulsion in him to undo that event in every mission he took on. Guilt like that was corrosive, and it could eat you alive.

Lucy had a share of her own, and she knew full well what it cost. She couldn't escape the thread of resentment that Sam Green's name dragged up in her. After all this time, the woman was reaching out from the grave to pull Lucy's friend away from the light he'd worked so hard to reach.

'We have evidence,' Farrier said grimly.

'Show me,' said Marc.

The lunch that had been brought to Esther McFarlane's room at the Hôtel de Paris sat untouched on its tray, the coffee turned stale and lukewarm, the cheeses and pastries wilting in the untrammelled golden sunshine beating down on the terrace.

She sat on an elegant rattan chair beneath a wide parasol, ignoring the food, ignoring the stunning view out over the quays of Monte Carlo, and the mass of yachts packed into Port Hercule's moorings.

Her thoughts were still where they had been when she left Edinburgh two days earlier. The digital tablet on her lap absorbed her attention, a complex report into drilling operations taking place at the Ninian oil field in the North Sea.

She was here in body, but in spirit McFarlane was beneath the frigid waters off the Outer Hebrides, down in the stone and earth of the seabed, thinking on how to tease out every last barrel of crude trapped there.

Esther was the current generation of a dynasty of Scottish industrialists that had started in the nineteenth-century farming bog head coal, and now held interests in gas and oil reserves around the world. She was an accomplished geologist as much as she was an uncompromising businesswoman, and when McFarlane needed to centre herself, rock and stone was what she returned to.

Geology had a form that she could grasp and understand, and studying the data on the tablet gave her focus. People and companies and all that came with them were far more difficult for her to parse. Esther had grown up in a family with a brisk attitude to interpersonal relationships, where the work was always the most significant thing. Her family was not only her parents or her siblings, Ruth and Jennifer. It was the workforce on the rigs, in the refineries and laboratories. Their fates were tied to the black gold they tore out of the ground, to the company that bound them together – and in turn, that company was irrevocably joined to the Rubicon Group.

If Rubicon crumbled, so would McFarlane Energy, and so would the lives of countless workers. Her family's fiefdom, for want of a better term, would come apart. That was something Esther could not allow.

She heard the delicate trill of a telephone back in her suite, and presently her assistant appeared at the terrace's open doors. Ryan Finlay was from Glasgow, but she didn't hold that against him. The rangy young man with dark eyes and close-cropped hair stood in the shade, with a handset in his grip.

'Call for you, ma'am,' he told her. 'It's *him*.'

McFarlane toyed with the idea of telling Finlay to decline the conversation, but her curiosity got the better of her.

She knew it would. McFarlane had been waiting for this call ever since she returned from her meeting on the beach.

'Give it to me and go away,' she replied, putting aside the tablet and waving Finlay off.

He did as he was told, but she sensed he was still close by, lurking out of sight inside the suite. Her assistant was good at his job, but he had a tendency to hover that she found tiresome. For now, she let that pass.

'*Good afternoon, Ms McFarlane,*' said the man on the other end of the line. '*How are you enjoying Monaco?*'

She listened carefully to every word, weighing each sentence and searching through them to study his diction. McFarlane believed that he was not a native English speaker, but that he had been educated in Europe to a high standard. The faint lilt in some of the words suggested a person of Far Eastern origin, but she was still uncertain. He was a puzzle, and she liked those.

'I had a feeling you would be in touch. You're calling to see how your present was received.'

'*Of course,*' he replied. '*I am interested to know how Ekko Solomon responded to the file I provided.*' There was a pause.

'*Ekko is such a measured soul, don't you agree? Composed to the point that one can be frustrated by him. Sometimes it is amusing to throw a stone into a calm pond and see what patterns the ripples make.*'

'You already know the answer,' she said warily. 'He wasn't best pleased.'

'*He likes his secrets.*'

'Aye, so he does.'

She stood up and walked to the edge of the terrace, leaning on the sun-warmed iron rail around the edge. Despite the heat, McFarlane felt a chill run down her spine. She had the uneasy sensation that whomever she was talking to was watching her at this very moment.

'All right, you have my attention. Who are you and what do you want?'

'*I will not divulge my identity for the moment. I have to maintain some distance. But as to what I want . . . I want the truth to come out, Ms McFarlane. I want to help you ensure the stability you seek for your people.*'

'That's generous of you.'

'*There is other material I could provide, other files,*' he went on. '*Material that shows exactly what kind of man Ekko Solomon is. You could make good use of it.*'

Questions rolled through her thoughts like dark tidal breakers. How exactly did this mystery man know what she wanted, how did he have access to information about Rubicon that even a member of the board of directors did not, and how did he know where to find her? She pushed those concerns aside.

'My father always told me, "Nobody gives you nothing" and he's never been wrong. What's the price of this going to be?'

'*We should meet, face to face,*' said the man. '*You are a shrewd judge of character. We will better understand what we can do for one another if we can first look each other in the eye. Do you agree?*'

'I agree.'

It would have been a lie to say anything else. As much as she sensed the danger in dealing with this unknown source, Solomon's reaction on the beach and McFarlane's own research into the Garza file convinced her it was authentic. If there was more like it – and there had to be, she was certain of it – then perhaps it could provide her with what she needed to finally end Solomon's adventurism.

'*I am pleased,*' said the voice on the phone, and there was amusement in it. '*I will contact Mr Finlay in a few hours with details of a location. Good day.*'

The line went dead and McFarlane found herself looking down at the boats in the marina, searching for a smiling face looking back at her.

The Leonardo made a languid turn over the roof of the mansion house, blasting the closely packed trees with the downwash from its rotors. A shiny black form like a lacquered wasp, the helicopter pivoted to drop cleanly onto a wide stone platform in the middle of the house's ornamental gardens, its undercarriage emerging from hidden bays in the nose and winglets.

Pytor Glovkonin stood unmoving as the hurricane-force winds plucked at the hems of his slate-grey Kiton suit, his hands clasped in front of him while his two bodyguards shielded their eyes from the dust kicked up by the arrival. The tall, imposing Russian oligarch was unimpressed by this show of power and presence. It was the kind of entrance he might have made himself, but with less panache. The helicopter's rotors wound down and he flicked a speck of grass off his lapel, before running a hand over the scrupulously maintained beard that did nothing to soften the harsh angles of his face.

Normally, Glovkonin would have sent his people out to greet this visitor in the manner of some king bringing a new petitioner to his court, but the power dynamic in this meeting was weighted in the opposite direction.

A trim, handsome man in a straw-coloured jacket and designer jeans stepped cleanly out of the helicopter's limousine-styled interior, catching Glovkonin's eye and giving him a jaunty salute.

The Italian, as Glovkonin thought of him, was a few years his junior and unfailingly confident with it. An engineering tycoon with a taste for fast cars, trophy wives and frequent divorces, on paper he would have appeared to be of similar status to the Russian billionaire. With any of those gauche rich lists or three-comma clubs their names would have been in the same stable, but what counted between them was something more ephemeral than money. The Italian bettered Glovkonin in one essential way. He had a seat at a very particular table that the Russian longed to join.

'Pytor . . .' The Italian spoke in English, their only shared language, and still he was able to ruin the Russian's name with his accented, indolent delivery. 'How are you, my friend?'

'Well,' Glovkonin replied, behind a thin smile. He gestured at the house and the groves of trees around them. 'Welcome to Corsica.'

'Do you know, I've never been before?' The Italian stepped in close, putting a hand on Glovkonin's shoulder and speaking as if he was confiding a secret. 'I suppose I should have before today. I hear the food is remarkable.'

Misha and Gregor, the Russian's thickset bodyguards, reacted to the Italian's overly familiar behaviour, their stances tensing as if they were attack dogs whose owner had been threatened. Glovkonin gave them a slight shake of the head as he allowed the other man to lead him away, and the two ex-Spetsnaz fell in step behind.

The Italian, he noted, had left his own security waiting by the helicopter. Only a secretary, an attractive blonde with a Germanic look about her, followed on.

'I want you to know that I appreciate you handling this personally,' said the younger man. 'The other members of the committee . . .' He made a *what-can-you-do* face. 'You know how they are. They've forgotten what it means to get their hands dirty.'

Glovkonin glanced down at the Italian's soft palms and wondered if he had ever worked a day in his life. The Russian knew the meaning of toil and struggle; he had lived through it in the bad years of the Soviet Union. This one had inherited every euro he had. Like the rest of the men who stood in his way, who held the status that Glovkonin coveted, the Italian was more akin to a monarch risen to power by birthright. He was no self-made man, even if he pretended as such, and it irritated the Russian to think his guest believed that lie would work on him.

'I intend my association with the Combine to be long and productive,' said Glovkonin, and the Italian winced as he used the group's informal name. They didn't like anyone to say it out loud, as if to do so would invite danger.

'Of course. And you've made yourself at home here.'

The Italian nodded towards the house as they approached the open doors to the great hall.

'We have made great progress,' he agreed.

The country estate lay towards the northern end of Corsica, up above the town of Bastia, an oasis of affluence shrouded by the thick woodlands and a treacherous hillside. Outwardly it was a convivial place, as good as any of Glovkonin's holiday residences, but beneath its faded opulence the estate hid a different face. Men would come here to train with weapons and tactics, safe from the prying eyes of police forces and spy agencies. Valuable computer data was held in server farms buried beneath the hill, off the grid and invisible to the world. It was one of a handful of 'embassies' secretly owned by the members of the Combine, a node in their network of power and influence around the globe.

Glovkonin had first heard of the organisation as a young man, and at the time they seemed like a fanciful concept. A clannish group of the rich and amoral, who saw the opportunity inherent in man's unerring ability to make war on his own species.

Armourers, gunrunners and quartermasters to the fanatical, the desperate and the hateful, the Combine's stewards were already among the wealthiest men on Earth. But money is its own end, a truth that Glovkonin knew all too well, and the Combine drew together their assets to help foster the instabilities of a troubled world.

They profited *greatly*. So the rumours said, beginning in the ashes of the First World War to the present day, stoking fears and fuelling conflicts on every scale. The Combine sought what Glovkonin thought of as *a stable instability* – that perfect state of grace forever balanced on a tipping point between chaos and order. In that condition, nations and non-state actors alike could be controlled, caught in a war that never ended, where victory could never be declared.

That was real power, he reflected, true wealth. And Glovkonin wanted it more than anything in the world.

A rich man only hates one thing, only really desires one thing, the Russian told himself, *and that is what he is told he cannot have.*

It had taken him years to get to this point, to be standing outside the circle of the Combine's controlling committee. Millions of dollars expended. Murders and lies and other crimes committed. And still it wasn't enough.

'But soon, though,' said the Italian, and Glovkonin almost flinched, as if the other man had plucked the words from his silent thoughts. 'Soon we'll need to see some concrete results, Pytor. The role you occupy – that of your predecessor, Celeste . . . She was noted for her ability to act with rapidity and ruthlessness. By contrast, your operations are taking much longer.'

Glovkonin smothered a sneer at the mention of Celeste Toussaint's name. He had engineered the assassination of the French media baroness in order to take her place in the Combine's cellular structure, and the Italian and his friends had to suspect so. That they let it happen and did nothing spoke volumes, and this thin excuse for chastising him was an irritation.

'The work can be done quickly or it can be done well. I prefer the latter.'

They passed through the halls of the great house, spaces modelled on the palaces of regency-era France, with ornately decorated walls and painted ceilings. Many of these had been turned over for use as military-style operations rooms, and the stark lines of modular computer units and encrypted satellite communications systems clashed aggressively with the eighteenth-century aesthetic.

The Italian paused in front of a bank of screens erected across a wall of faded portraiture, engaged by a display of live data coming from several of the world's key financial markets. Waves of green and red pixels moved to show the relative values of dollars and yuan, the fluctuation of gold stocks, steel futures and countless other indicators. It was the wealth of the world, washing back and forth in real time.

On a stock ticker along the bottom of the screen, Glovkonin saw the code for his own company – the Eastern European gas and oil conglomerate G-Kor – and smiled at the green numerals showing a value increase.

'You're having a good day,' said the Italian lightly. His tone was almost mocking, but then again, it always was. 'I would like to say more than that to my colleagues on the committee when I speak to them again.' The flippancy in his voice faded. 'You made a lot of promises. You need to make good on them.'

Glovkonin moderated his expression. 'The Combine have suffered setbacks in recent years,' he began, again enjoying the twitch in the Italian's jaw when he said the name. 'And most of them can be traced back to one source.'

'Rubicon.'

The Russian nodded. 'Not alone, of course. The Central Intelligence Agency have caused problems within the United States, but those have largely been contained. And then there is the British secret service, who continue to interfere with global affairs despite the irrelevance of their tiresome little island. But none are as constant a thorn in our side as the African and his band of mercenaries.'

The plot to use an Islamic terror cell to bomb a presidential rally in America; a scheme to take control of a portable nuclear device; a failed attempt to crash the economy of South

Korea; and in the last six months, the disruption of a planned false flag biological attack in Europe. Over the last few years, each of these operations had been guided by or benefited the Combine in some fashion. Each one had ultimately failed because of outside intervention.

'The British must be taught to mind their own business,' said the other man. 'But Rubicon is another matter entirely, it—'

'Rubicon needs to be obliterated, *da*.' Glovkonin liked saying the words out loud. 'To send a message.'

'Among other things.' The Italian studied him closely. 'Don't preen so much, Pytor. I know you have been advocating for Ekko Solomon's termination for a long time. You are being given the opportunity you asked for, so don't waste it.'

He bristled. 'We have not been idle. Key recruits are in place. Operations have begun. It is a matter of time before a point of critical momentum is achieved.'

'Time,' said the other man, with an airy sigh. 'It is not a limitless quantity, my friend. Remember that removing Rubicon from the board is not the end goal. Solomon's operation is an impediment to a larger work. While you are focused on Rubicon, the committee has a bigger picture to consider. You prevent us from moving forward.' The Italian looked around. 'Where is Lau? After the considerable investment we put into him, I would like to be reassured that he was worth it.'

Glovkonin opened his mouth to answer, but another voice beat him to it.

'I am here.'

A thin, gaunt figure in a linen shirt, deck shoes and casual slacks appeared from behind one of the server racks, materialising like a summoned wraith.

Lau – full name Lau Fa Weng – was in his early fifties, but the institutionalised cruelty of a harsh prison system had aged him beyond his years. The limp in his gait was exaggerated by a steel walking stick, but even with it the Chinese man moved with purpose, with a soldier's economy of motion. He gave a humourless smile without revealing any teeth, but the silence of his approach had given them pause. Glovkonin wondered how long had Lau been following them, listening.

The Italian's secretary reacted by putting herself between Lau and her employer, and abruptly Glovkonin realised he had misread the woman's function. She was only meant to *look* like an executive assistant. She was agile and watchful, the mask of blank vapidity she had worn gone in an instant.

The younger man said something *sotto voce* and the woman relaxed, but not all the way.

Lau inclined his head to her, a mutual moment of respect perhaps, and then he came to stand in front of the two men.

'I could tell you how grateful I am that your group has given me these tools,' he began, one long-fingered hand waving at the room around them. 'But as you said, our time is not limitless. To the matter of the moment, then.'

He led them to a workstation, where a digital tablet the size of a coffee table displayed false-colour imagery of a landscape. It was a ground-penetrating radar image, noted Glovkonin, the kind generated by orbiting satellites that searched remote regions for mineral deposits below the surface of the Earth. Sections of the map were cloudy, showing areas that had once been open trenches.

'What is this?' said the Italian, sounding disinterested.

'The dead,' said Lau, drawing a finger over the image, hesitating at the darker patches. 'Interred in shallow graves for decades.

This technology has been used by the United Nations to search for evidence of war crimes. I am doing the same, assembling proof.'

'To what end?'

'Burning down Rubicon would take a lot of gasoline and matches,' said Glovkonin, with a sniff. 'Better that we help it destroy itself, yes?'

Lau gave that non-smile again, fixing the Italian with a stare.

'You want Solomon ended. I will do that for you.' He pointed at the screen again. 'This is the way.'

There was something raw in his words, the Russian noted. A need that was growing with each passing day. At first, Lau had seemed almost indifferent to the task of destroying Ekko Solomon – a strange outlook, considering it was the African who had been responsible for all that Lau had endured. But in the weeks and months following his liberation from a *laogai*, the man's fire had begun to rekindle. Freed from captivity in the Chinese state gulag, he was rediscovering his desire for retribution, as the chance to settle old scores became real and achievable.

I am bringing out the worst in him, Glovkonin told himself, *nursing it back to health.* He smiled at the thought.

'I want you to understand what was taken from me,' Lau continued. 'Thirty years of my life, lost to pain and torture. Not for what I knew, but for punishment's sake. So I would be an example to those who might put themselves above the needs of the State and the People.'

That old, cold fury burned hard, glittering through the cracks in his façade, and in a matter-of-fact way he told them about the beatings, the degradation, and the endless mechanical process of the attempts to break his spirit.

Lau had a magnetism about him when he spoke like this, and in it, Glovkonin saw glimpses of the man he had once been. Thirty years ago, he would have been a force to be reckoned with.

'Believe me when I tell you, my life has no other purpose than to tear down everything Ekko Solomon has built in the years he stole from me. I will repay him in full.'

The Italian gave a nervous laugh and shot Glovkonin a look.

'Your friend here, he's quite intense! I respect that, the *passione per la guerra*, eh?' But then his humour waned. 'A good performance is fine enough, but we want to see action.'

'Before the week is out,' said Lau, looking to Glovkonin for a nod of confirmation, 'the walls of Solomon's palace will crumble.'

'A pretty metaphor,' said the Italian. 'You sound so certain. I am almost convinced.'

'I *am* certain,' Lau insisted. He nodded at the screen. 'After all, I know where the bodies are buried.'

The Italian remained for lunch, and then made his excuses and departed, the helicopter blasting away in a showy display of noise that mirrored the man himself. As the aircraft diminished in the teal afternoon sky, Glovkonin paused to study Lau anew.

He was dangerous, this one. The knowledge in his head was like plutonium – rich with power but toxic to the touch. He would need to be handled carefully.

'What you said, about how you were tortured,' said the Russian. 'How much of it was true?'

Lau's stories were so gruelling and grotesque that they seemed somehow improbable, even to a man who had grown up under the yoke of the Politburo at the height of the Soviet system.

Lau eyed him gravely. 'You lie a great deal,' he said, 'so you assume that everyone else also does so.' He turned away. 'I have no reason to be untruthful about anything.'

FOUR

Every security service had their own name for their places of work, varying from darkly derogatory to descriptive or cryptic.

Americans at the National Security Agency in Fort Meade called their facility '*the Puzzle Palace*'; for the French, the Direction Générale de la Sécurité Extérieure's home base was '*the Swimming Pool*' because of its proximity to the one used in the 1924 Summer Olympics; a glassy block in Moscow belonging to the GRU was known as '*the Aquarium*'; and MI6's art deco-style headquarters near London's Vauxhall station had been christened '*Legoland*' by some cynical soul serving within it.

In many ways, the building did resemble one of the plastic-brick construction sets in its final form. Sandstone-coloured walls made up of square panels, and grids of emerald glass windows formed a blocky bulwark on the South Bank of the Thames. It blended with the office blocks, hotels and apartments strung around it along the riverside. It was easy to overlook that Number 85 Vauxhall Cross went as far below ground as it did above, the unseen lower levels concealing the British Secret Service's external intelligence apparatus as it went about its duties.

Returning there was not something Marc Dane welcomed. The last time he had stepped through MI6's doors, he had walked in from out of the cold, his team dead, and unknown to him, the blame for their killings laid at his feet.

He missed London more than he cared to admit, missed the city he'd grown up in, fallen in love in, got drunk, hurt, laughed and cried in. But he didn't miss this piece of it.

Blackness engulfed the minivan that brought them from the airbase at Brize Norton as it left the street, and passed into an enclosed car park. A heavy, armoured gate dropped shut, and to Marc it was like a great castle portcullis coming down, sealing him off from the world. *Next stop, the dungeons.*

'Not happy to be home?' Looking at Marc from the front passenger seat, Lane didn't miss the opportunity to needle him.

'Do you have to keep talking?' Lucy interposed, from behind him.

'No one invited you, love,' Lane replied coldly.

'We kinda got past good manners when you drugged and kidnapped us,' Lucy retorted.

An argument had been brewing since they flew out of Portugal, and Marc stepped in to stop it before it finally kicked off.

'Let's just get this done. We need to check in with our office, let them know we're okay.'

'I'll see to it,' said Farrier, seated nearby. 'But we need to keep the circle tight on this, Marc. We have a renegade MI6 officer at large, and we don't want everyone and their dog knowing about it.'

Marc shot him a look. 'Rubicon knows how to keep confidences.'

'That's part of the problem,' Lane noted. 'They're an unknown quantity.'

The minivan halted and they climbed out, into an echoing grey space. Marc's gaze was immediately drawn to a nearby line of shabby, unmarked white vans. They were similar to any one of hundreds of other unremarkable delivery vehicles that roved the streets of the UK on any given weekday, slightly battered and scuffed, deliberately ordinary. You would have to look twice to see that they sat low on their axles, or notice the discreet blisters on the top of the cabs that concealed antennae for encrypted radio channels.

Marc knew the inside of those vans better than the council flat he grew up in. He had spent a long time in vehicles just like them, sitting in front of a monitor with a radio link in one ear, working communications, systems intrusion or drone control while a group of armed operatives were busy prosecuting a target.

That was who he used to be. A 'forward mission specialist', the guy in the van, the techie with the toy box. The one who stayed behind when others went in harm's way.

He could barely remember what it felt like to be that person. Too much had changed, too much blood had been shed. *What would that Marc Dane think of me?* He didn't have an answer that he liked.

The group were met by security, and for the second time since returning home Marc was searched thoroughly by grim-faced men with guns. When they were eventually satisfied, he and Lucy were allowed to ride up to the higher floors in a windowless elevator, with two armed guards flanking them.

One of the escorts stared fixedly at Marc, and finally he turned to face him.

'Can I help you with something, mate?'

'You remember me?' asked the man.

Marc looked him up and down. 'Not really,' he admitted.

The escort was the kind of bloke that Six liked to recruit for their tough-guy jobs. Former coppers or men out of the Parachute Regiment, good at taking orders and giving out hard jolts of controlled violence where it was needed, but not flexible enough to be field officer material. The man seemed vaguely familiar. He had probably been working here when Marc was part of OpTeam Nomad.

The guy reached down and slapped his calf.

'I caught a bullet, a through and through, right here. The docs told me I wouldn't walk properly again. But I showed those pricks. Eighteen months of fuckin' physio. Wasn't going to let them take my job.' He paused, then showed his teeth. 'Last time you saw me, I had a mask on.' The man held up the MP7 machine gun hanging off a strap across his chest, as if he was on an operation. 'On a roof. Block of flats in Walworth. It coming back to ya?'

'Oh.' And in a rush, it did.

Marc remembered a grimy, half-derelict housing estate in South London. He had been on the run, hiding out while a forger cut him new papers. A traitor in his own department, his former supervisor, had cooked the paperwork so an arrest warrant for Marc turned into a shoot on sight command. The escort was one of the men who had been sent to do the deed, and he would have, if not for the intervention of Rubicon.

'Huh.' Lucy leaned into the conversation. 'For the record? It was *me* who put you down.' At the time, Marc hadn't known the sniper was watching the whole scene unfold through a rifle scope. 'Dane here could have finished you off,' she added, 'but he didn't.'

The man's expression hardened. He hadn't expected that reply. He glared at Marc, lost for a comeback.

'You're not a small bloke,' Marc noted, refusing to be intimidated. 'You ought to thank the lady for missing the rest of you, yeah?'

The lift arrived and they filed out across a corridor, into a conference room that faced the river. The room was up high, a higher floor than Marc had ever visited as a serving MI6 officer, and through planes of armoured glass, he saw the shapes of the buildings on the North Bank of the Thames.

Lucy immediately moved to the windows, and Marc imagined that was some by-product of her shooter's instincts, always measuring and calculating sight lines and firing angles. Marc's own instincts went to a different place, as he immediately picked out the exit points and the places where surveillance gear was most likely concealed.

Presently, Farrier and Lane joined them, along with two more faces from Marc's past.

Talia Patel looked older than he remembered, but she still dressed the same, in expensive jackets and quality blouses. A well-presented East Asian woman in her early forties, Marc had always considered Talia a professional sort, friendly but not sociable, the kind of department manager that you felt comfortable knowing was on your side. She gave him a brief smile of greeting and came over to shake his hand.

'Marc, it's good to see you again. You look well.'

He nodded. 'I'm surviving. How are you, Talia?'

'The same.' Her smile faltered. 'It was difficult for a while after . . . the unpleasantness. But we moved on.'

Unpleasantness. Marc let the word fade. It was too vague, too bloodless, to encapsulate what they had actually gone through.

Along with a member of Marc's own unit, the head of K Section and the Tactical Operations Team programme – his de facto commanding officer and the man Talia had worked directly below – had betrayed them to the Combine.

Marc walked away from MI6 after that, but like Farrier and Lane, Talia had to live through the aftermath of that crushing deception.

So too had the last man to enter the room. Sandy-haired and of average height and build, Victor Welles dressed like an *Esquire* model, equipped with natural good looks and an ability to make anything he wore seem fashionable. All of that was counterbalanced by an expression that was perpetually on the edge of becoming a sneer, and a superiority in his manner that he did not care to tone down. A director in Six's internal security department, Welles had been instrumental in the hunt for Marc when he was framed by his boss. It had to be acknowledged that as much as Marc thought the man was an egotistical prick, in the end Welles had accepted the truth when it was revealed. He was one of those people who, despite being deeply irritating, was actually good at his job.

Welles gave Marc a brisk, sardonic once-over and didn't offer his hand.

'Dane, how's life in the private sector?'

'Better,' he replied, and decided to leave it at that.

The other man studied Lucy. 'And this is Keyes?' He shot a look at Farrier. 'I don't want her around for the briefing.'

Lucy sniffed. 'What, you brought me here for nothing?' She made a tutting noise.

'You don't get to make that decision, Welles,' Marc said firmly, before Farrier could reply. 'She and I work together. You want me to help you with your problem, Lucy stays.'

'It's like that, is it?' Welles replied.

'It's like that,' said Marc.

Welles paused. 'Fair enough. But don't get comfortable making demands.'

He took a seat and the armed guards stepped back.

'Right.' Farrier placed his hands flat on the table. 'Let's get started.'

He nodded to Talia, who was already busy at a digital notepad.

The windows darkened from pale green to deeply opaque emerald, and a blank video screen on one wall blinked into life. The screen cut itself into sections, each becoming a still image or a box of video footage. Marc saw a street map of Oslo lit up with path indicators.

'Tracey, give us the high points,' said Farrier.

Lane cleared her throat. 'Around five months ago, signals interception at GCHQ noticed an uptick in chatter relating to elements of former OpTeam missions.' She gestured at the screen. 'At first we thought it was some low-priority actors that Six had crossed paths with in the past making noise, nothing that seemed a worry.'

'At first,' repeated Welles. 'That supposition turned out to be very far off the bull.'

Lane went on, ignoring the interruption. 'Someone was poking around in the ashes. Confidential informants we had cut loose, contacts we were no longer using – a dozen of them were targeted by an unknown individual.'

Marc watched a series of poor-quality, long-distance images appear on the screen: views from city streets, railway stations, from the inside of cars. The same slight, athletic woman was in all of them, her face hidden by a hoodie or the bill of a baseball cap. His skin prickled, unable to stop himself anticipating the reveal of her identity. He could feel the moment coming, like a storm about to break.

Samantha Green. Could it really be her? Marc had seen her die, he had watched the light fade in her eyes.

Or had he?

'Unknown was designated as Echo-One,' said Lane. 'We now know she was gathering equipment, securing travel documentation and reaching out to dark net facilitators. Tooling up.'

Farrier gave a nod. 'Everyone she talked to had a connection that tracked back to an MI6 operation in the last five years. And those ops involved your former team, Marc.'

'Nomad,' said Lucy.

Farrier nodded again. 'We dispatched a team to track Echo-One, to determine her identity and intentions.'

'Intelligence led us to Tunisia,' said Lane, 'then to Norway. Team Paladin were on the ground at this stage.'

Marc remembered both of those places. Nomad's mission in Norway had been a penetration, going in to clone the laptop of a British businessman suspected of selling proscribed military software to the Iranians. Tunisia was a long-duration surveillance operation on an extremist training site, but for Marc it had become something else. Lengthy nights alone with Sam Green had brought them closer together than either wanted to admit.

It was the start of something complex and powerful between them. Something neither of them had been able to articulate. And then, before they could figure out the shape of it, she was gone in fire and smoke, and Marc was left with nothing.

'The subject was traced to Oslo.' Talia manipulated her data pad and more images appeared on the screen, overlaying the previous ones. 'The usual track and mark protocols were followed.'

'She used that against us.' Lane's tone turned cold. 'We learned to our cost, she has an intimate knowledge of our standard operating procedures.'

The digital photos told the story. First, they were shots of the woman through a torrent of rain, captured in motion. Then after-action stills and what could only be crime scene photos from the Oslo police. Marc saw the grisly, unidentifiable form of a woman lying against the blood-covered front seat of a car, with a stubby shotgun sitting in her lap. Then, broken bodies of men against steel tracks in the darkness of a subway tunnel, and finally, one more corpse slumped at the foot of a wall.

'Damn,' Lucy muttered to herself. 'She didn't do them clean.'

'As far as we can determine, Echo-One led four members of OpTeam Paladin to a pre-arranged location and killed them.' Farrier delivered the grim facts in short order. 'She displayed skills and knowledge commensurate with those of an MI6 tactical field officer.'

'When did this happen?' Marc's voice sounded dull and distant.

'Ten days ago,' noted Lane. 'Afterwards, the target dropped off the grid and all we have are some comms logs that don't mean anything, all coded references. She's ghosted, and until she sticks her head up again, we have no way to reacquire her.'

'Play the footage from the trail car,' said Welles.

Farrier blew out a breath, then nodded. 'Yeah, sure.' He looked in Marc's direction as Talia brought up another video window. 'I warn you now, you're not going to like this.'

'Just run it,' insisted Welles, and Talia tapped a button on her tablet.

The video showed a windscreen streaked with rain, and part of a car door and side window. Marc oriented himself to the display. It was the point of view of a camera sitting on its side on the top of the dashboard. From a smartphone, he guessed, placed there and left running.

He saw a woman lean into frame from the driver's side, and recognised the fur-collared coat she was wearing. The same one from the police photo, surrounding the crimson mess of a ruined face. The phone recording picked up faint audio of a wailing siren and the fumbling of a key going into the ignition.

'And here she comes,' said Welles.

A shadow moved into sight, a woman in a hoodie appearing at the side window. She had something in her hands, but it was hard to see it clearly.

The driver reacted, twisting around, and there was a sudden bark of gunfire and breaking glass rendered tinny and flat by the phone's low-grade microphone. Blood spattered across the inside of the windscreen and the driver fell away. The phone recorded wet, dying gasps as the driver's killer threw the murder weapon into the car. The woman in the hoodie hesitated, then reached in and stole a shoulder bag that had been sitting in the footwell.

For a brief moment, the killer was clearly visible, and Marc felt as if he had plunged into an ice-cold ocean.

The footage ended, and after a moment a still frame from the recording replaced it on the wall screen. Blown up and sharpened by image processing software, it revealed half a woman's face.

Hard blue eyes above a full mouth and a small nose, a face that could belong to the demure girl next door or the wild woman you met on a crazy night of clubbing. Marc made out scars on her cheek, the puckering and pinking of skin left behind after healed burns.

He wanted more than anything for it to be someone else, but it looked exactly like Samantha Green up there on the screen.

Marc's initial reaction and the sickened feeling in his gut told him that his instincts believed it was her.

'That . . .' He started to speak, faltered, and tried again. 'How can that be her? Sam died in France three years ago. I was with her when it happened.'

He recalled that terrible moment, holding her wounded and burned form as she struggled to hold on to life, then the monstrous crash of a grenade shell that blasted both of them into the stagnant depths of a canal. His last memory of Sam was her body sinking into the darkness, trailing streamers of blood through the dank water like ribbons of smoke.

'It would appear otherwise,' said Welles. 'The image is a 77 per cent match to what we have on file for Green. Good enough to be actionable.' He paused to let that sink in. 'One of our own. Back from the dead. Working against our interests.' He let his sneer show. 'Not the first time that's happened with Nomad, is it?'

'We can put at least three other kills on her,' said Farrier, pressing on. 'They were MI6 assets.'

Marc was struggling to take it in, and at length he sat down, across the table from his old friend.

'Why, John?'

'If we knew that . . .' Farrier trailed off.

'She's operating under an alias,' said Talia. 'She's using the name "Grace".'

'The same name as Green's mother,' added Welles. 'We have her surviving family under close surveillance in case she attempts to contact them, but given her training and personality, I consider that unlikely.'

Marc shot him a look, but stopped himself from saying anything he might regret. It was the right call to make, he thought, but it still felt shitty. Sam's parents had buried their daughter years ago and moved on with their lives as best they could.

'You were the last person to see her, Marc,' said Farrier. 'You're the only surviving member of Nomad. The only person still alive who knows her, who had a . . . a close relationship with her.'

'In the interests of full disclosure,' Welles told the room, 'be aware that my department is pursuing various lines of investigation, including the possibility that Dane and Green are working together. It'll be up to him to prove otherwise.'

'Go fuck yourself, Victor.' Marc let out the words in a low growl. 'A day ago I knew nothing about this. Maybe you could give me a bloody minute to get my head around it before you start throwing accusations!'

Lucy made a ticking noise with her tongue. 'So let me get this straight. An MI6 agent from Dane's old unit not only survived being blown up and drowned, she hid out for . . . what? Three years and change? And now she's back on the grid, and raking up stuff you would rather she didn't?'

'That's about the size of it,' said Farrier. 'Sam . . . *Grace* clearly has an agenda that isn't compatible with ours. We need to find her and lock her down before she does something that turns up on *News at Ten*.'

'With all due respect, that sounds like a *you* problem,' said Lucy.

Welles leaned forward in his chair. 'We've been polite until now, Keyes. But rest assured, this ministry is quite happy to make it into your problem—'

Farrier spoke over the other man. 'Victor! Be quiet for once in your life.' He looked across at Marc and Lucy. 'You're absolutely right. It is an *us* problem. I'm not going to even try to argue with that.' His gaze locked with Marc's. 'You have plenty of reasons not to want to get involved with this. But I'm asking you for your help. *Asking*,' he repeated, sparing Welles an acid glare, 'not demanding.'

'What if I refuse?' said Marc.

'Then you walk away.' Farrier frowned, and opened his hands. 'Just do me one favour first? Think it over before you decide.'

The dingy backstreets beyond the Metaxourgeio district were the parts of Athens that most tourists never saw. Above narrow lanes clogged with vehicles, the cracked and pollution-stained fascias of apartment blocks and cheap hotels rose up on concrete pillars, blotting out all but a sliver of the night sky. At ground level, metal security gates and untended doorways were covered with graffiti, and here and there, fast food vendors and electronics stores whose wares were of equally suspect origin crammed into alcove-sized spaces. It was late, and drinkers from local bars had spilled out into the streets in a vain attempt to cool off. The hard heat of the day was still present, motionless pockets of it trapped in the airless canyons between the buildings hours after sunset.

Cutting through the area, Sophocleous Street took its name from the Greek playwright of ancient history. The man in the dark cap walking stiffly along it, keeping to the shadows, wondered idly what Sophocles would have thought of the place, had he peered through time to see it.

Would the writer of tragedies see the decay of his city as another example of the same? In recent years, the changing fortunes of Greece and Athens had brought illegal immigrants and drug gangs into the area, and now they were bedded in, enough that the local police could barely keep a lid on the criminality.

The man in the cap was shorter than average, but thickset, and sometimes the thoughtless and the unwary misread his height and the colour of his skin as markers of an easy victim. It didn't help that he had a limp now, and he moved more slowly. He could tell there were eyes on him, measuring him up as possible prey.

Across the street, a gangly figure in a lime-green basketball player's vest whistled in his direction, mocking and threatening. It was a test, a strident hyena call sent out to gauge his reaction. Showing fear would label him as a target. If he ignored it and walked on, that too might have the same result. It was best to hope that the hyena would lose interest and find something else to occupy his attention. The man in the cap had no time for distractions from the locals.

He passed another group of rough men coming in the other direction, and they openly glared at him, bristling with territorial instinct. His face did not fit here, which meant they would most likely consider him a tourist. Outsiders were not welcome.

He pulled the bill of his cap down low. The name on the fake Republic of Korea passport in his pocket called him Park Ban-Woo, but that was a lie for people unable to tell the difference between one Eastern face and another. Hiroshi Saito had been born a Japanese citizen, but he had been exiled from his home country and the Osaka streets he grew up on a long time ago.

He stepped around a beggar on the pavement and continued towards his destination. Osaka had dark corners like this one, and he drew on his experience of them to navigate the Athens backstreets. The faces and voices might change, but the character of such places never altered. It was terribly familiar.

Once he would have moved through a place like this with a squad of killers at his side, and the animals would scatter. But he wasn't given that status any more. Saito had fallen from *enforcer* to *messenger*, and in doing so, he was forced to confront the reality of what he was doing. He had given years of his life in service to the Combine, to work off a debt that could not be repaid.

You were a fool to hope you would one day find a way out, he told himself. *Now you are in this until the bitter end.*

From the corner of his eye, he saw the hyena in the green vest talking with the men who had passed him, and the bleak thought dissipated. This was not the time to lose focus.

A couple of the men broke off to trail after him, but he gave them scant consideration. The taverna he had been looking for was up ahead, a hole-in-the-wall place marked by a sputtering, half-dead neon sign. He threaded his way inside.

It was a tiny, cramped space and too brightly lit for Saito's tastes. There were no shadows, no corners, nowhere to hide from the stark white light spilling down from the naked bulbs overhead. A blurry television set high up on one wall showed highlights from a soccer match, the watery sound from the speakers making the commentary hard to follow. Not that any of the drinkers inside were listening, their conversations loud and fuelled by glasses of raki and cheap, gassy beer.

His contact was at the bar and he had to look twice to be sure it was her. The woman's hair was a different colour from the photo he had been given, and the expression on her face was slack. On a stool at the side of the chipped wooden bar, she was laughing uproariously with a balding man, slapping his tattooed bicep. The woman who called herself 'Grace' was demonstrating anything but that quality. She acted like a fool-ish drunkard, blithely unaware of everything around her.

But then she saw Saito, and it was as if a different person suddenly took her place. She straightened, and the half-drunk act she was putting on melted away. The man reacted, slow and confused. She said something insulting to him, enough that he spat on the floor and shoved past her angrily on the way to the urinals out back.

Saito took the stool the other drinker had vacated and took off his cap.

'Alfa,' he said, asking the barman for a beer of his own.

She looked at Saito intently. 'You're obviously him.' Her accent was British, rough-edged and smoky. 'Bit old for an errand boy, aren't you?'

He leaned closer, speaking quietly. 'What happened in Oslo?'

'Everything that had to,' she replied. 'All dealt with. Do you have a complaint? The extraction was fine, I have my money.'

'You were paid,' agreed Saito. 'But the balance of the remainder is contingent on the completion of the entire operation.'

She chuckled. 'Your bosses afraid I'll drop out halfway and stick you with the dirty laundry?'

Saito toyed with his beer bottle but didn't drink from it. 'I am here to remind you of your obligations.'

'Are you now?' The woman sized him up. 'I know your type, yeah. All the crap about duty and shit, who owes what to who, blah-de-blah. But it's bollocks, innit?' She patted his knee and gave him a false, boozy wink. 'You're a chump if you think otherwise. No honour among thieves and cut-throats, Jackie Chan.'

'He is Chinese,' Saito corrected. 'I am not.'

'Whatever, mate.' She waved away his reply. 'I want an advance on the next payment.'

'That was not the arrangement.'

From his vantage point on the stool, Saito could see a group of men near the doorway. The drinker Grace had insulted was outside with them, and he caught the flash of a lime-green vest, a grinning face. He took a better, tighter grip on the beer bottle.

'It is now,' said the woman, as she absently ran a hand over her face. Where her dark hair hung down over her cheek, it didn't quite hide a streak of burn scarring that started at her throat and ended near her temple. 'The way I see it, I'm the bloody showstopper now, aren't I? You lot need me for your game, so that gives me a bit of leverage. You want me to play on, you gotta keep me sweet.'

Saito didn't argue the point. He pulled an unmarked credit card from the pocket of his jacket and slid it across the bar to her.

'Twenty per cent of the next payment, encoded in bitcoin as specified.'

She did a sleight of hand trick and the card was gone, just as someone on the television scored a goal and the bar patrons collectively booed their displeasure. Grace chuckled again.

'You had it ready. You knew I'd ask. You're a sharp one.'

'I am a pragmatist,' he noted. 'I prepare for all eventualities.'

'So what gives next?' She cocked her head, and he noted that she shot a look in the direction of the doorway. 'We sticking around? I hope not, because I've been here a day and already I'm done with the place.'

'The next phase is being prepared,' he told her, reciting the briefing he had been given. 'Target selection has been made. You will go to a staging area and prepare to deploy. Details will be sent to you via the usual channels. The rest of your team will meet you later, on site.'

'I get playmates?' She made a face. 'Who's that, then?'

'You do not know them, but they have worked for my employers on a number of occasions. They are very competent.'

'I'm in charge, though?'

'Of course,' he agreed. 'That is what you are being paid for.'

'Just checking . . .'

The hyena and the drinker came into the bar, moving as if they hadn't seen Saito or the woman, and before either of them could react, the bald man deliberately shouldered into him. The drinker dropped his beer and it shattered on the cracked tile of the floor.

Instantly, the man was yelling at him, stale breath washing over Saito's face. In the mix of English swear words and rapid-fire Greek he guessed the gist of the argument. The drinker was accusing him of knocking the bottle from his hand. He wanted immediate recompense.

The man in the vest put a hand on Saito's shoulder and told him to come outside. His other hand had something sharp and shiny hidden in the palm. A push-dagger, probably.

Grace switched seamlessly back to her drunken tourist performance and tried to laugh the whole thing off. The drinker shouted at her and slapped her hard enough to propel her face down to the bar top.

The man in the vest pulled Saito off his stool. In the tiny little drinking pit, they were only two steps from the front door.

Saito hit him across the face with the bottle and the man in the vest reeled away, snarling wildly. In the same instant, Grace punched the drinker hard in the belly, enough that he doubled over and vomited up some of the beer he had been imbibing.

'Back way.'

Grace stepped over the drinker and pushed to the rear of the bar, not waiting for Saito to follow. Tugging on his cap, he followed after her, down a constricted corridor and past reeking toilets, into a storeroom that opened out into an ill-lit alley.

Two of the men from the group Saito had seen on the street were waiting there, and they brandished empty ouzo bottles stolen from crates by the door.

Saito dodged the first blow aimed at his head, but the base of the bottle clipped the bill of his cap and peeled it off, sent it flying. He pivoted, and an old healed wound earned in Somalia jabbed him in his gut. There were fragments of a 7.62 mm round in there, stuck where the Combine's doctors had been unable to remove them. At times like this, the wound liked to remind Saito of his shortcomings.

Grace ran at the man threatening her and he didn't expect it. Her attack, combined with a slick of stale beer slops pooling on the ground, sent him down on his backside. Then she was on him, landing blows in the soft tissues of his throat.

Saito had no interest in engaging with these idiots, but the depressing inevitability of such an encounter could not be avoided. He resolved to end it quickly.

Hidden by his shirt sleeve, strapped to the inside of his forearm was a custom-made leather scabbard, and in it was a thick stiletto blade. The weapon was called a misericorde, a type of dagger once used in medieval Europe to kill unhorsed knights, by stabbing them through gaps in their armour. Saito jammed the heavy needle tip into the joint of his attacker's right knee, and the man's scream echoed down the alleyway. It was a good hit, but still Saito wasn't happy with it. His edge was growing dull.

Grace climbed off her assailant, as the man coughed up blood and struggled to breathe. She appeared to have crushed his larynx. As he choked and sputtered, she rifled through his pockets and took his wallet. She stole the few euro notes folded in it, and tossed the rest away.

Saito flicked blood off his dagger, eyeing her.

'The card I gave you is worth a thousand times that amount.'

'Old habits die hard,' she offered, turning as the drinker and the man in the vest finally emerged from the doorway behind them.

The face of the man in the vest was a mess of cuts and rage. The drinker, flushed pink and his eyes still watering, staggered to a halt as he saw the state of his two friends. He backed away, but Grace already had an empty ouzo bottle, and she clubbed him with it.

The bottle didn't break, but the drinker did. He fell on his knees, trying to block her rain of blows. Saito pointed his dagger at the man in the vest, whose own blade was far less formidable, and that was warning enough to stop him from intervening.

Finally, the woman stood on the drinker's right hand and broke two of his fingers. By that point he had lost control of his bladder and he began to cry.

'Give me that,' she said, holding out her hand, nodding at the misericorde. 'I want to finish up.'

Saito glanced to the end of the alleyway. No one had come to investigate the beating and the screams. He imagined they would be able to walk away and nothing more would come of this.

'There is no need.'

'I don't *need* to,' said the woman. 'I just *want* to.'

'No,' insisted Saito. He owed these opportunist thugs nothing, but Grace's casually vicious manner disturbed him. 'It will complicate matters,' he concluded.

She gave a theatrical sigh, like a child denied a favourite toy. 'Fine.'

She took the contents of the drinker's wallet as well and walked away.

At length, Saito sheathed his dagger and followed her, leaving the wide-eyed man in the vest to deal with the wreckage of his bad intentions.

FIVE

The icy porcelain at his back leached the heat from Marc's body, and the hazy form of stark white surfaces enclosing him drew inwards. The last gasps of breath escaped his mouth in smooth, steely bubbles, and then there was no air left, only the chill of the water pressing down on him.

Eyes open, staring at nothing, the wintry cold blurred his vision. It drew the life out of him, but it couldn't dull the memories.

He could remember *a stinging impact ripping the air from his lungs* and *patches of burning oil on the surface.*

He could see *Sam drifting in the dimness, her body falling away.*

Blood in a black haze. Like slow smoke.

In the freezing depths, his hand twitched. He had tried *to reach for her, their fingertips meeting briefly.*

Her face, ruined and blank, staring back at him. *The currents took Sam from him and dragged her down.*

When he couldn't hold on a moment longer, Marc bolted upright from beneath the water in the free-standing bath, throwing a cold wave over the edge. A small tide gushed out across the tiled floor of the bathroom, soaking a fallen towel where he had left it, swirling and pooling in front of the frosted glass door leading to the rest of the hotel suite.

He sucked in ragged, shuddering gasps of air as a shadow appeared at the door, a hand tapping on the glass.

'Hey,' said Lucy. 'You okay?'

'Not really.'

His voice was low and faraway. Dripping, fighting back shivers, Marc climbed out to find a dry towel and a dressing gown.

As he slipped it on, Lucy slid the door open and gave him a wary look.

'Whoa, it's like a meat locker in here.'

'It's not that bad.'

She shook her head. 'One close encounter with hypothermia was enough for me,' she retorted. The two of them had survived a night in the polar chill of the Icelandic wilderness several months ago, and for Lucy the memory was still fresh. She changed tack as he followed her out into the suite proper. 'Talk to me, Marc. You've barely said a word since we left Vauxhall Cross.'

He padded out across the carpeted floor, making a motion at his ear to indicate *they are listening*, and halted at the floor-to-ceiling window.

'I swept the place as soon as we arrived here,' she noted, gesturing at the two bedrooms leading off from the adjoining central space. 'And I have a masker running in case.'

Lucy pointed at her custom-model Rubicon-issue smartphone lying on the coffee table. Farrier had returned their kit on arrival in Britain, and every SCD operative in the field carried one of the so-called 'spyPhone' devices. Among its capabilities, it could generate a localised jamming field that interfered with most passive bugging devices.

Marc was using the threat of MI6 surveillance as an excuse to stay silent. She knew him too well to let the lie sit unchallenged.

'What were you doing in there?'

'When I can't get my head straight, I dive.' He gestured at his face, where he would have worn a regulator mask and goggles.

'Haven't done it for a long time, though. The quiet in the water
. . . gives me space to think.' He nodded towards the bath. 'That's
the next best thing.'

'What, half-drowning yourself? Did it work?'

'No.' He stared morosely out of the window, looking without
really seeing.

They were on the upper floors of the Park Plaza Hotel, less
than a mile down the South Bank from MI6 headquarters, and
now the sun had set over London, the city was a network of lights
and shadows stretching away into the evening. The Thames was
a band of black obsidian, reflecting the glow from the Houses of
Parliament on the far side, and the great wheel of the London
Eye, the capsules around the giant Ferris wheel changing colour
as they moved.

Being home should have meant more to Marc, but there was
nothing, no connection. Everything he should have felt was
being dragged away, caught by the inexorable gravity of what he
had seen in that conference room.

Samantha Green was dead.

Samantha Green was still alive.

The binary certainty of the choice was inescapable. Marc
knew what he had experienced when the Dunkirk operation
came apart. But now a totally different reality was unfolding, a
different truth taking its place. He'd hoped the ice cold would
shock him into some kind of clarity, but it had done nothing
but deepen his misgivings.

'They could have falsified it,' Lucy offered, seeing into his
thoughts as if they were being projected on the wall. 'I know you're
thinking that. After what we saw with Lion's Roar in Brussels last
year, I'm never going to take anything on video as true again.'

The far-right extremist group she referred to had been part of a false flag attack, and one of the tools of their atrocity was something called a 'deepfake', a software suite that could manipulate video footage in such a way to seamlessly overlay the face of one person over existing imagery of another. The technology threw everything digital into doubt, and it was possible the British security services had access to something similar.

'Yeah . . .' Marc gave a wan nod. 'But I reckon this is the real deal. There's no angle on Six faking it. What do they gain?'

'Just putting it out there,' she noted. 'Considering the potentials.'

'Don't worry,' he told her, 'the only person I really trust is in this room right now.'

'Good to know.' Lucy moved to stand by him. 'You don't have to be part of this, you know that, right? I mean, Farrier was the guy who recruited you back in the day, and maybe you feel like you owe him . . . Or maybe you want to show the people who kicked you out what you're really made of? Both are bad reasons to get involved.'

He shot her a look. *Did she really believe that?*

'That's not it,' Marc snapped, and there was a distance between them once again. 'Shit. I don't know *what* I'm thinking here.' He stared into the depths of the black river far below. 'Sam and me, we had something strong, something good. And just when we were starting to figure it out, she was gone. I didn't only lose a woman I cared about, Lucy. I lost friends and I lost trust . . . I lost who I was. I had a life and it was ripped right out of my hands.'

The deaths of the Nomad team had been the bow of a destructive wave that left Marc Dane's world in tatters. It almost claimed his life and that of his only living family, his sister Kate.

'I know you don't want to hear this,' Lucy began, 'but I have to tell you, Marc. You're stronger for having survived that. The person you were? The guy in the van who played it safe and stayed out of harm's way? That's not who you were meant to be.' She prodded him in the chest. 'This man? I see someone who lost a lot but didn't let it break him. You let it *remake* you. I know that because I went through the same thing.' She let him think on that, then added: 'A lot of people are alive right now, me included, because of who you are. Not who you were.'

'I'd like to believe that,' he said, after a moment. 'It's taken me a while, and I really thought I was finding a way past the regret, the anger . . . But then *that* comes up.' He jutted his chin at a military-spec computer tablet lying on the table near Lucy's smartphone. On it were files Farrier had pulled from K Section on the woman called Grace. 'And suddenly everything I thought was solid turns into sand.' Marc shook his head. '*Sam is dead.* That's been part of my truth for the past three years. But if she's alive, I can't be sure of anything.'

Lucy put a hand on his arm. Her fingers were warm to the touch against his cold skin.

'You can be sure of this,' she told him. 'I got your back.'

He drew away. 'No.'

'What do you mean, *no*?'

'I mean *no, I can see where you're going with this.*' He walked over and picked up the tablet computer, tapping through some of the digitised files. 'I'm going to do everything I can to help John and his team, even if Welles is still a wanker and Lane hates my guts. Because *I* need to know. You're not a part of this, Lucy. This is my bloody baggage, not yours. You want to back me up, and I appreciate that, but you don't have to get involved.'

Her jaw set, and she was about to throw back a hot retort, but Lucy caught herself.

'I figured I wouldn't be able to talk you out of it, you Brits are pig-headed that way. So, be advised. I *am* a part of this, like it or not. Because you need me to keep you alive, Dane. One time, you told me that you have to put your trust in someone, or else you get lost. That someone is me.' She shook her head. 'You don't get a say in it.'

Some of the weight on him seemed to lift, and despite everything, Marc found a crooked smile for his friend.

'Thanks.'

'Just don't push your damn luck,' she growled.

After sunset, when the gates were closed and the visitors were gone, quiet enveloped the elegant, tranquil spaces of the Hanbury Botanical Gardens. The wildlife in the trees would usually have the place to themselves as the evening drew in, the only sound rising from the waves below as they turned against the rocky beach at Capo Mortola, where the nature reserve met the sea.

It was one of the most beautiful sites along Italy's Ligurian coast, set a few kilometres between the border with southern France to the west and the city of Ventimiglia to the east. Built by a nineteenth-century English Quaker who had made a fortune in rebellion-era Shanghai, it was now a holding of the Italian government and a national treasure of the region.

It wasn't an easy matter to have a place like the Hanbury given over to a private meeting, but somehow the man Esther McFarlane had come to see managed it. That in itself spoke a great deal as to his influence, and as her car glided to a halt by the entrance, she took in the two white Mercedes-Benz sport utility vehicles parked nearby. Well-built men in black jackets stood around them with the watchful manner of career bodyguards.

McFarlane didn't wait for the door to be opened for her – she never did, as a point of honour – and climbed out. Her assistant Finlay scrambled after her, but she waved him away.

'You can wait here.'

Finlay rocked on the balls of his feet. 'Is that wise, ma'am?' He nodded towards the darkened entrance portico. 'Going alone?'

She frowned. 'A wee bit late to start having doubts now. I don't reckon our mysterious friend would bring me out on a night like this just to do me in.'

Despite her flippant comment, McFarlane had GPS transmitters built into the brooch on her jacket and her wristwatch, and a vial of powerful capsicum spray disguised as a lipstick in her clutch purse. Experience had taught her that a single woman travelling without protection was courting danger, and trust was not something she gave easily.

'Just keep your eyes open, eh?' She patted him on the shoulder. 'That's what I pay you for.'

McFarlane didn't grace the bodyguards with a look, and set off down the long stone staircase leading into the gardens proper. The full site took up all of the small cape, but her contact was meeting her nearby, at a water feature called the Fontana Nirvana. Her flat shoes clacked against the steps, and under the cover of the dimness she reached into a pocket to activate a recording app on her cellular phone. Satisfied that nothing of the conversation to come would be lost, she proceeded downwards.

The evening air was rich with heady scents from the perfumed gardens. Another time, she would have allowed herself the distraction of an enjoyable walk here. Right now, her thoughts were occupied by a torrent of questions.

The intelligence her unexpected benefactor had provided – the file on the cartel accountant Mateo Garza, and Rubicon's involvement in his disappearance – was exactly the sort of ammunition she needed to call time on Ekko Solomon's risky ventures in vigilantism.

Solomon gave little away, and for a long time McFarlane and the other members of the board of directors had chosen not to look too closely at what the African was doing. It was easy when the Rubicon Group's fortunes were on the rise. But it was no longer possible to ignore what was happening under the company's aegis.

Among Rubicon's holdings was an overt private military contractor, small but highly skilled, largely engaged in providing personal protection details, or kidnap-and-recovery operations in support of law enforcement. McFarlane had learned that PMC element was the cover for something else. Employees, hardware and resources were filtered through it to service Solomon's Special Conditions Division – essentially, a privately funded black ops unit that answered only to the African.

That idea alone was troubling: that one man, even someone as rigidly moral and unswerving as Solomon, could wield that kind of power. But worse still, the SCD was tied directly to the operations of the Rubicon Group as a whole, and its continued existence threatened everyone who owed their livelihood to the company. The longer it was allowed to operate freely, the greater the chance that something terrible would happen because of it, and Rubicon would be held responsible.

The more McFarlane looked, the more she found. The SCD had been involved in confrontations with terrorist groups, mercenary hackers and clandestine agencies from a dozen countries, and she had evidence that unauthorised intelligence gathering and other legally murky acts had taken place on Solomon's say-so. It didn't matter that the SCD was on the side of the angels. Even if the billionaire truly believed that it was his responsibility to defend the weak and bring evil to justice, there were other ways to do it. Being a philanthropist was one thing; being a vigilante was something else.

That someone outside the circle of Rubicon's board knew about this was worrying to her. Even the *suggestion* of such details leaking to the media was a grave danger, even if there was nothing that could be proven. If the SCD's actions were to become public knowledge, if solid proof could be presented, Rubicon would be declared in violation of dozens of international laws. It would be open season for legal and civil suits, and the value of the company's stock would plummet. Everything McFarlane and her fellow board members had struggled to build in their alliance with Solomon would be put in jeopardy.

She had to know more.

The path levelled out, and presently McFarlane arrived at the meeting place. Water cooled the air where it fell from the carved shapes of the fountain, and deep shadows ranged away in every direction. A man in a light blue Brioni suit stood near a stone balustrade, and he gave her a shallow bow as she came into the glow of the lights illuminating the water feature.

'Ms McFarlane,' he said, in the voice she recognised from their phone conversation. 'Thank you for accepting my invitation. I apologise for the theatrics, but it seemed to me that secrecy should be maintained.'

'Aye, true enough.'

Her suspicions had been on the money. The man was of Far Eastern extraction, Chinese most likely. He had that look about him that made it hard to accurately peg his age. She took in his greying hair and careful brown eyes that had seen a lot of life. Her instincts pushed the word *soldier* to the front of her thoughts, and she held on to that. In his middle fifties, she assumed, picking a median. He'd walked a hard road, evidenced by a stiffness in his movements and the steel stick at his side.

He offered her his hand and she didn't take it, keeping her distance.

'And you are?'

He let his hand drop, smiling slightly. 'My name is Lau. I am hoping you and I will be able to work together.'

'How much do you want?' She went for the first, most obvious option. 'To keep quiet about Garza?'

'Straight to business. I was told to expect that of you.' He gave a dry chuckle. 'Is that what you want me to do, Ms McFarlane? Pretend that Ekko Solomon is not running covert operations all over the world under your company's global network?'

She gave him nothing in return. If this was a blackmail attempt, it had to be quashed.

'I do not want to be paid,' said Lau. 'At least, not in the way that you might think of it.' He shook his head, and rested on the metal stick. 'I gave you the Garza file as a proof of intent. I have other information about Rubicon you would find interesting – material that would cause great upset if it were to leak out.'

'I'm here,' she said. 'I'm listening.'

'What would you say if I told you I could provide what you need to unseat Solomon from his stewardship of Rubicon? I can help you bring an end to his mercenary cadre and his reckless acts of intervention. Swiftly. Bloodlessly.'

'I don't know what you are talking about.'

His smile faded. 'Please don't insult my intelligence. I hope I have not made an error in coming to you. I am aware Solomon engenders great loyalty in his people, but I thought you were beyond that.'

He knows him. Something in Lau's tone, a faint note of wounded pride, told her that the Chinese man had a personal connection to Solomon, and she put that thought aside for later consideration.

'I have Rubicon's best interests in mind,' she continued. 'One man, no matter who he is, cannot be allowed to compromise that.'

'Agreed.' Lau's head bobbed. 'You want to keep your people safe, Ms McFarlane. A commendable goal.'

She walked to the edge of the fountain.

'You've got a handle on my motivations, but then I'm not quiet about them. What about yours, Mr Lau? I keep asking and you keep ducking me. What are you after?'

'I want justice,' he said firmly.

'Solomon says the same thing.'

'Ekko Solomon wants redemption,' said Lau, and that bitter flash was in his eyes again. 'That is *not* the same thing.' He took a breath, and his manner returned to its earlier detachment. 'He will sacrifice everything he touches for his own ends. His crusade. That includes you and your people. We both want him to stop. My reasons are my own, but they align with yours.' He looked around, and his voice dropped, as if he was sharing a confidence. 'You and I, we are being pushed by the agendas of others. We both wish to take back control.'

'And how do we change our situation?' McFarlane listened to herself ask the question.

For months now she had sought to bring the SCD's operations to a quiet end, and although she had never spoken openly of it, her thoughts did sometimes dwell on how Solomon's removal from the board would facilitate that in one single act. But unseating a king from his throne was no easy task – something every Scot who knew their history could attest to.

'You already know the answer,' said Lau, seeing it in her eyes. 'Are you willing to do whatever it takes? Even if you have to destroy Rubicon in order to save it?'

'Solomon is not Rubicon,' she told him. 'He's only one man.' A chill washed over her; doubt and fear crept into her thoughts. She decided to push forward to end the conversation, one way or another. 'If you have an offer, let's hear it. Otherwise, I'm walking away and you'll be—'

'I will be hearing from your lawyers?' Lau ended her sentence for her, and gave a humourless chuckle. 'I do have more for you, but you will not see it yet. The moment is not right.'

McFarlane scowled. 'You shouldn't have brought me here if all you want to do is drop hints. My time is valuable, and I don't take kindly to those who waste it.'

'Meeting an ally face to face is not a waste of time,' said Lau.

'Is that what we are?' She'd had enough, and turned to walk away.

'I will be in touch,' he called after her, but she didn't look back. 'When the moment comes.'

The lounge on the Park Plaza's upper floors had an excellent view of the river, and out on the smoker's balcony, Marc Dane leaned over the rail with a glass of neat Reyka in one hand, swirling the Icelandic vodka in slow circles.

'Careful,' said a voice behind him. 'Drop that and you'll brain some passing banker, and we'll be in the shit.'

Marc took a sip without looking up, staring out across the water. On Millbank, on the far side of the river, he could see Thames House. The headquarters of MI5, the sister agency to MI6, was a stately grey pile with sloping roofs in the neoclassical style. Even at this time of the night, lights blazed from the windows as officers of the country's internal security agency worked around the clock.

'I should have signed up with them, instead of Six,' he said, gesturing with the glass. 'Got a gig in some little cubicle over there, sifting intel takes and going down to Starbucks for lunch. Pub on Friday after work.'

'Nah.' John Farrier took up a position next to him. He had a drink of his own, and it would be a glass of Glenlivet single malt, if Marc recalled correctly. 'You wouldn't last a year doing desk work. You were always going to be a field man, like it or not.' Farrier looked out over the London skyline. 'I knew that, first time I met you.'

'Oh yeah?' Marc turned to study him. 'You found my measure, did you?'

Farrier had been, for want of a better term, Marc's recruiter, his conduit into the shadow world of intelligence operations. They had crossed paths in Afghanistan during Operation Herrick, when Dane was crewing helicopters for the Royal Navy and Farrier was part of a shady, nameless unit doing shady, nameless deeds in places off the battle map. A year after Marc had been demobbed, Farrier had come calling with a job offer.

'Like knows like,' said the older man, after a moment. 'We enjoy the cut of it too much, us two. More than is healthy.'

'I didn't want to be a field officer,' Marc insisted. Even to his own ears, the denial sounded hollow.

'Not about want,' Farrier noted, around a swallow of his Scotch. 'It's about need.'

Marc gave a snort, and opted out of the old argument before it got going.

'Okay, whatever you say, *Obi-Wan*.'

Farrier's smirk became a chuckle, a sound with genuine warmth in it.

'You've changed a lot, mate. In a good way, I mean. It's a shame it took everything it did to get you there.'

'I had a decent teacher.'

'Cheers for that, *padawan*.' Farrier saluted him with his glass. 'Won't lie, I've been keeping an eye on your exploits.'

After parting ways with MI6, it had been Marc's old friend who found him a job with a United Nations department tracking the illegal trade in nuclear materials; but even that had ended up leading Marc back to the Rubicon Group.

'Pays more than government work,' he noted.

'No doubt.' Farrier was silent for a moment. 'We've been picking up some of the pieces you dropped.'

'What's that supposed to mean?'

The other man made a face, an expression Marc knew of old. It was his way of signalling that he was talking around something he wasn't supposed to be talking about.

'Rubicon upset some rich people with big ideas and low morals, didn't they?'

The Combine. Farrier didn't need to name them.

'Six took advantage of that, here and there. Pushing back against some Russian wankers making inroads in Knightsbridge. Knocking off a few tangos. Hunting the Lion.'

The Lion was a nickname for a particular terrorist whose handiwork Marc had encountered and barely lived to tell the tale. Omar Khadir, a former Egyptian army officer turned nihilist radical, was rumoured to now be in the Combine's employ, but no one had confirmed a sighting of him in years. Others said that Khadir, along with the rest of his Al Sayf terror network, had been wiped out by the Americans as payback for their attempted bombing of the US capital.

'The Yanks got him,' Marc offered.

'No, they didn't,' the other man said quietly. 'Someone's protecting him. Using him.'

The thought of that sent a shiver down Marc's spine. Khadir had been a dangerous foe when left to his own devices. As a tool of someone with a larger agenda . . . Marc dreaded to think of what that could lead to.

'You know what this reminds me of?' He felt the urge to turn the conversation in a different direction, and went with it. 'That night in Odessa. With the French bloke – what was his name?'

'Villeneuve,' said Farrier. 'Like the racing driver.'

'That's him.' Marc nodded to himself. The man had been an MI6 asset embedded within a Ukrainian mining consortium, a group that the British suspected of funding radical pro-Communist groups in the UK. Farrier and Marc were part of a team sent in to extract him, but things went pear-shaped and they ended up getting stuck in a seedy waterfront hotel, waiting for a boot through the door that never came. 'He did not shut up all night.'

'Give the bloke a break, he *was* shitting himself,' said Farrier.

Villeneuve's cover had been catastrophically blown and the Ukrainians were on the warpath, coming to slot him before MI6 could get the man out of the country to be debriefed. For ten hours they had sat in a dank, unheated room, trading hits off a bottle of cheap vodka to stay warm while a gang of thugs swept the waterfront for them. At one point, the Ukrainians were in the room next door, high as kites, turning it over and jabbering in graphic detail about how they were going to kill the Frenchman and his British friends.

As dawn broke, the MI6 team decided to risk it and made a dash for the airport west of the city. It didn't go well, and the guns had come out. In the thick of it, only Farrier's guidance had brought Marc through it in one piece.

The first thing he did when he got home was to drink some *good* vodka, to wash away the taste of the fear.

Farrier wasn't the kind of person to ever say out loud that Marc owed him, just like Marc was never going to admit it. But they had a bond that had been forged in fire, a mutual respect that went beyond the oath of service.

He won't cash in that marker, Marc thought, *because he knows he doesn't have to.*

He took another long pull on the Reyka.

'You looked at those docs?' Farrier said, into the lengthening silence. 'I know you have an ear for that kind of music. What'd you find?'

Marc frowned. It was hard to look at the raw intelligence data on the woman with the 'Grace' alias, hard to sift it dispassionately and not see Sam Green at every turn.

'She has a plan,' he said, putting it into one thought. 'Her moves, they're not random. She's building to something.'

'Against us?'

'Can't tell.' He put down the glass on a nearby table. 'It doesn't track, John. If it's Sam, why didn't she just come in? Where's she been? What's put her on the offensive now?'

'You've gone through what she has,' Farrier countered. 'Left for dead. Cut off. You tell me.'

That truth knocked him off his train of thought.

'Yeah, I suppose I have. But that was different. People inside Six were working against me.'

Farrier drew a breath. 'I know this isn't easy for you, mate. You have history with this.' He shook his head. 'You know what? I never wanted to come anywhere near you with it. I told Welles and the Old Dog we could deal with it inside the family.'

The *Old Dog* was Sir Oliver Finch-Shortland, director of MI6's tactical operation programme, a man who worked at a level high enough to mingle with chiefs of staff and senior cabinet ministers. Tenacious in the most cut-glass of English manners, he was a formidable sort, and very much a *takes-no-shit* kind of fellow.

'And yet . . . ?' Marc prompted.

'You know Welles. You can always count on him to be a prick of the first water, can't you?' Farrier didn't wait for Marc to agree. 'He forced the issue. Even talked about trumping up some charges for a pretext so we could pull you in.'

'Of course he did.'

None of that was a surprise. There were still those in Vauxhall Cross who hadn't forgiven Marc for shining a light on the traitor in their midst, as if it offended them more to be caught out by one of the rank and file than to have a collaborator in the agency's upper echelons.

Marc pushed those grievances aside and took a mental step backwards. He had gone through the data on the tablet more than once since the morning's meeting in the conference room. He was caught by what he found there. Trapped between scrutinising the intelligence like the technician-analyst he once was, and seeing it through the lens of someone who had shared a bed with the subject in question.

'I can't square the circle,' he said, after a moment. 'Sam or Grace, or whoever. I'm not sure what to think.'

But that wasn't true, and something in his tone betrayed him. Farrier knew him too well to miss it.

'Don't bullshit a bullshitter, mate. Tell me what you got out of that.'

He sighed, and then committed himself. 'Her next move is going to be a meet, if she hasn't done it already. It's the pattern she's been following. Move, set-up, action, then check in with her contacts. *Repeat*.'

'Who's she talking to?'

'Can't give you that, too many variables. But there's communications logs you had in there, same lines of connection we used back when Nomad was up.'

Farrier nodded. 'GCHQ is trawling those, she'd know that.'

'Yeah,' Marc admitted, 'but I think she's hiding in plain sight. It's a very *Sam* thing to do.' He had left the tablet back in the suite, and he wished he had it to hand to show what he meant. In the end, Marc picked the cleanest explanation. 'Every tactical operations unit has its own shorthand, right? Informal comms protocols and set-ups that work for the team and the command hub back home, but don't go wider than that.'

Farrier nodded. 'I know what you mean.'

'There's no one from Nomad around to know how it went, except me. I saw the same practices we used in those comms logs. Real signals in among fake ones, set up so that prying ears can't tell the difference.'

'You think that . . . Grace is doing that?' Farrier almost said *Sam*, and barely stopped himself in time. 'Risky, isn't it? Following old routines?'

'It is,' said Marc, 'but when you're under the cosh, people tend to go with what they know.'

Farrier leaned in, a spark catching in his eyes as he saw that Marc might have a lead that Six had overlooked.

'So if you don't know who she's talking to, do we know where the messages are being sent?'

Marc nodded. 'I have an idea.'

Every encrypted message he found that fitted the pattern was headed with metadata pointing to the same place. A cluster of digital IP addresses on the island of Cyprus, in the eastern Mediterranean.

'Well, now . . .' Farrier finished his drink and reached for his phone. 'That's something we can work with.' He hesitated with the handset half-raised and gestured in the direction of the lounge. 'Someone's looking for you.'

Marc turned to see Lucy walking through the open bar area. She caught sight of him and came out to the balcony.

'Hey.' She glanced at Farrier. 'So I talked with head office in Monaco about releasing us to work with MI6 . . .'

'Both of you?' Farrier raised an eyebrow.

'There was some pushback. At first, Delancort was reluctant to allow two employees to be placed in harm's way.'

'We do that all the time,' said Marc. 'How much did you tell them?'

'Enough that Solomon offered to supply some additional resources.'

Lucy had Farrier's full attention now. 'Such as?'

'The Rubicon Group may not have a direct interest in this woman you're hunting, but we do look after our own,' she went on. 'This is important to Marc, so it's important to us. Rubicon is offering to assist the British government in apprehending this dangerous fugitive, in the interests of international stability.' The last she said in a flat, rehearsed manner.

Farrier gave a wry smirk. 'You know, there was a time when I would have said *no thanks*, but to be honest, a bit more manpower would come in handy. The Joint Intelligence Committee has been cutting our budget to the bone.'

'Welles won't wear it,' said Marc. 'Bad enough you're bringing me in.'

'Oh, sod him. I have operational authority, not that tosser.' Farrier offered Lucy a handshake, and she took it. 'Good to be working with you.'

'Likewise.'

'Okay, I'll set it up.' Farrier raised his phone and gave Marc a nod as he walked away. 'Get some rest, we'll come and get you in the morning.'

Marc shot Lucy a look when the other man was out of earshot.

'What's going on? You've pulled Rubicon into this now?'

'Not me.' Lucy made a *hands-off* motion. 'Solomon. He said he owes you. And he's the kind of man who makes good on his debts. Plus, it doesn't hurt to play nice with MI6.' She hesitated. 'The faster we get this Grace chick in cuffs, the faster we can close the book on everything, right?'

Marc frowned. 'However this goes,' he told her, 'it's not going to be that simple.'

Chin was afraid that his whole grand plan for the family getaway was collapsing.

An evening walk up the beach had done nothing to supply the solution he so desperately needed, and he trudged dejectedly back towards the scruffy little villa.

It had cost more than it was worth to bring his wife Tasanee and their son Jin to the resort at Prachuap Khiri Khan, even out of season, but he was anxious to mend their marriage. It had started badly, though, and gone downhill from there. Chin and Tasanee argued from the moment they left Bangkok, and the intermittent rain had only helped to sour the mood.

While Jin played quietly, they quarrelled. Tasanee brought everything back to the same place, every time. *You put your job before us.*

How many ways had he tried to explain it to her? *The job is what keeps a roof over our head, it feeds and clothes us.*

But she had grown to resent him for it, and Chin found himself accepting extra duties, preferring that to spending time with his family. When he was home, he felt like he was constantly being judged, by Tasanee's sharp glares and Jin's glum sighs. At the office, working on thorny coding problems or the intricacies of database structure, Chin could believe he was actually *achieving* something.

When he started to suspect that Tasanee was having an affair, he panicked. For all the distance between them, he still loved his wife, and the idea that she might take Jin and leave him for another man filled him with dread.

The whole point of this sorry little getaway had been to reconnect, to remind them what they meant to one another, but it was failing.

Chin was so wrapped up in his worries that he didn't see the foreigner sitting on the porch until he was on top of him. He jerked back in shock and tried to collect himself.

Even in the half-shadows, the stranger was imposing. He had a face carved from sandstone, hard edges and narrow eyes that gave him a feral aspect. Chin guessed he was an Arab, but little more than that. When he spoke, it was in accented, rumbling English.

'It is late for a walk.'

'Can I help you?'

Chin shot a look into the villa. The doors leading inside were open, the breeze off the water shifting the thin curtains.

'Keep your voice down,' said the man, nodding towards the rooms where Chin had left Tasanee and Jin asleep.

'What do you want?' Chin glanced around, wondering who would hear him if he called for help. Most of the other villas were empty. 'If you're after money, we don't have—'

'You do not have much,' said the man, as he reached for a black backpack. 'That might have been exploited, but you are quite honourable in your own way. If someone offered a bribe, you would report it.'

He produced a military-grade laptop computer, complete with a built-in satellite antenna.

'Bribes?' Chin shook his head. 'What are you talking about?'

The man went to his bag again, and when his hand came back there was a silenced pistol in it.

'Open the computer.' He glanced at the villa again. 'If you do not do as I say, I will kill them both.'

Chin managed a shaky nod and picked up the laptop with trembling hands. When the screen lit up, his stomach fell. He saw a remote relay of his office desktop displayed there, a mirror of the computer he used every day. The familiar field of blue with the globe-scales-sword symbol for Interpol in the middle.

His job in the agency's Bangkok liaison office as a minor civilian functionary was unglamorous, the work of a data-pusher, really. When they first met, Tasanee thought he was some kind of secret agent, but the dull reality of his work soon disabused her of that fantasy. Chin helped Interpol keep records of their investigators and their respective assignments in correct order, a job as unexciting as it sounded.

'A hacker could be paid to penetrate the firewalls,' said the man, 'but the simpler solution is someone like you.' He tossed Chin a flash drive. 'Use your log-in and password to access the personnel database, then insert the drive.'

'I . . . I can't . . .'

'Do you know who I am?'

The man rose to his feet and stepped into the light.

Chin blinked as recognition suddenly came to him. He had seen this man before, on the 'wall of infamy' back at the office, his face on a Red Notice.

'You're . . . Omar Khadir!'

The notorious terrorist was one of Interpol's most wanted. Chin didn't know the full story, but rumours said Khadir had led a campaign of suicide bombings across Europe for an Islamic extremist group, building to a planned strike in Washington DC that would have killed the President and hundreds of Americans, had it not been thwarted at the last moment.

It was unreal, impossible to believe that an internationally wanted mass murderer was standing there in front of him. And yet, there he was – and Chin knew full well what he was capable of.

'If I must prove my seriousness,' said Khadir, 'the boy will die first.'

'No,' Chin gasped. Sick with fear, he typed in the security codes. 'Look, look, I am doing it.' Fighting off the tremors in his hands, Chin used his access to connect remotely to the Interpol mainframe and plugged in the drive. He saw a progress bar fill as several megabytes of data were transmitted to the agency's central server, uploading a new personnel file. 'W-what is this for?'

'The final preparation for something larger.'

Khadir gave the answer dismissively, as if this had been a task beneath his skills.

'Please don't hurt my family,' Chin bleated.

Suddenly, nothing else mattered. All the arguments seemed trivial and pointless.

Khadir took back the laptop and the drive, exchanging it with an envelope.

'It is understandable, what you did.'

Numbly, Chin opened the envelope and found dozens of photos inside. He pulled out a few and the first thing he saw was an image of Tasanee's face. Her eyes closed, her mouth open in a gasp of pleasure. The picture had been taken with a long-lens camera, and it captured some of the man whose face was buried between her breasts.

'How emasculating for a dedicated father and breadwinner to see that,' said Khadir. 'Of course it would drive you to violence. You would lose all reason.'

The photos became more graphic as they spilled from Chin's hand. Tasanee and a man with darker skin, *a foreigner*, their rough sex taking them all over some nondescript hotel room.

'You . . .'

None of the photos showed the man's face, but there was no one else it could be. Chin shook his head, welling up with tears of rage and shame.

'You could not let her disgrace you. And you could not let your son live with that stigma.' In a sudden burst of motion, Khadir grabbed Chin and dragged him into the house, still speaking in the same quiet tone. 'There was only one thing left for you to do.'

Chin struggled, but it was pointless. He was small and unfit, and this man was like a lion.

Then Chin's gaze found the glitter of light on a puddle of blood, and he froze. Tasanee lay on her back, eyes open and staring at nothing, a dark entry wound in her throat. Jin was crumpled on the floor close by, and his son's nightshirt was soaked through with crimson.

Chin thrashed and clawed, but Khadir was already forcing his hand to grasp his pistol, pushing the barrel of the silencer into his cheek.

'It is a tragedy,' he said, and pulled the trigger.

SIX

The landscape beyond the runway at RAF Akrotiri was flat and open to the elements. A dry wind brought a tang off the salt lake to the north that Lucy could taste in the back of her throat.

Sunset was a couple of minutes away, and the lights on the perimeter of the Air Force base were burning steadily into the approaching evening. She walked towards the concrete expanse of the turning apron near a cluster of sand-drab buildings. Something about being on a military post called up a whole subset of behaviour patterns in Lucy that she was barely aware of. She carried herself a little differently, took in her surroundings in a more watchful manner. Familiar patterns, deep-rooted reflexes trained into her by the US Army, they came back easily and quickly, slotting into place.

Marc was out there, talking to his MI6 buddy, and the low mutter of their voices carried to her. She made a point of forcing herself to relax. They were in that phase of an operation where the adrenaline was still tanked in reserve, the waiting and the bullet-counting part of the deal. It could go long or it could be over in moments. The secret was not to over-anticipate. Just be *ready*.

Akrotiri was like any one of a dozen airbases Lucy had passed through in her career as an operator, one of those weird little kingdoms that belonged to a nation completely separate from the country that owned the dirt it stood on.

Like the haft of a broken sword, the peninsula extended from the southern coastline of Cyprus, ending at Cape Zevgari and Cape Gata at the azure waters of the Mediterranean. To the east of the thick outcrop of land was Episkopi Bay, and the cantonment that shared the name. To the west along the belly of the island republic was the Bay of Akrotiri, the borderline for a territory belonging to another nation that was over three thousand miles away.

On the flight out, Lucy had read the sparse acclimation briefing from their RAF hosts. Since Cypriot independence from the British Empire in 1960, Akrotiri had remained one of two 'sovereign base areas' in the country, held tight by the UK's military for obvious tactical and strategic reasons. Close to the Middle East and the vital waterway of the Suez Canal, Royal Air Force and British Army outposts stood in place to project power into the region, while US interests had to steam in aircraft carriers to rattle their sabres in the direction of Syria, Iran and Iraq. Decades after getting self-governance, the intricate politics of Cyprus had grown more complex, but still the bases remained as dislocated bits of old empire repurposed for a different age.

The sun was disappearing below the horizon, and Lucy scanned the darkening sky. She found what she was looking for in short order, spotting the running lights of a HondaJet HA-420 in the direction of the Limassol Salt Lake. The Rubicon aircraft was a compact, swept-wing executive flyer, its low-emission engines making its approach near-silent. The breeze pulled down the high whine of turbofans, and she knew who would be at the stick as it made a lazy, yet perfectly timed turn towards the runway.

'Ari's showing off,' said Marc, catching the same conclusion. 'You watch, he'll land it on points, just to look good in front of the crabs.'

'The what?' Lucy shot him a look. Since they had teamed up with the other Brits, Marc kept slipping back into UK service slang that she didn't follow. 'Crabs?' She mimed pincers with her fingers.

Farrier jerked a thumb at the RAF crew working out on the flight-line by the nearby hangar.

'Navy nickname for those guys.'

She frowned, not following the logic.

'So what do *they* call navy pukes like Dane here?'

'Andrew,' Marc said, checking the time on his battered dive watch.

'That makes as much sense as anything,' she replied, and decided not to press the issue.

'Well, we're all spooks to them now,' Farrier offered, as the HondaJet touched down and slowed, air-brakes flaring open.

For the most part, the officers and enlisted men that Lucy had encountered since their arrival in Cyprus had been cordial but distant. They gave her the kind of long-eyed looks that suggested they were wondering which three-letter agency she was working for, but they were experienced enough with those kind of visitors not to ask any questions. One of the facts not in the RAF briefing packet was that Akrotiri had a quiet history of hosting black ops missions and other shady stuff since the early days of the Cold War.

The HondaJet, painted in a dark blue livery with the Rubicon logo down the fuselage, rolled to a precise halt as Marc had predicted, stopping on a dime right in front of them.

'Smaller than I expected,' said Farrier. 'I thought your boss had an airliner, or something.'

'An Airbus,' said Marc. 'It's pretty slick. They base it out of Nice – bringing it here wouldn't exactly be discreet, would it?'

'True enough.'

The jet fell silent, and when the hatch dropped open, the first out onto the apron was the pilot. In his fifties, Hollywood-trim and good-looking in the manner of an older leading man, Ari Silber wore a short-sleeved shirt with captain's boards, tan trousers and deck shoes. He took a deep breath of the salty air and ran a hand through his tight, greying curls.

'We're late,' he began, with an apologetic shrug. 'Lot of eyes in the sky, had to come the long way around.'

Lucy nodded at that. The waters around Cyprus had more than their fair share of warships, vessels from half a dozen nations showing the flag around the Syrian and Lebanese coasts. But for Silber, navigating this piece of airspace was old hat. Before he had been recruited by Ekko Solomon to fly privately for Rubicon, he had served in the Israeli Air Corps as a pilot and later squadron leader in F-15I *Ra'am* strike fighters. Silber didn't fit the *Top Gun* stereotype of jet jockeys that most people expected, and Lucy liked that about him. He looked more the kind of man who should've been picking up a Best Actor award, or charming the panties off wealthy divorcees.

'Children,' he said, taking in Marc and Lucy with a fatherly nod, then he approached Farrier and shook his hand. 'Captain Aristotle Silber, call me Ari.'

'John,' said the other Brit. 'Good to meet you.'

'Pleasure.' Ari looked around, taking it in, sniffing the air. He grinned, and looked straight at Lucy. 'Funny, you forget how much you miss it.' He waved his hand, like a wine connoisseur taking in a fine bouquet. 'The smell of JP-8 fuel. To me, the perfume of an old flame. Sets my blood racing.'

Marc mentioned Ari's previous career, and Farrier gave a nod. 'I get you.'

But the pilot was already looking past the other man, towards the deployment area, where a pair of sleek RAF fighters were being worked on by their ground crews.

'What's this? Lightnings, yes?'

Another detail from the briefing was the mention of British F-35 jets deployed at Akrotiri as part of Operation Shader, the ongoing military effort against ISIS and Islamic militants in the local region. Ari looked at the aircraft with a mix of avarice and admiration.

'I'll stretch my legs,' said the pilot, and he wandered away towards the dart-like supersonic fighters, looking for one of his own kind to swap war stories with.

'Better tell the RAF lads to watch him,' said Marc, semi-seriously. 'They turn their backs and he'll take one of those birds for a joyride.'

He moved to climb into the HondaJet, as another man appeared in the hatchway.

'This is Malte Riis,' said Lucy, for Farrier's benefit. 'Our ground transit and security specialist.'

'Hello,' said Malte, his expression as neutral as ever, and it was clear he wasn't going to expand on that.

The Finn was muscular but not overly so, lean around the face and hard-eyed. He wore jeans, boots and a light jacket, and on a street in any major city you would have lost him in the crowd in seconds. He had that ability to fade into the background, perfected during his time as an undercover cop in his native Helsinki. Malte could drive pretty much anything with wheels and he was good in a fight, but he gave new meaning to the word 'taciturn'.

Lucy saw that he was carrying a Rubicon-issue gear crate, and intuited that he was looking for their staging area. She pointed towards the hangar.

'In there.'

'Okay.'

Malte stepped past Marc, granting him a nod, and went on his way. For him, that was the equivalent of a hearty handshake.

'Nice bloke,' said Farrier, 'but does he ever shut up?'

'You get used to it,' Marc replied, and boarded the jet.

Lucy let Farrier go next, and she hung back at the hatchway. Inside the aircraft cabin, it was cramped but well-appointed, and there were more hard-case containers piled up on the unoccupied seats.

Marc waved forward the last member of the Rubicon team on the jet.

'John, this is Assim, our cyber-ops guy.'

'I thought that was your gig,' said Farrier.

'Marc's the Alpha Geek,' said Assim, with a nervous smile. 'I'm in the rear with the gear. Assim Kader, delighted to meet you!' The rangy young Arab was dressed similarly to Malte, but on him the outfit hung as if it was on a clothes horse. He took Farrier's outstretched hand and pumped it. He had an open laptop computer in his other hand, the screen filled with panels of dense information. 'I hope you don't mind, but I can't really rest when I fly so I worked on the metadata Marc uncovered. I think I might have a time window for our target.'

The SCD's self-described 'hacker without portfolio' was Saudi-born and British-educated, and for Lucy, his perfectly enunciated English accent always seemed a little at odds with his manner. Assim was the product of expensive private schools and, if the stories she had heard were true, of ill-advised dalliances with the denizens of the dark net. He was smart as a whip, but not enough to get past his own hang-ups.

Farrier got the measure of him immediately, and shot Marc a look.

'Blimey. This guy is you ten years ago.'

Marc shook his head. 'Smarter than me.'

'I didn't like to say,' Assim said sheepishly.

'What else did you bring us?' Lucy asked from the doorway, nodding at the gear cases.

'Everything but a tactical kitchen sink,' Assim told her. 'Is there somewhere we can set up?'

'Follow me,' she said. 'The Air Force gave us a whole hangar.'

'Wait.' Farrier held up a hand. 'You said you have an idea of when Grace is going to be in the country?'

The mood inside the cabin shifted, turning serious.

'I think so.' Assim tapped his laptop. 'If I'm right, she's already here.'

'Then we need to move fast,' said Marc, grabbing one of the cases.

The hangar was usually turned over to the maintenance of one of Akrotiri's C-130 Hercules cargo planes, but for the duration of this mission the dusty, open interior had become a temporary base of operations for the combined MI6/SCD team.

The HondaJet sat off to one side, next to a pop-up geodesic tent made of sensor-opaque nanomaterials from one of Rubicon's hi-tech start-ups. Malte and Assim set up a satellite communications array and a workstation for cyber-ops, along with a rack of equipment and weapons, both non-lethal and deadly. The neighbouring MI6 'crib' was olive-drab prefabricated modules containing the OpTeam's equivalent gear.

Paladin had lost their field technician in Oslo to Grace's not so tender mercies, so it was quickly agreed that Assim would fill that role. But it didn't take long for Marc to see the lines of clear demarcation between the two groups of operators. Consciously or unconsciously, Farrier and his MI6 unit kept to their side of the hangar and the members of the SCD hung around the parked jet. Only Marc found it hard to settle, caught in the middle ground between the agency he had once been loyal to and the people he currently worked with.

'Boys and girls!' called Farrier, attracting everyone's attention. 'Time to firm up our plans, so gather round.'

Marc buried his hands in the pockets of his jacket and trailed after Pearce, the big guy he had encountered at the farm in Portugal. Marc pegged him as a former squaddie, all rugby full-back muscle and dogged focus. Pearce exchanged a nod with the two others who had been there that morning, the woman called Regis and the East Asian guy, Suresh.

Suresh had heavy bruising on the face and throat where Marc had put him down during his escape, and the man's right cheek was visibly swollen. Marc felt compelled to say something and fumbled an apology.

'S'okay,' Suresh said thickly. 'I would've smacked you about if it was the other way round.'

He had a soft Mancunian accent and his injuries made him look miserable. *Was he the type to hold a grudge?* Marc couldn't be sure.

'Won't happen again,' said Regis, staring daggers at a disinterested Lucy. 'You got the drop on us, that's all.'

'Actually, you got the drop on us *first*,' Lucy corrected. 'But it's good. No harm, no foul, right?'

'Sure, yeah.' Regis gave a nod, but not like she meant it.

'Okay,' began Farrier, halting the chatter with the tone of his voice. 'We know why we're here.'

He held up a tablet computer, and on the screen was a long-lens photo of their objective.

Regis's ire immediately refocused itself on the picture of the woman in the hoodie, like a weapons system tracking a new target.

'Echo-One,' said Farrier, 'also known as Grace, also known as . . . Well, *to be confirmed.*' He frowned. 'Make no mistake, we are dealing with a proper player here. Previous evaluations low-balled her skill level and lethality. Thank the higher-ups for that lack of salient data.'

A low murmur of agreement passed through the MI6 team. People were dead because they had underestimated this woman, and as Regis had affirmed, they were not about to let that happen again.

'Can we get a better look at her?' said Pearce.

'I can help, if you don't mind?' Assim put up his hand, like a kid in a classroom.

'Go on.'

Lane, Farrier's second-in-command, had virtually ignored the existence of the SCD operatives since the conversation in Vauxhall Cross, but now she was interested.

Assim brought an equipment case into the middle of the group, pulling from it a device the size of a beer can and what looked like a futuristic version of a conductor's baton. He set up a tall collapsible tripod, clipping the 'can' to the top, and threading in wires for power.

'We don't have a big board we can work off in here, of course, so this is the next best thing.'

He tapped a button and the device on the tripod projected a two-by two-metre square of white light onto the hangar floor.

The team stepped back out of the pool of illumination, and Assim thumbed buttons on the slim baton. Images wirelessly transmitted from his workstation appeared in the white square, instantly turning it into a video screen. Movements of the baton worked like the motions of a mouse, as he clicked open files.

'Bloody hell, he's the boy wizard with his magic wand,' said Regis, half-mocking, half-impressed.

'I was more the *Hunger Games* type, actually,' Assim corrected, weaving shapes in the air. 'Here we are.'

The image captures of Grace from the Oslo operation and elsewhere fanned out at their feet. Marc noted that there were a couple of shots from Samantha Green's official military record in there too, but no one called attention to it.

'What we have here is a dangerous individual,' said Farrier, drawing back control of the conversation. 'And as much as some of us would like to see her paid back in full for what she's cost our service, that's not why we're here tonight.' He paused to let that unpalatable truth bed in. 'This is a high-value target, and confidence is strong she's one of our own, *gone off the reservation* as our American colleague might say.'

Farrier inclined his head in Lucy's direction.

'She's out in the wild, agenda unknown,' added Lane. 'So our primary objective is the isolation and capture of target Echo-One for enhanced interrogation.'

She nodded in the direction of the base proper. There were facilities in Akrotiri where enemy combatants could be held, if there was a need.

Marc guessed that if they did manage to bring her in alive, she would bounce from there right into some nameless black site and never be seen again. He didn't like the way that thought made his gut twist.

'Secondary objective,' continued Lane. 'Learn whatever we can about who she's meeting here and what her endgame is.'

'Dane knows this woman,' said Farrier. 'He crewed with her back in the day. He's going to help us figure out which way she might jump, and his associates from Rubicon are going to back us up with tech and overwatch. Questions?'

Regis spoke up first. 'We know which side of the green line she's on?'

Everyone looked towards Assim, and he worked the baton again, bringing up a map of the island of Cyprus. A jagged, emerald-coloured band etched itself across the middle of the country, dividing it into the Greek-Cypriot south and the Turkish-Cypriot north.

'These are the United Nations buffer zones,' said the young man. 'Still in place since the coup and the invasion in the 1970s. Technically, the whole country is part of the European Union now, but in reality, the Greeks and the Turks do their own thing while quietly hating each other.'

'Old animosity runs deep here,' noted Lane. 'The division underscores everything on the island, so keep that in mind if you're dealing with the locals.'

Marc's knowledge of the situation was sparse, but he knew enough to be wary. Forty years earlier, a Greek-backed military takeover of the government had encouraged Turkey to invade, to defend their interests and their people living on the island. The fact that it also gave them a pretext to secure the territory was a bonus.

When the dust settled and a ceasefire was signed, Cyprus had been broken into the two parts shown on the projected map. Decades of UN-led attempts to heal the rift had made scant progress beyond easing freedom of movement across the border, and there were still no-man's-land regions edged with barbed wire, gun towers and armed soldiers along the green zones.

'Best guess is that Echo-One is on the Turkish side,' said Assim, answering the previous question. 'Comms traffic led to an IP address in Kyrenia, on the northern coast.'

'We can't count on the Turks for help here,' added Farrier. 'Their national intelligence organisation doesn't play nice with anyone except the Yanks and the Ivans, so that's out. Ideally, we want to do this thing without drawing their attention. Same with the Greeks. We know they're monitoring the British bases in Cyprus, so they'll have wind of us being here already, but they won't know why. We have to do this quick and clean, then get out before anyone starts asking difficult questions.'

Ari had found a folding chair and sat there, nursing a bottle of water. He slipped into the gap in the conversation.

'Perhaps it is worth mentioning that Rubicon Group has some connections here in the Republic?'

Lane gave him a sharp look. 'Do tell.'

'I don't like to talk out of school,' said the pilot. 'But the company has construction interests in both the north and the south. People on the ground, in an unofficial context, you know? Perhaps we could use them to—'

'No.' Lane cut him off before he could finish. 'Amateurs start asking questions and Grace will get wind of it and bolt. We cannot afford to lose this shot at her.'

'Just a thought.' Ari shrugged and fell silent again, letting the insult about 'amateurs' go unremarked.

Marc gave Lucy a sideways look, but her expression gave nothing away.

'Rules of engagement,' Farrier added. 'Defensive fire only, light small arms. We don't want anyone thinking the invasion is on again.'

'We know why she's here?' Suresh leaned in over the map.

'Speaking of difficult questions,' added Regis.

'Marc?' Assim glanced in his direction. 'Would you like to field that one?'

'Yeah, sure.' He swallowed hard. He hadn't expected to be called on so soon. 'So, OpTeam Nomad did a job in 2015 involving a Turkish organised crime gang with contacts here on the island. It's likely the . . . uh . . . target is following up a connection with that.'

'I see a lot of opportunity for trouble.' Pearce offered up the thought to nobody in particular. 'Turks, Greeks, UN, crooks and whoever else is hiding under rocks here. Whatever we do, we are going to end up pissing off *somebody*.'

'As usual, Colin here has summed it up succinctly,' said Farrier, tipping a nod to the man. 'So, once again for the cheap seats. Fast in, fast out, light footprint.'

'Assuming the target is meeting someone,' said Lucy, 'we gonna bring them in as well?'

'We'll stay fluid,' Lane snapped. 'React to the situation as it unfolds. You don't have to worry about those kind of details.'

'I'm pretty sure I do,' Lucy insisted. 'Most of my job comes down to who I shoot at, and who I don't.'

'Well, let me take a load off your mind right now.' Lane stepped around the projected map to meet the other woman head-on. 'When we go mobile, you're not coming with us.'

'Excuse me?' Lucy's expression hardened.

Marc couldn't hide his surprise. 'The whole point of us being here is to—'

Lane talked over him. 'Civilian advisors remain on base during field ops, that's the regs.'

'Are you capable of letting someone finish a sentence without interrupting?' Marc snarled. 'Rubicon is a private military contractor, and we're all experienced in the field.' He shot Farrier a look, hoping for some kind of support from his former colleague, but it didn't materialise. 'Why the hell else are we here?'

'Been asking that since Portugal,' muttered Suresh.

Lane nodded towards the HondaJet and the geo-tent.

'Your toys are nice, but don't make the mistake of thinking that's going to buy you onto the mission. You lot are just—'

'I'm just the pilot,' said Ari, with deceptive lightness.

'Just a driver,' added Malte, briefly breaking his silence.

'I'm just the . . . ah . . . tech guy,' said Assim, adding to the chorus.

Farrier let out a weary breath, and Marc saw right through him, catching up too late. This had always been the plan, he realised – to keep any Rubicon assets bottled up while the MI6 team undertook the mission proper.

'You can run tech and comms from here,' said the other man. 'Give us remote support during the shout.'

'I don't do that job any more,' Marc told him.

'No, we know what you do,' said Lane, finding the pace of her argument. 'You break the law wherever you go. Rubicon is a civilian corporation running military and espionage operations without oversight or legal governance. Now, we'll let you get away with that when it doesn't cause us any hassle, but that's not happening here.' She indicated the rest of the OpTeam. 'We have governmental permission to operate here. You don't. So back off and leave it to us, all right? We can handle this.'

'Like you did in Oslo?' Lucy sucked her teeth as her temper flared. 'We didn't come to this party to stand back and do nothing.'

'You're not doing nothing,' said Suresh. 'And with all due respect, you sort of invited yourself, didn't you?'

'Bollocks to that,' Marc retorted. 'If you're going in after Sam Green, I will be right there with you.' He pointed towards Lane and the others. 'Because let me tell you, none of you know how she thinks. *I do.* And trust me, you don't want me miles away, seeing everything second-hand through a bodycam. You want to bring her in? You're going to need my help.'

'And I'm his goddamn shadow,' added Lucy.

There would have been a time when Marc would never have argued the toss over something like this, but he wasn't that man any more. Somewhere along the line, he had stopped being the guy who looked for the easy way out, the safe path. It wasn't that he had changed, not really. It was more that old habits and old fears had fallen away. What remained was who he really was. And that man was not someone who would sit on the sidelines.

Farrier studied him, long and quiet, measuring his determination. Unspoken was a threat between them: that if the other man forced the issue and benched the Rubicon team, they would pack up and leave the MI6 officers to go on alone.

In the end, it would come down to two factors: could the Paladin team do this without the help of the SCD, having already failed once? And did John Farrier still trust the man he had recruited and trained?

At length, Farrier gave that wary nod again.

'All right, we make room for Dane and Keyes in the assault group.'

'I know you didn't miss what I said,' Lane began, giving Farrier a hard look.

'I appreciate your input, Tracey,' Farrier replied, 'but this is my call. Is that going to be a problem?'

To her credit, Lane was a good enough soldier that she swallowed her own feelings on the subject and gave a tight nod.

'No, boss. No problem.'

Suresh frowned. 'Welles isn't going to like it.'

'Welles doesn't have to know about it,' said Pearce.

The taxi driver was an older guy, deeply tanned, tubby and greying, and even his taste in strong cologne had not done much to cut down the odour of his sweat. He explained in broken English that a woman like her should not be travelling alone in a town like Girne, even if it was the tourist capital of the north. He repeatedly told her that she was pretty, in spite of her scars.

'You need protecting,' he said benevolently.

She couldn't miss how his free hand kept drifting to his crotch each time he leered at her.

She'd annoyed the man by using the Greek name for the place, and he corrected her sternly.

'Don't call it Kyrenia,' he told her. 'You will upset people.'

Then he laughed that off and asked her name, for what had to be the tenth time. She told him it was Natasha, and he made a strange face, momentarily uncertain if she was playing him for a fool. 'Natasha' was a nickname the locals used for Eastern

European girls who came in off the mainland to service tourists looking for pleasures of the more illicit kind.

He drove the long way around, making expansive movements with his hand, telling her he knew the best route even as he overcharged her. He said that some taxi drivers – not men like him, of course – would pick up foreign women and do terrible things to them. He mashed the brakes to show how easy it would be to stop the car and have his way, anywhere he chose to, in this town she knew nothing of. He talked about other women he had met, of how he had helped them and how they had rewarded him.

All the time, he was smiling. Because he was a good man, as he kept insisting, not like those others. He wanted to help her. He wanted her to enjoy her trip, and to that end, she could call him up any time if she needed a ride.

When they finally reached the address she had given him, on a dusty four-lane highway well away from the hotels and seafront favoured by visitors, he refused to unlock the doors.

'This is no place for you,' he told her, looking around at the handful of crumbling apartment blocks and sparsely populated storefronts. 'Let me take you somewhere lovely.'

But at length, she was able to pay him and get out, but not before he forced a business card into her palm and deliberately pawed her as the money changed hands.

Behind a diffident and vapid mask, she thought about using the steel-shelled pen in her purse to stab him through the hand so he would never be able to hold his cock again. But as amusing as that would have been, her goal today was to draw as little attention to herself as possible, and leaving this doughy pig screaming and bleeding would do the exact opposite. So she reluctantly decided to let him go on his way, wondering if he would ever understand how lucky he had been.

She gave him a last blank smile as he finally drove off. When the taxi was out of sight, she walked in the opposite direction until she found the building she was looking for.

A six-storey box of grimy glass windows and cracked plaster, the fascia of the nameless apartments was the yellow of nicotine-stained teeth. Abandoned balconies held drifts of grit and long-dead palm leaves, and the block's one attempt to show some architectural flair, with a decorative fin in a faux-futuristic Jet Age style, was falling apart to reveal the crumbling brickwork beneath.

Spaces for a cafe or shops on the lower levels of the building were shuttered behind rusted roller doors, and she had to walk around to the back to find a way inside. In the weed-choked alley, out of sight of the road, a gleaming white four-door Nissan Navara pickup was parked close to a breeze block wall. The truck was brand new and seemed out of place.

There was a combination lock on the back door, which she opened and secured behind her, taking care to make a noise when she did so. Coming quietly could lead to violence.

The airless hallway beyond ended in a staircase, and on a nearby wall someone had used a fat plug of quick-setting glue to affix a wireless security camera.

She made sure the camera had a few seconds to look at her, and then she climbed to the third floor. Each level had four apartments, but on the third there were holes in the walls, knocked through to give the current residents more space.

They were waiting for her, in one of the torn-open kitchens. Two men, cautious around her but respectful with it, the polar opposites of the taxi driver with his wandering hands and constant smirk. The difference was that they knew who she was, and what she was capable of.

The first man stood near a makeshift monitor screen, set up to take feeds from the stairwell camera and a few others dotted around the building perimeter. He was of average height and narrow build, swarthy enough to pass for Turkish, sporting a dark, close-cut beard.

'You're Grace,' he said, as if establishing the fact. 'Any problems getting in?'

His accent was deliberately hard to place, and she didn't waste time on it.

'No. What do I call you?'

She was already altering her posture, her tone of voice, doing it automatically to become the woman they expected her to be. Gone was the tourist girl who had ridden in the taxi, and here was the cold-eyed killer.

'Cord,' he told her, and she knew it was as much an alias as her own name. He nodded towards his companion. 'That's Vine.'

'Hey.'

Vine was shorter than the other man, and his face was pinkish, like it was wind-burned. He had a pistol in his hand, a Glock 17 semi-automatic distorted by the shape of a shell-catcher bag dangling off the gun's frame. Self-consciously, he put the gun down.

'Just being careful,' he explained.

She nodded. On the worktop there were three M4 carbines and neatly ordered lines of spare magazines, and Cord had apparently been in the process of filling more. Cord was wearing thin latex gloves as he transferred each 5.56 mm round into the spring-loaded mags, thumbing them into the slot one by one.

The M4s had bags on their ejector ports in line with Vine's handgun, black fabric shapes that resembled a sock, there to catch any spent brass before it spun away into the air. It was vital to control the amount of physical evidence they were going to leave at the target site, and policing the shell cases was just one element of that. Each of the firearms had been selected to be the correct make and model, one set of specifications in a long list that had to be adhered to, if the operation was to go as planned.

Satisfied with the weapons, she looked around the gutted apartment. Sheet plastic covered the floor in the areas where the two men had rested and prepared for the operation, and bright blue strips of duct tape marked off lines they had not crossed. It was designed to be a 'collapsible' location, where as much of their temporary presence could be erased with as few traces as possible.

Inside an open container, she found pairs of used tactical boots, worn enough to be comfortable and not obviously brand new. These were lined up next to over-suits made of black rip-proof material that could be worn under the armour vests and tactical webbing rigs that dangled from coat hangers on the walls. Like the guns, the other kit matched the specifications they had been provided. Another case held a pair of microlight quad-rotor drones.

She looked around. 'Where's the plastique?'

Vine pointed at a portable refrigerator in the corner of the kitchen.

'Keeping it cool.'

The bricks of plastic explosive could sweat in the wrong conditions, and she gave an approving nod.

The last items she checked were a trio of thin, skintight outfits that resembled gymnasts' leotards. When worn, they would cover around 70 per cent of a human body, drastically minimising the possibility of unwitting DNA transfer through lost strands of hair or skin cells.

Judging by their preparations, Cord and Vine seemed to be good at this, as the Japanese man she'd met in Athens had promised. That was fine with her. Working with professionals meant she could concentrate on her own part of the operation without having to micromanage theirs.

'Satisfied?' said Vine.

She nodded and glanced at her watch, aware of the time. It would be sunset in a couple of hours, and they had to be in place before full dark.

'Anything I need to be aware of?'

The two men exchanged a wary look, and she saw that there was something bothering both of them.

'While you were in transit, there was a development,' began Cord. 'Rubicon deployed one of their aircraft from France. It landed at a Royal Air Force base in the south, and it's likely they met with a British black ops unit.'

'They wouldn't be here if they didn't know something,' said Vine.

She cut straight to the question that hadn't yet been asked.

'We're not compromised, so don't be concerned about that. In fact, the appearance of MI6 and Rubicon here is an integral part of the operation. Without them, it doesn't work.'

'I don't follow,' said Cord.

'You don't need to,' she told him. 'Just do what I tell you, when I tell you to do it.' Her tone became steely, and the two men showed no signs of questioning it. 'This is what we want to happen,' she added, giving them a little more.

'The truck out back is ready,' Cord went on. 'Got the decals for when we get close.'

'Good.' She looked out of the dirty windows. Inside here, with the plastic sheeting and everything else, the air was close and warm. Vine seemed to sense that, and offered her an ice-cold bottle of water from a cooler crate. 'How long will it take to fold this up?'

'Full works?' Vine didn't wait for her to confirm. 'Thirty minutes. Fifteen if we cut corners.'

'Take an hour,' she told him. 'Be sure.'

'It's what we do,' Cord replied. 'From now?'

She nodded again, watching Vine closely.

He indicated the rifles. 'With this much firepower, I'm guessing this won't be a quiet job.'

'Correct.' She allowed a chilly smile to cross her lips. 'It's a kill mission. Get in, terminate the targets with extreme prejudice, then extract. There are some other elements that need to be addressed, but those are my concern, not yours.'

She heard the whip-snap of her own voice, and let the smile fade.

This was the part she liked the most. The moment when she became something *different*. The woman she had been in Oslo, in Athens, in the taxi – those personas were outfits she slipped into, then discarded when they were no longer needed. Everything about her was malleable and formless.

She was garbing herself in a new self, her body language, her expression and diction becoming what was needed for the job.

'What's the objective?'

Vine came closer as she removed a folded plastic-laminated document from an inner pocket.

'This.'

It was a satellite image of an airfield and a cluster of buildings. The resolution was high enough to pick out military vehicles and even individual soldiers walking patrol routes.

Vine studied the image and raised an eyebrow.

'That's going to make a lot of people very mad.'

'And then some,' she agreed.

SEVEN

From where she stood by the wing of the parked jet, Lucy could look right into the geo-tent where Assim had set up his gear, and watch the hacker working. The young Saudi bent over his keyboard, his nose up against a monitor filled with strings of computer code that were, at least to her, incomprehensible.

Marc was in there with him, and he stalked back and forth like a tiger in a too-small cage, shoulder-surfing and second-guessing everything Assim did. She had rarely seen the Brit wound so tight, not even when they had been jumping out of planes or running into firefights.

Lucy tried to see the situation through his eyes. Here was a guy whose entire life had been turned inside out by a cata-strophic mission failure, an event that saw him branded a traitor to his own side. Marc Dane had been carrying around the guilt and the anger over that for as long as she had known him, and he had finally started moving beyond that, letting the scars heal.

But his past wasn't done with him.

In what kind of fucked-up world does this happen?

Lucy asked the question of herself. The woman Marc thought dead and gone was apparently alive and kicking, and worse than that, she was killing her way through British agents like it was going out of style.

'So I'm guessing there's no word yet?' Ari stood on the lip of the HondaJet's open hatch, nodding in the direction of the geo-tent.

'When they know, we'll know.'

Marc and Assim had been at it for hours, attacking the data recovered from Grace's encrypted communications, tearing it apart for some inkling as to where exactly her meet was going to take place.

'You speak to him?'

Lucy frowned. 'Dane made it clear he's too busy for small talk right now.' She turned away and climbed into the jet, pushing past Ari and into the cabin. 'I need a drink,' she added, finding the fold-down minibar on the far bulkhead.

The pilot gave her a sideways glance. 'How is that a good idea before a mission?'

'Don't mother me just because you're Jewish,' she shot back, pouring a shot of Maker's Mark bourbon. 'You don't need to play the stereotype on my account.'

'What can I say? It's how I was raised,' Ari replied, with a smile that didn't meet his eyes. He refocused on her. 'So have you told anyone?'

'Told them what?' She savoured the drink's sultry burn on her tongue.

'That you're struggling.' His affable manner faded away, to be replaced by genuine concern. 'I know you, girl. Longer than anyone else. I know what you look like when you're wounded.'

'I'm good,' she said firmly.

Ari raised an eyebrow.

'Good enough,' she clarified.

Maybe it was true that she could have used another week or two back in the Delphi Clinic, but she wasn't about to admit it. She could fight past the tightness in her chest, like any other obstacle.

'He was there for you. You have to be there for him.'

There wasn't any judgement in Ari's words. He was too smart for that. He let Lucy find it on her own.

'I'm worried about Marc,' she said, finishing the bourbon. 'I've never seen him this ... this *driven* before. He's way too close.'

'He's not an operator, Lucy,' Ari noted. 'Dane doesn't have that training for compartmentalisation or whatever they call it, not like you do.'

'My point,' she said.

At length, Ari sat down on the arm of one of the big leather chairs in the cabin and ran a hand through his greying hair. He indicated the minibar and in turn Lucy plucked out and tossed him a miniature bottle of Tanqueray gin.

'Don't mention this to the boss,' he said, and swigged from it. 'I ever tell you about Mosche? A flyer in my squadron.'

Lucy shook her head and he went on.

'Mosche was a lot like our English friend. A hell of an instinctive pilot. Really bad at cards. A little reckless but good enough to pull it off, most of the time. Anyway, so there's this training mission we are on near the border. Long story short, the Syrians come up and goad us. Mosche lost his father in the Golan Heights, so he had an axe to grind, you know?' Ari's hands came up to mimic the shapes of aircraft in flight as the memory replayed for him. 'Mosche was fixated on a target and he flew himself right into the side of a hill. Killed instantly. I tried to talk him back, but by the time I saw what was happening, it was too late.' His usually bright manner briefly darkened. 'You do this for your friends. You stick with them, even when they put themselves at risk, because you believe you can talk them out of it. Don't wait too long to do it, though.'

Lucy tried to frame the right reply, but out through the cabin's oval window she saw Farrier and his people moving with sudden urgency. By the time she reached the hatch, Marc was already there, an unreadable look in his eyes. He handed her a lightweight plate carrier as she stepped down.

'All hands on deck,' he told her, shrugging on an armour vest of his own. 'We managed to decode a fragment of the email traffic Grace was sending. We have co-ordinates for the meet, but we're on the clock. It's going down an hour from now.'

'Get your kit and move!' Farrier called out across the hangar. 'Quick as you can, boys and girls.'

'Where are we going?' said Lucy, as she jogged after him, towards an unmarked vehicle in the shadows at the rear of the hangar.

'I'll explain on the way,' said Marc, without looking back.

Lucy turned and saw Ari watching her go.

'Be careful,' mouthed the pilot.

The white Nissan pickup turned off the main highway and slowed briefly as it bounced onto the airport road.

Grace dropped the window on the passenger side and leaned out, finding the edge of an adhesive plastic sheet plastered over the side door. She pulled hard and the whole thing came away, a layer of white ripping free to reveal the letters 'UN' in heavy black lines concealed beneath. Cord did the same on his side, and they both balled up the coverings and tossed them into the undergrowth.

In the evening light, the pickup was now a dead ringer for the same vehicles driven by the military patrols from the nearby UNFICYP garrison – the United Nations Peacekeeping Force in Cyprus.

Cord accelerated again, while Grace checked her pistol. Behind her, in the rear of the pickup's cab, Vine pulled the T-shaped charging handle on his M4, readying the carbine that lay across his lap.

'Masks,' she told them, as the guard post and barrier at the end of the road came into sight. A single soldier in a blue beret was walking out of the hut, a rifle over his shoulder and a flashlight in his hand.

Vine and Cord pulled thin fabric hoods up over their faces. Each one was made from a pale green material, and they had no holes for mouth or eyes. The breathable fabric was thin enough to see through, but opaque enough to hide their identities.

Cord shot her a look. 'What about you?'

'No need.'

Grace smiled, and tied her hair back so her scars were visible.

Up ahead, a sign in various languages declared that beyond the lowered gate lay Nicosia Airport, an area off-limits to civilians and unauthorised visitors.

Once, the airport had been the central hub for travel into and out of Cyprus, but that had changed after the Turkish invasion and the partitioning of the island. The site of heavy fighting in those days, the UN had been forced to make it a protected zone, and that declaration had never been revoked.

Now, while the majority of the airport buildings lay derelict and abandoned, a part of the old grounds on the far side of the runways had become the 'Blue Beret Camp' where UN troops remained to this day, maintaining a token force to watch over the buffer zone.

Soldiers stationed at Nicosia joked that the ghost town posting was like patrolling some abandoned movie set, but no one had fired shots in anger there for over forty years. Tonight, that silence would end.

The gate guard shone his torch at the pickup as Cord halted a few metres shy of the candy-striped barrier, and called out to them. No traffic was due this evening.

Grace stepped out of the vehicle, holding a digital video camera in her hand, and the flashlight beam washed over her. The guard hesitated; she wore dark, non-reflective tactical gear instead of the utility camos he expected.

He reached for the radio mike clipped to his shoulder, but Vine was already out and standing on the pickup's running board. He put a single round from his M4 through the guard's chest and sent him sprawling into the dust, the long sound suppressor on the carbine flattening the noise of the shot.

Satisfied she had captured the act on video, Grace moved to the pickup's flatbed and unpacked the two camera drones. Each one came to life in a buzzing whirr of black rotors and they shot vertically into the air, finding a vantage point overhead.

Grace clipped her camera to her tactical vest, drew her silenced Glock and crossed to where the injured guard lay writhing in pain. She finished him with a close-range shot through the forehead, before lifting the gate. Cord rolled the pickup forward and she climbed back inside. The drones hummed by, capturing everything they did.

'Who's flying those?' muttered Vine, as he closed the rear cab door, sliding back into his seat.

Grace didn't answer him, staring back down the approach road into the darkness.

'You're sure they'll come?' said Cord.

'They're already on the way,' she told him. 'I made sure of that.'

She didn't bother to explain about the message she had received twenty minutes earlier, from a contact observing RAF Akrotiri, describing an unmarked van hurtling out of the base at a high rate of speed.

Cord gave a nod and aimed the pickup towards the dark shape of the old terminal building. Headlights from another vehicle glittered in the distance.

The road rumbled beneath the wheels as Suresh pushed the vehicle as fast as he dared, guiding the high-sided transport through the sparse traffic on the northbound highway.

Marc shot a look into the cab, watching the lights along the road flash past.

'How far?' he asked.

'Fifteen minutes away,' said the driver. 'I can't push it any more than this.'

'Right.'

Marc turned away, moving back into the rear compartment. The interior of the Fiat Ducato was half-minibus, half-troop carrier, with mil-spec gear racked on the walls and low benches for the OpTeam members to sit on. The members of Paladin were in their operational gear as Farrier moved among them, checking equipment and getting them ready.

Regis had stayed behind with the rest of the Rubicon team, having reluctantly given up her seat to Lucy. Lane, seated next to Marc's partner, had not given either of them the courtesy of a look since they left the RAF base. The big guy, Pearce, rounded out their numbers.

Marc moved down the van, tugging on his armour vest to pull it into a more comfortable position. He tapped the wireless headset looped over his ear and spoke to the air.

'Radio check. Ari, do you copy?'

'*Reading you,*' came the reply. '*Five by five. Assim says the sat-comm net is coming into sync. We should have London in the loop in a moment, over.*'

'Brilliant,' grumbled Lane, hearing the same through her headset. 'We're gonna have Welles playing armchair general, aren't we?'

'Keep the conversation on task,' said Farrier, giving her a warning look.

He handed her an M4 rifle from one of the racks, and she deliberately lost herself in checking over the weapon. Farrier gave another of the carbines to Pearce, who did the same, and Marc waited, expecting the same.

Farrier made no move to arm them, and Marc frowned.

'What about us?'

'Let's hold off on giving you live weapons for the moment,' he replied, then changed tack before Marc could protest. 'You're positive about this location?'

'I'm sure,' Marc said firmly. 'And I'm sure Six have their own people double-checking our numbers as we speak, so if you want to wait . . .'

'Just bloody tell us,' snapped Lane.

Marc had Assim's projector gadget linked up to a digital tablet, and he used it to throw a video map onto the ceiling of the van.

'The co-ordinates in Grace's coded emails match up to this area.'

The map zoomed into an area in the middle of the island, right in the thickest part of the UN buffer zone.

'How'd you get this?' said Pearce, squinting at the image.

'Rubicon code-breaking software combined with email traffic captures from GCHQ, via MI6,' explained Marc. 'A minor miracle of teamwork.'

'Dark net comms aren't as secure as everyone thinks,' noted Farrier. 'Good for us. Bad for her.'

Marc went on. 'The meet is taking place at Nicosia Airport. It's a former civilian airfield now turned over to the United Nations peacekeepers in-country. There's an outpost there, a few helicopters on station. A token force.'

Lane held up a hand. 'Are you taking the piss? You expect us to believe that Echo-One is conducting an arms deal in the middle of a military base?'

'That's a pretty ballsy move,' said Pearce.

'It's what she was trained to do,' Marc retorted. Once again, he had almost said her name before he caught himself. 'Hide in plain sight.' He pulled other data into the projection. 'The broker she's been dealing with has known connections to rogue elements in the Argentinian military, and guess which South American country happens to be providing a large portion of the UN forces in Cyprus right now?'

'Grace's dark net contact is using his Argie army pals to move his wares.' Farrier rubbed his chin. 'Yeah, it does line up. Do we know what she's buying?'

Assim had only been able to pull partial fragments of the 'shopping list' included with the intercepted communications, and Marc threw them up to the projected screen from the tablet with flicks of his wrist.

'Magnetic breaching charges. Portable satellite navigation jammer. Intrusion kit for industrial automation.' He looked down the list as the van jolted across highway lanes and onto a minor road. 'Also, cold-water wetsuits, military-grade. A lot of marine-hardened gear.'

'That's the kind of kit you'd need to take a ship at sea,' offered Lane, her earlier tone fading as she shifted into mission mode. 'Cruise liner, oil tanker, whatever.' Suddenly, the acerbic MI6 officer was taking him seriously. 'That's her endgame, is it?'

'We can ask her when she's caught,' said Farrier.

'Am the only one getting a lot of stink off this intel?' Lucy had been silent through the rapid-fire conversation, but now she spoke up, addressing her question straight to Marc. 'I mean, correct me if I'm wrong, but MI6 have been tracking this woman for months now and got nowhere. Then suddenly it's Christmas, and we have her dead-on?' Lucy leaned forward in her seat. 'She already suckered in you people once and killed half your team. What if this is the same play?'

'*We have considered that, Keyes.*'

The voice of Victor Welles grated through their headsets, drawing a wince from everyone. His words were coming in via satellite transmission from Hub White, the operations command room in the lower levels of Vauxhall Cross, but the crisp digital signal made it sound like he was in the van with them.

'*Those concerns have gone through our intelligence analysts at GCHQ, and the validity of the data had been determined,*' he went on. '*It's good enough to be actionable.*'

'You mean, good enough that you're willing to risk our lives on it,' said Lucy.

'*Echo-One is on the run*,' said Welles, his tone turning flinty. '*We were close in Oslo, we rattled her cage. This intel capture is proof of that. Six applied the pressure and she slipped up. We've forced her to move up her timetable. She's on the back foot, and we're going to take full advantage of that.*'

'*You are very certain for a man thousands of miles away from where the action is.*' Ari Silber was still looped into the communications net, and he threw in a comment with wry disdain.

'*Get that civilian off the channel*,' said Welles, giving the order to someone back at Hub White, and Ari's connection was abruptly terminated. '*Now pay close attention. The JIC have given this sortie the green light, with certain caveats. We can't simply have a covert strike team roll up to a United Nations military base, and ask to be let in. And given the urgency of this matter, going through proper channels will be a prohibitively lengthy process.*'

Welles laid out the operational parameters in short, blunt terms: they were to remain beyond the Nicosia perimeter and observe Echo-One's movements, then move in and secure her when she was outside the buffer zone.

'And what about her contact?' said Farrier. 'It may be one of the UN deployment.'

'*That's above your pay grade. You have your orders, Paladin. Proceed. Hub White, standing by.*'

The line crackled as Welles fell silent again.

'That's bullshit—'

'He's wrong—'

Both Marc and Lane started speaking at once, muting their headsets so only the team in the van would hear.

Farrier silenced them both with a look.

'I'm not running a democracy here. This is what we're doing. Tracey, hand out the night vision gear. Marc, check our ETA.' When he hesitated, the older man's eyes hardened. 'You wanted in on this tonight, so you're going to follow my orders, clear?'

'Clear,' said Marc.

He switched off the projector and moved forward to the driver's cab, riding down the frustration that crackled through him.

'Blimey, what did you lot do to him?'

Farrier sat heavily in the seat next to Lucy and spoke to her in low, weary tones.

'What did *I* do?' she repeated. 'To Dane?'

'When I recruited Marc, he was a good soldier . . . *sailor* . . . you know. Did his bit, didn't kick off about it. But a couple of years in the private sector and he's ready to push back on everything.'

She glared at him, trying to see through to what the other man really meant.

'Yeah, well, your past coming back to bite you in the ass kinda pisses some people off.' Lucy spoke quietly, so their conversation would not carry. 'He thinks a lot of you, and you're taking advantage of that.'

'Am I?'

'We both know he shouldn't be part of this operation!' She spat the words back at Farrier. 'He's emotionally compromised. That makes him a liability.'

'I thought you and him were tight.'

'We *are*,' she insisted, 'that's why I'm looking out for my friend. More than you're doing.'

A flash of anger glittered in Farrier's eyes, then faded.

'You were an army officer. You know how it is to be in command of people. Sometimes you have to give orders that aren't in people's best interests, for the good of the job.'

'That's what you're doing? Manipulating him?'

'I'm making the most of his skills,' Farrier replied. 'Say what you like, but Marc got us next to Grace, or Sam or whoever the hell she is, in *days*. We've been on her for months and got nothing, as you so delicately put it.' He looked away. 'Yeah, he's a friend. And so were the officers we lost in Oslo. That's five families I had to lie to in their death letters, making up the usual crap about training accidents. All because of that woman. So if I have to put my mate through some grief to get my hands on her, I'm doing it.'

Lucy didn't have a reply to that. She knew if their roles were reversed, she would have made the same choices.

'He's different now,' Farrier repeated, glancing up at the cab. 'I mean, Marc always wore everything close to the surface. That's why he wasn't cut out to run assets and lie to them every day, or get buried in NOC missions. He wants a clear-cut fight.'

'This job ain't great for that,' Lucy admitted. 'Way too much grey.'

Farrier gave a slow nod. 'You are not wrong.'

Suresh put the van behind a stand of scrubland and the group deployed into the warm evening. The metallic rattle of cicadas filled the gloom, sounding off from the trees around them as they moved to a low rise overlooking the disused airport runway.

Marc squinted into a light-intensifying monocular, scanning the area until he located the old terminal building. A low, three-storey rectangle flanked by two skeletal towers, the structure was dark. The monocular turned everything into a lunar land-scape of white and grey, and through it he could make out the remains of the airport's name in a handful of dead neon letters.

'I see an aircraft down there,' said Pearce, from close by. He was observing the same area through a set of bulky night vision goggles. 'Looks like . . . a passenger jet? Is that the getaway?'

'Don't sweat it, it's just a shell,' Marc told him, spotting the gutted, rusting fuselage of an old Trident airliner. 'That thing hasn't flown since 1974.'

'Hub White, Paladin One.' Marc heard Farrier behind him. 'We have the location in sight and we are seeing zero, repeat, zero movement.'

'*Copy, Paladin One.*' The voice belonged to Talia Patel, and Marc visualised her half a world away in the Hub White command room, watching them through the eye of a satellite orbiting far overhead. Getting an RAF Reaper ISTAR drone over the operational area was out of the question. '*Maintain reconnaissance posture.*'

'Copy,' said Farrier.

'Can't see bugger all from here,' said Lane. There was nothing approximating high ground for miles in any direction, and it was making everyone edgy. 'Suresh, what do you see?'

Marc looked around. The driver was on top of the blacked-out Ducato, flat along the roof, with his M4's night scope pulled to his eye.

'I can see a guard post from here. No movement.' He put down the weapon. 'That seem right to you? Should at least be some bootneck on patrol over there.'

Farrier and Lane exchanged a look that communicated a mul-titude of questions.

'Go take a shufti. Quiet, like.'

'I'm a ghost, me.'

Lane patted Pearce on the shoulder and beckoned him to her. The two of them set off at a jog and disappeared into the bushes.

'Is this bat country?'

Lucy's question came out of nowhere, and Marc wasn't sure how to answer.

'Is that, like, US army slang for something?'

'No, dumbass, I actually mean are there bats here?' She pointed towards the airstrip. 'Because something is flitting around over there.'

Marc strained to listen, but the endless chorus of the cicadas made it nearly impossible to pick out any other sounds. He returned to the monocular and panned up the length of one of the towers. At the top, he could see the silver dishes of the old, broken floodlights that had once drenched the aircraft apron with illumination.

A black shape crossed his line of sight, blotting out everything for a split second.

'*Shit!*' He recoiled, as if the shadowy thing was about to grab him. 'Okay, yeah. Bats.'

'Movement,' Suresh called down from the roof of the van. 'I have two Land Cruisers on the road behind the terminal, coming up from the main camp. Looks like blue hats in both of them.'

Marc refocused in the direction of the building in time to see the white Toyota jeeps moving up along the line of the old runway.

'A patrol?'

'They're not in a hurry,' said Farrier, peering through his scope.

Lucy drummed her fingers on the dirt. Marc could tell she was uncomfortable being out here without a rifle in her hands. Then she stiffened.

'In the terminal, I saw something. North-west corner.'

The headset in Marc's ear crackled.

'*All call signs, Paladin Three.*' Lane's voice was quiet and wary. '*Guard post in sight. Going in for a closer look.*'

All through the drive out here, Marc's mind was set on a single thought: that Sam Green was somewhere under this same night sky, on a path he couldn't guess at, making choices that he couldn't understand. The need to find her and face her, to get some sort of answer, was overwhelming.

But now a creeping dread was rolling in on him, cold like a winter fog.

The Land Cruisers had halted by a blocky shape tucked in against the side of the terminal building, and through the monocular Marc made out a solider as he climbed out to investigate. A flashlight flared into searing white brilliance, illuminating a third UN vehicle, a pickup apparently abandoned by the wayside. Other soldiers exited the vehicles, looking around in all directions. Their body language communicated uncertainty and caution.

'*Paladin Four . . .*' Pearce's voice came over the radio net, clear and grave. '*Found the guard. He's dead. Belly shot and a close-range finisher through the nut.*'

'*Three confirms,*' said Lane. '*Gate's wide open. What's the call, boss?*'

Marc was still processing this new information when a series of flickers blinked briefly in the windows of the terminal building. The soldiers out by the vehicles spun and danced as high-velocity rounds tore through them. A split second later the dull cracks of the gunshots reached them on the low ridge.

'Oh, shit.' Lucy leapt to her feet. 'What the hell are they doing?'

Marc turned and found Farrier, his old friend's face etched with shock.

'John, call it in!'

'Hub White, Paladin One,' said Farrier, in a dead voice. 'Observing shots fired. UN troops . . . down. Unknown hostiles inside base perimeter, over.'

'*Copy.*' Patel took a moment to respond. '*Stand by . . . Situation is, uh, fluid.*'

But Lucy was already sprinting to the van.

'Keyes, what are you doing?' Farrier called after her.

Suresh jumped down from the roof of the van, in time to see her hauling a pair of guns from the weapons racks. She threw Marc another of the M4 carbines, having selected an SR-25 marksman rifle for herself.

'No!' Farrier raised his hands. 'Stand down!'

A distant cry sounded out to them across the airstrip, followed by another harsh clatter of rounds.

'*Boss, more shooting over here!*' said Lane.

Marc met Farrier's gaze.

'We're not going to stand around and do nothing, are we?'

'We don't know the situation . . .' The other man trailed off, unable to muster the conviction for his own denial. 'Ah, hell.'

'Yeah, that sounds enough like an order,' said Marc, rocking off his feet and into a run. Lucy was already with him as he skidded down the rise and over the dirt road marking the outer edge of the airport perimeter.

'*Paladin, move in.*' Farrier's voice came over the comm net. '*And don't make me regret this.*'

EIGHT

They moved quickly across the highway and through the derelict airport's unguarded entrance, Lucy and Marc and the members of Paladin advancing by the numbers.

The MI6 team were cautious but not slow, and Lucy recognised the signs of a well-trained unit in action. All of them had to be thinking the same thing – they had been caught off guard back in Norway and were wary of making the same mistake again.

This woman – Grace or Samantha or whoever the hell she was now – had shown herself adept at leading her pursuers into traps, and that thought preyed on Lucy's mind. As they moved past the rusted hulk of the abandoned airliner, she chanced a peep through the sight atop her rifle, searching for signs of movement.

This felt like an ambush in waiting, and sometimes the only way to break through a trap was to trigger it.

Lucy didn't like dancing to someone else's tune, but the alternative was to do nothing and let good soldiers die. That was not going to happen on her watch.

More sporadic gunfire crackled in the middle distance, closer to the dark bulk of the main terminal building. Everyone drew down, reacting instinctively, but the shots were not coming in their direction.

At her side, Marc had a low-light monocular raised to his eyes.

'I saw something by the east side of the building,' he noted. 'Shadows. Nothing definite.'

Lucy gave him a level look and spoke quietly. 'If she's here—'

'What?' His reply was short and sharp. 'I know what you're going to say.'

She asked the question anyway, to get it out of her head.

'If you have to take a shot, you can't hesitate.'

'The mission is to capture Grace alive,' insisted Marc. Every time he used that name, it sounded forced.

'From what I've seen, I don't reckon she'll give you the option, Dane.'

'We'll see.'

Lucy put her hand on his arm as he made to walk on, halting him.

'You need to be ready for it. You read me?'

Marc pulled away without answering and kept moving.

Up ahead, Suresh was crouched low, pawing at something on the cracked concrete.

'Fresh brass here,' he said, gathering up a couple of shell casings.

'Give it over,' said Farrier, and Suresh tossed a shiny cartridge to the other man. Farrier rolled it between his gloved fingers. '5.56 NATO round,' he pronounced.

'The Argentinians use a bigger calibre for their rifles,' said Marc, nodding at the Stoner that Lucy carried. '7.62, same as that.'

'The intruders are carrying M4 carbines like we are,' offered Lane. 'I recognise the sound.'

'Likely,' agreed Farrier. 'All right, break into pairs and push up. We'll sweep the building room by room.' He pointed towards the UN vehicles still idling by the front of the terminal. 'Suresh and Pearce, check out the trucks. Lane, you're with me. Keyes, you take Dane and go in through the west side. Everyone stay on comms, stay keen.'

Off a chorus of nods, the team split apart and set off, each pair breaking into a fast jog.

It might have been hours after nightfall, but the air was humid, and Lucy found her breathing becoming laboured as they closed in on the building. She grimaced and pushed past the sensation of tightness at the bottom of her chest. The scarring on her lungs was healing, but too damned slow for her liking. She felt a step behind, she felt *unfit*, and it annoyed her.

'You okay?' Marc was sizing her up.

Damn him for being observant, she thought.

'What's that?'

She covered his question with one of her own. Near the wall, a body lay slumped in the shadows.

Marc closed in, dropping to kneel by the corpse.

'He took two in the chest, one in the head.' He couldn't keep the sickened tone from his voice. 'Tight grouping.'

'That's an execution kill, like the guard by the gate,' said Lucy. The dead soldier's rifle lay nearby, the safety catch still set. 'What do you think? Grace made her deal with these guys and then double-crossed them?'

'Wouldn't they have been face to face, then? But the entry wounds are from the back, at range.' Marc shook his head. 'This doesn't track.'

'What do you think happened?'

He took a long moment before he answered. 'This poor sod was blindsided. I'm willing to bet they all were.'

As Marc stood up, the radio crackled.

'*Paladin One, entering building.*'

'*Two, entering building.*' Lane echoed Farrier's words. '*Stinks in here.*'

'Okay, moving inside,' reported Lucy, beckoning Marc to follow. But suddenly he was twisting on the spot, bringing up his M4 to aim into the sky.

'Did you hear that?'

'Hear what?'

'Not bats,' he said, in a low voice. 'Something else.'

There was only the low hum of the wind over the cracked asphalt.

'Come on,' Lucy snapped. She wanted this over and done with. 'We need to move.'

At length, Marc gave a reluctant nod and followed her into the desolate terminal.

'*Paladin One, entering building.*'

Regis acknowledged Farrier's words with a nod, but said nothing. From behind her, Ari watched the prickly English woman study a satellite photo of Nicosia Airport, tracing the shape of the terminal building with her finger.

'*Two, entering building. Stinks in here.*'

'*Okay, moving inside.*'

Ari heard Lane and Lucy over the net, and then turned back to Regis.

'You're going to have to explain to your people back in London what is going on,' he told her.

Hub White had gone uncharacteristically silent as soon as Farrier committed to entering the grounds of the UN base, and the pilot wondered what kind of conversation was going on at MI6 headquarters at this moment. *Nothing good*, he imagined.

'We're here to monitor, not to stick our oar in,' Regis replied, without looking up. 'At this point, we're doing damage control.'

Ari frowned. In the old days, he had a reputation in the IAF for going off-book, and every time it happened, he paid for it.

The only thing that had kept him flying was the fact he was very good at it, and even then his latitude had run out after a while. He wasn't sure how much rope MI6 were willing to give its people, but he was betting it wasn't much.

They're silent because they're covering their backsides, he thought, *establishing deniability if this goes balagan.*

He looked away, finding Assim craning over his laptop. The Saudi kid's hands were a blur as he typed a mile a minute, eyes glazed as he lost himself in the glowing screen, his expression distant. Ari knew that look: the younger man was on to something, and it wasn't good.

Careful to make sure Regis didn't notice, Ari pretended to get another bottle of water, using the motion as an excuse to move closer to the hacker.

'So something's off,' he said in a low voice that didn't carry.

Assim reacted with a start, so engrossed in his work he hadn't been aware of the pilot approaching him.

'Oh . . . uh . . . yes.' He blinked. 'How did you know?'

'Experience,' Ari said dryly.

Assim accepted that with a wary nod. 'I kept going over the intel we have in my head, and I don't trust it. It's too patchy.'

'Huh.' Ari's lip curled in a wry smirk. 'Son, this team makes a habit of *patchy*. For us, *patchy* is where we work, or hadn't you noticed by now?'

'Everything we have has been last second, quick-sharp,' Assim insisted. 'No time to double-check it. The man that Grace is supposed to be meeting, the dealer?' The hacker prodded an image on his monitor. 'I looked into his background, and all the data I can access seems to point one way.'

Ari saw his instincts being proven right, but said nothing, encouraging the younger man with a nod.

'The dealer is not here,' said Assim. 'Not in Cyprus. And if that's true, then what exactly is Grace doing at Nicosia in the middle of the night?'

Assim explained that the guy, a man who used the alias Nix from the mythic shape-changing creature of the same name, was currently registered as being under house arrest in Mexico City, guarded around the clock by agents of the Federal Police.

'And you're telling us this now?' Ari turned to see Regis standing behind them, arms folded and glowering. 'Your timing leaves a lot to be desired.'

Assim coloured slightly. 'I . . . uh . . . was waiting to hear back from . . . From a contact on the dark net. She's not exactly on the side of the angels, so it's difficult to get hold of her.'

'So our target is meeting with some go-between then,' said Ari. 'Nix may not be there in the flesh, but he can still deal from half a world away, right?'

'I don't think so,' Regis insisted, and swore under her breath. 'I think this is another bloody set-up!'

She rushed back to the sat-comm rig set up in the hanger and grabbed the handset. Ari trailed after her.

'How are you so sure?' he asked.

Across the way, Malte had been drawn by the raised voices, and the dour Finn looked grim.

'British intelligence has a whole file on Nix,' Regis shot back, as she stabbed a key code into the handset. 'He's old school. He runs a solid reputation by being on site for his deals. If he ain't here, something else is going on at that base.'

Malte looked in Assim's direction. 'False flag?' he offered.

Assim chewed his lip. 'It could be.'

'Hub White, this is Akrotiri.' Regis spoke into the radio, her words coming clipped and quick. 'Loop us back into the general net, we have new intel, likely critical, over.'

'*Akrotiri, maintain comms discretion.*' Ari recognised the voice of the man called Welles. His patronising tone carried across the miles from London. '*Pass your data through channels. Hub White is currently assessing the situation on the ground, over.*'

Regis turned off-mike for a moment, her tolerance for the man evaporating.

'Oh, for fuck's sake . . .'

'*Say again, over?*'

'Loop us in!' Regis snarled. 'I'm not making a fucking request!'

The heavy air inside the abandoned terminal building held the rank stink of decades-old mould and bird droppings. Marc took a sour whiff of it and began breathing through his mouth.

His boots crunched on a layer of blown-in organic debris and fallen flecks of concrete from the ceiling overhead, making it hard to move silently. A splash of white glow from the headlights of one of the parked trucks partly illuminated the main hall through the terminal, but the rest of the space fell to pitch-black shadows, so he pulled his night-vision goggles down over his eyes.

Turned monochrome by the NVGs, the building's interior took on a dead, skeletal atmosphere. The walls and structures were straight lines and right angles, the only circular shapes the faintly glowing light wells in the roof. Back in the day, this through-way would have been thronging with passengers, but now it was empty.

Here and there, broken bilingual signs stuck out over stripped-out alcoves and vacant kiosks. High up on the walls, long-forgotten billboards advertised brands that had gone out of business before Marc was born, others draped with the shreds of sun-bleached, rain-ruined posters for holiday destinations.

The place gave Marc the creeps, but not in a *haunted-house* way, more in the *last-human-alive* sense. It felt post-apocalyptic in here, like a piece of the modern world had died and he was walking around inside the corpse.

The bleak thought made him scowl and he shook it off. He kept his M4 pulled close to his shoulder, his head on a swivel as he advanced.

On the far side of the hall, Lucy was keeping pace. She pointed to the far end of the space, where a set of wide, rusting stairs rose up to the crumbling mezzanine level, the gesture giving the order: *That way.*

He nodded, taking point, moderating his breathing. They were halfway along the hall when two rifle shots sounded from deeper in the building, the reports attenuated by the concrete walls. There was a half-second pause and then a third discharge, and Marc's mind immediately snapped back to the dead man he had found outside. The murdered Argentinian soldier with the triple shot in him, *one-two* through the torso and then *three* to make sure.

'*All call signs, report if you have contact.*'

Farrier whispered the question over the radio, but no one replied. Whoever was shooting, it wasn't one of the MI6 OpTeam.

But Marc's attention was suddenly elsewhere, as he caught the sound of footsteps scraping on the departure hall's torn and ruined carpets.

A figure moved out of the remnants of what had once been a coffee shop, stepping into Lucy's path. It was another UN soldier, a junior officer, his face rendered into a pale sketch by the NVGs.

He was brandishing a pistol and he jabbed it in Lucy's direction, calling out in Spanish, demanding she drop her weapon. His voice carried, echoing off the walls.

Lucy let her rifle fall to hang on its two-point sling, raising her hands and flipping up her low-light goggles to make eye contact. The officer caught sight of Marc and flicked between the pair of them, the pistol's muzzle moving back and forth in nervous jerks. Marc aimed his M4 at the ground and kept still.

Any sudden movement could set this bloke off, and the soldier clearly thought the two of them were part of the group shooting up his base.

Lucy tried to explain it to him, keeping her tone even and clear, but he wasn't having any of it. The officer started shouting, and he came out into the hall, calling for his men.

Marc was the only one wearing NVGs, and so he was the only one who saw a thread of green laser light blink into being, drawing a twinkling line through the air to connect the soldier with the shadows up on the mezzanine.

'Shooter above!'

He bellowed the warning and spun about, trying to aim upwards, but the fearful soldier saw him move and opened fire in his direction.

The pistol shots went wide, burying themselves in the crumbling plaster of the walls, and whoever was the cold hand on the weapon in the gallery fired *one-two-three* into the Argentinian, marching the bullets up his belly, his chest, his throat.

Lucy was already returning fire out of cover, her SR-25 blasting chunks from rain-bloated wood and grimy glass panels. Marc saw the shooter flinch back and heard boots thudding away over the floor above.

'*Sound off!*' Farrier's voice crackled over the comm net.

'Contact, departure hall, single shooter!' called Lucy. 'Am pursuing.' She threw Marc a look, jabbing a finger towards the mezzanine. 'Check this guy, I'm going after that asshole.'

'Copy that.'

Marc sprinted to the injured soldier's side as Lucy took the stairs two at a time, banging up into the darkness. He slung his rifle and pulled at the medical pack on his tactical vest, dropping into a crouch.

The young officer's chest was rising and falling in jerky stutters. Blood, black as ink through the night-scope, came out of his mouth in wet gasps. The rifle rounds that hit him had cut straight through his lungs and heart, leaving mortal wounds that would end him before any help could arrive.

'Rossi?'

Marc read the man's surname off the tape on his fatigues, and the soldier tried to nod. Marc felt sick and hollow as he realised there was nothing he could do for the man, the damage to him so lethal that none of the anti-trauma kit in the med-pack would be of any help. The soldier grabbed his hand and squeezed it.

'I'm sorry, mate,' Marc told him, the words catching in his throat. 'I'm so sorry.'

In the next moment, Rossi's grip slackened and his breathing fluttered into nothing.

'*Fuck!*'

Marc let go of the dead man's hand and dragged himself back to his feet. Being so close to such a swift and violent end churned up a mass of old memories and suppressed fears, enough that it took a physical effort for him to tamp them down.

And that was when Marc caught the sound again, the same hornet-buzz at the top of his hearing, the same noise that had drawn his attention earlier, outside on the runway apron.

Moving slowly so as not to spook it, he angled his head until he was looking straight up at a splayed metallic shape beneath four spinning micro-rotors.

The drone was hovering high and well out of his reach, drifting beneath one of the light wells. The glow from the moonlight outside threw enough shadow to make it distinct, even through the filthy, grime-encrusted glass.

It was watching him.

A dozen questions crowded into his thoughts, but he pushed them aside. Marc knew from the UAV's design that it wasn't something MI6-issue, and he was fairly certain that the United Nations didn't employ this kind of hardware in their day-to-day operations.

So it belongs to Grace, he thought, *and that means I want it.*

Marc squared his stance, making it look natural, planting his feet firmly as he tightened his grip on his carbine. He would only get one chance to bring down the drone, and as good as he was, he wasn't as keen-eyed a sharpshooter as Lucy Keyes. He would need to try something different.

Now!

Marc twisted, bringing up the M4 to aim into the light well – not at the drone, but at the grimy glass dome above it. Whoever was running the UAV remotely took a second too long to react, and in that brief instant Marc fired off a burst of rounds. The glass above shattered and came down in a glittering shower of thick shards, striking the drone and sending it spinning to the ground.

He ran for the machine even as it bounced over the decaying carpet, the unknown operator trying vainly to right the thing with buzzing surges of power to the flickering props.

'Not this time!'

Marc stamped down on the rotors and felt the plastic snap beneath his heel. He scooped up the damaged device and wrenched off its radio antenna, severing any remote control, then held it up at arm's length. An unpleasant thought occurred to him: what if it had a self-destruct mechanism?

Behind him, boots crunched on the broken glass. Marc spun about, still clutching the drone, grasping for his rifle – and then he froze.

A figure in matte-black tactical gear, nearly identical to his own, moved around the edge of the moonlight falling through the light well.

She was aiming a Glock semi-automatic at his head, a long sound suppressor extending the silhouette of the pistol, staring fixedly at him through a fringe of short black hair. Laughing eyes turned cold measured him impassively.

She was a ghost, scarred by fire, staring him down.

Before he could stop himself, Marc raised the NVGs so he could look at her in the real light. The pale wraith he saw through the goggles became someone wrapped in shadows, but the lines of her face were unmistakable. That girlish aspect hiding a toughness that refused to be broken, that familiar confidence with which she held herself – all of it was Samantha Green. Standing right there in front of him.

Alive.

'Sam . . . ?'

The name slipped out of him in a gasp. He remembered stale water and fire smoke, and her body drifting away from him. The body they had never recovered.

She cocked her head, the motion so true that for a second he couldn't breathe. It was her, but some ruined and broken version of the woman he had cared for. The moonlight made the burn scarring on her face look like tattooed tribal patterning.

Sam, Grace, the woman – she looked him over, the pistol never wavering as she decided what to do next.

There were a million things Marc wanted. To go to her, to hold her, to ask her why, to call out for help. But in the end, there was only one question that mattered, right now in this moment.

'What are you doing?'

'Give me the drone,' she replied. There was no humanity, no connection in the words.

'I . . .'

For an instant, he looked away, down at the ruined machine he still held in his hand.

Blinding pain exploded across the bridge of his nose as she smashed the butt of the Glock into Marc's face. It came with such unexpected force that he dropped the drone and stumbled backwards over his own feet, skidding on the ruined carpet, down on one knee.

Bright stars of pain blurred his vision and he clamped a hand to his face as blood streamed from his nostrils. She snatched up the fallen drone with a sweep of the arm and made a *tsk* noise at the damage he had done.

'I've got it.'

'What?'

Then Marc realised she was speaking into a throat mike around her collar, to someone else out in the gloom of the humid night.

He blinked and saw her smile. It was exactly the expression Marc remembered, but stripped of the daring and the warmth that had made him feel so much for Samantha Green.

'Time to go,' she said to the air. 'Finish it.'

Marc pushed himself up off the floor, finally shaking off the inertia of the confrontation. Everything Lucy had warned him about was happening; the moment was here and he was going to let it slip away.

This had to stop. *He had to stop her.*

'Sam, no—'

The pistol dipped and she shot him in the chest at point-blank range.

'Drop your weapon and turn around!'

Lucy had chased the shooter across the rickety floors of the mezzanine level, leaping over gaps where the age-warped boards had broken and given way. She paced him as he tried to escape her, dodging around webs of old, corroded barbed wire left in place to fence off parts of the run-down terminal. She heard shots sound in the middle distance, back where she had left Marc, but she didn't dare stop. Lucy trusted the Brit to take care of himself.

Now she had her quarry, and he had nowhere to go but over a sheer drop, down to an abandoned departure lounge filled with rotting furniture.

The shooter came to a halt, balancing on the edge where a rusting guide rail had fallen away. He obeyed the first part of her demand, turning to face her. As he did, she heard the faint burble of a radio voice coming to him through an earpiece.

In the dimness, Lucy could make out his gear and his gun. Just as Lane had surmised, Grace's accomplice was carrying a M4 carbine. But that wasn't all. The man's clothing matched hers – the same generic tactical vest, and an identical black jumpsuit. The only strange thing was the mask. A peculiar hood that completely covered his head, coloured in a translucent shade of emerald. It had no gaps for eyes or mouth and it gave the shooter an unsettling, alien appearance.

'Do it,' she insisted, taking aim, 'and lose the Halloween get-up.'

The shooter's radio muttered something and he nodded, the blank head turning to study her. He moved his arm so Lucy could see that he was holding something in his free hand.

It was a slim silver cylinder ending in a stubby antenna, with a spring-loaded grip bar held shut by his fingers. Without a word, he let the bar snap open and dropped into a crouch.

'Shit!'

She had time enough to utter the curse before the first of a series of remote-triggered C-4 charges exploded.

The initial blast peeled a wedge of concrete and metal away from the building and down to the roadway outside, carving a huge ragged-edged hole in the upper floor. The shooter didn't wait, and seized his escape route, throwing himself over the drop, down into the lounge and across towards open space.

Lucy fired, but as she pulled the trigger a second charge blew and the floor beneath her feet vibrated.

Move or die, she told herself, and followed the shooter down as nearby support columns cracked and split.

'*Abort and exfil!*'

Farrier's shout echoed in the wake of the thunder, dragging Marc back from the cusp of unconsciousness.

His chest was on fire. The raw kinetic energy of the bullet had spent itself on his tac vest's armour weave, but that velocity had transformed into heat, melting the polymer strands that made up the protective layer. Marc smelled the hot stink of molten plastic, burnt cotton and coughed. The air was full of choking dust.

He was half on his feet when a hand grabbed his forearm and pulled him up the rest of the way. Blinking away the pain, he came eye to eye with Tracey Lane.

'You hit?' she snapped.

'Yeah,' he managed. 'Vest took it.'

'Then you can move your arse!' Lane shoved him, making him grunt with agony as she pushed him forward. 'This place is coming apart!'

The next charge blew right above them, detaching a complete piece of light well and accompanying roof in one solid mass. Marc saw the flash of detonation and reacted without thinking, shoulder-charging into Lane to shove her bodily out of the path of the falling debris.

Both of them stumbled across the throughway as bricks and steel crashed through the floor and into the basement level below, striking with the force of a wrecking ball.

The effort made Marc howl, and he feared that the old break in his ribs might have snapped again. He fought through the cloud of concrete dust, and Lane stayed close, the two of them supporting one another as they rushed to get out.

'I warned you . . . it was a set-up . . .' she managed, between ragged gasping breaths.

Marc could only nod and keep moving.

Lucy emerged into open air to the sounds of gunfire and the long, drawn-out rumble of collapse.

Ahead, she saw the white blur of a UN pickup speeding away across the overgrown runway in the direction of the main road that paralleled the base's northern perimeter. Suresh and Pearce were chasing the vehicle with rifle rounds, but nothing hit the mark and it was quickly out of range.

She limped towards them, pain lancing up through her leg where she had landed badly on one ankle, as waves of displaced dirt rolled up and over her. More muffled chugs sounded the triggering of the last few charges, and the airport terminal imploded, caving in on itself.

Metal screeched and glass pealed as the old building buckled and fell. She put a hand to her face as the night wind picked up the dust and drew it away.

Over the radio net, she could hear overlapping voices, and from the haze came lumbering shapes that formed into people. Marc and Lane pushed towards her, both of them pale and sweaty with effort.

'You okay?' Lucy offered a hand, but Marc waved it away.

'She shot me,' he managed, and that pretty much answered a whole bunch of questions.

'Where's Farrier?' Lane looked around, rising panic in her eyes. She tapped her radio. 'Paladin One, respond. Do you read me, over?'

'Oh hell, is he in there?' Pearce stared bleakly at the mass of settling rubble behind them.

'Look!' Suresh shouted and pointed, drawing their attention to another figure, shuffling towards the group from out of the choking dust.

Farrier walked slowly, planting one foot in front of the other, his head down and his hands clasped around his gut. The grey dust covered him, gummed to a mask of blood over his face, and to her horror Lucy saw that he was leaving a trail of wet red boot-prints over the cracked, debris-strewn asphalt.

'John?'

Marc took a step towards his old friend, and it was as if the sound of his own name was the signal for Farrier's body to give out.

The other man collapsed into Marc's arms. Lucy saw a length of metal rebar protruding from his gut, run through Farrier like a short-sword in the gap between the pads of his armour vest.

Over the radio, a voice from Hub White was calling for them to leave the area. They were already running, carrying their wounded back to the van even as UN vehicles raced towards the ruins of the airport terminal.

In the hills above Bastia, a light and summery rain fell from the night sky, streaking the windows of the old mansion house.

Glovkonin didn't notice it. The Russian stared into the projector screen erected in front of the leather couch where he sat.

He was there, but his mind was miles away, watching the live feed of the terminal building collapsing through the digital eyes of a drone. The video signal was clean and crisp. The little machines had performed perfectly.

A subsection of the screen was frozen in time on a single frame in the corner of the display, the moment just before the other drone had been downed by the Englishman. The still image had captured Marc Dane's face in all its detail, trapping him in a moment of determined resistance.

Glovkonin allowed himself a sneer. *Such wasted effort.* He hoped that the former MI6 officer was still alive, if only because it amused him to imagine Dane witnessing what was to come next. This common and unremarkable man, the lucky fool too clever for his own good, the irritant that lodged in his plans like a stone in his shoe.

Any victory would not taste as sweet without Dane understanding how completely he had failed. Once, on a rainy London street, the Englishman had shown the temerity to challenge Glovkonin, *threaten* him even. The Russian had not forgotten, and he would not forgive.

The men in the committee, they would have told Glovkonin that such musings were unproductive and unprofessional. *But what is the point of this*, he wondered, *if I cannot wring some enjoyment from it?*

The point of view on the main display came about, leaving the obliterated building behind as the drone sought out and pursued a white pickup truck that bounced across the rough ground, away from the chaos. He watched the truck smash through two layers of perimeter fencing and leap a gulley, skidding onto a public highway. The vehicle grew larger as the drone dived towards it, and at the last second the remote-controlled machine landed in the pickup's flatbed. The image feed turned dark. The sortie was over.

A moment later, there was a hesitant knock at the door, and Glovkonin nodded towards Misha, who stood silently nearby. His bodyguard opened the door to allow a tanned young man to enter, one of the technicians toiling away around the clock in the hall across the way.

The Russian eyed him, waiting for the man to speak. Normally, he paid little attention to the minor players in his dramas, but he knew something of this one. The man's name was Andre, a cyber-criminal of French extraction. He came begging the Combine for gainful employment after his mercenary hacker cadre had been destroyed during an ill-fated operation in South Korea. Andre was eager to please his new employers and unencumbered by morals, both useful traits to have at one's disposal.

'The drones are secure,' he began. 'We're downloading their memory caches now. The footage will be on our servers in thirty minutes, ready to be processed.'

Glovkonin gave an encouraging nod. 'And after that? How long will it take for the first package to be ready?'

'It'll be done before dawn.'

He considered the reply for a moment. 'Nine p.m. on the east coast of America. That will be ideal.' He waved the man away, already forgetting him. 'Get back to work.'

When Misha had closed the door again, Glovkonin retrieved an encrypted Blackphone handset from his jacket pocket and woke the device. After a cursory series of security checks, he made a call to another node on the Combine's protected network.

'*What is it?*'

Lau answered promptly, and the tone of his voice made Glovkonin's lips stiffen. The other man's manner was changing day by day. The gratitude and reticence he had first exhibited after his liberation was long gone. The Russian liked him better when he was grateful, like Andre.

'Do you ever sleep?'

'*Thirty years of prison life eroded the need,*' he replied. '*You are calling me because there is a problem, or because you wish to gloat. Which is it?*'

'You seem bad-tempered, my friend.' Glovkonin smothered his annoyance with a fake smile. 'Perhaps rest is precisely what you require.'

'*I will rest when we are finished. What do you want of me?*'

He settled back on the couch, the old leather creaking agreeably.

'To make you aware. The second stage of our endeavour has been a success. Work on the next phase is under way.' Glovkonin paused. He refused to allow the other man to sour this moment. 'Tomorrow, we fire the shot that will end Rubicon. You'll have your long overdue reprisal and I will secure my victory.'

'*An army of falsehoods has little substance,*' said Lau. '*I remain unconvinced.*'

'That prison time really has put you out of step with the real world,' said the Russian, unable to keep the acid from his words any longer. 'People will believe what we tell them to believe.'

'*If you say so. But the sharpest blade is always the truth, and I have something with a very keen edge.*'

'I enjoy your elegant turns of phrase,' Glovkonin allowed. 'Make that work when you have Ekko Solomon on the ropes.'

He cut the call and tossed the phone aside.

Lau had his uses, and a great deal of money and effort had been expended in order to bind him to the Combine's cause. *But the longer he lives*, thought the Russian, *the more the man he once was emerges.*

Once that investment had paid off, he decided, it would be time to discard everyone who did not know their place in the new order.

NINE

The RAF medical team carried the stretcher from the military ambulance and up the ramp into the back of the Atlas. Marc stood on the turning apron, watching the transport plane's crew secure their precious cargo in place, and the airstream from the aircraft's multi-bladed props pushed at him as they spun up to full power.

His last glimpse of John Farrier was an ashen and bloodless face beneath a breathing mask, his old friend reduced to a faded, pale copy of himself. The iron bar that speared through him had torn organs and ripped open intestines, causing serious internal bleeding. A blunt and uncompromising doctor from the base hospital told Marc in no uncertain terms that Farrier's odds of survival were slim at best, and as adequate as RAF Akrotiri's medical facilities were, he stood a better chance elsewhere.

The Atlas would fly him back to the UK, to the dedicated trauma unit at Queen Elizabeth Hospital. And hopefully, the doctors there would be able to pull Farrier back from the edge.

The cargo ramp closed and the ground crew signalled to the pilots. Marc backed away as the prop wash grew stronger, and the Atlas rolled into the predawn light.

He watched the aircraft set itself up at the end of the runway, listening to the humming skirl of the engines as it throttled up. Marc felt rooted to the spot, an unpleasant and familiar sensation stiffening his legs. He had to keep watch; he had to see the plane off and follow it until it vanished. If he looked away, that would be a kind of betrayal. He would be letting his friend down.

It was a foolish, childish thing to believe, but he couldn't break away from it. As the Atlas thundered past, wings tilting back to climb skywards, Marc was caught on the jagged edges of other moments, other memories of friends and loved ones clinging to life.

His mother, slowly fading in a featureless hospital ward. Lucy, wreathed in sweat, behind inches of polymer glass in a bio-containment room. Farrier's pallid face smothered by an oxygen mask.

Sam, drifting through dark waters and into the black.

Each time he hadn't looked away, hoping that force of will would help bring them back. But it didn't matter. He couldn't stop it.

Eventually, the transport plane was lost in the clouds, and beyond it, the glow of sunrise crawled up over the horizon. Released from his self-imposed vigil, Marc began the long walk back to the hangar.

It was impossible to miss the change in tempo at the airbase. They had returned to find the facility on high alert, the local warning state posted at SEVERE. They were met by armed members of the RAF Regiment, who escorted them into cover as quickly as possible. Now, hours after the chaotic events at Nicosia, the after-effects of the disastrous mission were still shaking out and the prognosis was grim.

On the way back, the mood inside the van was quiet, broken only by the wet gasps of Farrier's laboured breathing. The smell of blood, cordite and stone dust thickened in the heat, and none of them could find anything to say about how badly it had gone.

Twice now, Grace had led them into a trap, and to make matters worse, they had seen this one coming but still believed they could break through it. And Marc had believed that too, because he thought he knew the woman they were pursuing.

How was it possible for someone to change so much? Samantha Green had always played by her own rules, but the woman who Marc had confronted back there in the terminal was unknown to him. Behind that damaged face and those cold eyes, she wasn't the same person he had once held in his arms. But everything else about her – the way she moved, the way she spoke, the turn of her head and the tone of her voice – was the woman he remembered.

He felt a twinge of pain in his chest. The Kevlar weave of his body armour had taken the bullet she put in him, but beneath that his torso was an ugly swath of bruising, taped high and tight with bandages.

If she wanted you dead, that bullet would have been between your eyes, noted Lucy. *She made a choice back there, for what it's worth.*

'She didn't kill me.' Marc voiced the thought. 'What does that mean?'

There was no way to look at that fact that didn't make matters worse, and no way to avoid the truth. When the moment had come, he'd frozen. And now she was in the wind again.

Raised voices reached him as he approached the hangar. Marc recognised the whip-crack diction, common to a superior officer giving out a tongue-lashing to an errant subordinate.

Entering, he found a ruddy-faced man in duty camos wearing the barcode tabs of a wing commander. He was jabbing a thick finger in Lane's face, while a pair of junior base officers flanked him silently.

'There's a limit to the tolerance of our service,' he spat, 'and you bloody spooks have ridden right over it. Do you have any idea of the levels of shit that you have unleashed here?' The officer didn't wait for Lane to reply. 'I will not have my men lumbered with the blame for the mess you created, do you hear me?'

He glared around the hangar, finding the members of the Rubicon and MI6 teams and giving them a venomous scowl.

Lane looked like ten miles of bad road, fatigue lying heavy on her. Still, she tried to hold her own against the officer's bombast.

'Sir, it wasn't our intention to—'

'I don't give a toss about your intentions!' He shut her down with a snarl. 'The group captain is on his way in right now, and when he gets here, you'll give him a full and complete account of this clusterfuck of an operation you were running.' He paused for a breath. 'And then, *maybe*, we can find a way not to go to war with the bloody Argies all over again.'

The wing commander stalked away, pushing past Marc with his officers in tow, leaving an icy atmosphere in his wake.

It was Regis who cut through the sullen silence that followed.

'That bloke's a twat, but he has a point. Is someone going to explain what the hell happened out there?'

'Grace played us, end of,' Pearce said quietly, staring at the floor. 'She tried to finish what she started in Norway – wipe out the team.'

'It's not that,' began Lucy, shaking her head. 'If that's what she wanted, there's easier ways to fill some graves.'

'Oh, you're the expert now, are you?' Suresh turned on her, his tone lighting up with undirected anger. 'It was your idea to go in there, wasn't it? If we'd just stayed on station—'

'What?' demanded Lane, cutting him off. 'We should have stood by and let those soldiers get shot up?'

'Fat lot of good we did them, though!' Suresh shook his head. 'They still ended up dead. And it could have been us too. You saw what happened to Farrier . . .' He said the man's name and suddenly ran out of steam.

'Keyes is right,' said Lane, after a long moment. 'Grace didn't bring us all the way to Cyprus just to cross us off. There's another agenda here. We need to find out what it is, if we're going to salvage any of this night's work.'

'Why attack soldiers at a UN military base that hasn't seen action in years?' said Regis. 'Maybe she was double-crossing the Argentinians . . .'

'I don't think so,' said Marc. He pushed aside everything else, boxing up his emotions to concentrate on only the facts at hand. 'She faked the whole meeting with Nix to draw us in. After Oslo, she left enough crumbs of intel behind her so we'd take the bait and piece together where she was going. She knew who would be sent after her.'

Ari looked up from where he sat, on the folding steps leading into the parked Rubicon jet.

'So all that about buying weapons for a maritime assault was garbage?'

'In hindsight . . .' Assim gave a weak shrug.

'She wanted us here,' added Lucy. 'What does that get her?'

The trilling sound of a telephone issued out from the cabin of the jet, and Ari stood up, giving Lucy and Marc an *I got this* gesture as he disappeared inside.

'The drones?' Standing by a gear crate, Malte offered nothing more but a questioning look in Assim's direction.

In turn, the young hacker gave a slow nod.

'There were definitely unmanned aerial vehicles over Nicosia Airport tonight. I've combed through the local comms traffic and there are two distinct control signals buried in the feed. High transfer rates. A lot of data being transmitted.'

'We can dig into that, yeah?' Marc threw the question at Assim, and off his reluctant nod, he went on. 'Maybe back-trace the drones to wherever they were being operated from.' He paused, thinking it through. 'The one I saw, there was a definite lag to its movements, so that means whoever was flying the thing wasn't close by.'

'How can you know that from just looking at it?' Suresh's doubt bordered on mockery.

'I know,' Marc insisted. He had bitter experience of both being in control of and on the receiving end of military-grade unmanned aerial vehicles.

'We need more than guesswork,' said Lane. She was taking command now, stepping into the breach opened by Farrier's loss. 'In ten minutes, I have to be on a secure line to Hub White.' She glanced at her watch. 'And they are going to want something better than a weak tea replay of our collective fuck-up.'

'I'm afraid that conversation is not going to go the way you think.' Ari stood in the open hatchway, a wireless phone handset in his grip. His lined face was uncharacteristically pale. 'There's something you need to see.'

The narrow HondaJet's cabin was configured to manage five people, so it was standing room only to squeeze all of them on board. Lucy found herself at the front of the group with Ari and Marc, standing before a drop-down video screen hanging over the rear bulkhead. A live feed from a Russian news channel was playing out, with a serious anchorwoman recapping a breaking story.

'*For those of you just joining us, we have learned this hour of an unprovoked attack at a United Nations military base, on the island nation of Cyprus.*' A graphic popped up in the corner of the image, a globe rotating to show any viewers the relevant part of the world she was referring to. '*Footage has been released via internet and sent directly to a number of major news outlets.*' She paused before speaking again. '*We warn you that this report contains footage some viewers may find disturbing.*'

Other stations might have edited out what came next, but this network was more interested in driving up ratings with the raw and the shocking.

Lucy's heart dropped as the images switched to night-time aerial footage of a familiar rectangular building, and the expanse of bare concrete apron in front of it. Nicosia Airport looked as it had in the satellite images that were still sitting on a table out in the hangar. She heard a sharp intake of breath from Marc and she knew he saw it too.

'Is that . . . ?' began Suresh, but then he fell silent, his question answered as the camera's eye caught sight of the ruined lettering atop the derelict terminal, spelling out its name. The news anchor kept on talking, reiterating her warning as white 4 × 4s appeared in a lower corner of the frame. The camera shifted and sharpened focus to show the distinctive UN lettering along the sides of the vehicles.

'The drones,' Malte said again, with grim certainty. The video could not have come from anywhere else.

There was a jumpcut. Now the vehicles were stopped, and soldiers were moving around them. From out of nowhere, sparkles of muzzle flare blinked in the shadows and the UN troops broke apart in disarray. Bodies fell as they failed to find cover, others running for the shelter of the terminal building. The drone camera moved and found three figures advancing and firing, M4 carbines up and tight at their shoulders. It zoomed in, stabilising the image.

Lucy caught sight of someone and the recognition moved through her in an electric shock. She saw *herself* there, walking alongside Grace as if the two of them were part of the same kill team. The third shooter in the group wore Marc Dane's face.

She felt all eyes in the cabin on her back as the footage jerked through another series of cuts. Some of the following shots were from inside the ruined building, blurry images through greenish low-light filters: Lucy and Marc stalking down the throughway, weapons at the ready; Pearce and Suresh out on the apron, appearing to deliver execution headshots to wounded men; more dead soldiers lying where they had been cut down; Grace at the entrance gate, calmly killing the lone guard on duty.

'That is not what happened,' insisted Lane. 'Where are they getting this?'

The news report returned to the studio, and the grave-mannered anchor showed the right amount of dismay and concern as she launched back into her report. She spoke as footage of the terminal building's demolition unfolded on a screen behind her.

'*This video was supplied to our network via an anonymous source, together with information on the attackers, and we believe it originates from a principled whistle-blower within the international intelligence community. We are still in the process of confirming the veracity of this material, but it appears to clearly show figures identified as officers of the British security services, collaborating with agents of a private military contractor called Rubicon, in what can only be described as a deliberate and unprovoked attack on United Nations personnel.*'

'They didn't want us there to kill us,' said Marc, in a dead voice. 'They wanted us there for *this*.'

Esther McFarlane sat bolt upright in her hotel bed, pulling the cotton sheets tighter around herself in an unconscious attempt at self-protection. The chilly blue-green images on the television in her room were the only illumination, hard flickers of colour wiping out the soft glow through the windows from the Monaco skyline.

She mashed the channel-change button on the remote in her hand, advancing down the line of news stations. Each of the main broadcasters had some variation on the same report, from circumspect and grave in some cases to loud and accusatory in others. Everywhere she paused, the ticker chyron showed the name 'Rubicon' or the reports repeated the words that accompanied the damning video.

'*Additional details are becoming clear as we report on this apparent act of state-endorsed terrorism,*' said a sober-looking man on an Asian news feed. '*It is now being suggested that the motivation behind the attack may be connected to corporate holdings belonging to the Rubicon parent organisation in Cyprus. It is possible that a destabilisation of the tenuous Turkish-Cypriot peace that has existed for years in that island nation would be beneficial to Rubicon's corporate agenda—*'

McFarlane's smartphone lay next to her on the bed sheets, and it trilled incessantly as dozens of incoming text messages bombarded it. An initial call from her assistant, Finlay, had awoken her from a fitful sleep, with little more than a panicked warning to turn on the television, and now everyone wanted to talk to her, all screaming for some kind of explanation.

The moment felt unreal and dreamlike, but she knew too well to hope that this was some stress-induced nightmare. McFarlane picked up the phone and scrolled through the steadily increasing series of messages, many of them from reporters at the same networks currently accusing Rubicon of committing a terrorist act.

One message was tagged as a place name rather than a person – *Giardini Botanici Hanbury* – and it had no content, only a cellular number.

She calmed her racing heartbeat and muted the television, before tapping the call return tab. A voice answered before the second ring.

'*You have seen it, I assume?*' The Chinese man's words had no weight.

'You did this?'

Esther tried to keep her tone level, but it came hard. Anger and frustration and fear churned as the import of this grew clearer to her.

'*Does it matter who allowed the information to leak? Now it is out in the world and it cannot be called back. You knew that Solomon's agents would get out of control. The only question of importance at this hour is: how are you going to deal with this situation?*'

She fought back the impulse to throw the phone across the room. His tone was so metered, so damnably calm that it was like nails dragged down a chalkboard.

'I dinnae take kindly to being manipulated!'

Her native Scots accent cut through, the stress of the moment bringing it to the fore.

'*If you do not act now, swiftly and decisively, it will mean the end of Rubicon. The end of everything you have worked for. Is it necessary for me to repeat this truth? You know it as well as I. You must take control, or Ekko Solomon will drag you down with him.'* He paused to let that sink in. *'I promised I would help you. I will.'*

'What . . . ?'

There was a sound at the far end of her suite, out past the open bedroom door, in the direction of the hallway. McFarlane leaned forward, and she saw a shadow moving in the spill of light that fell under the suite's doorway from the corridor beyond. Someone was out there.

'I have sent you material that will be of use,' he told her. *'Forgive me, but I had to wait for a moment like this, because you would not have accepted it otherwise.'*

The shadow moved, and with a whisper of paper, a white envelope slid into the room under the door. The light changed as the shadow faded away.

'It is time for you to know the truth about Ekko Solomon,' said the voice on the phone. *'How you use this knowledge is up to you. But I think I know what choice you will make.'*

The line went dead, but McFarlane had already tossed the phone onto the bed. With the sheets still wrapped around her like a shroud, she padded into the hallway and recovered the envelope. Inside was a thin memory card bearing the seal of Interpol.

Her laptop blinked to life with a touch, and she sat before it, ensuring that the device was secure before inserting the card.

The contents were mostly high-definition photographs, large files dense with visual information. As an experienced geologist, she immediately recognised the formatting of ground survey images. The first few files were false-colour stills of deep-penetrating radar returns, but as she paged through, the character of the shots changed. They became images taken on location, then stage-by-stage shots of digs in various states of progress. *Red mud and dusty skies*; it looked like Africa.

Her hand rose to her mouth when she saw what had been buried.

'This is bullshit,' snapped Marc.

'I do not disagree,' said Assim, hunching closer to his laptop's screen.

Somehow, Lane had been able to convince the wing commander not to immediately throw the whole lot of them into Akrotiri's glasshouse in the wake of the news report. He settled for removing their weapons and placing them under guard, before marching her back to the base proper while a few men from the RAF Regiment were posted in front of the hangar. The big doors were now open, letting in the breeze and the morning light, but that was less for the team's comfort and more so their guards could keep an eye on them all at once.

The team had, disappointingly, broken back into its component groups. On one side of the hangar, Regis congregated with Suresh and Pearce, while Lucy, Malte and the rest of the Rubicon squad stayed close to the tent and the HondaJet.

Marc looked at the old Cabot dive watch on his wrist. Two hours now since the story had broken, and communications had gone unpleasantly quiet.

The silence from Hub White and Rubicon stirred up unpleasant memories of similar circumstances. Years past now, but the recall of it as strong as if it was yesterday. Marc's unit gone and him in the dark, unsure where the next shot would come from.

He'd done the dutiful thing, the right thing. Called in to MI6, hoping to request a rescue, trying to figure out what the hell happened. Silence answered. He was left hanging, forced to fend for himself.

This felt a lot like that, but now it wasn't just Marc Dane twisting in the wind. It was Lucy, and Assim and Ari and everyone else. It was Lane and Farrier and the Paladin team.

'We know what this is,' said Assim, drawing Marc's attention back to the screen. The young hacker had already downloaded the raw dump of the so-called leaked footage, cutting into it with surgical precision. 'This is the same thing Lion's Roar used in Iceland and Belgium. *Deepfakes*.'

Ari sat nearby, scowling at the mention of the violent extremist group.

'How does that even begin to be a thing?'

Marc shot the pilot a look. 'You've seen doctored photos. You know how that works, yeah?'

'Sure.' Ari shrugged. 'My kids do that all the time. Joke pictures of Ezra surfing off Niagara Falls and Leah walking the dog on Mars.' He pointed at the computer. 'But that is next-level falsehood.'

Not for one second did the pilot entertain the idea that the video might be real, and Marc was grateful for the man's unquestioning trust.

'The software combines one piece of digital footage with a completely separate one,' he explained. 'Manipulating a moving image, erasing something . . . In this case, adding something.'

'And all of it seamless.' Ari shivered involuntarily. 'So in this day and age, seeing is *not* believing any more, is that what you're telling me?'

'Pretty much,' said Marc. 'I tried to grab one of the camera drones buzzing around back at Nicosia, and now we know exactly why they were up there.'

'Grace wanted you where she did her killing, so it would match up.' Ari nodded as he thought it through. 'Better to hide the seams that way, I'm guessing.'

'He's right,' Assim noted. 'I mean, a deepfake program can patch images of one person's face over another from any source, but the closer the raw data is to the patch, the easier it is to do.'

'And the faster it could happen,' said Marc.

'You were in the same place at the same time.' Ari mimed a pair of scissors with his fingers. 'So they cut and stitched you, like cloth in my cousin Zussa's tailor's shop.'

'That's about the size of it.'

'But even the best needlework comes undone,' insisted Ari. 'It can't be perfect, can it?'

Marc and Assim exchanged a grim look.

'No. But it will take weeks of decompiling to prove beyond a shadow of doubt that the footage is fabricated,' said the hacker, 'and by then the damage will have been done.'

'Would anyone even believe you, after the fact?' said Ari, shaking his head.

'This is pure disinformation warfare,' concluded Assim. 'It is a targeted propaganda strike designed to discredit Rubicon and MI6.'

'The amount of effort needed to refute bullshit is infinitely more than the amount needed to create it,' muttered Marc. 'What else is in this pack of lies they put out?'

Assim brought up another panel on his screen.

'Actually . . . most of that material is authentic.'

The display showed scanned images of police records and military personnel files. Many sections were heavily redacted, but much of the salient data remained.

Marc saw pages from his own Interpol dossier, a leftover from his brief time as an international fugitive. There were details of a federal warrant in Lucy's name, and then excerpts that named Tracey Lane, John Farrier and other members of the OpTeam unit as officers of British intelligence. Sam Green was in there too, he noted.

He leaned in to read his file.

'This is terrific,' Marc said coldly. 'Our greatest hits collection, right out in the open.'

'But why would Grace . . . ? Why would she expose her own identity?' said Assim. 'That doesn't make sense.'

'Because she doesn't give a damn!' Marc retorted. 'That's an acceptable loss for her, you get it?' He sat heavily on the edge of a workbench and rested his head in the palm of his hand. 'Shit, I'm fucking exhausted by this.'

Saying it out loud drained the energy from him as the adrenaline and anxiety Marc had been cruising on dissipated. For a moment, all he wanted to do was find a shadowed spot in the back of the hangar and let sleep take him.

An alert ping sounded from Assim's laptop, and the hacker jolted with surprise. Suddenly he was closing data panels on the screen, scrambling to decode the contents of an encrypted email.

'What's that?'

Marc shook off the fatigue and fixed him with a hard look.

Assim coloured, and fumbled his reply.

'It . . . uh . . . It's something from a contact on the dark web.'

The young Saudi had the worst poker face of anyone Marc had ever known, and he utterly failed to conceal what he was doing.

'Let me see.'

'I reached out to some people I know.' Assim started with a pre-emptive excuse, trying to get his explanation in early. 'I thought I could get a quicker read on tracking the drone command paths if I . . . uh . . . *crowd-sourced* it a bit.'

Marc wanted to be annoyed at him, but he was too worn out to expend the effort. And there was something to be said for the *many hands make light work* model of intelligence gathering.

'Did it help?'

Assim nodded sharply. 'It might well have, yes.'

He pulled up a map graphic and overlaid the new data over it.

Marc saw Cyprus in the centre of the frame, a pair of blinking dots showing where the drones had been flying over Nicosia. A line drew back over the digital landscape to the northern coast, to a building in the town of Girne. It hesitated there as the computer continued to process the information.

'That's where the operator was?'

Assim shook his head as the trace line started moving again.

'Just a repeater. A local node to boost the signal strength.'

The trace bounced across to southern Turkey and a cellular exchange in Anamur, then around the country to other nodes in Ankara and Istanbul, crossing and recrossing its own path. It picked up speed, flicking to sites on the far side of the Black Sea in the Ukraine and Moldova, then back south again.

'They were definitely trying to obfuscate any tracking,' said Assim.

'Yeah, no shit.' Marc watched the line make a dive south until it terminated at a location on the Greek island of Rhodes. 'That's it?'

'Tracking sequence ends there,' confirmed Assim.

Marc blinked to clear his thoughts, glancing up towards the parked jet as he processed this new information.

Greece. We could be there in a couple of hours.

'Huh.' Despite himself, Assim gave a faint smile. 'My . . . ah . . . source has supplied more than just the trace.'

He pivoted the screen so Marc could get a clearer look.

The location where the trace terminated was a grungy commercial marina near the northern tip of Rhodes, on the edge of the town from which the island took its name, and attached to a map was content from a file stolen from a Hellenic Police server.

Marc skimmed the text. 'Says here there was an unexplained fire on a barge yesterday afternoon. It sank in the harbour, and the police are waiting on divers from the mainland to come and check it out . . .'

Assim cocked his head. 'Why is that relevant?'

'Because there's a witness statement mentioning a woman seen on board before the fire. The description talks about a white woman with dark hair and facial scarring.' Marc gave Assim a hard look. 'Where did you say you got this information?'

'I didn't.'

Marc held his gaze for a moment. 'Is this a *don't ask, don't tell* thing?'

'Most emphatically *yes*,' said Assim.

'And you trust this source?'

'Same answer,' said the hacker.

'Okay.' Marc hauled himself to his feet. 'You trust this, I trust you. Pack up the kit, we're going to Greece.'

He left Assim behind and called out to Lucy, striding quickly across the hangar.

'Hey! Where's Ari?'

Lucy caught the urgency from him.

'Catching some shut-eye, like we all should. What's the hustle?'

'Wake him up. Assim has a lead, we need to follow it.'

He waited for her to react, but Lucy shook her head, and looked past him, out towards the airbase.

'I reckon that's gonna be a tough sell,' she said.

Marc turned to see what Lucy had already spotted. Tracey Lane marched towards them with a face like thunder and a two-man armed escort at her heels. The guards waited outside the hangar, but Lane came in angry and looking for somewhere to dump it.

Lucy knew that expression. She'd seen it in the mirror enough times.

Lane didn't waste a second with preamble.

'It's as bad as you think. Welles has everyone back at Hub White scrubbing their feeds for incriminating data—'

'They should be trying to *clear* us!' said Suresh, but he fell silent again when Lane gave him an acid glare.

'According to him, Six are reviewing the situation, which for now means saying sod all and letting the accusations fly.' Lane cast a weary look in Marc and Lucy's direction. 'The long and the short of it is, we're on lockdown for the time being. Welles is coming out himself on the next available flight with his incident team, whatever that means.'

'It means his pit bulls from the ninth floor,' said Regis.

Victor Welles ran the department at MI6 whose primary function was to police the officers of the agency, and investigation of a catastrophic mission failure like this one was squarely in his purview.

'I've been here before,' said Marc, under his breath. 'I have no desire to do it over again.' He spoke up. 'That's an interrogation for all of us, Lane. You know it and I know it . . .'

'We don't have time for that crap,' said Lucy.

'Welles will handle the debrief,' Lane continued, 'and we'll go from there.'

'What about our target?' Pearce broke his sullen silence.

Lane looked away. 'Other assets will be tasked with that. Like I said, we're stood down until this is cleared up. Six can't have us in the field right now if our faces are plastered over the news.'

'We stand here with our thumbs up our arses and we lose our lead!'

Marc advanced on Lane, and for a second Lucy thought he was squaring up for a fight.

'Back off,' warned Lane, but he shook his head.

'What lead?' said Regis.

Marc filled them in on the information Assim had dredged up from his anonymous dark web buddies on the drone control trace and the barge in Rhodes harbour.

'The way I see it, we have half a day at best to get there and sweep for whatever Sam left behind.'

'And what makes you think that won't be the prelude to another ambush?' Lane made an angry, cutting gesture at the air. 'Your ex roped us in twice, Dane, laid down a false trail just like that one. You want to go for three fuck-ups in a row?'

'This is different,' he insisted.

'How so?'

The question escaped Lucy before she was even aware she'd asked it. But once it was out there, she didn't want to call it back. As much as she trusted Marc, Lane had a point. Their quarry was making a habit of the sucker-punch play, and they would be fools to let her do it again.

Marc seized on the question. 'Because she knows how this is supposed to shake out. An OpTeam mission fail means *hold for evaluation*. She knows those protocols! She knows we'll be taken off the board. But if we keep going, keep chasing her—'

Lane made a hissing noise. 'Did you miss the bit where I said the word *lockdown*, Dane?'

Marc was silent for a moment. He glanced at Lucy, and she knew he was going to go next.

'I heard it. Now you hear *this*.' He leaned in. 'We don't work for MI6, remember?' Marc gestured at the other members of the Rubicon team. 'We don't have to jump when that prick Welles cracks the whip.'

'You think you can just fly out of here?' Suresh got up, eyeing him.

'We have good intelligence.' Assim stood with his laptop, gripping it like a shield. 'We have to chase it down.'

Suresh gave him a withering look. 'Stay out of this, nerd.'

Lucy expected Lane to kick off angry, but she went a different way, matching Marc toe to toe.

'You know Welles already has a serious dislike for you and Rubicon. He thinks you're loose cannons. You make a run for it and you prove him right!'

'We're not running from anything,' said Marc, 'and I am long past giving a toss about what Victor Welles thinks of me.'

'You reckon you can still get to Grace? Get to the bottom of this?' Regis asked the question on everyone's mind.

'That's the idea.' Marc kept his eyes on Lane. 'Are you going to try to stop us?'

The question hung in the air, the tension in the hangar pulling drum-skin tight, and in that instant the simmering rivalry between Paladin and the SCD operatives was laid bare. When Lane didn't answer Marc's challenge soon enough, it was Suresh who sounded off.

'Why are you so eager to be gone all of a sudden?' He pointed at the jet. 'Are you afraid something else is going to come up? Something you don't want found out?' Pearce protested, but the other man was on a roll and talked right over him. 'Maybe you're in it with Grace or whatever the fuck she's called. Maybe you set us up.'

'Maybe *you* set *us* up!' Assim blurted out the retort.

Lucy had to intervene before someone did something stupid.

'Cool down, everyone. Look, no one likes this, but what we have now is a bunch of bad options.'

'You're not allowed to leave,' said Lane, slow and clear.

But something had shifted behind her eyes. Marc saved her life back in the terminal building. Was she weighing that up, measuring the debt?

'You're not going to get in the way,' Marc replied. He said it matter-of-fact, not like a threat, and Lane didn't counter.

'Those apes will give it a shot.' Pearce jerked his chin in the direction of the RAF guards out on the apron.

'Not if we give them something else to think about.'

Regis rose to her feet. Suresh started to complain, but the other woman shut him down with a glare.

Lane scowled. 'Well, we're already in deep shit. A little more isn't going to make much difference.'

The black smoke from a burning tyre doused in flammable engine degreaser coiled up from behind the hangar. It did the trick, drawing the attention of the RAF guards long enough for Ari to start the HondaJet's twin over-wing engines.

Normally, the business of setting up the swift little executive jet for take-off was an involved and measured process, but Ari threw the manual aside and went back to his fighter pilot roots, spinning up the aircraft to power even as it rocked against the chocks holding the wheels in place.

Assim and Malte were already on board, strapping in for what was going to be a hostile departure. Lucy bounded up the stair ladder ahead of Marc, but he hesitated on the lowest rung, turning back to see Lane standing behind him.

'This is the best you'll get from me!' she called, over the rising whine of the jets. 'So don't waste it!'

'Come with us!' He hadn't thought to make the offer until that second, but as soon as he did she knew he meant it. 'We could use you!'

'Idiot,' she snapped back, as Pearce pulled the chocks and threw a salute to the cockpit. 'Someone's gotta look out for John.'

'Yeah—'

'Dane!' Lucy bellowed at him from the open hatch as the jet began to roll. 'What the hell, man? Get in here!'

She grabbed a handful of his jacket and pulled.

Marc lurched into the cabin, and dragged the hatch shut behind him. Up at the front of the aircraft, Ari had the cockpit door open, and through a side window Marc saw the guards coming back at a full-tilt run. But the jet was already out of the hangar, and Ari gave a nasty chuckle as he put more power to the engines, sending a heavy pulse of exhaust wash into their path.

The guards staggered and fell as loose debris from inside the hangar whipped into the morning air.

'This is your captain speaking,' called Ari, as calm and steady as any commercial airline pilot. 'You know the drill. Seatbelts on, seat backs up, tray tables down, all that whatever. Hold tight, children, because this will be a fast one.'

Marc dropped into the closest chair and secured himself, chancing a look towards Lucy across the cabin.

'If this doesn't work, this is going to be a real short trip,' she muttered.

The jet lurched as Ari pushed the throttles forward, and Marc let the sudden acceleration press him deep into the leather chair.

A voice spoke up behind him. 'Even if we g-get off the ground,' said Assim, forcing out each word, 'wh-what is to stop the RAF sending one of those F-35s after us?'

'Nothing,' said Marc. 'So we'll have to fly below radar and move fast.'

'Here we go!' Ari sounded almost cheerful as the jet's nose tilted upwards and they shot into the air. 'This is my favourite part!'

'He's enjoying this way too much,' growled Lucy.

Marc watched the ground flash away to become blue waters beneath their wings, the white wave tops close enough he could have reached out and touched them. They were low, a lot lower than he was comfortable with.

'Are we c-clear?' called Assim.

'Ask me again in a couple of hours,' said Marc.

TEN

Marc's feet touched the muddy bottom of the harbour, and he moved slowly, careful not to stir up any silt. He let himself float there, listening to the hiss of air through his regulator and the pulse of blood in his ears.

The midday sun fell down through the water above, throwing the shadows of the moored boats on the surface across him. He turned in place as Malte settled close by. Like the Finn, Marc was making do with tourist-quality gear rented from a shabby little dive school a few miles down the coast from Rhodes. It wasn't the best kit, but they couldn't afford to be choosy. An over-generous rental fee had got them use of skin-suits, vest, masks and short-duration air tanks, and most importantly, with no questions asked.

He signalled Malte to follow him, and the other man gave an exaggerated nod. They drifted towards the black bulk of the ruined barge, and Marc looked it up and down, thinking through his next move.

Sometime in the past, the old craft had been converted into a houseboat of sorts, but that was being generous with the description. It was a rusting, decrepit tub, thick with barnacles on the underside and patched in dozens of places. It sat at a steep list, with a quarter of it afloat and the rest beneath the water. The mooring was in the deepest part of the harbour, and Marc assumed that it had been meant to sink all the way.

The fire on board had done a lot of damage, but it set the barge into a kind of half-capsize that put out the flames and left it in its present, not-quite-destroyed state.

Marc swam up to the rail on the submerged deck and took hold. He blinked behind the mask, working the regulator in his mouth and failing to get comfortable with it.

A brief, deep sleep on the jet was the only rest he'd had in the last twelve hours, and he was feeling it. They were in the shallows here, a few metres down, but still Marc was labouring each breath.

You shouldn't be doing this, he told himself. *You get tired and you make mistakes.*

But what the hell else could they do? Lucy was up on the dock, covering them and watching for the local cops. Ari was back at the airport with Assim, doing their best to maintain the lie of the fake flight plan the hacker had spun up. Nothing the SCD team were doing on Rhodes was good enough to withstand any solid scrutiny from the Greek authorities. This was about as quick and dirty as it could be, and all of them knew they were one mistake away from arrest and incarceration.

Marc found a collapsed skylight and pointed it out to Malte, who nodded again. Switching on a waterproof flashlight tethered to his wrist, Marc pushed off with a deft flick of his fins and dropped inside.

The barge's interior was a mess. The main open section was completely flooded, and through a side door Marc saw a shimmering mirror, indicating the area of the boat where a pocket of air was still trapped. Everything loose had been stirred up by the sinking, creating a slow-moving snowstorm of rubbish and gritty particles.

The torch beam picked out what had probably been the main living and sleeping area. Burn-damaged chairs, a smashed television and a collapsed workbench were visible past a curtain of floating, discarded blankets.

Malte followed him in and settled on the deck, but then kicked off again in a sudden gush of bubbles as the barge gave a low moan and shifted alarmingly. The wreck was dangerously unstable.

The Finn gave Marc the *I'm OK* signal and Marc returned it. Slow and steady, the two of them spread out and scouted the compartment.

Sam had been here and set this place alight on her way out. Marc considered that grimly, trying to put himself in her mindset. It wasn't the best way to sanitise a location, but it was expedient. Burning it down should have destroyed anything left behind, and that might have worked if the barge itself hadn't taken on water too soon.

There was a chance that something, some clue, was still in here. He held onto that hope, even as another, more candid part of himself wondered if this was a waste of effort. Sam Green was trained the same way Marc had been, trained to make sure every location was left as clean as possible for just this reason.

He moved through a web of ruined, shredded paper, remnants from whatever files, photos and maps Sam's team had been using. None of it was salvageable, legible.

Light moved over the floor, and Marc turned as Malte drifted towards him. In his hands, the other man held blackened, melted blobs of plastic. He offered up cracked circuit boards and heat-seared panels for Marc to inspect. All of it had been in the middle of the fire, most likely doused in kerosene before Sam had struck the match.

Marc took the ruined bits of hardware. The first was the slagged, useless remains of a compact digital printer. He shook his head and tossed it away. But the second item was something else. He gripped the torch and shone it down.

Malte had found part of a satellite communications unit, the broken thing still trailing wires.

A wireless comms node, thought Marc. *This is what was talking to those drones in Cyprus.* The presence of the device as good as confirmed the lead that had brought them here, but it opened up a whole new problem. The node was internet-enabled, which meant that whoever had been flying the UAVs over Nicosia could have been on the other side of the world.

Still, it was something. He handed it back to Malte with another *OK* and the other man stuffed it inside a mesh bag hanging from his belt.

They split apart and moved on. Marc checked the time on the Cabot watch at his wrist, and peered at his air gauge. They'd both been down for around fifteen minutes, and the small tanks had maybe twice that in breathable air.

He pushed to the bow of the sunken boat. The barge's frame narrowed here, the fire-scarred walls closing in, and the metal kept up a constant groaning, creaking chorus as the wreck refused to settle.

A shape hit Marc across the goggles and he jerked back in shock, bringing up his hands in self-defence. Drifting there ahead of him, paper booklets moved through the beam of the flashlight like fat, lazy moths.

He grabbed one. It was a Singaporean passport, the bright red cover catching the light. Others floated around him, in different colours from different nations, stirred up by the motion. Most of them were burnt and ruined, but some were still legible.

All of them had variant versions of the Sam-or-Grace face on the identity page. Names, birthplaces, hair and eye colour changing, and none of them with visible facial scarring.

Marc grimaced behind his mask and salvaged a few for later study. He cast around, shining the flashlight into the corners.

Think like her, he told himself. *What was she trained to do?*

If the barge had been a staging area, and the presence of emergency papers seemed to suggest that, then it stood to reason that Sam had prepared the attack on the UN base right here.

She would have needed maps and imagery of the area. Tickets and travel documents. Any physical examples would have been shredded or burned, but digital assets were a different matter.

The first phase of standard operating procedure for sanitising a location was *erase everything*, but control-alt-delete only went so far. It wasn't enough to wipe hard drives and memory sticks, because even dead data could be resurrected with the right tech. There had to be physical destruction as well.

Marc floated down to a makeshift kitchen in the lower section of the barge. Lying on the deck, he saw the bright yellow gun-shape of a cordless power drill and nearby, metallic bricks the size of hardcover books.

He scooped one up. It was a removable hard drive unit, riddled with holes where the drill had been used to Swiss-cheese it. He let it drop. The drive was useless, the fragile magnetic platens inside it fractured beyond any hope of recovery.

Then his gaze fell on a microwave oven fitted to a shelf. He pulled open the door and wisps of tainted water billowed out. Blobs of plastic and metal that had once been smartphone SIM cards and USB memory sticks littered the inside of the appliance.

His eyes widened. Two of the memory sticks were relatively intact, and that meant that they might still be recoverable. Marc clawed at them, but he couldn't get a grip, his neoprene gloves slipping. The sticks were fused to the floor of the oven, and if he tried to chip them out with his dive knife, he risked destroying them completely.

He gripped the frame of the oven and pulled, putting his weight behind it. Loose bolts sheared off and it shifted, but so did the shelving, and a whole section of the wall broke away. The barge rumbled in response and the deck tilted.

Objects migrated down and away from Marc, falling in slow motion as his unwitting shift in weight set off a chain reaction down the length of the wreck. The barge was rotating, this time leaning fully into a capsize.

Light flashed in Marc's direction. Malte was up at the other end of the compartment, close to the open skylight, signalling him to get out. Marc waved him away, signing *Swim Up*, and went back to the microwave.

With effort, he hauled the weighty metal box to him and pushed off the deck. It was hard work to move with it, and he banged into the low ceiling, then off a support girder. Marc held onto his salvage even as the drag of it pulled him down like an anchor. Each kick of his legs seemed harder than the last, the exertion making his breathing rough, sending pennants of bubbles out behind him.

Silt and debris rolled into the compartment, killing visibility, but Marc kept pushing up and forward, towards Malte's hazy torchlight.

The Finn met Marc halfway, his pale eyes wide behind his mask. There was no dive sign for *What the Hell Are You Doing?* Malte's expression communicated that well enough.

Marc shoved the metal box towards him, and the other man got the message. Between them, they shouldered it through the skylight, even as the barge reached complete inversion. Marc's hard-won prize sank towards the bottom and they scrambled after it.

Moving by feel in the silt-fogged water, Marc's fingers found the frame of the metal box and grabbed on. The barge was coming down on top of them, serenely sinking the last few metres to the bottom of the harbour.

The two divers kicked hard, moving low and fast, away from the wreck before it could crush them into the mud.

The boat settled heavily into the sediment, displacing a shock of water that sent Marc and Malte reeling.

Lucy watched the sapphire-blue waters of the harbour turn opaque as the barge went under, a bloom of stale green-brown silt erupting to smother it.

The muscles in her legs twitched, her first impulse to dive off the quay and go in after her teammates. She almost did it, but rocked back at the last second. She had no gear, no way to see clearly down there. A Navy SEAL she'd known during her time with JSOC had once warned her that going into the water unprepared, no matter if it was far at sea or next to shore, was asking for trouble.

A group of fishermen who until now had been idling further down the breakwater started calling out in alarm, jabbing fingers in the direction of the sinking barge. It was attention she didn't need, but there was nothing Lucy could do. Someone was going to get the cops, that was a given.

'Ah, hell.'

She shrugged off her jacket and took a step back, sucking in air in preparation to jump, but then two goggled heads burst from the muddy water, near a narrow slipway close by.

Marc and Malte were carrying something between them, struggling to haul it out of the water. She dashed down to the slipway as Marc came up, kicking off his fins.

He spat out his regulator.

'I need ... I need a ...' Marc was breathing hard and he couldn't finish his sentence.

For the first time Lucy saw what he was carrying.

'Is that ... ?' It most definitely was a cheap microwave oven, the cracked case leaking seawater, the door flapping open uselessly. 'You have the sudden need to heat up a burrito?'

Marc dropped the microwave on the concrete quay and staggered towards an emergency locker bolted to a tall bollard, shedding his mask, buoyancy vest and air tank. He broke the glass over the locker's latch and wrenched it open. Inside was a powder extinguisher, a lifebuoy ring, and he pulled them out, discarding them in search of what he wanted.

'Aha!'

Marc dragged a stubby fire axe from the locker and marched back to his piece of salvage.

'What is he doing?' Lucy asked Malte, who answered with a shrug.

Marc attacked the microwave with swooping blows of the axe, breaking it into pieces, and Lucy started to wonder if lack of sleep or some kind of diver narcosis had temporarily fried his brain.

'Got it,' he reported, ripping out a section of the appliance, waving around the bit of scrap like it was a trophy. 'We can ... probably go now.'

'Police,' said Malte, nodding in the direction of the harbour centre.

A patrol car was pulling to a halt at the other end of the break-water, cops getting out to meet the animated fishermen.

'We came here for that?' Lucy glared at Marc.

'Oh yeah,' he replied, still breathing hard. 'See, this—'

Lucy raised a hand. She had a hundred questions, but now was not the time for them.

'Leave the gear and move,' she snapped, sprinting towards the road. 'You can explain it to me on the way.'

Many of the richest Monaco residents had expansive homes in the hills around Monte Carlo. Opulent penthouses, apartments and villas vied with one another to fill the territory with the biggest, the most expensive, the most lavish, but Ekko Solomon had never felt the need for such a domicile.

Perhaps it stemmed from an early life where he had owned nothing material beyond the clothes on his back and the rounds in his rifle, but the African saw little value in surrounding himself with things. Most of his art collection stood in museums, not private galleries. He thought of his cars, yachts, and his aircraft as tools. The monuments of Solomon's wealth were in plain sight, in the factories and hospitals and laboratories built with Rubicon's successes.

He had no home, at least not in the sense that others would think of it. Two floors of Rubicon's corporate headquarters on the Avenue de Grande Bretagne were turned over to his private use, but Solomon's quarters were elegantly spare in aspect.

Clean, crisp and modern, the apartments were characterised by tall windows, wide open spaces and minor elements of decor that recalled the lands of his birth. That was his only nod towards possessions – a few rare artefacts, some Makonde carvings, an ivory *lupembe* hunting horn and nothing else. Even then, he saw himself more as a caretaker of the objects, rather than their owner.

Solomon had always moved through life carrying with him what he needed. Anything more would hold him back from the path he had chosen. He did not measure his life by the dollars in his bank accounts or the reach of the corporation he had founded. Solomon found worth in only one thing: the balancing of the scales of the world.

And now that was awry, the balance in danger of tipping past a point of no return.

In the silent, open atrium at the heart of his apartments, he sat on a heavy suede chair and leaned forward, elbows on his knees, a crystal glass of dark bourbon clasped in his hands. A single drop had yet to pass his lips.

Solomon had always known that his crusade would make him a target. A man of his power and influence could not rise as high as he had without making enemies. There were those he had outbid, outmanoeuvred or outfought, nursing their enmity and wishing an end to him. There was the hatred he had drawn simply because of the colour of his skin and the circumstances of his birth.

Rubicon had fought its own small wars before, in boardrooms and corridors of power, sometimes in the ghost realm of cyberspace or down a darkened alleyway with the chug of a silenced bullet. Solomon had done all that and worse; he held back secrets and dark truths for the promise of a greater good. In doing so, he had made many enemies.

They were coming for him. The footage of the Nicosia attack was burned into his thoughts. His most trusted people, cast as killers and terrorists. His organisation, branded as conspirators in partnership with a supposedly corrupt intelligence agency.

It was all lies, of course. But it seemed the days of reasoned doubt and rational challenge were long gone. The world was a riot of the credulous and the mendacious, driven by emotion over fact. Too many were seeing and believing, but not questioning, in an age when truth was the rarest commodity. Every day, the powerful spewed blatant falsehoods in such explosive profusion that they drowned out even the merest chance of challenging them.

And now that tide of deceit was rolling over Rubicon.

Solomon's gaze turned inward, his thoughts searching through countless bleak possibilities, sifting every potential outcome. He could not escape the sense that these were only the opening shots, the thunder rumble of an oncoming storm.

That worse was yet to come.

A soft click behind him signalled the opening and closing of a door, but he did not acknowledge it. Reflected in the golden glass of the windows, Solomon's aide Henri Delancort came into view, and the younger man's face was set in a worried frown.

'I'm sorry to disturb you, sir,' he began. 'It is just . . .' Delancort trailed off, his usually prim manner briefly crumbling. '*Merde*! There have been new developments.'

'Go on.'

Solomon watched his reflection, as Delancort read from a digital tablet in his hand.

'Legal Operations received a formal warning from Interpol that Rubicon is now the subject of a major criminal investigation. They'll be calling for complete access to company records next.'

'Of course they will.' At length, Solomon turned to study him. 'There's more.' He wasn't asking a question.

'The Dow Jones and the Nikkei indices have yet to stabilise. The negative impact on Rubicon Group stocks in the wake of the Nicosia report has been . . .' He faltered, grasping for the right word. 'Substantial.'

'It is just money, Henri,' Solomon told him. 'What about our people?'

With a flick of his wrist, Delancort would have been able to reproduce the content of his tablet's screen on the digitally enhanced glass of the apartment's windows, but he knew Solomon, and knew that he would want to hear the words said aloud.

Delancort sighed. 'We have only one Special Conditions Division team in the field.' He didn't need to say which, and off Solomon's nod, he carried on. 'They'll be landing at Nice in approximately thirty minutes.' He paused, then spoke quickly. 'There are arrest warrants in effect for some of them. Sir, there's still time to route the aircraft to a non-extradition location. If Rubicon impedes an active Interpol investigation—'

'I know the risks. But I want my people safe. I need to look them in the eye.' Solomon turned away. 'Kader has set up a cover story for their flight. I want you to move them quickly. Bring Dane and Keyes here as soon as possible, and keep it quiet. No one outside this room is to know where they are, am I clear?'

'Yes sir.' Delancort's discomfort was obvious, and for a moment Solomon thought he would push back. But then he continued with his briefing. 'The Argentine Republic, the United Nations Security Council, and the Republic of Cyprus have condemned the Nicosia attack in the strongest possible terms. They've demanded explanations from Rubicon and the British government. In addition, Argentina and Cyprus have frozen Rubicon Group assets within their national borders.'

Solomon weighed that consideration. In material terms, that last act was of little consequence to the company, but it had a strong negative effect regarding the global perception of Rubicon.

'Our construction project in the Cypriot green zone . . . ?'

'Already closed down by local law enforcement.' Delancort's frown deepened. 'You should also be aware that our monitoring teams have noted an uptick in online chatter.' He made a sour face. 'A number of so-called alternative news sites are disseminating stories suggesting that the Nicosia incident is directly connected to Rubicon's investments in Cyprus. They're accusing us of engaging in an attempted false flag attack, in order to support Turkish control of the North.'

Solomon nodded grimly. 'More disinformation, designed to obfuscate the truth.' He looked up. 'And the footage that was released?'

'It is already with our imaging lab in Palo Alto,' said Delancort. 'They're working to deconstruct it as we speak.'

'That will matter very little if no one cares,' he noted.

Delancort gripped his tablet tightly, and finally cut into the silence that followed.

'Sir, we have to get in front of this before it is too late. We have to look at the realities of the situation . . . We must consider what is best for the organisation.'

'Henri.' Solomon's next words were cold and hard. 'I would hate to think you might suggest I throw my people to the wolves, so that Rubicon might gain some breathing room. That would go against the principles we stand for.'

'I am only suggesting that we consider every available option,' he managed.

A chime sounded on Delancort's tablet, ending the thread of conversation for the moment, and he tapped at a pop-up panel. His frown deepened.

'A message. From the board of directors.'

Solomon nodded. He had been expecting this since the moment the news story was broadcast.

'And so it begins,' he muttered.

'Esther McFarlane has called an emergency meeting of all senior Rubicon Group board members,' said Delancort. 'For tomorrow morning.'

'The summons to the gallows,' said Solomon, finally taking a sip from the glass in his hand.

ELEVEN

Military service had taught Lucy how to grab rest when she could. In a career operating in regions that would have to clean up to be considered hellholes, she had developed that feline skill of being asleep, but awake enough to snap out of it in a fraction of a second.

She blinked to full awareness, ignoring the brief but seductive pull back into dark oblivion. Lucy was dreamless, or so she liked to believe. If there was turmoil going on in her subconscious while she was out of it, it stayed there, and for that she was grateful.

She slipped off a long sofa in the unlit, empty conference room, casting around to find a clock on the wall. It was the dead of night. Whatever had woken her, she couldn't place it. She decided it was her body's way of paying her back for the abuse she put it through, kicking her out of a comfortable REM sleep when she least expected it.

Those weeks in the clinic made you soft, woman, she thought, scowling at the notion. Too much downtime had allowed her body to exert control over her will, and that wasn't going to cut it any more. She stifled a yawn and took a deep breath. Her lungs tightened, warning her to go slow, but she pushed past the moment. She moved to a spot in front of the room's window to do some stretches.

Outside, the streets of Monte Carlo were lit like fading embers. Even a place like this needed to sleep once in a while, and in the predawn hours the casinos and the hotels were dialled down to their lowest beat, probably accommodating vampires or the few hedonists too stupid to go to bed.

She gave herself a silent, internal debrief as she worked through her moves. Everything was a blur of activity after Akrotiri. The hop over the Med to Rhodes had been a turbulent, low-level rocket ride, and then there was the barge and Marc's crazy salvage operation. But he turned out to be on the money, in spite of her misgivings.

By the time they were back in the air and running under a fake flight plan to France, Marc had teased out the broken fragments of two USB flash drives from the guts of the broken microwave oven. He showed Lucy slivers of blackened circuit board and microchip that looked to her like the shiny carapaces of dead insects, insisting that there was still actionable intel on them.

Zapping computer memory was a good way to wipe its content, but as the Brit noted, it wasn't foolproof. Nothing short of dissolving the drives in a bucket of acid could guarantee 100 per cent erasure.

Lucy didn't like trusting the mission to something with so much 'maybe' coming off it, but there was little else she could do. Slim chances were the stock-in-trade for the Special Conditions Division, like it or not.

After landing at Nice they executed a rapid deplaning, with Malte and Ari remaining in Rubicon's hangar at the airport, while Marc, Lucy and Assim fled before too many questions could be asked.

She didn't like the thought of putting Malte and Ari in the line of fire, leaving the two of them to face the gendarmes. But neither man had their faces on the news and that hopefully gave them enough plausible deniability to stay out of jail.

She still felt shitty about it. Lucy knew what it was to walk around with a target on her back, and she didn't want that for anyone else. She owed Malte Riis too much, and Ari Silber deserved better. In the pilot's case, it was the last thing a good man with a wife and kids deserved to be stuck with.

So far, the cops had not come calling to the Rubicon tower, which meant that the world at large didn't know where Lucy Keyes, Marc Dane and Assim Kader had gone to ground. But every hideout had a diminishing level of protection the longer it was in play, and any investigator worth the name would have the building at the top of their checklist. Someone would put two and two together, and the proverbial knock on the door would come.

We need a plan, and soon, she told herself.

Her warm-up complete, Lucy left the darkened conference room and padded out onto the main floor of Rubicon's crisis centre. Normally, the space would be manned by a handful of techs working 24/7 at sat-com, surveillance and monitoring desks. Right now it was a ghost town, with all but a couple of screens running in standby mode. The staff were gone, sent home or temporarily reassigned in the wake of the Nicosia attack, and the emptiness made Lucy uncomfortable. It felt abandoned and dead, like the dusty halls of the derelict airport terminal back in Cyprus.

But not quite *empty*, though. She caught the soft rattle of a keyboard and the faint double-clicking of a mouse. Homing in on the sound, she found Assim in front of a brightly lit monitor, obliviously manipulating complex lines of computer code.

'Hey,' she said, announcing herself, and the young Saudi practically shot off the chair in surprise.

'Bloody hell!' He gave her a shaky glare. 'Don't sneak up on me like that. Oh gosh, I nearly wet myself.'

'Wasn't sneaking,' she noted.

'You do it without even realising,' retorted Assim. 'It's rather unsettling.' He wiped his brow and took a moment to calm down.

'Why are you even awake?' she demanded. 'Do you know what time it is? Do nerds ever sleep?'

'That is a lot of questions.'

'Pick one.'

'We've been reconstructing bits of data from the damaged flash drives. A lot of it is rubbish, but it's not a complete wash.' Lucy noticed that pages from the fake passports Marc had taken from the barge were showing on another display, scanned images of them blown up to ten times resolution. 'There's some stuff there that looks like travel documentation, but the most interesting take is *this*.'

He brought up a data panel filled with more lines of code, and looked at her as if she should have been impressed by it.

Lucy studied him levelly, waiting for Assim to remember that not everybody had a degree in computer science.

'Okay, so I harvested metadata from these files, like the digital equivalent of a label? It has the encryption signature of a STRAP 2 document – you know what that means?'

'You're gonna tell me,' she said.

'The STRAP protocol is the security rating system used by British intelligence agencies.' Lucy turned towards Marc's voice, as he walked in from out of the shadows. He looked pale and sweaty, but there was hard focus in his eyes. 'Which means the digital docs on those drives had to originate from inside the UK intelligence sphere.'

'You should be resting,' Lucy admonished. 'Shit, we all should be.'

'Couldn't sleep.'

Marc waved that away with a vague motion. He positioned himself next to Assim, peering over the younger man's shoulder.

Reluctantly, Lucy gave in to the reality that she wasn't going back to that comfortable sofa any time soon.

'Okay, so Grace either stole, bought or otherwise acquired top secret MI6 files.'

'Show her the picture,' said Marc.

Assim nodded. 'I was able to partly restore an image.'

He tapped a key and up came a grainy photo of Tracey Lane. It was your classic mugshot, the sort of thing that would be on an ID pass or in a criminal record.

Lucy made an educated guess. 'From her personnel jacket?'

'The lady wins a prize.' Marc nodded back at her. 'Yeah, it looks like what we rebuilt are bits and pieces of OpTeam crew files.'

'I sent out the hounds for fragments of names for the rest of Paladin.' Assim's prim English accent held a note of triumph. 'And came up trumps!'

Another screen-in-screen showed positive hits for the words LANE, REGIS, SURESH and FARRIER.

'I got the bally lot of them,' he noted.

Marc put a hand on his shoulder. 'Mate, you're a smart bugger but sometimes you sound like a P. G. Wodehouse character.'

Assim started to protest, but then thought better of it.

'The public school system has a lot to answer for.'

'She had files on the MI6 officers coming after her,' said Lucy. 'Us too?'

'Could be,' offered Marc. 'There's a lot of data that's totally unrecoverable on those drives.'

Lucy nodded. 'Makes sense. Grace is running a con. If I was her, I'd want to know as much as I could about my marks.'

'But she ... Samantha Green *already* knew these people.' Lucy could see it was hard for Marc to say her name. 'She served alongside them in K Section, like I did. John Farrier recruited Sam from Army EOD the year before he brought me in.'

'It's not just the members of Paladin she had information on.'

Assim replaced the search panel with another. The call sign NOMAD was highlighted, along with a series of other names that included GREEN and DANE.

'I've copied everything we have and forwarded it to Lane,' said Marc, his tone turning stony. 'But I don't know what it means, or why Sam would have this. Seems off to me.'

Lucy sat heavily on one of the workbenches, and looked him in the eye. In the back of her thoughts, an unpleasant idea had been gathering weight, picking up momentum as it took on a spiky, solid reality that she couldn't continue to ignore. Marc met her look and said nothing, and she knew right then and there that he was seeing it too.

Dane picked up on threads of information faster than anyone Lucy had ever worked with, intuiting connections where others would see random events. And that meant that if she spotted something, he was already ahead of her. He just couldn't bring himself to say it out loud.

'We've been so busy focusing on our target that we didn't stop to look at why this is happening,' she began. 'What's her objective?'

'Grace is a rogue with an axe to grind,' said Assim.

Lucy shook her head. 'That's the easy narrative, the simple choice. It's more complex than that.' She held Marc's gaze. 'Isn't it?'

He took a long moment before he told Lucy what she already knew.

'Everything that has happened up to now was to get us where we could be framed for a terrorist attack. Enticing MI6 by picking at old Nomad contacts, pushing them off balance by killing their officers.'

'And drawing you – and Rubicon – into the game,' added Lucy. 'They dangled some bait and goddamn it, we took it hook, line and sinker.'

'What do you mean, *they*?' Assim's brow furrowed.

'Sam was the stalking horse,' said Marc, his manner turning grim. 'That's obvious now. Which means, this is much more than a rogue officer looking for some payback. It's bigger, it's been planned down to the last detail. We're in the middle of an orchestrated attack, on *us*. On Rubicon and MI6.'

Assim considered that soberly for a moment. 'Which raises the question . . . *Cui bono*? We have made a lot of enemies. And that's just since I signed up.'

'Okay, I'm gonna come right out and say it,' Lucy broke in. 'This thing has the Combine's fingerprints all over it.'

'It does fit their profile,' admitted Assim. 'They have a long and storied history of false flag operations. It's practically their hallmark.'

'You're making a big leap,' said Marc, but it was a weak deflection and Lucy called him on it.

'They know us,' she insisted. 'They know you, Marc. That dick Glovkonin and his billionaire boys' club have the resources and the reach. They know what buttons to push. I mean, what better way to drag you in than to bring your—'

'Enough.' Marc held up a hand to stop her talking. 'Just . . . *enough*, Lucy, okay?'

'Let's say it is the Combine.' Assim didn't get the message, turning in his chair, his fingers working at the air as he became lost in the problem. 'We would need to know for sure, of course. But the circumstantial evidence is compelling, especially the deepfake tech and the use of proxy operatives. I can dig into this.' He nodded to himself. 'There are people I can reach out to.'

Lucy was going to say something about the dangers of mingling with black hat hackers on the dark web, but given their current circumstances, it seemed a moot point. She turned to Marc, but he was walking away, the room's long shadows swallowing him up.

Lau's phone trilled and he fished the device from his pocket. Two words in English script – GREEN LIGHT – appeared on the screen and he smiled thinly.

The office inside the police headquarters on rue Suffren Reymond was modern and light, but narrow and condensed like the majority of real estate in Monaco's expensive environs. Lau rested on the windowsill, considering a cigarette as he squinted into the darkness outside.

The four operatives Glovkonin had provided waited patiently nearby. Three men and one woman, no two alike in build but all of them identical in terms of manner.

A soldier knows soldiers, Lau reflected.

The four security specialists wore black tactical trousers, combat boots and military jackets. Each had a hi-tech set of polarised glasses that also contained a radio bead, a wireless eye-tracking device and a built-in digital camera. They holstered

semi-automatic pistols beneath their jackets, and the only identifying mark on their clothing was a discreet coloured flash on
the right cuff and a patch on one shoulder. The patch was white
on black with crimson trim, showing the design of a stylised
vulture – the corporate logo of ALEPH, a Moscow-based private
military contractor.

Lau worked his phone with a thumb, tapping a fast-dial key
that would immediately connect him to Glovkonin, and the
phone buzzed to indicate the line was secure.

'*Report*,' said the Russian.

'We are in position,' said Lau. A strange sensation whirled
through him, a mixture of anticipation and building fury.
'I hope you are prepared.'

'*Are you?*' said Glovkonin. '*I've invested too much for anything
to go awry.*'

'You will get what you want,' Lau replied.

He gave the ALEPH operatives a sideways look. They were
under his command, that was true, but he did not doubt that the
Russian had given them orders that superseded his. He could not
allow himself to forget that Glovkonin saw men as his tools. Lau's
presence here was not a partnership, more a temporary alignment
of shared goals. It would be a grave mistake to lose sight of that.

And yet, it was difficult for Lau to think too far beyond the
next hours. Years of captivity – decades of it – and all that had
sustained him was a dogged refusal to die and a cold ember of
hate. He imagined that ember cupped in his hand, a cinder of
dark fire, seething and burning. The glow of it brightening now,
as his moment of truth moved closer.

'*I will remind you – for my own sake, you understand – to be
mindful of our objective.*'

'I know what must be done.'

'*You do. But it is easy to become caught up in the emotion, yes? Your great patience has been taxed to the limit. So promise me you won't shoot Ekko Solomon dead the moment you lay eyes on him.*'

The idea of that made Lau lick his dry lips.

'I will try to restrain myself.'

Through the glass office walls, he saw a group of police officers approaching, some of them in the black and red caps of the uniformed division, others in the tactical gear of Monaco's Specialised Intervention Unit.

'*You are to prioritise securing the computer server containing Solomon's Grey Record files, am I clear?*'

'I understand.'

Lau had been briefed in detail about the clandestine database and what it contained.

The Combine were very interested in that particular prize. Not only would it tell them exactly what Rubicon knew about their operations and where any security leaks in their organisation might be, but it would also give them thousands of man-hours of useful intelligence on Rubicon's other targets of interest – many of whom were direct rivals of the Combine. The material could be used for blackmail, assassinations, and worse.

'I will contact you again when I have it,' Lau told him.

He cut the call as the door opened, and put on a wan smile.

The lead officer from the SIU gave Lau and the ALEPH team a wary look. He was the tallest man in the room, and his manner made it clear he was accustomed to being obeyed. He, like all his officers, was clearly unhappy about being called in to prepare for the forthcoming operation in the middle of the night.

'Let me make this clear,' he said without preamble. 'I don't like having armed contractors in our principality. It sets a bad example.'

He put withering emphasis on the word *contractors*, pushing it to get a response.

The female ALEPH operative leaned close to her colleagues to translate the officer's words into Russian, but her stone-faced comrades showed no reaction.

'Your name, sir?' Lau took a couple of steps, using his cane to support him.

'Dupuis,' the officer said sourly, as if unwilling to give even that much away.

Lau adopted the same mild tone he had used on a lifetime's worth of bored and belligerent prison guards.

'Monsieur Dupuis, many private security staff are employed by the more affluent residents of Monte Carlo and its surrounding wards. If you can work with them, I hope you can work with us.'

He made a show of offering up the Interpol identity card that the Combine had provided, designating Lau as an official investigator dispatched by the agency's liaison office in Bangkok.

Quite how the Combine had been able to falsify the card and the paperwork required to back it up was unknown to Lau, but it was airtight. Along with the credentials, Lau also carried a legitimate Interpol Blue Notice, an alert document naming Ekko Solomon as a person of interest in an investigation into the Nicosia attack. Monaco's criminal police division had grudgingly accepted the notice, and now they were about to execute it.

Dupuis chewed his lip, and Lau saw how this would go. The SIU officer was being pressured by his commanders to keep this quiet, to do nothing that would disrupt the smooth running of the principality and frighten the indolent rich who fed its coffers. It would not do for Monaco to be seen in the world's eyes as a safe haven for corporate criminality.

These people are greatly invested in appearances, Lau noted. *I can make use of that.*

'Interpol will take full responsibility for this operation,' he said, granting Dupuis a cloak of deniability. Lau indicated himself and the ALEPH operatives. 'With your permission, I will serve the notice personally. Mr Sigalov, Mr Gera and Mr Adaksin will provide general security . . .' He gestured to the three men, who responded with a nod to the sound of their names. 'And Ms Milost will act as close protection for me.'

The woman inclined her head, brushing a thread of short dark hair back behind her ear, revealing a pale cheek.

'We anticipate no real opposition,' she noted, her Moscow accent blunt and without affect.

Lau began moving again, ending the conversation.

'Everyone understands this is a delicate situation,' he concluded. 'Trust us to handle it discreetly.'

Marc found an empty conference room and went to the window, leaning forward until his forehead rested on the glass. The cool aura of the night air pushed through, and he drank it in like it was a tonic.

Marc imagined the cold spreading over him, down his body, into his flesh. Turning him numb, until he couldn't feel a thing. He welcomed it.

Succumb to the chill. Lose yourself in it.

Anything to get away from the questions he couldn't answer and the emotions he couldn't master.

I've led us into this mess, he told himself. *And for what? Chasing the memory of a woman I thought I knew, and a relationship that doesn't exist.*

'I know this is hard for you,' Lucy stood in the doorway behind him, 'but you have to put your history aside, Marc. There's people out there who wanna end us, and they're using you against yourself.'

'You were right,' he told her. 'Back in London, I should have walked away.'

'Don't beat yourself up over that.' She moved closer to him. 'We're all of us who we are, for better or worse. There's no world where you turned your back on this. It's wired into you.'

'That doesn't make me feel any better.'

'I would have done the same thing if it was my brother or my mom.' She shook her head. 'The Combine – their whole deal is finding pressure points and exploiting them. You know that better than anyone.'

Marc gave a nod, recalling how his sister Kate and her family had once been used to coerce him. He'd made sure that could never happen again, but his enemies were smart enough to find a different angle of attack.

'We've been fucking up their plans for long enough,' he said. 'Makes sense, they'd get sick of it after a while.'

'We made ourselves too big a pain in the ass to ignore.' She showed her teeth. 'Should we be flattered?'

He sat heavily on a long sofa, his dark-adapted eyes picking out Lucy's shadow in the half-light.

'You know, I tell myself I knew Sam Green but I must be a fool. She was always wild, always following her own path through life, and sod everything else.' Marc sighed. 'But as hard as I try, I can't square up the woman I knew with the person I saw in Nicosia. How could she work with the Combine after what happened to Nomad? For all her faults, Sam was never ruthless. She wasn't callous. She couldn't do what Grace has done.' He let that thought drift away.

'People change,' said Lucy. 'The Samantha Green you cared about, that ain't her. That woman is gone.'

'What else am I wrong about?' he said, the bleakness of the realisation reaching up inside his chest. 'I've been running after the illusion of something I never really had to begin with.'

Did Sam feel the same way I did about her? Was I seeing a connection between us that wasn't there?

Lucy sat down next to him.

'Let go of the ghost,' she said, after a long moment. 'And we'll deal with what comes next, like we always do.'

Her hand was on his, and that made it a little better. But as he turned to look at Lucy, a sharp trill sounded from the smartphone in his pocket.

'What now . . . ?'

Marc pulled out the phone and glared at it. A string of hash-symbols and non-numeric characters showed where a caller ID should have been, immediately making him tense. He tapped the answer key and waited.

'*Dane.*' Tracey Lane's voice was rough with fatigue, rendered metallic by encryption systems at the other end of the call. '*Don't talk, just listen. I don't know what Farrier sees in you, but I respect him so that counts for something.*'

'Is he all right?'

'*I said don't talk,*' she shot back, then paused, her tone softening slightly. '*He's still in a coma. Docs say he'll come out of it, but in his own time. You know John, always does it his way.*' When Lane went on, she was back to being blunt and quick. '*This shit we're in . . . Six is scrambling to put the blame somewhere else. Welles is throwing Rubicon under the bus, and sticking it to John because he can't defend himself. He's going to Whitehall today to give a statement, and your mates won't come off well, believe me.*'

Marc's jaw set in a grim line. 'Thanks for the warning.'

'*Now we're even,*' she told him. '*And we're done. I have to protect mine, you understand?*'

'I do—'

Lane never heard Marc's reply, as the line abruptly went dead.

TWELVE

'The board is ready, sir,' said Delancort.

He stood on the threshold of the apartments, and in the corridor Solomon's bodyguards were waiting.

Solomon stood, taking a moment to smooth the line of his jacket and adjust the cuffs.

'No blindfold for the condemned man?'

Delancort showed a pinched, false smile at the gallows humour, but said nothing.

'I will make do.'

Solomon marched past his assistant, and paused in front of the guards. The two men were well-built figures in suits of similar cut to Solomon's, and for years he had employed them as his personal close protection detail. But today, he was going to meet a threat that neither of them were equipped to deal with.

'Gentlemen,' he said, 'you are relieved. Take the rest of the day off.'

'Sir?' One of the men shot his employer a wary look. The dark-skinned Brazilian was an ex-commando, and fiercely loyal. 'Are you sure you want to do that?'

Solomon patted him on the shoulder, then glanced at the other guard, an American who had joined Rubicon from a career in the Military Police.

'This is not Ancient Rome. My Praetorians do not need to stand with me if I fall.'

He walked on, leaving the men behind, with Delancort rushing to keep up with his long-legged strides.

The central meeting room on the seventeenth floor of the Rubicon tower was a masterpiece of understated design, a minimalist assembly of chrome and white leather seating around a long table of bleached blond wood. Low morning sunshine, the glare lessened by the smart-glass of the broad windows, filled the space. To Solomon's eyes, the combined effect seemed sterile and bloodless. Ironic, considering that by the end of this meeting, he expected there to be plenty of metaphorical blood on the pale carpet.

He scanned the room, seeing familiar faces, each wearing a mask of professional detachment, each of them offering perfunctory handshakes or nods performed for the sake of decorum.

So this is how it will be, he thought. *All cards played close in this game. I expected no less.*

He sat at the head of the table, and Delancort took a seat to his right. Just beyond Solomon's reach, the woman who carried the axe this day was studying a sheaf of closely printed pages in a file; Esther McFarlane had called the meeting, pulling in every member of Rubicon's governing body to discuss the corporation's future. That all of them had come in person attested to the seriousness of the matter at hand.

McFarlane didn't look up at him, distractedly pushing a thread of henna-red hair back over her ear as she marshalled her thoughts.

Whetting her blade, Solomon told himself.

To the left, Gerhard Keller rested his fingers in a steeple. The German financier remained grave and silent. Under any other circumstances, the broad, barrel-chested man would have been thrilled to be in Monaco, indulging his prestigious numeracy skills at any one of a number of gambling salons. Instead his gaze was turned inwards, and Solomon imagined Keller's mind ticking over like a mechanical counter, as he dwelled on the losses incurred by Rubicon's wounded share value. Keller was a good man, but sometimes he had to be reminded to see past balance sheet numbers to the realities of the world around him.

Keller sat across from Victor Cruz, the other man's deep tan turning his face uncharacteristically sullen. The Chilean energy innovator's typically thoughtful demeanour was absent, his mood as far off beam as Keller's was from his usual median.

There was something accusatory in the way that Victor studied Solomon, as if holding in a question he could barely contain. *How could you let this happen?*

Solomon had been asking himself the same thing since the incident in Cyprus became public knowledge.

'Here we are again,' said McFarlane, still staring down at her papers as her assistant hovered nearby. Like Solomon, she had brought her aide into the meeting room. 'It only seems like yesterday when we were enjoying a nice cocktail on your boat out there, Ekko . . .' She gestured vaguely in the direction of the windows and the bay of Monaco. 'And you were making assurances that Rubicon's operations would not be jeopardised by the exploits of your pet project.' She finally looked up at him. 'The Special Conditions Division. I've never really liked the idea of Rubicon having a hand in private military contracting. The whole *mercenary* thing feels boorish and needlessly macho. But the fact that you have a subdivision of that dedicated to your own agenda is just . . .' She trailed off, shaking her head.

Solomon opened his mouth to speak, but Keller headed him off.

'Before you move to defend yourself, know that we understand what the SCD was intended for. You've said many times that it is the moral responsibility of the wealthy to look after the poor. Those of us with agency and strength are obligated to protect the weak and the oppressed. And sometimes those actions might require drastic measures. We do not dispute that.'

'I do,' snapped McFarlane. 'I'm sick of hearing myself say this! We're a Fortune 500 conglomerate, not an international peacekeeping agency. Rubicon is not a playbox of toy soldiers made to indulge vigilante fantasies! It's one thing to protect our own interests and that of our employees, it's quite another to go looking for trouble.' She closed the folder and held it in place with the flat of her hand. 'You know, we could sit here and I could list the intelligence agencies around the world that have been pissed off by the exploits of the SCD. The criminal and terrorist groups that we have made enemies of. The governments who now consider us rivals instead of business partners.' She pointed at Keller. 'Gerhard could put a dollar figure on it, no doubt, explaining what we've lost in earnings. In the name of Ekko Solomon's crusade for justice, and whatever sense of redemption he is grasping for, he's sent armed agents into sovereign countries, had cybercriminals spy for him . . .'

'And then there is the database of secret intelligence files maintained by the SCD.' Keller looked at a digital notepad in front of him, searching for the name. 'This so-called Grey

Record. The existence of that alone is a violation of dozens of international laws.'

'You've put us at risk,' McFarlane told Solomon. 'Over and over again. We warned you to hold back. You didn't.'

'And now, this is where we are.' Cruz broke his silence, shaking his head. 'This attack in Cyprus . . . This blood on our hands!'

'It is a fabrication,' Solomon insisted, glancing at Delancort.

His aide spoke up. 'Our technicians are working to prove that—'

'It happened!' Cruz's voice rose, silencing Delancort. 'Men are dead, damn it! Real people with real families, soldiers who were killed for nothing! A military base in a nation that we trade with was bombed, and the whole world sees the faces of your private soldiers in collusion with rogue spies! The British have already disavowed this, and now every eye turns to us for an explanation. Do you have one?'

'This is an attack on Rubicon.' Solomon stiffened, working to maintain an even tone. 'Our enemies are moving against us, and their aim is nothing less than our destruction.'

'It's an attack on *you*,' countered McFarlane. 'Enemies *you* brought to our door. And now we're paying the price.' She shook her head again. 'I warned you months ago that one day you would cross a line that could not be walked back. *This* is that day.'

'Our division plays into their hands,' insisted Solomon. 'It is what they want.'

'Who are *they*?' said Keller. 'The Combine?'

Solomon half-expected McFarlane to dismiss the notion of that group out of hand, as some fevered conspiracy theory. But she did the opposite.

'We should have stayed out of their way. Left it to others to deal with the Combine. Now we're in their sights.'

'You've spoken of our ethical imperative to do right.' Cruz made a visible effort to calm himself. 'But at what cost? You have gone too far this time, Ekko. The truth is, it doesn't matter if that drone footage is real or not. Rubicon is seen as culpable, and no one is standing with us. Everyone who wants us to fail is pouring fuel on the fire. Our reputation is collapsing. We are bleeding money on the stock market. Something must be done.'

'I advise that all elements of the Rubicon Group's private military contracts be terminated as of today,' said McFarlane. 'We get out of the PMC business. Close protection, kidnap and ransom, escort services, the lot of it.' She made a cutting gesture. 'Wound up and done. And that includes every last piece of your Special Conditions Division. Not a suspension, not a temporary halt, not like last time. Your private little war is over.'

'I will not allow that.' Solomon placed his hands on the table. 'You do not have the power to enforce such demands.'

'Not alone,' said Keller. 'But together, we do.'

'I'm calling for a vote of no confidence in Solomon's leadership of this organisation,' said McFarlane.

'Seconded.' Cruz gave a nod. 'I am sorry, but this is the only way forward.'

'Are you in here?'

Assim burst through the door and into the conference room, almost falling over his own feet in haste.

He cast around and found Marc and Lucy lying together on the wide couch, with Dane's jacket draped over them like a blanket. His expression fell into one of open shock.

'Oh. *Ah*. I didn't expect to find ...' He coloured a little. 'Awkward.'

Shaking off sleep, the two of them disentangled from one another, stifling yawns and stretching. Marc grunted at the stiffness in his back.

'Ugh. Not as comfortable as it looks ...' He found Assim staring at them and gave him a quizzical look. 'What?'

'I didn't know you two were in here,' replied the hacker, his tone becoming conspiratorial. 'Together.'

'Why'd you say it like that?' Lucy eyed him. 'It's not like you caught us—'

'Of course not.'

Assim flashed a weak smile, and briefly thought about the money he had in the office pool on exactly when Marc Dane and Lucy Keyes were going to *get caught*, as it were.

'I told you to get some sleep,' said Lucy.

'I thought about it,' Assim admitted, 'but then I ate a whole packet of caffeine tablets and suddenly it seemed less important.'

'Keep that up, you're gonna have a heart attack. You'll be dead before you're thirty,' Marc admonished, getting to his feet. 'Why did you come looking for us?'

'We have a big problem,' he told them.

'That's not news.' Marc exchanged looks with Lucy. 'Be more specific.'

He beckoned them to follow him back into the crisis centre. Now lit by daylight, the empty space seemed even stranger than it had in the dark, vacant and echoing.

'I've been monitoring a lot of feeds.' Assim's words were coming machine-gun quick. 'Back channel, black core, dark web, shadow mirrors, Prism and Tempora hacks, you know ...'

'His blood's gotta be 50 per cent stimulants by now,' Lucy noted.

'No doubt,' agreed Marc.

Assim didn't register their comments.

'One of the things I did, I know I shouldn't have because it's technically a sacking offence, but I thought that these were special circumstances and it would be okay, well, not okay, but at least forgivable—'

Marc clapped both hands on Assim's shoulders.

'Mate. Take a breath. Calm down and explain.'

Assim made a visible attempt to steady himself.

'I hacked us.'

Lucy raised an eyebrow. 'Rubicon?'

'Got into the building's security feeds. Including the ones that no one is supposed to know about. And I also secretly implanted a ghost app on Delancort's phone and turned it into a listening device, just in case. Because I was worried something bad would happen and it did.' He blinked. 'It did – I mean it is – happening. Right now.'

Marc went cold. 'Let's see.'

Five floors beneath the crisis centre, the atmosphere in the conference room was strung tight.

The pinhole camera hidden in the driftwood sculpture at the far end of the room had a fisheye lens that gave it a distorted view of the entire space, and so it was able to capture warped versions of every expression and every gesture as the board members cast their votes. An audio pickup built into the middle of the table recorded the silences between their words, the sharp intakes of breath.

Solomon sank back into his chair. On an intellectual level, he had always known a moment like this might come, but he had never truly believed it. Rubicon's corporate charter was his creation, the power of the board's vote something he had insisted on being part of those rules. The possibility that the people Solomon had hand-picked to support him would turn their backs on him seemed like a faraway, implausible event.

Not so now.

'Ekko, please,' said Keller. 'Don't make this any harder than it has to be.'

As he spoke, McFarlane's assistant took a call and answered with a few terse words, before leaning in to whisper something to her.

'Officers from the Monaco police force are in the lobby, and Interpol agents are on the way,' she said. McFarlane kept her hand on the folder as she spoke. 'Security and Legal have been ordered to co-operate fully with them. They're waiting for the investigators to arrive with warrants, and then they'll be cleared for full access. The police have asked us to make sure you remain in the building until then.' She paused. 'So we have a small window of opportunity here.'

'For what?'

Solomon kept his voice level, but behind his calm exterior, old and long-buried instincts were awakening.

'For you to be open with us, before we take a formal vote.' McFarlane glanced around the room.

'We know about the jet's arrival at Nice,' said Cruz.

McFarlane's gaze turned back to Solomon.

'Dane, Keyes and Kader, where are they now? I know you think you're protecting them, but you're making a mistake. Their names are on those Interpol warrants alongside yours.'

Solomon's jaw set and he said nothing, betrayed nothing. He wondered how McFarlane would react if she knew that Dane and the others were a few floors above them, hiding in plain sight.

At his side, Solomon felt Delancort tense. His aide was the only other person in the building who knew the location of the three SCD operatives.

When she saw Solomon's stony expression, McFarlane's ire rose, her cheeks colouring.

'You think any of us want to be doing this? You gave us no choice, man! You got us into this mess!'

'It is a lie,' Solomon repeated. 'You have trusted me in the past. Trust me now.'

Cruz watched in rigid silence and Keller put his head in his hands, emotionally drained by the experience, but McFarlane had only just begun her tirade.

'I can't,' she told him, angrily flipping open the folder, and fanning out the papers within it. 'Because you've been lying to us for a long time, and it's only now that it's becoming clear.'

'What is this?' said Delancort, reaching out to pull one of the pages closer. It was a geological map, annotated with details of what could only be the locations of mass graves. '*Mon Dieu* . . .'

'You have that uplifting story about the boy from poverty who became a man in wartime,' said McFarlane. 'And the man who built a fortune out of nothing. But there's blood and bodies beneath it, Ekko. You hid it from us.'

Keller took some of the papers and turned ashen as he read them.

'This . . . This is Corte Vermelho. Rubicon's original coltan mining holdings in Mozambique.'

'No.' Solomon had worn a mask of stillness and calm for so long that when it cracked, the moment shocked everyone in the room. 'No! You don't understand.' He struggled to control his reaction. 'That was a long time ago, it was different then!'

'How many people died?' said McFarlane. Her tone was matter of fact, but the question cut as deep as a knife wound.

Solomon had buried the guilt so deeply that perhaps he had convinced himself that it no longer existed. Now it rose up and grasped his heart, claws of ice seizing him, as potent as the day it had happened.

For a moment there was blood and powder and dirt in his nostrils, the sense-memory unfolding in full effect.

'The mines where you made your first millions,' said McFarlane. 'And the men who were killed there were your responsibility.' She leaned in, glaring at him. 'Are you going to look me in the eye and say this is a lie too?' She tapped the pages with a long finger. 'It's mass murder, Solomon. Just like at Nicosia.'

'That is not . . . a lie.' He said the words, unable to stop himself. 'You are right. I was responsible.'

Keller's shock rendered him speechless, but Cruz was on his feet, at the door, calling in two uniformed security guards.

'Escort Mr Solomon to his apartments,' he told them, biting out the words. 'He is to remain there while the board discuss this new information!'

Solomon barely heard the words, unable to look up from the damning images across the table. He finally tore his gaze away to meet McFarlane's, recovering some of his wits.

'Who gave this to you?'

'Does it really matter?'

All accusation was gone from her voice, leaving only the bleak reality behind.

The guards flanked him, and Solomon submitted. For now, he had been outplayed.

'What the hell is Corte Vermelho?' said Lucy.

'No idea.' Marc watched the hacked camera feed from the conference room, seeing Delancort leap to his feet to follow Solomon out into the corridor. 'Shit, you know what this is? It's a corporate coup d'état, and we're right in the middle of it.'

'He didn't give us up.' Lucy sat heavily on one of the empty desks near Assim's bank of monitors. 'So nobody knows we're here.'

'So far,' said Assim, typing furiously into a clattering keyboard with one hand, pointing to a smaller screen with the other. The monitor he indicated was partitioned into video windows, each showing a feed from a Rubicon security camera. 'But the police will search the building.'

Marc saw images from the lobby of the Rubicon tower, the underground car park and the plaza outside. Uniformed policemen were visible in each location, some of them talking into walkie-talkie radios. All the exits were covered.

At least, the exits that were public knowledge.

'There's other ways out of here,' said Lucy, intuiting Marc's train of thought. 'The bike park, for one.'

She was referring to a moped bay in a nearby alley. Behind a hidden hatch, a narrow tunnel that appeared on no city maps connected it to a false air vent on a lower level of the Rubicon tower.

He eyed her. 'You want to do that? Cut and run?'

She shook her head. 'Nah. Had to put it out there, but that wasn't gonna fly.'

'Corte Vermelho,' called Assim, spilling out more rapid-fire words as he brought up new data on his screens. 'Location of a now-played out mining concern in Mozambique, East Africa, site of a sizeable coltan strike in the late 1990s, considered to be the first major success for what was then Rubicon Mines, the root of what would now be . . . uh . . . all this, the Rubicon Group—'

'Solomon's big score,' said Lucy. 'But McFarlane talked about bodies.'

'Mozambique was in the throes of civil war back then,' said Marc. 'And Solomon's never made a secret of the past he had there.'

It was difficult to imagine the suave, urbane businessman Marc knew as the younger man he had once been, once a child soldier in bloody brushfire conflicts, who had grown to become a leader in his own right.

'What McFarlane said . . . ? I can't believe he's capable of that.' A shadow passed over Lucy's face, a moment of stark doubt that Marc felt too, as a knife in his gut. 'Not him.'

Marc wanted to deny it too, but something stopped him. As much as Ekko Solomon was selfless in his cause, there was a side of him that remained forever hidden.

Something John Farrier had once told Marc came rushing back into his thoughts. *For all that man's good deeds and high ideals, he's not the noble crusader he paints himself. Solomon is a very dangerous bloke. He's got a lot of secrets trailing after him.*

Were they seeing that now?

'This is the next hit,' said Lucy, staring into the middle distance. 'First, they draw us into that mess in Cyprus with a rope-a-dope. Now the uppercut, going for Solomon.' Her hands contracted into fists, unconsciously mirroring the blows she was describing. 'Next comes the knockout. We have to get off the ropes.'

'New arrivals out front,' said Assim, nodding at the monitor. 'Oh, they seem serious.'

Marc leaned in to get a good look. A police van halted on the Avenue de Grande Bretagne, spilling out a squad of cops in tactical gear. With it came a silver Mercedes G-Wagen, and the figures that disembarked had a whole other aspect to them.

'Is that the Interpol contingent?' Assim wondered.

'Not in this life.'

Marc recognised the swagger before anything else, the tell-tale *fuck-you* attitude that certain PMCs drilled into their operatives. But the man leading the four hired guns, the one the police deferred to, was something else entirely.

An older East Asian gent, well dressed and weathered, his age hard to peg through the video feed. He walked with a stick and a steady, purposeful gait, halting for a moment on the threshold of the Rubicon tower to look up and take in the whole thing.

The man smiled unpleasantly, like someone would if they were twisting the knife for the hell of it, and then carried on inside.

'Can we run facial recognition on that guy?' Lucy was already prodding Assim in the shoulder. 'Looks like he's the one calling the shots.'

'Can't risk it, I have to be bloody careful,' said the hacker. 'I don't want to raise a red flag on the system with too much activity. Someone will come looking.'

'Marc.'

Lucy called his name but he didn't turn away. His attention was on one of the security contractors, the only woman in the group. She was careful, making sure she didn't get caught square in the camera's field of vision, but he found himself watching her until she disappeared out of frame.

'Marc,' Lucy repeated, coming over to his side. 'You see their outfits? The patch on the shoulder?' She answered her own question. 'Only Ivans would be wearing combat jackets in seventy-degree heat.'

'Our old pals the Vultures,' agreed Marc. 'The Combine's rent-a-thugs.'

The SCD team had run afoul of the Russian mercenary force before. Marc recalled a particularly unpleasant high-speed chase through the Polish countryside where he had experienced ALEPH's tactical doctrine first-hand, which involved applying large quantities of bullets to any problem they encountered.

'So if they're not Interpol—' Assim began.

'It's exactly what we thought,' Marc broke in. 'The Combine set this up from the start.'

When the door opened, Solomon looked across the room with a frown, expecting to see Delancort on the threshold once again.

But it was too soon, he reasoned, surely? Could the board vote against him and seal his fate so quickly? It had to be unanimous, and as much as Gerhard Keller and Victor Cruz had been perturbed by recent events, he could not believe that they would commit to this without some kind of debate. Esther McFarlane's position was as clear as glass, but he hoped the other two men would at least deliberate before ousting him.

But it was not Henri Delancort who walked into his private apartments.

It was a ghost.

'Hello, old friend,' said Lau Fa Weng. He moved stiffly but with certainty, measuring out each step with a steel walking stick. 'Look at you! Lord of all you survey.' He stopped and gestured around with the cane. 'Not for much longer.'

'*Lau.*' Solomon had not spoken the other man's name in years, and as the word slipped past his lips, he felt giddy, he heard blood roaring in his ears. 'You are here . . .'

'I am not dead. That must astonish you.'

'I . . .'

A hurricane of questions burst open in Solomon's thoughts, and it took a near-physical effort for him to hold them back. His shocked mind raced as he struggled to process what was in front of him.

He remembered the last time he had seen Lau. Bloody and beaten, being dragged in chains into the belly of a droning cargo plane. The instant when their gazes locked – the two rebels, two friends after a fashion, one the betrayed and the other the betrayer. Decades ago, but the memory prickled Solomon's flesh, like acid against his skin.

Puzzle pieces snapped together. The attack on Solomon's organisation, on his people, on him – there had been a strange sense of the personal about it that he had been unable to explain. Now it made sense.

He said the only words that he could.

'I am sorry.'

A brief and terrible rage flashed in Lau's worn face, but then it was concealed.

'I do not care for your apology, Ekko. I do not accept it.'

Solomon took a step closer to the other man. There was no point seeking to excuse the inexcusable. To do so would have insulted both of them.

'My people have no part in our dispute,' he said gently, building each reply with care. 'You and I . . . We can settle this.'

'I am not the only one who wants your empire in ruins,' Lau said coldly. 'If it were just you and I, Ekko . . .' He shrugged. 'It might go differently. But that is not an option.' Lau reached into a pocket. 'I have obligations. What I owe to you is not the only debt I must repay.' He produced a small-frame revolver, and removed all but one bullet from the six chambers. 'But I will grant you this favour.'

Lau held out the nickel-bright gun in the palm of his hand, like an offering.

The inference was clear and unequivocal. For a moment, Solomon considered it. He would remove himself from the chessboard, becoming the king that surrendered itself. But it was foolish to believe that if he took his own life here and now, no more harm would come to what he had built. The fall of Rubicon was already in motion, he saw that now. He met Lau's gaze and he understood.

'You know me, old friend,' said Solomon, deliberately echoing the other man's words. 'I am not a coward. I always turn my face towards danger.'

Lau's brittle expression cracked. 'I will take from you what you cost me. And you will watch it happen.'

The revolver vanished back into his jacket and he walked away.

Just before he reached the door, Lau hesitated, and spoke without turning around.

'If you had known, Ekko, that I was still alive . . . would you have come to liberate me?'

They knew each other too well for anything other than the truth.

'No,' said Solomon.

'We can't call out for help,' said Lucy, stalking around the silent crisis centre, thinking aloud. 'Have to assume comms going in or out are gonna be dead or monitored by the threat force. We need to get *gone*.'

'We can't just leave,' Assim blurted out, shaking his head. 'That would be a bad idea!'

Marc tried to give him a sympathetic look.

'Solomon's resourceful. You know the kind of man he is, he'll have an exit strategy.'

'I am not talking about Solomon!' Assim's hands blurred over his keyboard. 'I am talking about the servers!' He threw Lucy an imploring look. 'The Grey Record!'

He brought up a schematic of the Rubicon tower's upper floors, directing their attention to it. Lucy saw the levels below them as the virtual model of the structure turned, glimpsing the air column that ran the height of the building and the green-power solar arrays up on the roof, near the helipad. In the middle of the animated architectural drawing was a blocked-off section, fittingly filled in with dull grey pixels.

'Do you know what is on those servers?' Assim continued, without taking a breath. 'File after file of surveillance data, not to mention reports on every member of the SCD, the missions . . .' He ran out of steam, shaking his head again.

'But it's encrypted, right?' said Lucy. 'Unreadable to anyone without the right keys.'

'The SCD is not just you people going out and doing all that *kinetic* stuff,' Assim went on. 'It's digital! We watch non-state actors and rogue nations, corporate malefactors and organised crime groups. It goes into the Grey Record and we sift it for weak points or actionable intelligence. Some of it gets passed anonymously to law enforcement and security services, but what can't be dealt with by them is . . . It's what you get given.'

Silence fell among them as they considered the same grave possibility. It was dubious enough for a group like the Special Conditions Division to have access to that kind of material. If Lucy was honest with herself, she had never been able to square the circle with regard to Rubicon's covert information gathering, but she had silenced her concerns with the assurance that what was learned would only ever be used for a just cause.

But if that kind of intelligence fell into the hands of a group with no moral compass, and no compunctions about using it . . . The thought made her feel sick inside.

'Solomon's biometrics give him access to the Grey Record,' said Marc, thinking it through. 'He's literally a living key.'

'How'd you know that?' Lucy eyed him questioningly.

'Because . . . After the first time I heard about it, I tried to hack the firewall. You know, just to take a look-see.' He paused, looking uncomfortable. 'I didn't get far. It's air-gapped, isolated from outside intrusion, layered with cutting-edge encryption software.'

'You could be sacked for that,' Assim retorted.

'Report me to Human Resources later, yeah?' replied Marc. 'The point is, Solomon could be . . . *compelled* to unlock the server.'

The Brit didn't need to elaborate any further. Lucy had seen enough enhanced interrogations in her time to know that everyone had their breaking point, even a man like Ekko Solomon.

'So wipe it.' Lucy made the decision without a moment's hesitation. 'You can do that, right?'

'Not with a single keystroke, no,' said Assim. 'It's not designed like that. The server is virtually hacker-proof, as Marc learned, and that means it can't easily be erased.'

'Well, how *is* it designed?' she demanded. 'And how do we go fuck it up?'

'You have any C-4 on you?' said Marc, only half-joking. She shook her head.

'I don't have a plan for . . . ah . . . that contingency,' admitted the hacker, and he tacked on a hasty addendum as Lucy took a warning step towards him. 'But I can come up with one! I need ten or twenty minutes and some more coffee, probably.'

'The cops are already sweeping the building,' Lucy noted, pointing at the monitor. 'So twenty minutes is a luxury we don't have.'

'Then I'll buy us some time,' said Marc, gathering up his jacket. 'I got an idea. It's a bit of a risk, though.'

Lucy scowled at his flippant tone. 'Oh, that's original.'

THIRTEEN

Sigalov crossed the building's atrium, giving the Monaco cops a hard glare as he passed. The mercenary had been recruited into ALEPH right out of the Bratva clans, stepping up from his criminal life as a *brodyaga* and into an elite hunter-killer squad. But he would not forget the bone-deep hatred of police learned on the streets of Saint Petersburg, no matter what country they came from or what badges they wore.

The local *musor* moved out of his way quickly, and Sigalov liked that just fine. The word meant *trash*, like other criminals in other countries called the police *pigs* or *filth*, and that was how he always thought of them – as something he would scrape off his shoes. Maybe if it turned violent, some of them might get caught in the crossfire, he mused. *What a pity that would be.*

Milost threw him a nod from where she stood, arms folded in front of her as she pretended to listen to the French cop, Dupuis. He was still salty about being put in second place, but at the same time he didn't want to take responsibility for what was going on. That gave Sigalov even more reason to dislike him.

One of the white-shirted cops reacted to something, his hand dropping to the pistol holstered at his waist, and Sigalov spun to intervene. A skinny, wolfish-looking man walked in from across the street with his hands raised in surrender. He had dirty blond hair and a searching gaze.

Sigalov knew who he was. The Chinaman had briefed them on a number of 'targets of interest', and this one was high on the list: the British spy, Dane.

The mercenary pulled his gun in a quick motion, the Stechkin pistol coming up to aim at a point right between the other man's eyes. Sigalov was aware of Milost coming around behind the man, outside his line of sight, her gun already out. Dupuis started complaining about the weapons, but the ALEPH operatives ignored him.

'Stop,' Sigalov snarled, in thickly accented English. 'Get on your knees.'

'All right, tough guy. Settle down.' Dane made no move to obey. 'I came to you, didn't I? But I'm not talking to the monkey, I want the organ grinder.'

Sigalov didn't know the idiom, and the confusion showed on his face.

But Milost understood.

'He wants to talk to Lau,' she said in Russian.

Dane jerked in surprise at the sound of her voice, twisting around to see her aiming her pistol at his chest. His eyes widened and Sigalov saw his own confusion mirrored in the Britisher's expression. The arrogance Dane had arrived with vanished in an instant, and he was staring at Milost like he knew her, like something was very, very wrong.

'Hey, you,' said Milost, her accent mimicking Dane's. 'We gotta stop meeting like this.'

'Sam . . .' he said, half-whispering, one hand reaching up to her pale and unblemished cheek, faltering halfway. 'Your face . . . What happened to all the scars? You were burned . . .'

'Those were never real, love.' Her lip twisted, and she gave him a mocking, patronising look. 'I'm not who you think I am.' She pushed her gun into his sternum. 'Don't blame me for wanting to look pretty.'

Milost threw Sigalov a nod, and he grabbed the Britisher by the shoulder, hauling him away in an iron grip.

Ari Silber looked up from the A350's pre-flight checks as a silver G-Wagen entered the open hangar, halting near the fuel bowser. He leaned forward, catching sight of two women and a man in black combat jackets as they jumped out and advanced on the aircraft.

Malte Riis was down there with the ground crew, and the Finn immediately moved to intercept the new arrivals. Malte looked up at the Airbus's cockpit and mouthed a single word. *Trouble.*

'*Chara.*'

Ari sounded out the curse and cast around, wondering what his next move should be.

After arriving at Nice, he'd leaned on Rubicon's good relationship with the airport management to get the little HondaJet straight into cover and out of sight, all the better to stay hidden in the wake of the team's less-than-legal departure from Cyprus. But once the smaller executive jet had been safely parked in the corner of the cavernous Rubicon hangar, he set straight to work on readying Ekko Solomon's other private aircraft for immediate departure. No order had been given, but he knew from experience how quickly circumstances could escalate around the Special Conditions Division.

The bigger Airbus A350–900 was a twin-engine airliner with a fifteen thousand kilometre range and a cruising speed of five hundred knots, and her flight deck was Ari Silber's usual office. Converted for Solomon's personal use as both an office in the sky and a mobile crisis centre for SCD operations, the A350 was self-sufficient and packed with military grade systems that could help it avoid detection and deflect attack. But none of that was any use while the bird was still on the ground.

With Marc, Lucy and Assim in Monaco, Ari didn't need to wonder what was likely to come next. They were in the middle of something dangerous here, and they had to be ready to move at a moment's notice.

The arrival of these black-jacketed thugs told the pilot his instincts were right on the money.

He slipped out through the galley, and stayed in cover by the forward doorway, straining to hear the conversation down on the hangar floor.

'Who is in charge here?' said the man. He had oily black hair and wraparound sunglasses that seemed a size too small for his head.

Malte jerked a thumb in the direction of the Airbus.

'We are working with Interpol,' said one of the women.

She was muscular, unsmiling and narrow-eyed. The other woman, a taller brunette with her hair up in tight braids, matched the taciturn Finn for his silence.

As if to underline the woman's words, the man in the sunglasses produced an identity card. Malte glanced at it, and even at a distance, Ari could see he wasn't impressed.

'You will suspend aircraft operations immediately,' continued Sunglasses.

His accent was Ukrainian, Ari guessed, and Muscles sounded like a Muscovite.

So, Russian mercenaries, the pilot said to himself. *That's not ideal.*

'We are here to secure this hangar and everything in it. You understand?'

Sunglasses was beginning to get annoyed with Malte's silent treatment.

A prickle of fear tightened over Ari's chest and he drew back into the cabin, running the same kind of rapid mental threat assessment he used to in his days of flying fighters.

If these mercs are here, then they're in Monaco as well. If no one stopped them coming in, that's a bad sign. This has to be a move against Rubicon, cutting off exit routes . . .

He wondered about Marc, Lucy and the others. The fact that they hadn't contacted him was worrying.

Ari returned to the cockpit for his Rubicon-issue smartphone, but when he attempted to call the SCD team the communication was immediately cancelled. *Not good.*

He could hear raised voices in the hangar. He didn't have much time.

Ari's wife answered her phone on the third ring.

'*You're back?*' she said, her voice like honey.

He sat on the arm of the co-pilot's chair and schooled his own reply.

'Not exactly, *ahuva*. It's complicated.'

Her tone became severe. '*Ari Silber, you are going to tell me what is wrong right now.*'

He grinned ruefully. Bless her, but Vada was like a heat-seeker, able to lock right onto him whatever chaff he tried to use to obfuscate. Twenty years of marriage had made him transparent to his wife, and he loved her for that.

'Vada, do you remember what it was like when I was deployed? I told you there might come a time when you'd need to take the children and get away, no questions asked.'

He heard her take a shaky breath. '*We left that behind. There's no war here.*'

'No, we didn't. And I'm afraid there is.' He could hear boots coming up the boarding stairway. 'Do it now, my love. Please?'

She didn't question him; she knew he meant what he said.

'*All right.*' Vada fell silent, and for a moment he could hear his son Ezra and daughter Leah playing in the background. '*Ari, I'm afraid.*'

'No, wife. You're brave.' He had to fight to keep his voice steady. 'I love you. I'll be with you again as soon as I can.'

He cut the call as the brunette with the braids appeared in the galley space. Ari stood up, feigning surprise, palming his phone.

'Hey, you can't be up here!'

'You are the pilot?'

'He went home for the day,' Ari lied. 'I'm ground crew.'

He plucked at the orange high-visibility vest he was wearing, grateful that he had left his shirt with captain's boards hanging up in the crew closet.

She waved an ID badge at him.

'Shut down the aircraft.'

'I can't do that!' He made a deliberately big, expansive gesture of denial. 'We're in the middle of an engine systems diagnostic! Shut it down halfway and you'll have explosive jet fuel pissing out all over the hangar – you want that to happen?'

None of that was true, but Ari gambled that Braids here didn't know anything about aviation.

Fate came up in his favour.

'Just you on board?' She made a face but she didn't question the story. Off his nod, she stepped back. 'Okay, you stay in there and when you are done, shut it down. Understand?'

'Sure, sure.'

He watched her stalk away down the length of the cabin, then shot a look out of the cockpit window. Malte was still in view, silent and unresponsive as Sunglasses stood in front of him making annoyed jabbing motions with one hand.

Trouble indeed, thought Ari.

Marc's plan had been simple. Emerging from the hidden escape tunnel across the street from the Rubicon tower, he walked back in, right through the front door and gave himself up. He was gambling that he could play off ALEPH against the Monaco police and chew up their time while Lucy and Assim set an exit plan into operation.

That fell apart when he saw *her* face again. Sam, or Grace, or Milost, which was what the mercenaries were calling her.

He'd told himself he would be ready the next time they crossed paths, but that turned out to be wishful thinking. She stopped him dead, like she had before.

There she was, standing opposite him as the express elevator rose to the tower's upper floors. The scars from the horrific burns she had suffered during the catastrophic Dunkirk operation were gone.

Had they ever really been there? Because if this woman wasn't Samantha Green, then . . .

'Who the hell *are* you?' He couldn't break away from staring at her.

'Take a photo,' she replied, in an authentic North London drawl. 'It'll last longer.'

Then she switched to Russian and said something to the broad, bald-headed bruiser who had threatened him down in the lobby. The other man sniggered, eyeing Marc with a predatory sneer.

They stopped on the lower conference level, and he was pushed out into a busy scene. Marc saw police officers from the Monaco SIU and a dozen regular cops, some of them interrogating Rubicon's security staff, others poring over floor plans of the tower as they plotted out their search of the premises.

Nobody intervened as Marc was marched to an isolated room. His escorts waited outside, and Marc found himself alone with the suited man he had seen earlier on the monitors.

'Take a seat, if you wish.'

The man was making himself tea, keeping a narrow table and chairs between them.

Marc automatically sized him up as a potential aggressor. He was old and wiry in that way that a lot of Chinese men could be, but there was something deceptive in his build and movement. Marc glanced at the metal cane by his side. As a weapon, it could be lethal in the right hands.

Marc had been careful to leave his kit behind with Lucy, so he scanned the room, looking for anything that might come in useful. Some heavy objects, the little tea urn . . . If push came to shove, he could improvise, but with two armed guards outside the door there were not a lot of opportunities.

Marc deliberately did *not* look in the direction of the abstract sculpture at the far end of the room, where he knew a security camera was hidden. He would have to trust that Assim could find him in this one out of hundreds of individual rooms inside the Rubicon tower.

Instead, his gaze kept slipping back towards the frosted glass door, and the silhouette of the woman standing guard in front of it.

Who the hell are you? The question echoed around and around in his head.

The older man sat, and told Marc his name was Lau. He flashed an Interpol badge, but he did so with such disdain that Marc had the immediate sense it was a fig leaf of a cover.

'Your name is Marc Dane,' said Lau. 'Royal Navy helicopter crew, turned MI6 field technician, turned private intelligence operative. Do you find your work with the Rubicon Group rewarding, Mr Dane?'

'You meet a lot of interesting people.' Marc kept his tone steady. 'You see a lot of the world.'

'You tell a lot of lies,' added Lau. 'That is the stock-in-trade of a spy, isn't it?'

'You tell me. Been with Interpol for long, have you?'

Lau chuckled, not even bothering to deflect the veiled accusation.

'Truth is such a malleable thing, I have found. I have spent years in cages, because some men wanted one truth to be false and another to be correct.'

Marc's gaze drifted to the door again, and he pulled it away.

'Sad story,' he offered. 'What's it got to do with me?'

'Secrets are cages too, Mr Dane. You've been inside one for quite a while now, without being aware of it. Ekko Solomon has been lying to you about who he is since the day you met him.'

Marc tried to hide the flash of doubt that coursed through him, but Lau was watching for it. He had known it would be there.

'Solomon is not a good man. He is a killer, with a great deal of blood on his hands. There are graves upon graves in the African dirt that he is responsible for filling.'

'Oh yeah?' Marc shook his head. 'Let me guess – you have proof? Good for you. These days I don't trust anything I haven't seen for myself, and even then I'm still doubtful.'

'Only weak men need to armour themselves with lies.' Lau's reply was icy. 'Solomon knows his own guilt, and I think you suspect it. All this?' Lau gestured around at the walls with his teacup. 'You know why it exists? It is nothing more than Solomon's elaborate attempt to shield himself from his past, and a pitiful effort at atoning for it.' He took a sip. 'A great hubris for one to have such ego that it draws others into the orbit of his penitence. Solomon risks you and those like you in his attempts to balance the scales of his guilt. It is a rich man's vanity.'

'I don't know you,' Marc replied, after a moment. 'But I reckon I know who you work for.'

'Rubicon would not exist without me,' Lau told him. 'I was there at the beginning.' He put down the cup, unable to hide a grimace. 'I have my own scales, Mr Dane. I am here because only I can carry the truth. Only I can open the cages.' He leaned back in his chair, studying Marc through hooded eyes. 'But enough of me and enough about Ekko. You are the question at hand, you and the choice you make next.'

Marc caught Lau's use of Solomon's first name, the odd cadence to it. It took him a second to put it together, and then he was sure. *They were friends once. You can't hate an enemy that much.*

'In the spirit of truth, I will be direct,' said Lau. 'Ask any question you wish, but first, let me say this. I personally bear you no malice, but you have become ... What is the phrase? *Collateral damage.* This is the reality for you. All you can do is think of how to mitigate harm to yourself and your comrades.'

'You'll answer any question I put to you? Truthfully?'

Marc's expression showed his obvious disbelief.

Lau met his gaze with a nod, guileless and open.

'There is no value in lying to you, not now. You have already lost.'

'Who is the woman?' He couldn't stop himself from blurting it out. 'Grace.'

'She is a fake.' Lau nodded again. 'But you know that, I think. You are perceptive, even if you let your emotions get in the way.'

Marc stared into her shadow through the glass barrier, seeing her all over again.

'How . . . ?'

'I do not know her true name. I believe she is American, a product of the Central Intelligence Agency before she escaped to pursue her own ends. A mimic, trained to fully inhabit a given identity. She has a quite specific psychopathy that allows her to do so almost flawlessly, but it has also left her devoid of what you and I would consider morality.' He smiled to himself. 'A *huli jing*, of sorts.'

'The nine-tailed fox,' Marc said quietly, struggling to process what Lau had revealed.

The name he used was of a mythological shape-changer from Chinese legend, a dangerous animal spirit.

'You understand,' said Lau.

'Why this subterfuge?' Marc pushed off the window, animated by sudden anger, advancing on the older man. 'Baiting a trap for MI6? Oslo and Nicosia?'

'Two birds with one stone.' Lau became dismissive. 'I am told the British have become troublesome of late. Some last spasm of imperial ambition making itself known before they become irrelevant. The woman's deception brought them in, and through them, you.' He pushed his empty teacup away across the table. 'You were given the rope to hang yourselves. The woman to entice you, the threat of a terrorist plot in Cyprus to entice Ekko. He must be discredited utterly, you see. That is the only result that will suffice.'

Marc's hands tightened into fists. 'People died because you and the Combine want to settle scores, is that it?'

'It is that.' Lau didn't flinch at the mention of the Combine. 'Do you want to live, Mr Dane? Do you want Ms Keyes to live? Your sister and brother-in-law and nephew? They can be put within the Combine's reach, if required.'

'You can't touch my family . . .' Marc growled. 'They're protected.'

Lau continued as if he had not spoken. 'That is what the Combine does. They are meticulous. They close up every avenue of escape until the only path which remains is the one that benefits them. You are deluded if you think you can oppose them, you and Ekko alike.'

Marc's fury seethed, but it had nowhere to go. He thought about grabbing the teacup, smashing it into Lau's leathery, blank face. But what would that get him?

A radio crackled, and Lau removed a walkie-talkie from inside his jacket. He listened to a snatch of conversation.

'I am afraid this discussion is at an end. The Rubicon board of directors is about to make a momentous decision, and I wish to be there to see it.' He eyed Marc. 'Yes, I think you should be there too.'

'And then what?' Marc spat the question at him. 'You get to take the castle, yeah? Like some conquering warlord coming for the throne. But what happens next? You reckon Glovkonin is just going to *give* Rubicon to you? Believe me, the guy doesn't work that way!'

And for the first time since he entered the room, Marc saw that Lau did not have an answer.

The board cast the vote, and Delancort watched it happen like it was in slow motion, like a film of something delicate shattering into millions of pieces. It felt unreal.

McFarlane's position had never been in doubt, but despite his simmering anger and disappointment, it still took Cruz a while to nod his head towards her. Then Keller, the German taking the place of the deciding vote, was left to cast his ballot. He talked for a while about how sorry he was, but after a few sentences Delancort tuned him out.

It didn't matter what was said, or what justifications were being given. Ekko Solomon was being severed from his stewardship of Rubicon. The action moved on inexorably, as if it had always been destined to play out this way, leaving Delancort to reflect on where that left him.

'The ayes have it,' said Finlay.

Delancort's opposite number, McFarlane's thin Glaswegian assistant, announced the result with what might have been a sneer, if one looked at it closely enough.

'And we're done,' said McFarlane, leaning forward over the table. 'Gentlemen, I know this was difficult, but this is the only way we could proceed. We can no longer allow Ekko's personal crusade to jeopardise the Rubicon Group. We have thousands of people who rely on us – our staff and our specialists, their families, and everyone who benefits from what we create. One man cannot put that at risk.' She glanced towards Delancort, then away. 'We've turned a blind eye for long enough. We gave him a chance.'

'More than once,' muttered Cruz.

McFarlane nodded. 'No more plausible deniability. We take responsibility for this mess by excising it and moving forward. By the order of this board, Ekko Solomon is dismissed from his post as chief executive officer of the Rubicon Group, and the activities of the Special Conditions Division are to end immediately. Permanently.'

'Interpol will accept that?' said Keller.

'If we are fully transparent with them, we may be able to avoid the worst of the legal issues,' she added.

'There will be fines, penalties, at the least,' said Cruz. 'Rubicon will not escape censure.'

'Better that than prison time,' offered Finlay.

McFarlane gave him a sharp look and he smiled weakly, realising he had overstepped the mark.

But what the woman said next made Delancort's ears prick up.

'I've been in contact with Interpol's lead investigator. He assures me that if we are completely open with him, it will go a long way towards mitigating the damage that Ekko has wrought.'

'Damage?' Delancort said the word without thinking, as the conference room's door slid open.

'What else would you call it?' An older Chinese man picked out his comment as he entered, moving stiffly with a pair of bodyguards behind him. 'Solomon brought all this to the brink of destruction.'

Delancort's eyes widened as he saw Marc Dane hustled into the room by one of the bodyguards. The Englishman's hands were secured in front of him with a thick plastic zip-tie.

'What is he doing here?' said Cruz, indicating Dane. 'And who are these people?'

'I'd like to introduce Mr Lau, from Interpol.' McFarlane nodded in the older man's direction. 'In the interests of transparency, I have to inform the board that we have been in communication over the past week. He brought me some troubling information that led me to act to remove Solomon from his position.'

From the corner of his eye, Delancort saw Gerhard Keller's face drain of colour as he studied the new arrival. Dane seemed to pick up on it too, but for his part Lau never once looked in the portly German's direction.

'I am investigating cases involving war crimes and terrorist activities,' Lau began, pacing out his words. 'By now, you will have heard the name Corte Vermelho. The location of a mine owed by Rubicon in its early years. Interpol is tracing the participants in a mass killing that took place there in the 1990s. Ekko Solomon is a person of interest in that investigation.' He adjusted his position on the metal stick he used to walk, letting his statement sink in. 'There is also the developing situation in Cyprus and Rubicon's connection to it.' He glanced towards Dane. 'Your employee is going to help us with our inquiries into that. He wisely surrendered himself a short time ago.'

Dane looked up and met Delancort's gaze. They were the only two people in this room who knew there was more to that, who knew that Assim Kader and Lucy Keyes were also somewhere in the tower. Was Dane watching him to make sure he kept his silence? He broke eye contact, glancing back at Keller.

'Everyone believed you were dead,' the German said quietly, staring fixedly at Lau. 'It's what Ekko told us . . .'

'I know,' Lau said, inclining his head. He approached the conference table. 'As Ms McFarlane said a moment ago, in the interests of transparency I should make it clear who I am. My full name is Lau Fa Weng. I co-founded Rubicon with Ekko Solomon years ago, before I was removed from the equation.' He gave Cruz and McFarlane an indulgent, fatherly smile, ignoring the surprise on their faces. 'That was before your time. Before Herr Keller's too, if truth be told. I won't bore you with the details, but suffice to say, I am uniquely motivated to see the facts come to light in these matters. I am a victim of Solomon's single-mindedness, as you have been, just like those poor souls at Corte Vermelho and elsewhere.'

'You never told me any of that.' McFarlane's voice was low and rough.

'It was not necessary,' he replied.

'Surely your personal interests compromise your involvement in this investigation?' Delancort studied the older man, looking for the gaps in the truth he was presenting to them. 'Your objectivity?'

'On the contrary, Mr Delancort,' said Lau. 'It makes me the perfect man for the job.'

Finlay's attention had turned wholly towards Dane.

'What about the active members of the SCD? Keyes and the others?'

'That is a most important question.' Lau turned to study the Englishman. 'Will you answer truthfully, Mr Dane? If you do otherwise, I promise you will be inside a police cell within the hour. And that will be all you see for years to follow.'

Something in his tone hinted at a familiarity with such things.

'I dropped them off in Tahiti,' said Dane, with a regretful shrug. 'It's a magical place.'

'Marc . . .'

Delancort's dislike for the cocky ex-hacker came flowing up to the surface in that moment, his irritation flaring. He couldn't recall ever having referred to the man by his first name before. It did not matter.

How dare he make idiotic jokes when this situation is so grave?

It was typical of him to be cavalier, to risk everything on a gamble, as if he lived a charmed life where the numbers always came up in his favour. But none of that was true. Dane was reckless, and a magnet for trouble. From the start, Delancort had been at odds with him, and with Solomon's choice to make Dane part of Rubicon. He was only going to make it worse.

Which meant there was only one decision to make.

'Kader and Keyes are here, in the building.' Delancort said the words before doubt could set in. 'I believe they are hiding in the crisis centre while it remains inactive.'

'You self-serving prick!'

Dane recovered after an instant of shocked silence, spitting the insult across the room at him. He rocked forward, impotently furious, but the balding bodyguard grabbed his shoulder and reeled him back before he could do anything aggressive.

'Thank you for that,' said McFarlane. 'Better late than never.'

'Hedging your bets, Henri?' Finlay asked the question from the side of his mouth, earning him another stern look from his boss.

Lau exchanged looks with his operatives.

'Bring Gera and Adaksin up here. Two teams.' The dark-haired woman gave a nod and stepped away to speak into a hand-held radio, and Lau turned back to the board. 'The more accommodating you are, the easier this will go.' He focused on McFarlane. 'You are aware that Solomon has a private computer database used for the logistics of his clandestine operations.'

She gave a wary nod, and Delancort felt his gut tighten. *He means the Grey Record.*

'Interpol have a warrant to seize it,' Lau went on. 'I trust that will not present a problem?'

'We can make it available to you at a later—'

Lau cut her off with a sharp jerk of the head.

'No. I need to access it today.' Before she could answer he continued. 'You did promise full transparency, Ms McFarlane. I would hate to think you are going to renege on that.'

'Of course,' she said, at length. 'There are two security ciphers. Ekko has one . . .'

Delancort felt the blood drain from his face.

'I have the other.'

'I told you they would be here,' said the woman, as Lau left the room with his team. 'Dane's friends.'

'Oh. Yes, of course.'

He paused, sparing her a fraction of his attention. There were so many moving parts to this endeavour, and it was vital for Lau to remain alert to the changing circumstances.

He had few illusions that Pytor Glovkonin and his comrades in the Combine would consider him a spent force once the taking of Rubicon was complete, something the Englishman's angry words had brought back to him with chilling effect.

Lau would have to ensure he made himself invaluable to the Combine, if he wished to survive. If fate were to be just, then Solomon's position should be his, but prison had dulled Lau's appetite for such a life.

At this moment, all he wanted was to be the architect of his old friend's destruction. Lau would find something beyond that in the ashes, when the time came.

He leaned closer to her, so their conversation would not carry. The Russians called her *Milost* and Dane had called her *Grace*, but those were cover identities. He had little interest in digging beneath them beyond one salient point.

'You have some history with Dane.'

'Not that much,' she noted. 'Someone else's, really.'

'Would it stop you from killing him?'

She rolled her eyes. 'Give me some credit.'

'Take him with you to the crisis centre,' said Lau. 'Threaten his life to force the others to surrender. Their comradeship is a weakness you can exploit.'

'Yeah, I thought so too.' Her accent wandered away from its Russian baseline, briefly becoming fluid and malleable. 'And after?'

'Eliminate them. Make it look like an escape attempt.'

Marc stood with his back to the rear wall of the elevator as it began to rise, his gaze flicking to the bald-headed thug and then back to the woman. To Grace.

'I know who you are now,' he told her.

She gave a dismissive laugh. 'Oh, I doubt that.'

'You stole the face of someone I cared about, and for what?'

'For money, honey.' She grinned at him from beneath the black wig she wore, and it sickened Marc that he could still see a little of Sam Green in her expression. 'Yeah, sorry and all, but your former girlfriend?' Her accent shifted to mimic Sam's voice. 'Dead and gone, Marc.'

She sounded so much like her that it took him a moment to find his voice.

'You're a heartless snake, aren't you?'

'People always say that,' Grace replied. 'But they don't get it. You have to feel something, y'know? To get into who a person is. You have to sense a little of what they felt. So I do that, I pour all of them into the hollow in me.' She ran a finger down his arm. 'I know what Sam felt. I know who she was.'

An oiled, metallic snap-click pulled Marc's attention away for half a second, as the other ALEPH operative drew and reloaded his gun. He removed the standard-size magazine for his Stechkin APS and inserted a new one as long as Marc's forearm, filled with 9 mm ammunition. The Soviet-era pistol was capable of firing hundreds of rounds per minute, and loading it like that meant the user was expecting a war.

'Hey.' Grace snapped her fingers in front of Marc's face, drawing him back. 'Don't be sad. Think of this as a way to get some closure.'

'Stop talking like her,' he grated. 'Just fucking stop!'

'You wanna know what I figured out about Samantha Green by living in her skin for the past six months?' She pulled her own gun and followed the other man's example, loading a heavy-duty magazine. 'All she gave a shit about was her job. Everything else – her mates, you and whatever you thought you had together?' She prodded him in the chest. 'It was *sport*, Marc. It didn't mean anything.'

He looked away, up to the ceiling of the elevator car, finding the plastic half-globe of a security camera nestled in one corner.

'You don't know her,' he said.

'Funny,' she replied, as Sam's accent melted away and merged back into something Russian and husky, 'I was going to tell you the same thing.'

The lift slowed as the indicator ticked up to the floor one below the level of crisis centre. Marc guessed at their tactics: they would get off here and go up one flight via the emergency stairwell, hoping to blindside Lucy and Assim by coming in from behind them.

He had no way of knowing if they were still there, or if Assim was active inside the Rubicon tower's systems. *Are they watching through the camera?*

'Sigalov!'

The woman saw Marc glance up and pointed out the security eye to her colleague. The balding man nodded back and reached up to smash the little camera with the butt of his gun.

'Must be careful,' she added. 'Your friend Kader, I hear he's very talented.'

'He figured out who you were,' Marc retorted. 'I should have listened.'

'Love is blind,' she said airily. 'It makes you stupid.'

Marc felt the lift come to a stop.

'So does arrogance.'

He had been counting the floors since they left the conference level, and something didn't add up.

The elevator doors sounded a chime and slid open, to reveal not an office level, but the open atrium of the crisis centre. And standing right there, in half-cover behind an overturned desk, was Lucy Keyes with a short-frame shotgun.

Marc threw himself out of the firing line as Lucy pulled the trigger, pumped in a fresh shell, and fired again, in the space of the same half-second.

Sigalov was caught with his pistol aiming the wrong way, and he took both rounds in the middle of his mass. The impact from the solid-slug rounds blasted him back across the inside of the elevator car, and his hand went into a spasm. The ALEPH mercenary's death-grip on his weapon set it off, bullets shrieking wildly across the floor, out into the corridor, up the wall of the elevator, into the roof. The fully automatic Stechkin pulled Sigalov's arm up with the force of its muzzle climb, as the gun spewed brass ejecta into the air.

Shrinking away from the chaos, Marc slammed into Grace, bringing down his zip-tied hand in a sharp, jerking motion that snapped the plastic lock and freed him. Grace tried to traverse her own weapon towards him, but both of them were too afraid of being hit by Sigalov's uncontrolled gunfire to do more than avoid it.

Shots from the Stechkin punched through the lift controls and the doors hissed shut before it sank back down the shaft. The gun's slide snapped open, every round spent, and Marc had an instant to reflect on the miraculous fact he was still alive before Grace clobbered him with her pistol.

He staggered back, almost falling over the dying man on the floor. She threw herself at him, and more by luck than judgement, Marc met her midway. Grace was smaller than him, and she didn't have the training that Sam Green had possessed. If she had been Sam, this would have been a harder fight.

Marc threw a vague punch that did little but move things around, and Grace bounced off the elevator controls. The lift obediently halted with another melodic chime, and she took the opportunity to knee Marc squarely in the balls.

He swore loudly and hit her again, this time with feeling. Grace fell back, out through the open doors and into an office level. Rubicon staffers working nearby fled when they saw the weapon, and Marc slammed the flat of his palm into the *door close* pad as Grace fired a three-round burst in his direction.

The shots clattered off the closing doors and the lift began to rise again. In the sudden quiet that followed, Marc teetered on the brink of adrenaline crash, slumping against the wall.

The bald guy was dead, staring blankly into nothing, dark blood pooling around him amid drifts of broken plastic and spent shell casings. Marc wrenched the Stechkin from the mercenary's clawed fingers and searched him for ammo. As he got back to his feet, the lift returned to the crisis centre once again.

He exited warily, finding Lucy off to one side with the smoking shotgun still in her hand.

'How did you do that?'

'Assim spoofed the level counter in the elevator,' she explained. 'Made them think they were going where they wanted, when he was really bringing them to me.'

'You saw us on the camera, then?'

'So that was *her*?' Lucy peered past him, dispassionately surveying her handiwork inside the lift car. 'Where's she at now?'

'Still mobile,' he admitted. 'She's not who I thought.'

'Tell me later.' Lucy beckoned him to follow. 'Assim has the exit plan good to go.'

'No, I do not!' the hacker said hotly, as they crossed the room to where he was hiding, boxed in beneath a desk with his laptop open before him. 'I told you, I had to put that aside to keep tabs on Marc.'

'Appreciated,' said Marc, 'but, mate, we have to go right now. Grace is gonna ring the dinner bell any second and then everyone will be coming up here.'

'It's not ready,' Assim insisted.

'So we'll run it on the go,' Marc told him. 'Come on, what do we have to do?'

'Have you ever had an electric shock?' Assim gave them both a worried look.

'Yes.' Marc and Lucy replied in chorus. They had been on the wrong end of tasers and cattle prods more than once.

'Well,' he said, offering up the words in his clipped, careful English, 'if we screw up, this will make that look like baby kisses.'

FOURTEEN

'You made the intelligent choice, Henri.'

McFarlane's assistant stepped up to walk alongside Delancort.

'What is that supposed to mean?'

Delancort quickened his pace up the wide spiral staircase leading to the Rubicon tower's apartment levels.

Finlay showed an expression that he seemed to think was friendly.

'It's not easy to do what we do, is it? Be the confidant, the aide-de-camp? They expect our loyalty.'

'And who are you loyal to?'

Delancort cut him dead with his waspish retort.

A few steps behind them, Lau and one of his black-jacketed thugs were following, but the old man moved with effort and it slowed him down. Lau and his men couldn't hear the exchange going on ahead of them.

'I put my employer first.' Finlay's fake emotion dropped off his face. 'Don't you?'

'I suppose that depends who exactly is writing your cheques.' He shook his head. 'Why are you even here?'

'To keep an eye out.'

Finlay gave an arch sniff as they entered the next atrium, and gestured towards Solomon's executive rooms.

'He's in there,' he told Lau. 'Just where you left him.'

Delancort saw another black-jacket standing in front of the door to Solomon's apartment. The man had a canine look about him, and he was holding a gun out and ready in his right hand, his arms crossed before him.

'Where are the police?' said Delancort, but he already knew the answer.

They were elsewhere because Lau didn't want Monaco law enforcement to see what was happening.

'How does the server key operate?' Lau was a little out of breath, but his tone was severe. 'Explain it to me.'

'An electronic card.' Delancort knew there was no point in refusing or delaying his reply. 'It enters a code, it reads my thumbprint. Then there is a voice authentication.'

'You and Ekko must both do this?' He nodded, and Lau pursed his lips in thought. 'I will need to persuade him.'

The man guarding the door stepped aside as they approached, and Lau led the way in, his cane tapping across the floor.

Solomon rose from where he was seated in the middle of the open living room, adjusting the sleeves of his jacket.

'Ah.' He took in Delancort's face with a curious expression. 'It is done?'

'You're out of a job, Mr Solomon.' Finlay couldn't help himself, laying on a little smirk with the pronouncement. 'The board voted.'

'Of course they did.' Solomon kept his eyes on Delancort. 'Steps had to be taken.'

Lau halted by a wall, idly examining a Xhosa wood carving.

'I want your Grey Record, Ekko. Surrender it.'

'You know I will refuse.'

'And you know I can find ways to compel you.' Lau cast around, his gaze finding McFarlane's assistant. 'Are you going to make me prove it?'

For the first time, Delancort understood why Finlay was really there. Lau had to keep Delancort intact to use his key card, but the haughty Scot had no such protection. One of the black-jackets reached inside his coat and came back with a hand knife with a wide, spade-like blade.

Finlay blinked. He had yet to catch on.

'You believe you hold the advantage, but you do not,' said Solomon. 'That has always been your failing, my friend.'

A garbled sputter of radio static issued out from inside Lau's jacket, and he pulled out a walkie-talkie, still resting his other hand on his stick.

'Report?'

Delancort heard a woman's voice, a Russian accent speaking urgently. The two bodyguards tensed. Something was wrong.

And then he realised there were other people in the apartment with them.

'Step away from the door,' said Marc, sliding out from the shadows on the far side of the room.

He had a stolen Stechkin pistol aimed at the guard on the right, and even if the guy didn't understand English that well, he got the inference.

The other one, the one with the dagger, twisted in place to meet Lucy as she came around a high rack of bookshelves. She had her compact shotgun cocked and ready to fire.

'Drop it,' she ordered, and the ALEPH operative reluctantly let his weapon clatter to the floor.

'Ah.' Lau mimicked Solomon's earlier motion, adjusting his jacket and his balance on his walking stick. 'Well done, Ekko. You always did know how to lay a good trap for me.'

'This is not chess,' said Solomon. 'You have made this war.'

'*You* did that!' Lau's face suddenly twisted into a snarling mask. 'When you gave me up!'

'We need to get out of here, sir,' said Lucy, looking towards Solomon.

'Yes, rather!' said Finlay, becoming animated.

'Not you,' she added.

But Solomon did not move.

'I have not been honest with you.' He looked between Marc and Lucy, regret filling him. 'About a great many things.'

'He is a liar and a murderer,' said Lau, bringing his moment of fury back to heel. 'He betrayed me. He will betray you when the circumstances merit it.'

'*Sir,*' insisted Lucy, her attention shifting. 'We have to go, *right now.*'

Later, Marc would recall this moment and see that Lau was savvier than he realised. The old bloke had been military, and he must have seen some of that in the way Lucy carried herself. Lau decided that the former sniper was the greater threat in the room, so he waited for that instant when she took her eye off the ball.

Lau moved faster than a man of his age and in his condition had any business doing. He whipped up the metal stick in a flashing arc that knocked aside a table lamp, smashing the tip into a fire alarm trigger on the wall.

Hooting sirens and flashing strobes were set off, but Marc was barely conscious of that, as the guard he had drawn down on pivoted to attack him. The man was his size but he was all muscle and spitting violence. He ran into Marc with a shoulder-charge, shoving him back into the shadowed corner of the apartment.

Maybe the ALEPH guy was counting on Marc being caught off guard; maybe he had been told that Dane was just a tech and he didn't have it in him to use a weapon in anger. It was true that most ordinary people, even when push came to shove, couldn't kill someone up close. To do it, you had to have that hesitation about taking a human life burned out of you by training, or hard-earned experience.

Maybe the ALEPH merc thought that would happen, that he'd get the automatic pistol right off him. But when Marc looked back, what he would remember was no conscious thought, no actual pause between reaction and action.

With the Stechkin's muzzle pressed right against the mercenary's chest, Marc squeezed the trigger and the pistol released an angry, roaring burst. His would-be killer tumbled away, his torso turned into a mess of crimson.

He was aware of Lau knocking Finlay out of his way with another blow from his stick, the bony old man barrelling out of the door and back into the corridor. Across the room, Lucy struggled with her guy; the ALEPH operative put his hands on the shotgun and they were turning around it, wrestling the weapon back and forth between them.

It went off with a thunderous bellow, blowing through a glass coffee table, the sound and fury of it causing Delancort to throw up his hands to protect his face.

Lucy let the gun go – it was no good to her now, the chambered round spent – and the black-jacket was momentarily put off balance as he got what he wanted. The ALEPH merc was quick and he spun the gun into a club as Lucy ducked low, skidding over the floor, grabbing at the fallen dagger.

He hit her across the shoulders in the same second she buried the blade in his thigh, and the man fell with a scream.

Lucy wrenched the shotgun from his nerveless fingers and backed off.

'Pull that and you'll bleed out in five minutes.' She pointed at where she had left the dagger lodged deep in his muscle, dangerously close to his femoral artery. '*Ponimayu?*'

'*Da,*' he gasped, panting and clutching at the oozing wound.

Marc walked away from the body of his assailant, shaky and sick at his own actions. The sudden brutality of the fight left him feeling like he wanted to vomit. He swallowed the impulse, breathing through his mouth.

'Where's Lau?'

'He fled.'

Solomon helped Delancort to his feet, and waved towards the open door.

'We should go after him—'

'You killed that man!' Finlay shouted over Marc, red-faced and caught between indignation and horror, desperately trying to claw back some composure. 'Good God, it's all true! You people are a bunch of wild dogs!'

Lucy looked up from where she was securing the injured ALEPH operative.

'He's not coming with us, is he? I don't like whiners.'

'No.' Marc tore a length of electrical cable from the bottom of the smashed lamp and coiled it up. 'Wrists,' he told Finlay.

'What?'

'Show me your wrists!'

Marc realised he was still gripping the Stechkin in his hand, and he put it aside. His skin prickled where the gun's hot exhaust gas and the back-spatter of blood had hit him.

Finlay obeyed and Marc used the cable as a quick and dirty restraint, securing the man to the table.

'I'm not the enemy!' said McFarlane's aide. 'Why are you doing this to me?'

'Because you're not one of us.'

The explanation was simplistic, but it was true, and Marc saw a reaction in the other man's eyes that told him he had struck a nerve.

'You are making a big mistake.' Finlay became stiff and formal. 'Are you really going to let yourself get hanged for some rich man's vanity?'

A rich man's vanity.

The words brought Marc up short. Lau had used exactly that phrase when describing Solomon and his endeavours. Marc stepped back, studying Finlay with a new intensity.

'What is it?' said Delancort, seeing the change come over him.

'We're leaving,' Marc replied, with finality. 'Come on, Assim's waiting.'

Lucy loaded fresh shells into the shotgun and waved it in the direction of Finlay and the surviving ALEPH operative.

'Trust me, none of you wanna follow.'

But Solomon hesitated. He looked drawn, and for the first time in Marc's memory, he seemed worn down and tired.

'There is truth in what he said.' He nodded towards Finlay. 'You risk everything for me, and there is much I have not told you.'

'Yeah . . .' Marc knew there would have to be a reckoning, but this wasn't the time or the place for it. 'Explain later, though?'

'Escape first,' added Lucy.

The elevator deposited them at a floor that didn't actually exist.

Lucy shot Marc a questioning look as the doors opened somewhere between the twenty-seventh and twenty-eighth tiers. He gave her a shrug and stepped out, with Solomon and Delancort following on behind.

Warm, machine-scented air hit her like a face-full of oily cotton, and there was an abrupt moment of giddy vertigo when she realised where they were. A skeletal metallic deck, little better than a glorified set of catwalks, crossed over the throat of the tall air chimney that ran down the core of the Rubicon tower.

Lucy looked through the steel grate supporting her boots and into a long concrete tube studded with spinning fans and metal baffles. The building's elevator spine was built into the airway, part of a system that was designed to manage waste heat and keep the tower as power-efficient as possible. She remembered a little about it from a brochure she'd once read, but this was the first time Lucy had actually seen under the skin of the skyscraper.

The 'ghost floor' was built around a steel cube the size of a small car, held in vibration-dampening clamps in the middle of the shaft where air could flow freely around it. Thick cables snaked away, vanishing into the walls. Lucy circled the cube, seeing through vents in the side to racks of blinking electronic hardware within. It was a computer server, and by the look of it, the tech was high-grade.

'Hardened against electromagnetic pulse,' said Marc, stepping up beside her. 'Self-supporting internal power supply. Inch-thick bulletproof and fireproof carbon-fibre shell. A digital bank vault.'

She frowned. 'I was hoping for something we could, y'know, fit in a backpack?' Her voice echoed oddly in the air shaft, and she patted the side of the cube. 'This thing, we'd have to winch it out with a helo, like back in Seoul.'

'Trying to forget that,' Marc admitted. 'If we had the time, we could pull all the hard drives one by one. But that's not really an option here, is it?'

'No.' Behind them, Solomon studied the cube gravely. 'We cannot save this. And we cannot leave it for our foes.'

Lucy raised an eyebrow. 'I thought we—'

'Nope.' Marc cut her off with a shake of his head.

'You have the means?' Solomon shot Marc a warning look. 'I will not put our people at risk. There are still hundreds of Rubicon staff in the building!'

'Don't worry, we're not going to blow up the tower,' said Marc. 'Well, I mean, that's not Plan A . . .'

'Hello!' Lucy looked up as a shout filtered down to them. 'Watch out below!'

She saw Assim, framed as a black shadow against an open hatch high up at rooftop level. He was guiding something through, and presently the ends of two thick, serpentine cables found their way down to the metal floor.

Solomon nudged one of the cables with the tip of his shoe and gave a slow nod.

'Ah, I see.'

'Can someone explain it to me, please?'

Delancort stood with his arms close around himself, moving nervously from foot to foot.

'Those cables connect to the solar cell farm on the roof,' said Marc, giving Assim a wave that the hacker returned. 'Directly to the battery capacitors up there. There's enough stored charge in them to run this building for days.'

'*Oui*, I know, I wrote that press release.' Delancort's reply was testy. 'What are you doing with them?'

Marc pointed to one side of the cube, where an access panel was situated next to a standby console.

'You're going to open that, and then we're going to plug these in and run a few hundred thousand volts through that delicate silicon.'

Lucy made a buzzing noise through her teeth.

'That sounds extremely unsafe,' said Delancort.

'Oh, shit, yeah.' Marc's head bobbed. 'I mean, really, really fucking dangerous.'

Solomon walked to the console, pulling a slim key card from an inner pocket.

'I will destroy it before I see it in the hands of the Combine.'

Lau stumbled through the doors of the conference level and into the midst of Dupuis and his men, cursing himself.

His will was strong, undimmed by years of confinement, but he felt fury at the weakness in his flesh. The beatings, the malnourishment and the frigid prison cells had damaged him beyond recovery. He would never be the man he once was.

He was in pain from the exertion of fleeing Solomon's apartments, but it was better that than allowing himself to lose the game. Lau was within striking distance of his goal, his promised revenge. He would die before he allowed it to slip from his grasp.

Dupuis came striding over, demanding to know what was going on, but Lau waved him away with the cane, searching for the woman in the black jacket.

'Sigalov is dead,' she told him, dropping her voice to a conspiratorial hush. Cuts and contusions on her face spoke of the violence she had been a party to. 'Almost took me down too. Dane's friends played us. Led us into a trap.' She sneered. 'They're learning.'

Lau's anger, washing in and out like an ocean tide, briefly peaked again. He snarled a stinging gutter curse and bit down on the urge to spit.

'Yes. They were waiting for us in Solomon's quarters. Adaksin was killed, perhaps Gera as well.'

'*Shit.*' Grace's Russian accent slipped, her Milost identity discarded like a shed skin. 'This is coming apart. What do you want to do, old man?'

'We must contain the situation.'

He was going to say more, but Dupuis forced himself back into the conversation, his colour rising.

'What are you doing, Lau? We're getting reports of weapons fire on the upper floors, and the elevator systems are not responding!'

Lau banged the tip of his stick on the floor with a crack of sound as loud as a gunshot.

'Listen to me! There are terrorists in this building! They have killed three of my men and several civilians! They must be dealt with. We have no idea what they may be planning!'

'We need this tower sealed tight!' Grace called out at the top of her voice, backing up the story he was spinning. 'Call in your men! Make sure no one gets in or out!'

'Do what she says!' Lau barked, and Dupuis hesitated half a second before obeying. Lau turned back to Grace, speaking so only she would hear him. 'Where is our third team?'

She looked at her watch. 'They should be on station by now, holding over Cap Martin.'

'Get them here,' he growled.

Solomon inserted his key card into a slot on the console and held it, so the sensor in the card could read his thumbprint. Marc watched as he leaned close to the panel and spoke a string of words into a hidden pickup, activating the security system's voice recognition function.

'*When we are born, we cry that we are come to this great stage of fools.*'

'Huh,' muttered Lucy. '*King Lear.*'

Marc shot her a sideways look. 'I didn't know you were the Shakespeare type.'

'Saw the movie,' she noted.

A set of magnetic locks in the server's access hatch released, and Solomon stepped away, gesturing to Delancort.

'Your turn, Henri.'

Delancort had his key card in his hand, tapping it nervously against his chin.

'I am not sure I should,' he said, at length. 'This is not right.'

'Seriously?' Lucy turned to glare at him.

Delancort sucked in a deep breath, steeling himself. He couldn't stop from glancing at Marc, openly distrustful.

'This is spiralling out of control. People are dead. People are trying to kill us. We need to go to the authorities!'

Marc felt compelled to argue back.

'In case it's slipped your mind, don't forget the local coppers are going along with Lau and his mercs! They think this is Interpol, not the bloody Combine!'

There was something about Delancort that always brought the worst out in Marc. He couldn't carry on a civil conversation with the man for more than ten seconds. The dislike between them ran deep and neither one wanted to try and bridge the gap. Today, that was rising to the surface.

Delancort threw up his hands. 'So we ignore the law and do what you say? Because that has worked out so well in the past, has it not?'

'Henri, please.' Solomon's expression was grave. 'You hold the second key because I trust you implicitly. But I need you to do this.'

Solomon's honesty seemed to wrong-foot Delancort, and he blinked.

'I suppose I have no choice. It seems that is always how it is.'

He shook his head and moved to the console, inserting the key card.

'*Chacun voit midi à sa porte*,' he said, speaking the words with a weary sigh.

Lucy cocked her head. 'What's that a quote from?'

'It is a French proverb,' explained Solomon, as the remainder of the mag-locks released. 'It means *everyone sees noon at his own door.*'

'Deep,' said Marc dismissively. 'Okay, back off and I'll take it from here.'

He crouched down to gather up the ends of the thick power cables, and yanked them across towards the server module as the hatch retracted into the frame. A whiff of chilled air and ozone gusted out into the shaft.

'You got this?' Lucy didn't appear convinced.

He nodded at a service ladder running up the side of the elevator channel.

'Get them to the roof. I'll be right behind you.'

'Are we ready?' Assim shouted down from the open hatch high above. 'I am quite exposed up here, I do not want to hang around!'

Marc pushed past Delancort as he followed Lucy and Solomon to the ladder. Dragging the cables was more effort than it seemed, as they caught on support girders and Marc had to whip them across to get them into position.

He jammed the heavy-duty electrical connectors into ports below the main server bus in the middle of the cube, snap-locking them in. Next, he shut off the fire safety system and pulled the overload buffers, tossing them down the air shaft and into oblivion.

Marc stood back, his gaze passing over racks of brick-sized hard drives. Each one was an encrypted data store, the equivalent of a digital safe deposit box filled with hundreds of thousands of man-hours of potentially volatile covert intelligence. The entirety of the Grey Record, the collective memory of the Special Conditions Group, sat silently before him.

Al Sayf's attempted bombing of the National Mall; the Exile device in the caverns below Naples; Ghost5's cyber-attack on South Korea; the Shadow bioweapon; and the rest of Rubicon's battles in their covert war. Every mission they had undertaken, every injustice they had recorded, every enemy still to be challenged – it was in there.

And now I have to destroy it in order to save it, he told himself. But the alternative was far worse. Marc's chest tightened when he thought about what a man like Pytor Glovkonin could do with a database like that. *That's why he didn't wreck Rubicon out of hand. He wants this in one piece.*

Marc marched away, across to the middle of the gridded deck. He shouted up to Assim.

'Do it!'

'Get clear!' called the hacker.

He shook his head. 'Gotta make sure it works!'

Above, Marc could see Solomon, Delancort and Lucy at the top of the ladder, within a few metres of the roof access.

'Three! Two! *One!*'

On the last shout, Assim threw the scissor-switch that made the cables go live, and for a long second, nothing happened.

Marc rocked on the balls of his feet. Had he missed something in the connections?

Then the pungent ozone smell came back, acrid and harsh in the back of his nostrils. He tasted it as much as he smelled it – the bitter sting of overheating plastic and circuitry.

A low and unpleasant hum built up, resonating in his back teeth, and as Marc retreated towards the maintenance ladder, the server began to obliterate itself.

Fat blue-white sparks gushed from the faces of the stored drives, searing commas of purple after-image on his retinas, and barking cracks of noise sounded up and down the air shaft. The humming rose into a basso drone that made Marc wince. Sheets of yellow, smoky fire curled out from the racks, and with a crunch of displaced air, the server module went up.

A howl of electrical feedback shook through the deck and the service lights winked out, the lifts grinding to a halt. For a moment, the only illumination came from the sunlight pouring down the air shaft, but then emergency battery backups clicked on, pouring a sodium-bright glow over everything.

The choking grey smoke from the burning server stung Marc's lungs as he started up the ladder, his boots clanging off the rungs. It was hard going, but he didn't look back, and by the time he reached the top the fail-safe chemical powder extinguishers were firing, dousing the flames below. But they were too late to stop what Marc had set in motion.

'Got you,' said Lucy, offering a much-needed hand to haul him up the last half a metre to the roof.

'Cheers.'

Marc shielded his eyes from the bright sunshine as his vision adjusted, stepping away from the open hatch. A pennant of smoke had followed him up, and it rose vertically into the air with no breeze to deflect it.

The rooftop of the Rubicon tower was a glittering field of black and silver solar panels shimmering in the morning heat. On the far side of the upper tier, a crimson EC120 helicopter sporting the Rubicon Group corporate logo sat waiting on a hexagonal helipad. Marc set off at a jog, threading through the rows of panels without waiting to see if the others were following.

He scrambled up on to the helipad, circling to the pilot's side of the aircraft. Marc was certified on the Eurocopter, and it would be swift enough to put some much-needed distance between them and Lau's plans. He was already mentally plotting his flight path when he came around the nose and stopped dead.

'No, no, no . . .'

Marc's gut filled with ice as he saw a service panel beneath the chopper's engine compartment hanging open and unsecured.

'What's wrong?' Lucy was coming up behind him.

He stared blankly at the empty space. 'They pulled the fucking battery!'

Lau was a sharp one – he would have to be to play chess with someone like Ekko Solomon – and he'd seen this move coming. Somewhere in between swarming the tower with cops, Lau had sent his ALEPH black-jackets up here to sabotage the helicopter in the event of an escape attempt.

'So we are going nowhere?' Delancort gave a heavy sigh. 'And this is the inevitable end result of recklessness. A rash ploy fails and there is nothing else left!'

Marc wasn't certain if the other man was addressing him, but it certainly felt like it. He rounded on Delancort with fire in his eyes and his fists cocked.

'For once in your life, shut your mouth.'

'And if I do not?' Delancort glared back at him. '*Imbécile!* You brought us to this!'

Marc returned his cold stare. 'You want to go back down there and watch them take apart everything we've bled for?'

Before Solomon's aide could answer that, Assim called out, pointing into the sky.

'We have more company coming!'

The distant double-thud of rotor blades reached Marc's ears and he looked in the direction of the sound. Out over the bay, a black helicopter was coming in on a wide, curving approach.

'It is ALEPH?' said Solomon.

'Likely.'

Marc gave a grim nod. He estimated they had less than five minutes before the other aircraft was over them.

'They know where we are, then . . .' said Assim. 'That's not good.' He pivoted back to stare at the smoke billowing out of the open hatch. 'So, we try something else? I might still be able to co-opt the lift controls.'

'We'll have to risk it,' began Marc, but Lucy put her hand on his arm and shook her head.

'We have another option.'

She moved to a bright yellow storage bin near the edge of the roof and kicked open a latch. Inside were racks of what looked like small backpacks, each one the same reflective colour as the bin. She tossed one to Marc and he caught it with both hands.

It was a lightweight, one-shot escape parachute, an 'egress rig', to give it its technical name. At once, he knew what Lucy was suggesting.

Assim fumbled the catch on his and his dark eyes widened.

'Oh good grief, no.' He offered it back to Lucy. 'I am not doing that.'

'Why is jumping from a great height always your go-to plan?' Marc weighed the chute in his hand.

'What can I say? I got the taste for it in Delta.' She spoke quickly. 'C'mon, let's hustle.'

Solomon already had his rig on, and the brightly coloured gear looked utterly incongruous over the cut of his expensive suit.

'Where is our landing zone?'

He peered over the edge of the roof, scanning the city below.

'Can we get to Port Hercule?'

Lucy looked to the south, to the glittering waters of the marina.

'The *Hermes* is moored at the quay,' said Delancort, glaring at the chute by his feet. 'But you'll never make it down there.'

Marc pulled on his rig and secured it, before turning to Assim.

'This is the only way, mate. Trust me, it's not as scary as it looks.'

'You b-bloody liar!' stuttered the hacker, but he reluctantly followed suit.

Marc double-checked him to be sure.

'Good. Just keep your eyes on the person in front of you, use the cords to steer left and right.'

'And for crying out loud, bend your knees when you touch down, 'cos no one's gonna be carrying your sorry ass if you break your legs.'

Lucy covered it with sarcasm, but her unease was real and she shot Marc a concerned look.

Both of them knew that making a regular jump from an aircraft was dangerous enough. Doing it over a city, where invisible thermal air currents rose up from the streets below, added a lot more complexity.

Delancort thrust his chute rig back into Marc's hands.

'I will not participate in this insanity.'

'Henri . . .' began Solomon, but the other man shook his head.

'No.' Delancort backed away a step. 'To hell with this! There is a point I will not go beyond!'

'Now?' Lucy glared at him. 'You're chickening out right now? Shit, man, your timing sucks.'

'It is not cowardice!' Delancort shouted back at her. 'This is my choice!' He looked towards Solomon. 'The board are *right*, sir. You have gone too far. I have tried to pull you back, time after time, but I failed to do so! Please.' He opened his hands. 'I beg you, stop now. If you do this, it is the end of everything. The end of Rubicon. Of everything we have built.'

'We are trying to *save it*, Henri,' said Solomon.

'I know you believe that.' Delancort looked away. 'But you are wrong.'

Marc's jaw stiffened, and he tossed the spare pack away.

'Fine. He's made his decision. He wants to pick the wrong side? That's up to him. We don't have time to debate it.' A sharp tug on the D-ring pulled the rig's smaller pilot chute into Marc's hand, and he gathered it up, ready to deploy. 'We're going.'

'Five-second intervals,' called Lucy, flipping her legs over the guard rail. 'Assim, Solomon, then Marc, that's the order.

'I'm not really sure . . .' muttered Assim, but Lucy drowned him out with a yell.

'Go!'

She threw out her pilot chute and jumped into open space. She went through a split second of free fall and then the main chute unfurled into a wide arc of yellow canopy. Lucy pivoted smoothly through the air, angling away across the parkland and towards the Beaux Arts domes of the Casino Monte-Carlo.

Marc had to give Assim an ungentle shove and the hacker let out a scream as he fell off the edge, but his emergency chute popped on cue and he wobbled into Lucy's wake. On the next count of five Solomon jumped as if he had been born to it, tacking expertly into the line.

Marc moved himself into position, ticking off the numbers. Out in the lead, Lucy was making good progress, cutting confident S-turns through the air to line up her descent with the marina.

'Dane!'

Delancort shouted out his name in a warning as a metal door banged open on the far side of the rooftop. He saw SIU officers in tactical gear boiling out of an access way, brandishing their weapons. Grace was with them, her gun tracking right to him.

A burst of bullets sparked off the metal of the guard rail inches from Marc's arm, and he fell, tumbling off the edge of the Rubicon tower.

FIFTEEN

A sheer wall of gold-tinted glass flashed past as gravity pulled Marc towards the streets below. The little pilot chute was ripped out of his hand by the violent rush of air, vanishing into his wake.

The ground seemed terrifyingly close, and the heart-stopping gap between jump and release felt like an eternity. But then the canopy opened, kicking him in the back with the force of it, and he lurched around. A rising thermal coming from a tall apartment block pushed him off course and he struggled to counter it. For one giddy moment, Marc was afraid he'd screwed up his path, fearing that he would come down in the park – or worse, collide with the side of a nearby hotel.

He tugged on the steering cords, levelling out, and found Solomon's neon-yellow canopy ahead of him. Beyond that, the sun was in his eyes and there was no sign of Lucy or Assim's chutes. He hoped that meant both of them were already down and safe.

Marc risked craning his neck around to look back towards the Rubicon building. He caught sight of figures in white shirts spilling out across the ground-floor plaza, as uniformed officers from the Monaco police sprinted for their cars. It was going to be tight, keeping a lead on the local cops. If Marc went down short of the dockside, he was as good as caught.

Something else flickered in the corner of his vision, but it was gone before he could get a good look at it, disappearing behind an office block. He had the vague impression of a boxy fuselage beneath two counter-rotating blade discs.

ALEPH reinforcements, he guessed.

As he passed over the park, Marc widened his turn to stay in his tail-end spot of the chain. Ahead, Solomon followed a line that took him over the rainbow-coloured roof of the Auditorium Rainier III and down onto the quayside, as cleanly as if he'd been riding on a rail.

Marc resisted the instinct to stiffen up as the ground drew closer, staying loose and ready for the landing. His approach lacked the same style as Solomon's point-perfect touchdown, and he forced a messy last-second adjustment to avoid the arm of a construction crane jutting out from a nearby building site.

Tourists and dog-walkers out for a morning stroll scattered in panic as Marc came fluttering down from the cloudless blue sky. He overcorrected and barely avoided hitting the edge of the jetty, but the steady breeze off the sea shoved him back and he landed hard. He felt the shock in his knees and ankles, hissing in pain, fighting it down.

He tore off the rig and left it where it fell, sprinting to Solomon. Lucy was coming their way, supporting a panting, drenched Assim on one shoulder.

'He landed in the water,' she explained. 'Better than the alternative.'

Assim's eyes were wide with the adrenaline racing through his veins and he grinned from ear to ear.

'That was incredible! I want to go again!'

He laughed, still punchy from the rush of the jump.

'This way,' said Solomon, pointing up the quay.

Usually, Solomon's hundred-and-five-foot giga-yacht *Themis* dropped anchor at the nearby Lucciana Jetty, but the boat was out of the water in some Italian shipyard getting a refit.

And even if we had it here, it's a big target at sea, thought Marc.

With the Combine gunning for them, he wouldn't put it past them to employ heavy firepower against the fugitive members of the SCD.

'Please tell me the Swedes finally delivered that submarine you ordered,' Lucy said breathlessly, as they ran towards a covered boathouse.

'I regret the A26 remains incomplete,' replied Solomon. 'A pity. Stealth would be of great use at this moment.'

Behind him, Marc heard the thudding beat of helicopter rotors echoing off Monaco's towers, and the skirl of police sirens.

'Right now, we'll take whatever you have.'

Solomon punched a code into a keypad and the boathouse door slid open. Inside, bobbing in a gentle swell, lay a long, sleek, silver-grey shape with a forked prow. It resembled the talon of some giant animal, a racing form that seemed to be going supersonic even when it was at rest. Picked out in black, a line-art sketch of the Greek god Hermes covered the twin bows of the powerboat.

Marc gave a low whistle. 'Yeah, this'll do.'

'A Skater 46,' said Assim, giving a knowing nod. 'Top Catamaran hull in Open and Superboat classes.'

'You a boat nerd too?'

Lucy jumped into the passenger deck as Marc set to work untying the lines.

'Little bit,' admitted the hacker, scrambling after her. He hesitated, glancing back over his shoulder. 'You think Delancort will be all right?'

'As Marc said, Henri made his choice.'

Solomon took the pilot's chair and started the *Hermes* up, the four outboard motors at its stern coming to life in a throaty rumble.

Marc yanked the switch to open the boathouse door and leapt aboard with the last bow-line.

'How fast can this thing go?'

Solomon frowned. 'I have not had the opportunity to find out.'

Lucy looked up as the sound of sirens and shouts reached them.

'You have now.'

Silber's phone buzzed in his pocket and he jumped. The pilot shrank back into the galley of the Airbus and slid the device into his palm, careful to stay out of sight of the ALEPH operative moving around the aircraft.

The message from his wife was simple, but it still broke his heart.

Gone to the beach. All happy. V.

That was the code they had agreed on. Back when he had been a combat pilot, they had quietly decided on an innocuous secret message that could be shared between them in the event of something terrible occurring. Ari had always told Vada that if he needed her to get out of the city, no questions asked, if he knew that war was coming, the signal would be *go to the beach*.

He tried to visualise her now. In the car, probably across the border into Italy or France. Smiling and keeping their children content, all the while hiding her fear.

All happy meant *we are okay, we are safe.*

Ari let out a slow breath, feeling a dread he hadn't known he was holding in go with it. He dwelled on the message a moment more, then deleted it – but he couldn't stop himself from flicking to the phone's gallery to find a photo of his family. Just to look at their faces for a moment.

From the cabin beyond he heard the crackle of a radio. He put away the phone and chanced a look.

The ALEPH operative with the braided hair had her back to him, holding up a walkie-talkie to her ear. Another woman's voice rattled from the handset, orders streaming out in urgent Russian.

Ari's grasp of the language was basic, but good enough to get the gist. There was a situation developing, something about 'targets on the water' and an escape attempt. Braids asked if the targets were on their way here, and the radio voice responded in the affirmative.

He drew back into the galley and leaned into the oval window looking down to the apron of the hangar. Ari saw the other operative, the one he'd christened Sunglasses, holding up a radio of his own and listening in to the same conversation.

Then he heard the voice telling them to take no chances with anyone at the airport. The man down on the ground gave a nod and drew a pistol from inside his jacket, looking up at the jet's flanks.

Ari ducked away, hoping that he hadn't been seen. This was it. Whatever he did in the next minute would mean the difference between seeing Vada and the kids again, or . . .

He pushed that thought aside and dashed across the galley, sliding into a narrow stairwell that led into the Airbus's lower deck. Behind him, Braids glimpsed the movement and shouted out, but could not dare to halt.

The level below the mid-galley was a steel-lined space fitted out with lockers and secure containers. Ari knew where to go, mashing the thumb of his right hand against a sensor pad and typing in a six-digit code on a keypad with his left. A single locker popped open as he heard heavy boots on the deck above him, glimpsing a shadow fall over the stairwell.

'Come up here!' shouted the woman.

Inside the locker was the short, tubular form of a Kel-Tec KSG shotgun and a rack of stun grenades. Ari pulled the gun from its spring-loaded clip and flicked off the safety.

He loathed having firearms aboard his aircraft. Bullets and planes were a bad mix, especially at altitude when a single round could go through its intended victim *and* the thin fuselage, causing catastrophic decompression.

And that was why the KSG was the only gun on board he allowed to be loaded at all times: because the specialised shells racked in it were the pilot's personal recommendation. The bullpup shotgun had two magazines; in one were non-lethal 'beanbag' rounds that fired balls of heavy wadding rather than lead shot; in the other were the shells that Ari had selected for this situation.

Braids gave up waiting for him to obey, and she came down in a rush, not taking the short flight of stairs, but jumping over the rail to land cat-footed in the middle of the lower deck. It was a good move and it might have taken him by surprise if he was the ordinary ground crew tech he'd pretended to be.

Ari Silber was a warrior, and he was ready. He squeezed the KSG's trigger and a thick yellow cylinder blasted out of the barrel, hitting the ALEPH agent squarely in the chest.

Needle-sharp tines at the end of the shell pierced her jacket and the super-dense battery inside the shell discharged. The round was a tiny, high-voltage taser, packing enough power to lock her muscles and send her into twitching shock. She tried to turn her own pistol towards him, but her body refused to work.

Ari rushed to her, tearing the gun from her hand as she sank to the deck in a quivering heap. She cursed him through gritted teeth, struggling to fight back. The pilot used his weight to push the mercenary into the floor and found a zip-tie to secure her hands behind her.

'Get up,' he ordered, as her tremors subsided. He force-marched her back to the main deck at the barrel of the shotgun. 'Where are your friends?'

'I will not help you,' she gasped, still shaky from the taser hit. 'Surrender n-now, while you still can.'

'That doesn't work for me,' he explained. He gave her a shove towards the conference room and the exit door beyond it. 'Time for you to get off my plane.'

She threw a look over her shoulder, and past him. Braids was good, he had to give her that, enough that he almost missed the subtle shift in her stance as she prepared herself for a fight.

Ari pivoted, holding the shotgun close, and saw the other ALEPH operative coming up behind him, the big woman with the loud voice.

Must have got on board through the rear cargo ramp, the pilot guessed, not that it mattered now.

Ari fired, more to give Muscles something to think about than to hit her, and another bright yellow slug buzzed angrily down the cabin, deflecting harmlessly off the wall.

The other ALEPH operative didn't share Ari's reluctance to use lethal force; she had her full-auto pistol out and ready, and let off a three-round burst.

The pilot threw himself into the cover of a narrow toilet cubicle, but the woman with the braids did not react so quickly. One of the bullets meant for Ari hit her in the throat and she toppled over, her hands still tied behind her back, rendering her unable to reach up to staunch the gush of blood.

The sound of gunfire snarled through the air and Malte saw a wave of panic pass over the ground crew on the hangar floor. They broke into a terrified scramble, fleeing out the open doors and into the daylight.

'You!' The man with the sunglasses, the one who had enjoyed shouting point-blank into the Finn's face, came into view from beneath the wing of the Airbus. He was holding a pistol with an extended magazine. 'Do not move!'

Once, Malte had been a police officer, and he passed his cop's eye over the ALEPH mercenary, his stance and his red-cheeked, snarling expression. Malte knew the signs. The man came from criminal stock. It was there in his street-brawler attitude and poor gun control, and if Malte's evaluation needed confirmation, he had it from the blurry bits of prison tattoos peeking out around the man's cuffs and collar.

'How many of you here, prick?' barked the gunman.

Malte raised his right hand and showed him four fingers.

'You talk shit,' said the other man, despite the fact that Malte hadn't uttered a word.

He came closer, making motions with the automatic pistol. It was more evidence the man had too much aggression and too little training. Someone taught by law enforcement or the military would have known to keep their distance, and use the threat of the weapon to control their target. This one wanted to get right into Malte's face, just as he had earlier.

When a muffled blast of gunfire sounded inside the jet, the thug couldn't stop himself from looking in that direction, and Malte went for him.

There were trays of tools lying unattended within his reach, and he grabbed the edge of the nearest one, tipping it in an artless throw towards the gunman. The ALEPH mercenary was momentarily wrong-footed as wrenches and screwdrivers pelted him, giving Malte enough time to snatch up a pair of combination spanners.

The gun was coming back at him as he crossed the distance to the other man, and he used the heavyweight vanadium steel tools to crack down on the thug's forearms.

The mercenary gave a low howl, losing his gun, staggering back a step. Malte kept up the attack, and the other man fumbled for a replacement weapon.

His hand clasped around the shaft of a rubber-headed mallet and it came humming towards the Finn's head. Malte ducked back, but not enough to avoid a scrape. The mercenary spat and went on the offensive, but it was the wrong play.

Malte advanced, jabbing the open claws at the ends of the spanners down in a double strike, hitting his opponent across both clavicles at once. He was rewarded with the damp crunch of fracturing bone, and again the ALEPH merc cried out. Malte shoved him into a parked fuel bowser, and got a hand around his throat.

The mercenary scrabbled at the Finn's tightening grip, losing his sunglasses in a frantic attempt to escape the sleeper hold.

'No,' said Malte, and he kept on squeezing until the other man fell limp.

The cabin floor creaked as the heavyset ALEPH operative moved closer, and Ari realised that he had acted without thinking it through, trapping himself in a space with no other exit.

Any second now, Muscles would be close enough to point her gun around the corner and let off a blind-fire blast of shots that would end Ari.

The pilot gave a humourless smirk, cursing himself. Being riddled with bullets on a cramped airliner toilet wasn't how he wanted to go out.

Not the heroic ending I would prefer.

Then he thought about Vada and the children, and a new determination came to him. Carefully, he flipped the thumb-switch that shifted the KSG's loader mechanism, selecting the shotgun's second magazine. Then he aimed the weapon at the far wall, tilting the muzzle into an acute angle.

The floor creaked again, and he saw a shadow shift.

Now!

As fast as he could work the trigger and the slide, Ari fired shot after shot into the wall. The heavy beanbag rounds struck the bulkhead and careened off in wild ricochets. Caught around the corner in the narrow corridor, the second ALEPH agent had nowhere to go, calling out in alarm and flinching back as they bombarded her.

Ari pushed off the toilet seat and swung around, colliding with the mercenary and knocking her down with the smoking bulk of his shotgun. The woman landed hard, but recovered instantly, swinging up her pistol.

Before she could pull the trigger again, Ari shot her point-blank in the head with another wadded round and she reeled back, her nose broken, her eyes rolling up to show the whites.

'And stay there,' said the pilot, panting hard.

He heard footsteps clanking up the boarding ladder and racked the last round in the magazine, but it was a familiar face that hove into view.

Malte, looking a little worse for wear himself, hesitated over the still form of the woman with the braids as he checked her over, then threw Ari a look and made a throat-cutting gesture.

'This one is unconscious,' said the pilot, pointing his weapon at the other woman. 'What about the third, the man?'

'Dealt with.' The Finn didn't elaborate.

'All right then.' Ari blew out a breath. 'Unload these two and make sure all ground connections are disengaged.' He swung the shotgun over his shoulder on its strap and started walking forward. 'We're getting out of here.'

Malte frowned, meeting the pilot's gaze. He said nothing, but both men knew the unspoken question hanging in the air.

Were the others on the way?

Ari answered it anyway. 'We have until airport security catches up with us. After that . . .' He trailed off.

Malte gave him a nod, and set to work.

It turned out that *fast* was an understatement; but that was okay, because Lucy liked the speed.

Solomon's racer moved like a rocket, revving up to full throttle once they cleared the harbour wall and hit open water. She couldn't help herself, and let out a whoop as the *Hermes* sped over the wake of a passing sailing boat and caught air. It skipped across whitecaps and Solomon leaned into the swerve, aiming the catamaran prow in a north-westerly direction.

Within moments they would officially be beyond the Principality of Monaco and into French territorial waters, and from there it was a straight shot up the shoreline to the international airport at Nice Côte d'Azur.

It was a gamble. *Hell, everything they had done over the last three days had been that.* The hope was that the Maritime Gendarmerie wouldn't be able to scramble a patrol boat to intercept them first.

She looked to Marc, who crouched in the passenger compartment over his Rubicon-issue spyPhone. He said something into the device, then looked up at her.

'Sent a message to Ari. Dunno if he got it . . .'

He caught himself and fell silent before he said something negative.

'He'll be there!' Lucy called back, pitching her voice up over the roar of the engines.

'Yeah.' Marc did something with his smartphone, then spoke up so all of them could hear. 'I need everyone's comms gear right now.'

Lucy handed over her phone and the smartwatch networked to it. Assim was reluctant, but he followed suit. Solomon didn't look back, steering the *Hermes* with one hand, briefly taking the other off the throttle to pass Marc a phone plated in rose gold.

The boat bounced over more wake turbulence as it knifed through deeper waters. They were closing in on the main shipping channel, where the big freighters and cruise liners ruled the waves. The *Hermes* was an extremely fast minnow in comparison.

The Brit weighed his gathered loot in one hand, and then tossed it into the speedboat's foaming slipstream.

'No sense in helping them track us,' he noted.

'Yes,' said Assim, 'but the people who want us dead know exactly where we are going.' He pointed in the direction of Nice. 'So if we—'

Whatever he was going to say next was swallowed up by the snap of splintering fibreglass as a high-velocity bullet struck the stern. In quick succession, a second shot hummed over their heads and shattered a windscreen panel.

Solomon immediately put the *Hermes* into wild zigzag turns, the force of it throwing everyone in the passenger bay against the racing restraints holding them to their seats.

'There!' shouted Lucy, finding the shape of an aircraft moving low in the sky at their 7 o'clock position. It was a peculiar-looking thing, an ungainly rectangular box held stable beneath two sets of counter-rotating blades.

Marc pulled a pair of field binoculars from a storage bin and twisted around, peeking up over the lip of the hull to spot the helicopter.

'It's a Helix,' he called back, 'Russian, Kamov Ka-32, flying ALEPH colours.'

'So much for getting away clean,' she muttered. 'Shooter?'

He nodded. 'I see an open hatch at the rear . . . I see a rifle . . . *Shit!*'

Marc ducked and a heartbeat later they heard the hum of another round pass over them.

'It's gaining on us.' Assim dared to take a quick look himself. 'Can we outrun it?'

'We go straight and full throttle, we give them a clear target,' said Solomon.

Marc gave a nod. 'But every second we don't, we're letting them close the net.'

Lucy looked down at the Stechkin auto-pistol and the stubby shotgun stowed in the gunwale.

'We have nothing that can hit them back from this range.'

Marc snapped off his safety belt and slid across the deck to Solomon's side.

'See that?' He pointed towards a massive slab of white-painted steel half a mile distant, an enormous roll-on, roll-off car carrier steaming southwards. 'Get us to it?'

'Hold on.'

Solomon gave the steering yoke a savage twist that made the *Hermes* launch itself off the waves like a leaping dolphin, coming about to aim directly at the cargo vessel.

The speedboat shot away, but now they were presenting a longer aspect to their pursuers in the Helix. Lucy saw the flash of muzzle flare from inside the helicopter's cabin and she ducked. A shot thudded into the hull with a noise like nails driven through wood.

'We can't hide behind that thing!' she yelled, as the car carrier loomed larger. 'It's heading in the wrong direction!'

Marc was emptying the contents of the storage bin on the deck, and he shoved the loaded Stechkin across to her.

'You're the best shot we have. You'll have to get all the rounds on target.'

She flicked another glance at the Helix. It had gained some height, enough that it would be able to pass straight over the cargo ship.

'It's still too far away!'

'I know!'

Another rifle round kissed the *Hermes*, and this time Assim cried out in pain as splinters of fractured hull raked his shoulder. The shots started coming thick and fast, the sniper on the helicopter giving up on accuracy in hopes of scoring a lucky hit.

Lucy's estimation of ALEPH's mercenaries reluctantly jumped a few notches. The shooter would have to be good to even get a round close to target, firing at a fast-moving speedboat from inside the juddering perch of a hovering helicopter.

The sniper kept pouring it on, and Lucy heard cries of alarm from crewmen up on the car carrier's deck as wild shots clanged into the steel hull of the big ship.

Solomon took them right through the foaming, stormy wake at the car carrier's aft, banking on the speedboat's velocity to punch them through the turbulence before it flipped them over. For one stomach-lurching second, the *Hermes* pitched into a thirty-degree roll, then slammed back down into the sea with a bone-shaking crash. A gush of salt water and spilled marine diesel came over the bow, drenching the lot of them.

'Get in as close as you can!' shouted Marc.

Solomon turned hard, pivoting the speedboat into line with the cargo ship. The smaller craft scraped against the hull of the larger one, and Lucy looked up. It was like a sheer, thirty-metre high cliff made of ageing, white-painted steel. Off towards amidships she spotted the orange blobs of hard hats popping up as curious crewmen peered outboard.

With the car carrier blocking the view, the sniper on the Helix had no visual on them. Solomon chopped the throttle, killing most of their forward momentum, letting the ship's slipstream pull them along with it.

The speedboat's engine note fell to a low mutter, and Lucy caught the sound of double rotors in the air. The heavy beat told her that the Helix was hovering, the pilot inching it cautiously over the cargo ship.

'Here it comes.' Marc found the bright red plastic flare gun he was looking for and jammed a signal cartridge into the breech. 'We get one go at this.'

'I got it.'

Lucy wriggled out of her safety harness and checked the Stechkin, flicking its selector to fully automatic fire. She put both hands around the lower frame of the gun, gripping it as firmly as she could.

The ALEPH helicopter came into view, passing over the flank of the car carrier, a fat black bumblebee droning against the clear blue of the sky. She estimated the distance to target was maybe fifty metres, inside the effective range of the pistol.

It was close enough now for Lucy to see the figures in the cockpit, and one of them reacted in shock as they spotted the drifting speedboat right beneath them. But Marc was already firing, the lazy, fizzing arc of the flare slicing up and over the hovering aircraft. The flare head burst into smoking crimson fire above the rotor blades, blinding the aircrew as Marc gave the word.

'*Now!*'

Lucy squeezed the Stechkin's trigger and the gun tried to leap out of her wet grip. She fought it down, leaning into the drumming recoil, and fired into the belly of the Helix. In half a second, the magazine was empty and her hands were seared with exhaust vapour, but the helicopter was adrift, turning drunkenly on its axis. It sank low, clipping one of the cargo ship's masts, and vanished out of sight, crash-landing on the upper deck.

Solomon didn't wait, and pushed the throttles to the stops. The *Hermes* made a wide turn and set into an arrow-straight course towards the peninsula of Saint-Jean-Cap-Ferrat and the airport beyond it.

Marc scanned the airport complex as it came into sight, taking a juddering survey of the runways lined up along the coast. It was hard to get a clear view, but he saw aircraft moving around on the apron, white and silver darts reflecting the bright sunshine.

He searched for a particular tailplane sporting the blue streak livery that signified the Rubicon Airbus A350, and spotted it on the move near the main terminal building.

'He's already rolling!'

'Guess Ari got the message?' said Lucy.

'We will have to hope so.'

Solomon angled the speedboat towards the seashore, without slowing down. Nice Côte d'Azur Airport was partly built on reclaimed land, and the section that faced the sea was concrete and rocks. There were no quays or inlets where the *Hermes* would be able to dock, but Marc realised that Solomon wasn't going to let that stop him.

'Be ready.'

The speedboat hurtled towards the shore at maximum speed, barely giving Marc enough time to strap in. Skipping over the top of the waves, the forward velocity and shallow draught of the vessel pushed it out of the water and into the air as Solomon deliberately beached the craft.

A horrible crunching and grinding vibrated up through the deck as the *Hermes* tore its keel to bits on the stones. Speed bled off to nothing, slamming Marc and the others against their straps. The boat shuddered to a halt and sagged to starboard, the broken hull giving a last, dying groan.

'Out!' shouted Marc, smacking the quick-release switch with a balled fist.

He grabbed Assim, ignoring the injured hacker's cry of pain, and shoved him overboard. Lucy and Solomon scrambled down after him, and together the four of them jogged across a grassy border, to a service road running parallel to the longer of the airport's two runways.

Marc had grabbed the binoculars on his way off the *Hermes*, and swung them up, finding the Airbus again. It was passing the end of the other runway, and he grinned; but that fell off his face when he spotted three airport security vehicles racing to catch up with the Rubicon jet.

'We have to get to them before the cops box them in,' said Lucy, catching the sound of sirens on the breeze.

'Those chaps . . . might give us a ride,' said Assim, forcing out the words between each breath.

He pointed with his good arm to a Toyota pickup with a huge FOLLOW ME sign in the flatbed, as it screeched to a halt a short distance away. Two men climbed out, one speaking into a radio, the other yelling in angry French.

Lucy, as usual, cut to the quick. She aimed the Stechkin pistol in the direction of the pickup crew.

'*Agenouillez-vous!*' she barked, and they dropped to their knees on the tarmac, unaware that the gun was empty.

Marc climbed into the driver's seat, the other three into the flatbed, and he stamped on the accelerator.

Ari's unscheduled aircraft movement had shut down the airport as well as putting it on high alert, which meant there was no other traffic out there and nothing to stop Marc taking the shortcut across median strips to the main runway. He spun the wheel and the Toyota lurched onto a parallel course with the rolling Airbus.

The airport police units were coming in fast, closing their window of opportunity. Marc cut across the path of the airliner, slewing wide and around, so that whoever was in the cockpit would see the vehicle and who was on board.

'Come on, flyboy, it's us!' he grated, reversing the motion, cutting back the other way.

The bright running lights on the jet's forward undercarriage flashed *one-two-three* and Marc felt a rush of relief.

'He sees us!' shouted Solomon.

The airliner bumped to a sudden halt, the blades of its Rolls-Royce Trent engines still idling.

Lucy banged on the top of the cab.

'Right side, right side!'

Marc guided the pickup around the nose as the forward passenger door rotated inwards. He looked up to see Malte lean out and survey the group with a hangdog expression.

In the next second, the end of a collapsible escape ladder came tumbling down to the runway. Lucy and Solomon helped Assim out, but Marc stayed in the cab, revving the engine. He could see the security vehicles. The three cars had halted, the officers inside uncertain of what was taking place.

Turning the other way, Marc saw more cars powering down the runway from the opposite end, hoping to block them in.

'Marc, we gotta go!' Lucy shouted from the base of the ladder.

He nodded and vaulted from the pickup's cab. His action seemed to trigger something, and the trailing cars burst into motion once more. Marc was the last one onto the ladder, and barely got his feet on the rungs before the Airbus started moving again. The keening shriek of the engines pitched up and that meant only one thing – Ari was powering up for take-off.

He felt the ladder shift even as he hauled himself up it, and then he was being dragged into the cabin by Solomon and Malte. Lucy slammed the door shut behind him and gave a shaky, nervous laugh.

'Well, shit. We missed duty free.'

The weird tension of the moment broke and Marc snorted.

The familiar two-tone chime of the aircraft intercom sounded, followed by Ari's smooth, professional tones.

'*Ladies and gentlemen, please take your damn seats and strap your backsides in. I'm making my second illegal take-off in as many days and it is going to be bumpy.*'

They made it to the common area and belted in as the Airbus reached speed and the nose tilted into the air. Marc saw flashes of white and strobing yellow lights as vehicles veered into the grass rather than risk being struck by the airliner, and then they were off the ground.

The deck sloped at an angle far steeper than any regular passenger flight would have experienced, as Ari pushed the A350 past its usual tolerances. Out through the window, Marc saw dark ocean and pale sky.

'We made it,' he said quietly, suddenly aware of his heart drumming in his chest.

'This far,' said Solomon.

'Is this really necessary?' Delancort held up his hands, showing the police-issue handcuffs around his wrists. 'I am co-operating.'

'I will be the judge of that.'

Lau walked to the conference room window, glowering out at the sun-drenched streets below. The Rubicon tower was still in semi-darkness, its systems out of action until the power grid could be reactivated.

'I tried to convince them to surrender,' Solomon's aide began again. 'I do not know what else I could have done.' He looked around. 'If I could speak to the board—'

'They are in protective custody.' Lau cut him off with a sharp reply. 'Everyone in this building is a suspect,' he amended, belatedly adding something to play to the fiction of Interpol's involvement.

The conference room door opened, and the woman called Grace stood on the threshold. She was grimy and cold-eyed, and she shot Delancort a wary look as she walked in and closed it behind her.

'Speak,' Lau ordered. He did not care what Solomon's aide heard.

'They've escaped,' she said without preamble. 'Nice Air Traffic Control just filed a formal alert. Solomon's aircraft made an unsanctioned departure, last seen heading south-west over the Med.'

Lau's bony fingers tightened around the handle of his walking stick, gripping it so hard it caused him physical discomfort.

'You were supposed to prevent that,' he hissed.

'I did the best I could,' she retorted. 'But it's above my pay grade to jump off a roof.'

'They will send the Air Force after them,' offered Delancort.

'I did not ask for your opinion,' said Lau, without taking his eyes off Grace.

'That jet's loaded with electronic countermeasures and mil-spec gear, right?' she added. 'They reprogram their ID transponder and they can ghost into any commercial traffic they want.' She gave Delancort a hard look. 'Now might be the time to start exploring other options.'

Solomon's aide shifted uncomfortably in his seat as the room's lights flickered back on. Lau looked out through the frosted glass door and saw that power had returned to the entire floor, and perhaps the whole building as well.

Then the cellular telephone in his pocket vibrated. Warily, Lau drew it to his ear.

'Yes?'

'*I am disappointed,*' said Glovkonin. '*I wanted this done cleanly.*'

Lau turned away, glaring out at nothing once more.

'I told you to give me more men.'

'*And what would you have done with an army? Invaded Monte Carlo? This was meant to be bloodless.*'

'Ekko forced my hand. He sabotaged the tower's power grid.'

'*Yes, I am aware.*' Lau wondered how that could be so, but said nothing as Glovkonin paused. '*He thinks he is safe. But there is nowhere he can go I will not find him.*'

Lau maintained his silence, waiting for the question he knew was coming.

'*What is the status of the Grey Record database?*'

'Uncertain,' said Lau. 'There was an electrical overload, a fire. But I will tell you now – it is worthless. Ekko destroyed it.'

He enjoyed a thrill of spiteful amusement at informing the Russian that his prize was lost.

'*How can you be certain?*'

'Because it is what I would have done. He would not flee his castle with those riches still in it. He has denied them to you.'

Lau heard something brittle shatter, and imagined Glovkonin back in the halls of the Corsican manor house, hurling a crystal glass at the wall in impotent rage.

He let that fester for a moment.

'I know Ekko Solomon,' Lau continued. 'And I know that this story does not end here. He is a man of secrets. Many of them.'

Glovkonin was silent for a moment.

'*I want that intelligence.*'

Lau found Delancort's reflection against the office window and studied him dispassionately.

'I have a place to start.'

SIXTEEN

It was late afternoon by the time the local police had completed their sweep of Solomon's apartments, and Lau stood alone in the wreckage, surveying what he had taken from his old comrade.

The elegant, minimalist space had been turned over in search of what might have been hidden there, but Lau knew that nothing of value would be found. Ekko was too meticulous to leave behind something obvious that could be held up as a smoking gun, as evidence of his extra-legal activities.

Not that it was required. The Combine fostered entire agencies of people whose jobs were to sow disinformation and build false truth out of nothing. That was, after all, how this takeover had been engineered from the start. Lies and deceptions set in motion to entrap the self-righteous. It had worked perfectly.

Glovkonin was angry at losing the information in Ekko's files, but that did not concern Lau. His personal victory was near complete, tarnished only by Solomon's escape.

'I have what was yours,' Lau said to the empty room. 'What was always meant to belong to me.'

He turned as the apartment door opened, and the woman McFarlane entered. Her aide stood warily in the corridor, unwilling to re-enter the rooms where he had been witness to such violence and bloodshed.

'What do you want?'

Lau dismissed her with the question, studying the places where police markers taped off the locations of bodies, bullet casings and blood spatter.

'You owe me an explanation,' she seethed. 'You lied to me!'

'I told you what you needed to hear,' he replied. 'Anything more would have confused the issue.'

'Confused?' she shot back. 'You didn't think it bloody well relevant to tell me you were once Ekko Solomon's business partner? And that he shafted you?' McFarlane shook her head. 'Dear God, I knew you were holding something back, but this?'

'We used each other to get what we wanted,' Lau said coldly. 'Do not pretend otherwise. You wanted Solomon gone. Rubicon is now free of him and his blind crusade. Take the win, Esther.'

She baulked at his casual use of her first name.

'I'm not some child you can pat on the head and send on her way. I want to know why you did this!'

Lau balanced on his walking stick, staring down at a few scattered shell casings among some fragments of broken glass. He poked the spent brass with the tip of his cane and considered her demand.

In thirty years, he had never really told the story.

Hornet.

That was what they called it: *Operation Ma Feng*, named after the huge winged insects that swarmed in China's forests. They were great black creatures with flickering wings that had terrified Lau as a child. He had been six years of age when he saw an old woman killed by a swarm that attacked her because she disrupted their nest.

But the hornets were not only killers. They were industrious. They built intricate homes for themselves. They colonised and conquered. They acted with a strict collective will.

They were a fine metaphor for what the People's Republic of China intended to do on the African continent.

In the early 1990s it was a land of unexploited riches and oppressed peoples who had been misunderstood and mismanaged by short-sighted Soviets and self-obsessed Americans. Only China, a nation born to understand the long view of history, could see its true potential. A potential that could secure the future of the People's Republic as the next century's sole superpower, if only the chaos could be tamed.

Lau remembered a mess of spent bullet casings at his feet. There had been gunfire, confusion and death.

The guerrillas ambushed Lau's team on the road from Niassa. Insurgents, remnants from the Front for Liberation or the Mozambique Resistance Movement, or one of half a dozen other paramilitaries – in the melee that followed it was no longer important.

All that mattered to the men who attacked was that Lau's group were outsiders. Not whites, not Europeans or Westerners, but alien to them all the same. Perhaps they had seen through the veil of the team's cover legend and guessed that this so-called 'business mission' and their 'land surveys' were nothing of the sort. At the last township, there had been soldiers among the locals, and it was possible they recognised Lau and his comrades as military men, even out of uniform.

Or perhaps it was just poor timing. There were few people in north-eastern Mozambique who were not part of the civil war, and in that flashpoint, *'foreigner'* had become interchangeable with *'spy'* or *'mercenary'*.

They were soon overrun. Their hired guards died in the first salvo of shots from the trees, and their vehicles were expertly ruined with bullets through the radiators and tyres. As a punishing rain fell down upon them, beating the dirt road into a ribbon of mud, Lau was certain he was going to die there.

What surprised him was how little fear came with that realisation. A good son of the People's Republic should have wept to think he would perish unknown and forgotten so far from home, in a land so alien it had no ghosts. But Lau felt something else in that moment.

He felt *free*.

Zheng Ma – that skinny wretch, that rat of a man who would be the seed for the problems that came after – had crouched in the back of the Land Rover and trembled with abject terror. He clutched at Lau's arm, whispering that he did not want to die, he should not have to die, that he was too important to die. But no one here cared where he was from or who his family was.

Lau shook him off and counted the rounds in his Type 59 pistol. Too few bullets and too many men out there with murder on their minds. He took a breath of stale, wet air and steeled himself to go down fighting.

But then Lau saw other men coming. Other rebels, carrying rifles and shouting in fury. Leading them was an African no older than he, whose rain-swept face shone like polished teak wood and showed only fearlessness.

The three of them sat in the Airbus's conference room, in exhausted silence. Malte worked on bandaging Assim's arm, patching up the lacerations around his shoulder where splinters from the hull of the *Hermes* had cut him, while Lucy slumped in the chair, resting her head on the circular wooden table in the centre of the cabin.

Marc stared blankly at the artwork that dominated one wall of the room, a rich landscape in oils depicting the African veldt. Despite the beauty of the piece, it had always struck him as sparse and distant. It mirrored his own feelings, a sense of emptiness that came over him as the rush and fury of their escape faded.

What the hell do we do now?

The question that no one had asked, but that none of them could ignore, drifted in the brittle silence. Finally, Marc could stand it no longer and his frustration propelled him to his feet.

'I need . . .'

He hesitated.

What? A stiff drink? Twelve hours of sleep? A deep dark hole to crawl into? All of the above.

The curtain partition leading to the front of the jet slid open and revealed Solomon. Like the rest of them, he was tired and worse for wear. His jacket was gone, his trousers torn in several places, his tailored cotton shirt stained with dirt and sweat. But his face told the real story. His gaze passed over them, and in it was a mixture of gratitude, dread and resignation.

'Captain Silber has reprogrammed our IFF transponder to confuse any tracking,' he began. 'We will follow a staggered course along international borders to obfuscate our route.'

Marc accepted that with a nod. The latter was a tried and tested ploy used by military spyplanes, flying a course in the interface zone between the boundaries of two nations to avoid tracking by either one. Air traffic controllers, who were always overworked and understaffed no matter where they were, would see the jet on radar and assume it was talking to ATCs on the other side of the border, and vice versa.

Sticking to the blurred lines between radar coverage zones could get them away from the more densely populated airspace over Europe, but it would only work for so long. It was a tactic but not a solution.

'Where we headed?' said Lucy, taking a long breath.

'South,' said Solomon, confirming what Marc already suspected. 'Across the Sahara. I have given Captain Silber co-ordinates . . .' He stopped himself before he said more. 'We have enough fuel for a day's flight.'

Marc's pilot instincts kicked in, and he mentally calculated how far that could get them.

Not far enough to escape the Combine's grasp, he thought.

'We cannot risk connecting with any elements of the Rubicon network.' Solomon settled into another of the seats. 'We must assume that all SCD assets are similarly compromised.'

'So Rubicon is . . . lost?' Assim sounded plaintive.

'The Combine made their K-O move,' said Lucy. 'That guy Lau was their hitter, and he walked right in through the front door.' She looked to Assim. 'We have to consider ourselves rogue. As of now, Rubicon belongs to the Combine.' She paused, coldly considering her own words. 'And that is as bleak as shit.'

His work done, Malte stepped away from Assim's side and gave him a nod.

'Well,' began the hacker, 'at least we destroyed the Grey Record files. That's one thing they didn't get.'

Marc watched Solomon as Assim spoke, and the flicker in the other man's eyes answered a question that had been bothering him since they fled Monaco.

'That's not true, is it?'

The fatigue in Solomon's gaze was instantly gone, and he fixed Marc with a hard look.

'The more instances you have of a bit of data, the safer it is. The more copies of something that exist, the less chance there is of it being lost forever.' Marc looked back at Solomon. 'So I don't believe for one second that the server we cooked in Monaco is the only place that held the Grey Record.'

'As usual, Mr Dane, your insight does you credit.' Solomon leaned forward in his chair. 'A backup does exist. It mirrors the content of the Monaco server, along with several black budget caches.'

'We're going after it,' said Lucy.

Solomon nodded. 'When the Monaco server went offline, an encoded fail-safe was sent to the backup, causing it to disconnect from external communications. By now it will be in total lockdown.' He paused again. 'It represents the only power we have left. Securing it is a matter of survival.'

'So no connections in or out, no way for anyone to log on and access the data remotely.' Assim shifted uncomfortably in his chair. 'That means a physical intrusion, actually on site, to get to it.'

'I'm assuming you didn't just stash it in some branch office in Mombasa?' said Marc.

'It is in Mozambique.' Saying the name seemed to age Solomon. 'In the north. I chose a place . . . A place that I know well enough. It is in a concealed location that only two people are aware of.'

Lucy frowned. 'Who's the other person?'

'It's Delancort, isn't it?' Marc answered before Solomon could reply, and at length he gave a brisk nod. 'Great. What's to stop him spilling that to Lau or McFarlane, or whoever's running Rubicon now?'

'I do not believe Henri will give up that information,' said Solomon.

'Did you believe he was going to turn on us?' Marc snapped. It was a cheap shot, but his fatigue was making him irritable. 'It doesn't matter. If the Combine are inside Rubicon, the first thing they'll do is take the network to pieces, looking for leads on us and anywhere we'd go. They'll find that fail-safe eventually.'

'The situation is complex,' Solomon countered. 'Henri did what he thought was right.'

'Yeah, well, that doesn't cut any ice with me.'

Marc kept his focus on the other man, unwilling to yield any ground.

Malte sensed the growing tension in the room and rose, nudging Assim to come with him, and the hacker reluctantly followed.

When it was the three of them, Solomon went to a cabinet and poured them each a drink.

'There are facts you need to know,' he said at length.

'The accusations,' offered Lucy. 'Lau talked about war crimes. And your past with him . . .'

Solomon nodded. 'It is true, in its way.'

'Then you need to explain it to us.' Marc's tone turned grave and flint-hard. 'If we don't trust each other now, we've got nothing.'

Solomon's gaze turned inwards.

'When I met Lau Fa Weng for the first time, he was a bullet away from his death. And we changed the courses of each other's lives.'

The insurgents from the north had been a thorn in the side of Solomon's militia for months, pushing recklessly into their territory from hideouts near the border with Tanzania and striking with wild abandon.

Solomon's closest comrades – big and bellicose Barandi and even the more level-headed Simbarashe – wanted to take the fight to them. He had resisted, knowing that there were other battles to be won, but then the insurgents had forced his hand on the road to Niassa.

They had come too far and done too much to be allowed to escape unchallenged. Solomon's soldiers broke their ambush and in turn, broke them. The ones who were not shot fled into the undergrowth, and left him with the problem of what to do with the Chinamen they had been trying to kill.

Barandi's bloodlust was up, but Simbarashe saw the value of taking the foreigners hostage. Western corporations always paid fat bounties for the release of their agents, calling it a 'passage payment' instead of ransom money. China's powerful men would do the same for their people, he assumed.

They took them to their encampment, and for the most part the Chinese made no trouble, remaining watchful and respectful among the guns of Solomon's men. Simbarashe believed that was because they understood who was mighty here, but Solomon saw differently.

He saw how they watched, measuring and calculating. Especially the one called Lau, the nominal leader of these so-called businessmen. These were not what they appeared to be. Solomon had practically been born a soldier, and he smelled that same spoor on these men.

Lau's coolness impressed him. Here was a man, thousands of miles from his homeland in a place utterly alien to his experience, and yet he remained in control of himself. He was almost comfortable here, Solomon reflected.

They talked and they played chess, and Lau seemed in no hurry to leave. Solomon found himself liking the man; day by day, they drew back the layers of each other, finding something kindred.

Why are you really here, in my nation? Solomon asked him that one night, as they drank warm beers and listened to wood crack and spit in the campfire. *Why did your masters send you to Africa?*

Because I am not Chinese enough to serve in China.

Lau's reply was bitter and rueful. There was foreign blood in him, he explained, from a grandmother born in a bordering country. And perhaps there were foreign thoughts in his head. Not much, but enough for the men in power to deem him only worthy of duty in other lands.

I am here because I am considered disposable. You know how that feels, Ekko?

As a man grown to be a warlord, from a boy traded into slave-soldiery, he knew that very well. The sense that one's life was valueless destroyed everything; it made nothing matter. It gave power only in one place – in the manner of how you would die.

Or so Solomon had believed, until the day he killed the man who owned his life. On that day, he reclaimed his future. He took back not only the right to choose how he would die, but how he would *live*.

Soon he had some men with him, then some land and some power. Then some villages and mines and farms who looked to him for guardianship. With each new step, he drew a path towards a better tomorrow.

The insurgents came back that night, seeking revenge and hoping to kill the valuable hostages into the bargain. The ploy was devious and unexpected, and it caught Solomon's militia-men unprepared. The enemy almost succeeded.

But when the shots flashed brightly in the darkness, Solomon did not stop to think when he threw a rifle to Lau and let the other Chinese take up arms. Together, they killed every last insurgent who had dared to attack them. And by dawn, the thorn in Solomon's side was torn out.

'I presented Ekko with something that no one had ever offered him,' said Lau, limping to the conference room window as his walking stick clicked over the floor. 'A partnership of equals.'

'The group's foundation was backed by agents from Communist China?' McFarlane was incredulous. 'I can't believe that!'

'You do not understand.' Lau made a negative noise, a clicking of the tongue. 'That is a simplistic interpretation. Circumstances were far more complicated. Where it began – and what we did to bring it to pass – that is not important.' He eyed her. 'What is it that horrifies you? The fact that the roots of Solomon's empire were founded with bloodstained money? You are not so naive. Ethics and morals are an expensive indulgence. Rich men can enjoy them, the poor and the desperate seldom have the choice.'

'Most rich men don't bother with them either,' she muttered.

'Yes. A perverse truth, is it not? But not one that Solomon was willing to accept. He had different plans, and for a while I believed I could follow that same path.' He shook his head with a bitter chuckle. 'Foolishness on my part, of course. It seems I was the naive one.'

The men whom Lau served were often of narrow thinking. To them, victory was a binary construct. For every success, there had to be someone who failed. For every winner, there had to be a loser. It was beyond their hidebound mindset to conceive of a victory where *all* might profit from it. By their lights, mutual benefit was a sham. They would be happy to pretend that there was advantage on both sides, but that was a phantom promise. Their long views only showed a world where, in the end, it was China that stood alone and victorious.

That Lau thought otherwise was partially why he was out here on this mission into the wilderness. But ironically, it was also why he was best suited to warp the mission's end towards something more in line with his own way of thinking.

Solomon was well educated for a self-taught bush general, and he was cunning and thoughtful. He devoured books on history and geography, soaking up knowledge like a sponge. Lau saw an echo of himself in the African, he could not mistake it. Two men so different in birthright but so alike in instinct.

They were incapable of lying to one another. It was as if each man was glass to the other. It became the bedrock of the comradeship that was forged between them.

And so Lau's offer had no artifice to it.

China seeks a foothold in Africa, he told Solomon, seeing no point in obfuscating the reality. *It can be here, in your country.*

Lau and his men were only one group of scouts operating across the continent, looking for resources to secure, like the mines rich in iron, bauxite and rare earth minerals so vital for modern electronics. They were the pathfinders.

You can be part of this, he said. *We can make each other wealthy and influential. Command of land leads to guns, guns lead to power, power leads to freedom.*

At first Solomon was angry. *We do not want to be colonised again. Other nations tried that. I have no desire to repeat history.*

But this is not colonisation, insisted Lau, *this is a partnership*.

He promised a path between their nations where power was on an equal footing, and he meant it. Because this was as much an escape for him as it was a way for Solomon to forge the future he wanted.

China would never truly honour Lau's service to his nation, never recognise the sacrifices he had made. Never reward him with the life he deserved. But here, far beyond the gaze of the Dragon, he could find some measure of what he was owed.

'I agreed to it,' said Solomon.

A shaft of light through one of the windows played across his face as the jet made a gentle turn, briefly illuminating him before passing on and plunging him back into shadow.

Marc and Lucy exchanged glances but said nothing. There was much more to come, they could both sense it.

'Of course I agreed,' continued Solomon. 'If I had not, Barandi would have slit my throat and taken the offer in my stead. I could not have allowed him to give rise to the worst traits of our people.'

'So Lau gave you, what? Hardware? Weapons?'

Lucy looked distant, as if she was trying to picture it in her mind's eye.

Solomon gave a nod. 'Soon we had bricks and cement to rebuild houses and construct hospitals. Machines to help us open up the mines. And we had the guns we needed to ensure we kept them. Our territory grew and we became almost respectable.'

Marc looked back at the painting on the cabin wall.

'How long was it before Beijing started asking for something in return?'

'At the time . . .' Solomon frowned. 'They were far away. And in our arrogance, Lau and I believed that we could stay one step ahead of them.'

He chose the name because of a story he had known as a boy.

Before the dissolute priests at the orphanage sold him and the other children to the local warlord as fresh cannon fodder, Solomon had learned to read.

What drew him back time and time again to the orphanage's meagre library were the tales of ancient civilisations that had become dust and old stone. In a book about the Roman Empire, one story captured his imagination: the tale of how Julius Caesar, when commanded to disband his army and return to Rome, instead marched across the dividing line of a river in northeastern Italy and committed himself to an act of open rebellion.

Caesar refused to accept the orders of weaker men, choosing a path that would lead to civil war because he knew it was for the good of the empire. He declared *alea iacta est* – *the die has been cast* – and ignited the fires of a revolution.

The name of the river was *Rubicon*. And that strength of character, that will to defy all in the name of what was right – it was everything young Ekko aspired to be.

When Solomon and Lau made their pact, both men knew that, like Caesar, they had crossed a point of no return. There could be no turning back from the choice, and they had no intention of doing so.

Solomon wanted the power to bring peace to his embattled country, and Lau wanted purpose. In Rubicon they found it, giving a shape to something that would one day grow from a collective of mines and farms to an international megacorporation.

But that was in the future. In the beginning, the story was very different.

Barandi and some of the others resisted until they saw the benefits of Chinese assets making real differences in the poverty-stricken villages and outlying hamlets. The rising tide lifted all boats, and for a while it seemed that all was well. But as the months drew on, Solomon saw tension among Lau's men, a conflict that crystallised in disagreements between his new comrade and Zheng, Lau's second in command.

Lau was adaptable and intelligent, and he adjusted quickly to life in their country, but Zheng railed against it. He detested the food, the weather, the people, and he resented the orders that had forced him to come to Africa.

Solomon disliked Zheng as a matter of course, and the two of them kept a wary distance from one another. He learned from Lau that the man was the son of a highly placed official in the Chinese Communist Party, sent on this mission as a punishment for his indolent, self-interested manner. Zheng was a disappointment to his father. He was a spoiled child of a man accustomed to getting what he wanted without working for it, dispatched to Africa with the intent that the bush would teach him some humility. But all Zheng did was complain and scheme, his arrogance hardening as he was forced to live alongside foreigners he considered to be little better than animals.

Zheng's attitude had its roots far away, in the corridors of power in Beijing. The men who commanded Lau's mission grew dissatisfied with progress in Mozambique, seeing too little return for what they considered to be too much investment. Their long view began to shorten, turning towards Nigeria, Chad and Uganda, nations they considered more easily manipulated to

follow China's ends. Lau wanted to build real and genuine connections with Solomon's countrymen, but gradually Beijing's
hunger for resources overcame other concerns.

Even as they worked to build a better future, as possibilities
rose of new deposits of coltan and rare minerals in the mines
near the River Lugenda and Corte Vermelho, Solomon sensed
time falling short on a clock he had never set running.

Lau remembered most clearly the earth around the mine works.

The ground beneath his feet was rich and heavy, a dense red
the colour of the terracotta warriors he had once seen in Xian.
When the rains came, that earth became mud carved by slug-
gish trails of water the shade of arterial blood. And when blood
was shed across it, the colours merged into cloying, thick matter
that stained his clothes and his skin.

Zheng Ma died there, choking out his last, weeping in agony
with Lau's bullet in his belly. His blood seeping through his field
shirt, mingling with that of the men he had killed. The metallic
stink of death rising despite the damp air.

Looking back at that moment, it appeared that Zheng's death
was the inevitable endpoint for all that had come before, but at
the time it seemed impossible.

The day started badly. For weeks, the miners at Corte Vermelho had been deliberately slowing their work after word got
out that there might be new deposits of mineral wealth beneath
the ground. The men wanted more money to go deeper, work
longer hours, and take the risks that came with it.

Always angry, always spoiling for a fight but sly with it, Zheng
made sure that Solomon's comrades were miles away when he
took a truck full of armed men to the mine. He left word for Lau

that he was going to 'correct' the lazy natives and put them back to work. He took only Chinese men, with rifles and the heavy machine gun from the encampment's armoury. He was tired of pretending to be a partner to these foreigners. He wanted to put terror in their hearts, to remind them how little their lives mattered and who was in charge.

Zheng had not known compassion in his life, or grown up in a place where his wants and needs had not been immediately met. The seething resentment churning inside him at his father's refusal to let him return home found expression in acts of cruelty. He was careful to conceal these thoughts, taking it out on raiders or thieves. But on that day, he no longer cared enough to hide it.

Solomon took jeeps loaded with his men to the mine, racing at dangerous speeds along the waterlogged roads. Lau was at his side, silent and fearing the worst, fears made real as they crested the ridge near the mine and heard the popping of pistol shots on the wind.

When they reached the pithead, there were already dead mineworkers lying in the mud. Each had fallen from a kneeling position, shot through the skull in the manner of military execution taught by the army of the People's Republic. Zheng screamed and berated the rest of the workers, his mask of apathy dropping away to reveal the loathing he had for the Africans.

He turned that rage on Lau, screaming at him, calling him a traitor. The heavy machine gun was unveiled and drawn on Solomon and the workers. Zheng declared that Lau was unfit to lead the mission any longer.

For months now, Lau had been stalling commands from Beijing to abandon operations in Mozambique, ignoring his recall orders.

The Dragon was far away, he told himself, *and I am too small to matter.*

Zheng knew this. The demonstration taking place at the mine was his coup d'état, his way to take control and remove Lau in one action. He had no interest in Lau's attempts to defuse the situation. Zheng *wanted* it to escalate. He was *counting* on it.

One detail Lau had never been certain of was the identity of who fired the first shot. It might have been one of Solomon's men, pushed to rage by the shouting, braying little man standing in front of the truck. Or it could have been one of the *Ma Feng* team, encouraged to violence by Zheng's bombast.

The wet air was suddenly filled with the fizzing shriek of weapons, drowning out Lau's cries to cease fire. The machine gun opened up and so did the rifles in the hands of Solomon's men. The brutal crossfire took lives on either side, cutting down the workers pinned out of cover between them. Lau saw unarmed civilians shredded by the heavy RPK in the truck, and cursed Zheng's luck as the little man found protection behind a mine cart piled high with ore.

Until that moment, Lau's oath had always been loyalty to China, to the Party and the People, even if the love of his nation had been withheld from him, like the cold regard of a distant, unfeeling parent. To go against that, to put the life of any foreigner before one of his own, was a line that could never be crossed.

Lau took his pistol and charged through the chaos, finding Zheng where he cowered in the mud. The other man seemed confused as Lau aimed his gun at him, and he took that emotion to the grave.

The shot was a sudden crack of thunder among the commotion, bringing everything to a halt. Zheng cried and wept and died. It was an act that could not be undone.

The die was cast.

Solomon's men secretly buried the dead in unmarked mass graves near the mines, in fields where debris from the works scarred the earth.

Countless families were destroyed by the killings, lost in a few seconds of fire and madness. The horror of it sickened Solomon to his core, and in his shame he knew that he bore much of the responsibility for what had happened.

The first shot had been his.

For one furious moment, as he stood there in the mud and the hissing downpour, Solomon's control slipped from him. He saw Zheng, a weak and venal man concerned only with what benefited him, threatening to destroy what Rubicon could become. The AK-47 in his hands bucked hard as he pulled the trigger, but the accursed maggot moved too fast and the round missed its target.

The shot was the signal for hell to be released, and the air became thick with death. Solomon wanted to believe that he had shouted out, desperate to call back what he let loose, but that would have been a base lie.

In truth, he fired until the slide on his Kalashnikov locked open. He spent his ammunition on the men who had stood with Zheng, heedless of the innocents in the way. So great was his fury in those seconds that he could not control it, nor did he want to. It tapped into something dark within him, back to the empty place where his soul had faded during his life as a child soldier.

It would have been easy to march into that abyss once more, and if he had, Ekko Solomon would not have dragged himself out a second time.

The shock of that realisation brought him stillness, and in that silence one more gunshot sounded. Zheng perished at Lau's hand and the madness was at an end.

The cost of that day's work came at a price Solomon had no choice but to pay.

A week passed after the disposal of the dead, and as night began to fall the mutter of insects was cut by the heavy whirr of rotor blades. From out of the western sky came stocky Russian-made helicopters in olive drab, military transports with no visible insignia. One of the aircraft put down outside Solomon's encampment and disgorged squads of soldiers in helmets, body armour and savannah-coloured camouflage, while the second orbited away, heading in the direction of the nearest township.

The soldiers carried the same weapons that Lau's contacts had provided to Solomon's militia, but where the guns given to the Africans were used and battle-worn, those in the hands of the soldiers were parade-ground clean. These were elite warriors, killers of a breed far removed from the bush-hardened fighters Solomon stood with.

Their commander removed his helmet and, despite years of age between them, the resemblance to Zheng Ma was unmistakable.

Which of you killed my son?

He asked the question in flawless Portuguese. His name was Zheng Ko, and he knew far more than he should have. The man showed no emotion as he made his threats. The Dragon had come to claim what belonged to it, in blood and treasure, and the transaction was brutally simple.

Zheng Ma's murderer would pay, and Solomon would pay, and Solomon's people would pay, and this would be allowed to happen or worse would come to pass.

To accept that demand is to willingly place chains around our own necks.

Solomon drew his pistol and his men brought up their guns. The Chinese did the same, the moment echoing what had taken place at the mine.

What was the stronger pull? Solomon wondered. *To friendship and to a kindred spirit, or to home and nation?*

He and Lau had become brothers, after a fashion, their bond forged by shared adversity and shared vision. Solomon was born in this land and he had shed blood for it all his life. To give it up now to a coloniser power would betray everything he believed in. But to challenge these invaders could spark a bloodbath that would end the lives of countless innocents.

So he surrendered Lau, knowing full well what the alternative would bring.

He told Zheng Ko the truth about his son's killing, showed him the gun that had fired the shot. Simbarashe brought Lau to them in chains, and Solomon did not meet his gaze as he gave him up.

He expected to see Lau die then and there, but whatever anger Zheng Ko might have had was shuttered away and controlled.

Lau will pay for his defiance, the soldier told him. *Dying here will mean nothing. He will be taken home to be made an example of.*

The other helicopter returned, and Zheng Ko allowed himself a smile.

There will need to be reparation, he noted. *You took our benevolence and abused it. Someone will have to pay.*

Solomon shook his head, knowing that only strength would rule this moment. There would be no obedience here. There was only defiance.

The second helicopter landed, and from it spilled a squad of Zheng Ko's men in disarray, under the guns of Barandi's war band. Wounded, disarmed and humbled, they had come to his township to teach a lesson and in turn they were taught not to underestimate Africa. Barandi's men hijacked the helicopter, captured the men and brought them back, to set an example of their own.

Solomon had the Chinese soldiers released, and out of the night came more and more of his militia, drawn to defend the encampment. Zheng Ko found himself outnumbered with twenty fighters to each of his elites. He looked into the eyes of the fearless.

Leave with what you carry, Solomon told him. *And do not return. Others may give you what you want, but not us. Not here.*

You are one man, said the soldier. *You are not Africa.*

No, admitted Solomon, as he stood at the head of two hundred rifles. *But I am enough.*

The air in the conference room had become arid, and Marc felt a tension across his shoulders as he gripped the glass in his hand too tightly.

Of all the possibilities he had wondered at, this was not what he had expected. Ekko Solomon, the man he had come to trust and admire, was guilty of everything he had been accused of.

'In the months after, as we solidified control, I learned that Lau had secretly surveyed the mines. They were richer than we could have hoped for. With that wealth, Rubicon was given life. And I vowed that I would use it for a just cause.'

'No wonder he hates you.' Marc let his reply come unfiltered. 'You gave him up. And when the men in Beijing realised they couldn't hit back at you, they took it out on him. They turned Lau into a walking warning – someone they could point to and say *this is what happens when you defy the Dragon*.'

'I did what I thought was right,' said Solomon.

It wasn't lost on any of them that he was echoing what he had said about Delancort hours earlier.

'They didn't give you a choice,' said Lucy, with an abrupt nod. 'There was a hard call to be made, and you didn't flinch. Lau would have done the same thing.'

'No . . .' Solomon shook his head. 'No, he would not. He was different from me. And I took that away from him.'

'This is why Rubicon is your penance.' Marc fixed him with an unflinching, accusatory glare. 'I always knew you were trying to atone for something.'

Solomon's eyes flashed, a mote of anger cutting through the haze of his remorse.

'I am born from blood and war,' he growled. 'And I have done much that I regret! But I do not seek forgiveness, Mr Dane. I strive to rebalance the scales.' Then the moment passed and he broke Marc's gaze. 'One does not escape guilt – one can only hold it at bay. I know you both understand that.'

Marc reached for a retort but found nothing. The rawness of Solomon's revelations, of his confession, were difficult to process but it rang true. And with the cold, unflinching clarity that came in its wake there was nothing left to do but focus on the here and now.

'To survive this, we must trust in one another,' said Solomon.

Lucy looked towards Marc, searching his face.

'Like you said, we've got nothing else left.'

SEVENTEEN

'When will I be allowed to leave?' Delancort glared at the sullen young police officer. 'I have been here for over a day!'

He gestured around the office where the black-jacketed ALEPH thugs had installed him in the aftermath of Solomon's escape.

After the power failure, the corridors of the Rubicon tower were empty, echoing spaces. Most of the staff had been processed out through police interviews and discharged. Whole sections of the building were dark and sealed off with security tape. Henri was forbidden to venture up to the crisis centre levels or the executive quarters, and he wondered what was going on there.

'This is intolerable!' he began again. 'If I am a suspect, arrest me and charge me with something! If not, let me go!'

'I have orders to keep you here,' said the policeman. 'You want me to put the cuffs back on? Sit down and be quiet.'

'I refuse!' Delancort's voice rose to a crack-throated shout. 'You have no right . . .'

He trailed off as a by-now familiar clicking sound signalled Lau's appearance, the older man leaning heavily on his walking stick.

Lau looked tired, but his eyes were clear and hard. He was being driven by a will that gave him energy beyond his years. He dismissed the police officer with a flick of the wrist and closed the door. He stood, rail-thin but still imposing, preventing Delancort from leaving.

'I apologise for neglecting you,' he said. 'Other matters required my attention.'

Delancort launched into a replay of his complaints to the police, but Lau's expression soured with disinterest. The aide changed tack, going on the offensive.

'How long before they discover you are not actually an Interpol investigator?'

The corner of Lau's mouth quirked upwards in a faint smile.

'You do not know what you think you know.'

'I can hazard a guess as to who is running you, Mr Lau.' Delancort composed himself. If he could not demand his way out of this room, he would try to reason his way to freedom. 'Don't pretend otherwise, it is insulting to both of us.'

'No one *runs* me,' Lau warned. 'Do not make the mistake of believing that your opinion is of any importance here.' He tap-tapped his cane on the floor. 'There was a terrorist incident. People have been killed in this building! And I am the man that decides who is culpable. If I decide it is you, do you think anyone will listen to what you say?' He nodded at the city outside, where the daylight was fading. 'I speak a word, and ALEPH removes you from the world. Gone.' He made a biting motion, snapping with his teeth. 'Swallowed up in some nameless black site.'

'Where are the board? Where is Esther McFarlane? I want to speak to them.'

Delancort's attempt to meter his tone was failing.

'The Rubicon Group's directors are helping me with my inquiries, and it is your turn to do the same,' Lau replied. 'I will start with a simple question. Where do your loyalties lie, Mr Delancort?'

'To Rubicon.' His reply was instant, reflexively swift.

'Not to Solomon?'

'My loyalty is to my employer.' Delancort licked his lips. He did not like the direction the conversation was taking, and he tried to take control of it. 'Say what you came here to say! I am tired of playing games!'

'There is a backup of the Grey Record database. How do I access it?'

The blood drained from Delancort's face. It was worse than he thought. He had expected to be challenged on something he did not actually know, such as Solomon's whereabouts or his plans following the flight from Nice, but not *this*.

Lau held up a hand. 'Yes, let us dispense with the playing of games, the obfuscation and the denials. Do not waste my time pretending you know nothing of it.' That quirk of a smile rose and fell again. 'It is insulting to both of us.'

With the secure server in Monaco rendered worthless, and Rubicon's resources denied to him, or worse, being used against him, Ekko Solomon's options were scarce indeed. There were few places he could go to ground, fewer still where he might seek some way to protect himself.

Delancort felt suddenly light-headed, detached from the moment, as the import of what he knew became clear to him.

'Ekko is finished,' said Lau. 'This struggle is already over. All that remains is for you to choose where you will be standing, when the dust settles.'

As nightfall approached the hills of Corsica, the Italian returned to give Pytor Glovkonin a repeat performance of his strutting routine.

His helicopter dropped out of the sky with great drama, the glossy shape glittering as it caught the lights of the mansion house. Presently, he disembarked with the German woman in tow, and the secretary-bodyguard studied Glovkonin blankly with her doll-like, predatory eyes.

'I was passing,' lied the Italian, 'and I simply had to congratulate you, my friend!' He slapped Glovkonin on the back with false bonhomie. 'You must be pleased, eh? I expected to see a smile on that face!'

'When we are done,' he replied. 'It is too soon to celebrate.'

'Ah, so *you* say!' The Italian chuckled. 'I say, enjoy each victory as it comes to you. Like savouring each sip of a fine wine.' He looked around, as if seeking something. 'Speaking of which . . . Have one of your men bring us something to drink, eh? I know you have a few bottles of good rosé in the stocks. Perhaps that Sciacarello?'

Glovkonin nodded to his bodyguard Misha, who stood waiting near the helipad, and the man stepped away. He didn't dwell on how the Italian knew the exact contents of the mansion's wine cellar. It was another calculated statement, intended to remind Glovkonin of his place.

'Let's walk and talk.'

The other man led him into the ornamental gardens, and Glovkonin allowed it. A cool breeze was coming in off the sea, gently stirring the trees.

'Are they satisfied?'

Glovkonin decided to cut to the immediate matter, and looked out over the steep hillside.

'Our friend Lau was as good as his word,' said the Italian, with a flat chuckle. 'Rubicon is in disarray. Solomon has fled.' He eyed Glovkonin. 'So far, you have delivered what was expected. Consider the committee pleased, Pytor.'

It took a lot for him to ignore the other man's patronising tone.

'I keep my promises.'

'Yes.' The Italian smiled as Misha returned with the wine on a silver tray. He took a glass and toasted the air. 'Here's to success.' He sipped and gave the bodyguard an indulgent nod. '*Perfetto!*'

Glovkonin took a glass for himself, for appearances only. Wine was the drink of self-indulgent aristocrats and old men. He preferred something stronger.

Get to the point. He wanted to say the words out loud, and the Italian seemed to sense it.

'We have taken full advantage of the opportunities this scenario presented.' The Italian took another sip of wine. 'Ah. Our financial assets in Europe and the Far East have been deployed to manipulate market trends and share prices. The value of Rubicon Group stock has been severely depressed by news of their misdeeds!'

Monitoring the Nikkei, Dow Jones and NASDAQ indices, Glovkonin was well aware of Rubicon's tainted fortunes. The company board were distancing themselves from Solomon, without need of external coercion from Lau and the ALEPH thugs. Esther McFarlane, the interim chief executive officer, had made a statement assuring the public that all issues would be dealt with quickly. But investors were already cutting and running in droves.

The Italian gave a sigh. 'Confidence in Solomon's company wanes. We will continue to exacerbate that situation. It will become, as the British call it, a *carve-up.*' He made a slicing motion with an imaginary knife. 'And what we do not take from Rubicon, we will break.'

Glovkonin said nothing. He too had arranged for his financiers at G-Kor to bet against Rubicon's fortunes, shorting stocks to his best advantage.

'I am afraid you won't make as much from their troubles as you expected to,' said the Italian. His unsettling ability to read Glovkonin's train of thought was becoming annoying. 'But don't worry, we have it in hand. What benefits our organisation, benefits all within it.'

Glovkonin covered his irritation with a pull from his glass. He swallowed the overly sweet wine along with his resentment and presented a bland expression.

'Of course.'

The Italian turned his back on him, staring off towards the great house.

'There is still the matter of the intelligence data accumulated by Rubicon's private security division. I am told there have been complications in its recovery.'

'I have it in hand.' Glovkonin could not resist echoing the other man's words.

That seemed to amuse the Italian. 'I am pleased to hear it. I would hate to return to the committee with news that would mar our successes today.' He turned back to face him and the amusement was gone. 'The database in Monaco is ruined. How do you hope to reconstitute it?'

'There is a copy.'

Glovkonin relished the look on the Italian's face as, at last, he told him something he did not know. It was clear the other man had come here believing that the Grey Record was destroyed, and planned to use that failure to undercut Glovkonin with the other members of the Combine's committee. He took pleasure in correcting that assumption.

'Shortly before you arrived, Lau contacted me with information on an approximate location. I have already set a plan in motion to retrieve the data.'

'Very good . . .' The Italian recovered smoothly, but now there was a brittle note to his performance. 'We will deploy our resources to secure it.'

'That is not necessary.' Glovkonin maintained his detached aspect. 'I have operatives in play.'

'Operatives . . .' The other man picked out the word. 'Oh yes. The Japanese, your little samurai? Or is it the other one, the Arab assassin? Is he still alive? I forget . . .'

It was a poor attempt to rattle him, by showing that the Italian knew more about Glovkonin's assets than Glovkonin did about the Italian's.

Saito, the Japanese, had been a Combine agent long before he fell under Glovkonin's direct command, so it was no surprise the Italian knew of him. The Arab, as the other man referred to him, was Omar Khadir, the former terrorist cell commander with the now-defunct Al Sayf extremist group. That organisation had been wiped out by the Americans, but Khadir lived because Glovkonin protected him. In return, he became Glovkonin's personal knife in the dark. Khadir had been the one to kill Glovkonin's predecessor in the Combine hierarchy, and both of them shared a mutual hatred for Ekko Solomon.

He let the comments pass.

'Solomon has made a virtue of staying out of sight, but no man can be truly invisible. Over the years I have gathered extensive research material on him. His personality, his history. No one can escape their past, my friend. I will find Solomon, I will find the data, and soon neither will be of concern to anyone.'

The Italian put on a false smirk. 'Extensive material, eh? Do you keep such dossiers on all your enemies?'

'Of course,' said Glovkonin, and this time his smile was genuine.

Assim Kader and sleep had an odd relationship. He could go for days without it, a talent he honed in his youth during boarding school all-nighters, and it was a definite benefit when pulling a round-the-clock hacking session.

The only problem came when he crashed. That backed up sleep debt came down like a dense, cottony wave, and he was off to a dreamless abyss. He lost nearly fifteen hours this time, putting his head on one of the beds in the Airbus's guest cabins when they were still above the Med, and waking up to find them somewhere over the border zone between Malawi and Tanzania.

He wasted no time getting back to work, beginning with the black hat's breakfast of champions – a stale sandwich from the galley and a mug of dense coffee to wash down a handful of nootropic capsules. The pills were a cocktail of methylphenidate, Piracetam and *Panax ginseng*, brain-enhancing drugs that acted like vitamin shots for his grey matter. Assim wasn't 100 per cent sure they actually worked, but they were better for him than his on-off cigarette habit.

He found a seat in the common area and booted up his laptop. No one else was around, and he guessed the rest of the team were getting rest while they could. Assim considered checking in on Captain Silber up in the cockpit, but forgot about that when he saw a particular MESSAGE WAITING flag blinking on his screen. The flag displayed a distinctive icon, a stylised musical note, and its appearance made Assim's mouth go dry.

He checked again to be absolutely certain that he was alone, then logged on via the jet's on-board encrypted satellite router. Moving out through a series of data proxies, he connected to the wider grid of the internet.

The email message itself was heavily coded, but he had a one-time digital key that opened it without issue. There was no text in the correspondence, only an attached photo. It was a big file, a large, high-resolution image of a cute kitten playing with a ball of string. But for the size of the file, it could have been the kind of trivial thing anyone might post to their social media feed. On first look, it was meaningless.

There were no instructions explaining what to do with the image file, but Assim didn't need them. He had already agreed a delivery process with the source providing him information along the dark web's clandestine back channels. Everything so far had been gold. He expected no less. His source was one of the best net rangers out there.

The kitten picture went into a decoder program, and pixel by pixel, it transformed into pages of text. Through a process called steganography, the covering image was stripped away until the real data hidden within was revealed.

Assim's eyes widened as he read what the source had purloined for him. Most of the material came from a partly redacted file with CIA security headers. It referred to an asset with the codename 'Regal', a woman deployed undercover in Europe as part of a programme to probe for intelligence leaks in the EU security community. As he dived deeper into the document, Assim became more and more certain that Regal was the woman they had been tracking in Cyprus. *The perfect mimic*, he thought, *she doubled for Marc's ex.*

Regal was extremely good at her job. The file commended a mission where she assumed the identity of a French military liaison and under that woman's name, placed several software implants on a computer mainframe in their embassy in Germany.

But then Regal began to show signs of 'intransigence, disinterest in mission goals and questionable morality'. Assim wondered what the latter meant, given the reputation of the Central Intelligence Agency for its own dubious moral compass.

One day Regal didn't report in to her handler. The next the CIA knew about their asset was when the wife of a prominent Emirati prince apparently masterminded a million-dollar jewel heist in Abu Dhabi. The wife was found four thousand miles away on the same day, and swore her innocence, later describing a Spanish woman as the culprit. The Spaniard was a match for Regal.

'Is that her?'

Assim jerked in shock. He had been so engrossed in the file, he hadn't heard Marc approaching. He looked up at the other man, seeing the weary resignation on his face. Behind Marc, Assim caught a glimpse of Lucy getting something to eat from the galley.

'It looks that way.' Assim turned the screen and Marc dropped onto the couch next to him, leaning in for a closer look. 'I asked around for intel on this Grace person,' he said, using the woman's other alias. 'This is what came back.'

'Where's the data from?' said Lucy.

'The CIA by way of ... um ... my less than legal source.' Assim didn't elaborate beyond that.

Marc gave him a sideways glance, but didn't press the point. He read on in silence for a while, then sat back with a sigh.

'Matches up with what Lau said. She's a professional double. Trained by the Americans, but she cut loose and turned freelance.'

Assim saw the hollow look in Marc's eyes, and he felt a pang of sympathy.

'I'm really sorry.'

Marc shook his head. 'For what? That she's not really Samantha Green? Forget it,' he said sharply. Then Marc looked in Lucy's direction and that distance in his gaze went away. 'What's done is done.'

Assim felt like he was supposed to say something, but he didn't get the chance. Without warning, the fading light through the cabin windows abruptly shifted. The deck tilted so steeply that Lucy fell into the wall, and Assim scrambled to grab his laptop before it skidded off the low table and away across the carpeted floor.

Lucy grunted as she hauled herself up. 'What the hell . . . ?'

'*Everyone belt in!*' Ari Silber's voice barked out the command from a speaker in the ceiling. '*I'm afraid our girl has attracted some unwanted advances . . .*'

'Who did what?'

Assim didn't immediately understand what the pilot was getting at. The airliner continued to turn hard, the fuselage rattling alarmingly as it pivoted.

Marc ignored Silber's order and lurched across the cabin to the nearest window, pressing his face up to the clear plastic to scan the sky outside.

'There's something out there,' he called back. 'Other aircraft.'

The radar sweep displayed on the A350's cockpit monitor showed the steady progress of two arrowheads as they continued to vector in on an approach course.

Ari leaned across to the cockpit window and looked east-
wards as the Airbus levelled out. He searched the low cirrus
clouds for any sign of the incoming interceptors, but saw nothing. He blinked heavily. Fatigue was weighing on him. So far, his
only respite had been to catnap in short bursts over the duration
of the flight, but it was no substitute for real rest.

The challenge had come over the guard channel within a few
moments of crossing the northern border of Mozambique, like a
nasty surprise. The Airbus's reprogrammable IFF transponder was
supposed to be masking Rubicon Alpha One's true identity, telling
the world it was a chartered air cargo flight on its way to Johan-
nesburg. Operating under that false flag was, by all definitions of
international air law, hugely illegal, but it had never failed to work.

Until now. The timing could not be a coincidence.

The cockpit door thudded open and Ari glanced back as
Marc came rushing in. The Englishman didn't wait to be asked
and took the co-pilot's seat, slipping awkwardly into position as
he scanned the control panel.

'What's the flap?'

Ari pointed a thick finger at the radar screen.

'Say hello to the Forca Aérea de Moçambique.' He reeled off
the name with a flourish. 'Who are suddenly taking a serious
interest in our otherwise unremarkable aircraft.'

'Fighter patrol,' said Marc, with a frown. He fiddled with
a switch on his side of the cabin, adjusting a display screen.
'This feels familiar . . .'

Despite Marc being a helicopter pilot by training, Ari was willing to give a rotor-head like him the benefit of the doubt and
allow him into his office. Marc had been a good, if itinerant, stu-
dent on the occasional long-distance flights they shared, and last

year he'd shown some real mettle when called upon to handle an emergency landing aboard a hijacked commercial jet.

'They were waiting for us,' Ari told him. 'The first radio call didn't come from air traffic control or a military command asset. The lead pilot challenged me directly.'

The usual protocol would have been for an aircraft of dubious status to get a warning from the nearest ATC. Unless they were in airspace over a war zone, military intervention was typically a way down the list.

'What did he say?'

Ari opened his mouth to reply, but the man he was talking about decided to insert himself into the conversation.

'*Unknown civilian aircraft in our sector, this is F-A-M. State your identity, heading and fuel status, over.*'

The voice of the interceptor pilot was husky and quick, muffled by the cover of an oxygen mask.

'He said that,' Ari explained. 'And I gave him the answer already.' He toggled the radio. 'F-A-M intercept, this is, uh, CargoTransit Nine Nine Heavy. Did you not copy our last? We have responded to your challenge, what is the issue, over?'

'There they are.'

Marc jabbed a finger out at the evening sky and Ari found a pair of sleek shapes in a two-ship formation off the port wing.

He recognised the characteristic 'lawn dart' silhouette. The camouflaged aircraft were MiG-21s, Russian-made fighter-interceptors. Ari had frequently crossed paths with the type of same aircraft flying Syrian or Egyptian colours, during his time with the Israeli Air Corps.

'I see heat-seekers on their rails,' added Marc. 'And drop tanks. That could mean they've been loitering up here for a while.'

Ari nodded. 'I have no doubt.'

'This might just be bad timing . . .'

The Englishman didn't have the conviction to sell the point. Instead, Marc pulled some maps from the chart bin and began leafing through them.

'Mama always said to me, *Ari, never forget it can always get worse.*'

As if to make dear Mama's point for her, the lead pilot radioed again.

'*Unknown civilian aircraft, this is F-A-M. There is a problem. You are suspected of smuggling and aiding terrorists, very serious. You will change course to . . .*' The pilot fell silent for a moment, possibly conferring with his wingman. When he returned, the pace of his words picked up. '*Yes, you will change course to Lichinga, where you will land immediately, do you understand, over?*'

'Lichinga . . .' Marc ran a finger over the map, quickly finding the location. 'That's an airport, south of our current position.'

'Civilian, not a military base,' said Ari. 'How about that?' He considered the situation. 'He sounds pretty rattled, eh? This smells fishy. No ATC challenge, no real explanation, and now trying to divert us to some random airstrip.'

'The nearest military airbase is at Nampula, off to the southeast,' said Marc. 'If this was a proper intercept, he'd divert us there.'

'Good point.' Ari keyed his microphone. 'F-A-M intercept, Cargo Transit Nine Nine Heavy responding. We can divert to Nampula, that runway is more suited to our aircraft—'

The interceptor pilot didn't allow Ari to finish, and barked out a reply.

'*Negative! You do as I say! Descend to land at Lichinga or you will be shot down, these are your orders!*'

'Rude,' muttered Ari. 'This fellow seems quite highly strung.'

'Let me give him a poke, yeah?' Off a nod from him, Marc slipped on a radio headset and added his own question. 'F-A-M intercept, we are carrying a cargo of . . . uh . . . tractor parts, we have nothing to do with smugglers or terrorists.'

'*Do not argue!*' the interceptor pilot spat back. '*We know who you are – we were told! Divert course or we will deal with you!*'

The trailing MiG peeled off, while the leader dropped back.

'I think your mum was right,' said Marc, after a moment. 'Someone's tipped off these blokes to look out for us. And that's a whole new problem.'

From out of nowhere, a flash of white tracer arced across the nose of the Airbus, cutting through the sky like bolts from some sci-fi blaster. Ari and Marc both recoiled in their seats, and the jet shuddered as the lead MiG-21 followed a heartbeat later, thundering across their path to veer up and back around.

'*That was your only warning,*' said the voice over the radio.

Ari gripped the flight yoke and put the jet into a slow southerly turn, weighing the situation.

'If the Combine have someone inside the local military,' he began, 'if they've activated them, how much do they know about our intentions?'

'This could just be a couple of fighter jocks who've been offered a bag of cash to put us down somewhere,' countered Marc. 'I mean, the Combine aren't omnipresent, but their money is.'

Ari glanced at the radar, seeing the MiGs drop into formation behind them.

'The outcome is still the same. We are in the shit.'

'I don't disagree.'

An indicator on the control panel lit up orange-red and a familiar high-frequency tone sounded in the cockpit. Both former military aviators, Ari and Marc knew the sound of a missile threat alert. Civilian jets like the Airbus A350 didn't come with that kind of detection gear as standard, but Solomon's private aircraft had a lot of special modifications. One of the key devices was a MAW – a Missile Approach Warning system, technology that used passive laser detectors, capable of picking up the output of infrared heads on the tips of the deadly heat-seekers.

'He's going for a lock-on,' said Marc. 'We really pissed him off!'

'Countermeasures are on the right side panel,' Ari snapped, jabbing a finger in the direction of the console. 'I'm going to pretend our girl here is a fighter jet, you make with the distractions.'

Marc shot him a look. 'I know you're good, but even you can't outfly two MiGs with this bus.'

'Sad but true.' Ari reached for another sub-panel at his side, powering up another of the jet's clandestine systems. 'But we can shake them up . . .'

The MAW warning changed from a wheedling high-low cadence to a steady call, indicating an imminent attack, and Marc swore under his breath. He reached for the countermeasures console and pushed a release button marked *I-R.*

'Flares away!'

Pop-open panels beneath the tail of the Airbus ejected a scatter of silver tubes, which burst into blinding white fire as they fell into the jet's wake. The magnesium flares burned sun-hot, instantly giving the interceptors a huge false return for their heat-seeking missiles.

From inside the rear cabin, Lucy saw the brilliant white glow and knew exactly what it meant. More than once she had flown into the airbase at Kandahar, aboard a C-130 spitting 'angel' flares to baffle Taliban anti-aircraft launchers. She gripped the armrests of her seat and did the same thing she had then, putting her faith in the pilot to get her down in one piece.

'Ya Allah!' gasped Assim, from the seat next to her. 'Are we on fire?'

'Not yet,' said Solomon.

He and Malte had joined them moments after Marc sprinted off to the cockpit.

The Finn said nothing, staring straight ahead.

'That is not very reassuring,' Assim added.

Lucy was only half-listening. Through the window, she made out one of the interceptors veering wildly away, but the lead was still tucked in close, too close for a missile attack.

But near enough to use his guns.

A white spark lit up along the MiG's midline as the pilot triggered the interceptor's 23 mm autocannon, and fresh bursts of tracer bracketed the Airbus.

Marc felt the rounds hit the jet more than he heard them, the thick bullets smacking the fuselage with enough force to send a shock all the way forward to the co-pilot's seat.

A scattering of crimson indicators bloomed across the control panel, but Ari was already on top of it, his hands dancing over the field of switches with the dexterity of a concert pianist.

'All right,' said the pilot, icily calm despite the danger. 'The gloves are off now.' He shot Marc a look. 'Have you been briefed on the Stinger?'

'I thought that thing was still being tested.' Marc suddenly realised what Ari had been fiddling with before the gun attack, and forced himself to focus. 'Does it actually work?'

'Yes, and I don't know. Solomon's technical people fitted it a few months back, but we never had a hot check, so you might consider this a field trial.' He jerked his thumb at a shrouded panel at the rear of the flight deck, next to the jump seat. 'Go, get in there!'

Marc did as he was told, scrambling out of the co-pilot's position, and dragging himself back over the sharply canted deck as Ari made another turn.

Unlocking the jump seat panel revealed a multifunction digital screen and a stubby joystick. It was styled like an arcade video game, but the tech was military specification.

A power level monitor told him the battery packs in the hold were ready to discharge, and he flicked on the screen. Like an eyelid opening, the display blinked and suddenly Marc had an inverted view looking along the curve of the Airbus's ventral fuselage. The horizontal tailplanes were visible in the middle of the screen, blanked with an overlay cross-hatched in red. He gave the joystick an experimental flick, and the view shifted.

Down on the belly of the Airbus, a panel slid back to let a hemispheric turret emerge, the half-globe resembling the bulbous eye of some mechanical insect. It turned to track the trailing MiG, passive mass and motion sensors picking out the pursuing jet as it moved against the darkening sky.

Marc saw what the turret saw, catching sight of the interceptor as a sharp-angled shadow weaving right and left as it tried to stay in the Airbus's 6 o'clock position. It didn't help that Ari Silber was doing manoeuvres with the Airbus that would have given her designers a heart attack.

The ground rolled hard around the display panel and Marc was shoved back into the jump seat by the force of another banking turn. He saw what Ari was up to, extending his angle to lead the MiG into making a wider pass.

The interceptor pilot fell for it. Marc pictured him smiling behind his oxygen mask, looking for the payback he was going to give them for that trick with the flares.

Mate, you don't know the half of it.

Marc tapped the pre-fire control and a green light blinked. A set of cross hairs dividing the screen into quadrants drifted over the cloudscape and he steadied them on the shadow of the MiG. The Stinger didn't need to make a direct hit on its target; a glancing pass would do just as well.

'Ready. Ready. *Firing!*'

Marc squeezed the push-button trigger on the joystick and the screen whited out.

There was no sound of discharge, no recoil, no flash of light.

The beam from the emitter in the turret was invisible to the human eye – an oxygen-iodine laser in the 4000 megawatt range. It was too weak to burn through metal and inflict any physical damage on the pursuing MiG, but that wasn't the point. The laser's energy was specifically tuned to excite molecules present in the canopy of any attacking aircraft, so the effect of a successful hit briefly turned the pane of the MiG's windscreen into a flashgun.

For a split second, the inside of the MiG's cockpit lit up like a sunburst. The FAM pilot reacted with a scream and clapped one hand to his face, but he was too late to save his vision. Distorted purple after-images crowded his retinas, rendering him temporarily blind. Raging angrily into his microphone, the pilot fought with his plane, unable to read his controls.

'Good hit,' reported Marc, as the monitor returned to an active state. 'Target one is veering off, motion is erratic.'

'He'll get his sight back in a few minutes, if he doesn't fly himself into the dirt in the meantime.'

Ari searched the radar for the other jet. He hoped the other pilot would do the decent thing and form up alongside his buddy, to talk him through his predicament.

Instead, the MAW signal began to wail again, as the second MiG ignored his wingman and came around on an attack run.

'He's staying out of gun range,' said Marc, trying to follow the other jet with the turret.

That meant they would be facing one or more air-to-air missiles.

'I'm taking her down,' said Ari. 'The ground clutter will mask us.'

Marc nodded. 'I can't hit him at that distance.'

Ari shook his head. 'Forget it. Run the countermeasures instead.'

'Roger that.' Marc swapped seats once more, as the MAW's wailing grew louder.

'*You are going to die.*' The voice snarled over the guard channel. '*He said, tell Solomon that he should never have come back!*'

'Shut that idiot up,' muttered Ari, and Marc switched off the radio. 'I ever tell you my war story about the turkey shoot?'

'The what?' Marc shot him a confused look. 'Ari, this is not the time!'

'Oh, no,' he disagreed, 'it is. Helps me concentrate.' The Airbus's altimeter spiralled down as they descended over the savannah. 'See, the Syrians were putting SAMs into the Bekaa Valley, so we flew out to show them the folly of their intentions and—'

A flashing red alert blinked twice and Ari caught his breath.

'He's launched!' called Marc. 'One off . . . No, two!'

Somewhere behind them, a pair of AA-2 Atoll missiles were loose, their seeker heads finding the heat signatures from the Airbus's Rolls-Royce engines. At full burn, there were only seconds before a fatal impact.

The pilot continued his story, as if they were out on some pleasure flight.

'So I said to my wingman . . .' Ari gulped in a breath as he worked the throttle cluster. '*Eli*, I said, *it's good as long as you don't hear the bad sound,* and he said to me, *Ari, what's the bad sound?'*

'It's *that*,' said Marc, as the MAW began to scream.

'It is,' agreed Ari.

'Counters away!'

Marc didn't dare wait a moment longer, and he flicked the switches to send another torrent of anti-missile flares out into the Airbus's jet stream.

The first Atoll took the bait, sensing the bloom of heat and light, and it pivoted like a falling arrow, straight into the fiery mass of the flares. Losing its lock-on, the missile began to waver, before it finally lost all sign of its target and plunged towards the ground, blasting a shallow crater in the hillside.

The second missile hit the tail end of the flare bursts and its primitive control system became confused. For a second, the sky around it was filled with too many potential targets burning brightly, so many so that it could not tell where its objective lay. But the second Atoll's warhead had been primed with a proximity fuse instead of an impact trigger.

It exploded in mid-air, below and to one side of the Airbus, beneath the tip of the starboard wing. A cloud of shrapnel and fire ballooned, the force of the detonation shoving the wing upwards and clawing across the underside of the jet.

The missile detonation acted like a colossal shotgun blast into the starboard-side engine, ripping it apart. The fast-spinning turbine blades inside the engine cowling fractured and splintered, magnifying the damage done. Shards of razor-edged metal tore up through the wing and control surfaces, while dislocated bolts became bullets that cracked windows and punched holes in the fuselage.

The Airbus gave a low animal groan, and it skidded sideways through the sky. Trailing streamers of black smoke and pieces of metal, the jet began a terminal fall towards the dark wilderness below.

Agony rolled through Marc's skull, down his neck and across his shoulders. He was aware of blood streaming from a cut above his eye, and everything felt thick and slow.

Ari was calling his name and he rocked back in his seat.

Something blew up, said a ghostly voice in the distance. *Did you hit your head?*

A hard, cold wind shrieked around him in a banshee howl, pulling at the shattered remains of a broken window on the starboard side of the cabin. The air was thin and polar cold but breathable, and Marc blinked away his daze, seeing blood smeared on the control panel in front of him. He had the nauseating sense that he had lost time. There had been an abrupt lurch to port, and he remembered sudden pain and sparks of fire behind his eyes.

'You okay?' said Ari, around a wet cough. 'Lost you for a minute.'

'Yeah . . . ?'

Marc focused on the first thing he saw – the view out over the nose. The rolling plans of African savannah below them were parting to offer up a narrow ribbon of brown roadway in the middle of nowhere. The Airbus was dropping towards the ground at a giddying rate and Marc shook his head, as if that might dispel the image. He regretted that instantly, the pain returning with a vengeance.

'Don't worry, I'm just putting her on the deck.' Ari's voice was tight. 'Gear down . . .'

He pulled the lever to deploy the undercarriage, wincing with the effort.

'That's not a runway,' Marc said thickly.

It was hard to get his thoughts in order, each one moving too slowly.

Do you have a concussion? The ghost voice asked another question.

'No, but close enough, eh?' Ari drew back on the throttle. 'Flaps, Marc, can you . . . ?'

'Flaps, yeah.' He leaned in and deployed the control surfaces, grimacing at the number of red lights that came on. 'Done it.' Marc gritted his teeth, ignoring the pounding in his head.

Out through the missing window and the ragged tear in the side of the flight deck, Marc saw the black flashes of tree canopies streaking past, and unconsciously pulled tighter on his seat restraints.

'Brace, brace!' shouted Ari, his voice echoing back down the length of the plane over the on-board PA. 'Marc,' he said, without looking up from the controls, his voice dropping low. 'Talk to Vada for me, will you?'

Who is that?

For a moment, Marc couldn't connect the name with anyone he knew.

The Airbus hit the hard-packed dirt road and bounced off it. There hadn't been rains in this part of the country for some time, so the ground was parched and dusty. A cloud of earth erupted around the aircraft and swirled into harsh vortices. Flames licking at the gutted shell of the starboard-side engine blazed as the jet briefly left the ground and then came down again with a tortured, grinding crunch.

The second impact destroyed the tyres in the main landing gear, each one bursting like a gunshot. The surface of the track began to break and churn as the Airbus's brakes and thrust-reverser fought to slow it down. But with its mass unbalanced by the loss of one engine, the plane skidded and the nose veered off the road.

The forward landing gear crumpled and snapped clean off, forcing the nose into the ground. Kinetic force instantly transferred down the length of the fuselage and the Airbus shuddered into a hard yaw motion, flicking the port wing back and up while the ruined starboard wing dug into the ground and tore open.

For a moment, the jet rocked off to the right and then collapsed back into the deep gouge it had made in the dark earth. Washes of unspent aviation fuel sprayed across the hull and the ground, turning it to toxic mud. Inside the ruined engine, the hungry fires took on new life.

'Get them out!' Ari shouted at Marc, and the Englishman gave a distant nod, freeing himself from his straps. The younger man's face was a mask of blood and he seemed dazed, but he was alive and he could move, and for Ari Silber the most urgent thing right now was to make sure his people were safe. 'Go!'

'Okay.' Marc staggered towards the cabin door. 'You ... coming?'

'Right behind you,' he lied. 'Remember to talk to Vada.' He choked on his wife's name.

He listened to the thuds and bangs as Marc vanished down the length of the jet. He could see from the panel that one of the rear exits had already been deployed.

'Lucy,' he said to the air, tasting copper in his mouth. 'You two, you'll work it out.'

Now he was alone, Ari dared to look down at the puddle of sticky crimson pooling in the footwell beneath his seat. The hot, throbbing pain in his thigh was breathtaking.

His life was leaking out; his own aircraft had killed him, and that seemed funny. Ari managed a laugh amid the tears streaming down his face.

He could see the piece of metal, the shard of turbine blade that had knifed through the canopy and lodged in him. The femoral artery was down there, he recalled from field medical training.

A man takes that hit, his instructor had said, *call the rabbi, not the medic.*

It was a very, very bad hit. He could smell it, the blood along with the fuel-stink and the smoke. Was he going to burn before he bled out? Which would be the quickest?

He pictured Vada, Ezra and Leah, and under his breath Ari whispered the words of the Shema and the Verses of Unity. He wanted to tell them how sorry he was.

But the fire was coming.

EIGHTEEN

The sun had only been above the horizon for an hour, but the streets of Djibouti were active. It was a market day, and trains of women in headdresses and brightly coloured clothing thronged back and forth. Many carried bundles, bound to sell or trade, most of them heading towards the harbour to meet up with boats coming in from Yemen, neighbouring Somalia or ports further afield along the Red Sea corridor.

Observing from the upper floor of a crumbling two-storey colonial building, Saito scanned the pedestrians for any sign of the final arrival. It was a testament to her ability to blend in that he did not notice her until she was walking up to the door directly beneath him.

The woman who called herself Grace looked up, peeling back a length of bright orange cloth to reveal her face. She smiled as if she had scored a point from him, and inclined her head.

'She's here,' he called, and from below he heard Cord reply in the affirmative.

Saito closed the blinds and walked back to the inner balcony as Grace strode in below. The building had once been a hotel of some kind, with a cafe on the ground floor, but that had been gutted and boarded up. The open lower level made it an ideal staging area for operations in the Horn of Africa, and Saito had used it before. The locals knew well enough to ignore any foreign visitors who passed through, and bribes to the police kept it out of the public interest.

Grace shed the rest of her garb as she walked, revealing desert-shade tactical gear beneath it. A pistol hung from her hip in a low-visibility holster, and Saito saw that she also carried a combat dagger in a forearm sheath.

'Sorry I'm late,' she began, in a flat, unreadable accent. 'Traffic.'

Cord gave a grunt that could have been his equivalent of a laugh. His companion, the one Saito knew as Vine, threw the woman a nod of greeting. It was less than a week since the three of them had been deployed for the operation in Cyprus, but none of them commented on it. Saito didn't expect the sort of barrack room chatter common to other mercenary units. The Combine didn't employ those kinds of people, preferring to work with professionals at the more reticent end of the spectrum. Money paid for silence.

Still, Grace could not resist giving him another of those smiles.

'You called, I came, Jackie Chan. It was hard to resist the offer of a bonus that big.'

'She must be good.' A figure stepped into the room from the rear of the building, tall and imposing even in the careworn robe he wore. Omar Khadir looked the woman up and down, measuring her for purpose. 'If the Russian thinks we need her.'

'Glovkonin knows quality,' said Grace, briefly shifting to a pitch-perfect Muscovite intonation. 'What can I say? I am impressive.'

Khadir glanced up at Saito, then away.

'Indeed.' He walked to the middle of the room, where hard-case crates containing weapons and other gear had been neatly stacked. 'As we are here, can we begin?'

'Sure, whatever.'

Grace's pronunciation became mid-American as she sat heavily on an old chair and drained a bottle of water. Cord made his grunting noise again.

Saito glanced across the group.

'You will travel to Harare under one-time snap cover identities.' Off his nod, Cord distributed plastic packets containing passports, money, credit cards and pocket litter. 'Our contact in Zimbabwe has an aircraft prepared for your use. Crew will be provided.'

'Copy that,' said Vine.

'Khadir maintains operational control on the ground,' Saito continued. 'Your team will cross the border into Mozambique, and commence an active search to trace any members of the Rubicon Special Conditions Division who may still be alive. The location of the crash site and details of the surrounding area are in your packets . . . I will follow in two days.'

'Is there confirmation that anyone survived the crash?' Cord flicked through the pages, coming across a blurry satellite image of burning wreckage. 'We don't want to deploy for nothing.'

'Confirmation is what you are going to deliver,' said Saito.

'Say we find survivors, what then?' Vine looked towards Khadir. 'We do them quietly, or does there need to be some theatre? Are we sending a message?'

'We will proceed as circumstances permit,' said the Arab.

'To be clear, locating any Rubicon personnel is a means to an end. The main priority is to find the concealed storage facility they are looking for. Use whatever means that will give you that information.' Saito paused, allowing the orders to bed in. Torture was a tool he considered to be unreliable and highly distasteful, but he knew his opinions would be of little interest to this audience. 'Other, non-kinetic assets are searching for the same location through supplementary methods. You will be updated if those avenues prove successful.'

'And when we find this facility?' Grace cocked her head again.

Khadir answered for him. 'We secure the contents and kill whomever is left.' He glanced at Grace and the other men. 'I have one additional stipulation. If Ekko Solomon is there, I will be the one to end him.'

His tone made it clear that this was not to be questioned.

'You got a personal beef?' Grace was just on the right side of mockery. 'Oh yeah, I heard about that. His people fucked up your big showstopper back in DC, right? Guess you owe him.'

'Every effort is to be made to take Solomon *alive*,' Saito insisted, drawing a hard look from Khadir. 'Personal considerations are irrelevant. Is that understood?'

At length, the Arab gave a sullen nod.

'Very well.'

'Gather your equipment,' said Saito, cutting off any further conversation. 'A van will be here to pick you up in forty minutes.'

Awkwardly, he made his way back to another of the upper rooms. The heat of the day did not do well with the injuries that had forced him out of the field, sending jagged tics of discomfort up from the bullet splinters lodged in his flesh. Saito dry-swallowed a couple of painkillers and walked back to the shuttered window.

Behind him, the floorboards creaked as someone approached. He didn't need to turn around to know Khadir had followed him.

'There are some further details,' he said. 'For your attention only.'

'I assumed as much,' noted Khadir. 'The Russian is fond of nesting his plans inside one another. Like those toy dolls.' He took a breath, controlling his simmering anger. 'I was promised the kill, Saito.'

'And you will have it. But on Glovkonin's terms, not yours.' He paused. It offended Saito to be the conduit for the Russian's deceits, but he had little choice but to do as he was told. He lowered his voice. 'Glovkonin feels that the woman, Grace, is a liability. She is loyal only to herself.'

'Unlike us,' Khadir said quietly. 'I, loyal to my rage. You, loyal to your duty. Both of us trapped by our own natures.' He smiled thinly, and looked down at his hands. 'But unlike you, I can be freed from my burden. When Solomon dies that debt will be paid in full.'

'He may be dead already,' countered Saito, tamping down his irritation. 'Our reports on the crash are incomplete, but it is clear the aircraft was incinerated.'

'I choose to hope he survived,' said Khadir. 'Fate owes me the opportunity to be the instrument of his murder.' He eyed Saito. 'What happens to you when Rubicon is no more? *Ah*. Nothing, of course. You will remain locked in your path, obeying Glovkonin's orders no matter how objectionable you find them.'

'As you say,' Saito replied, 'I am loyal to my duty.'

'What does he have over you?' Khadir said softly. 'It must be compelling.'

'You will never know.'

At length, Khadir saw that Saito would not rise to his bait, so he let the point lie.

'If the Russian wants the woman dealt with, then why bring her out here and promise her money? There are easier ways.' He mimed a throat-slitting action.

'She has proven useful,' Saito admitted. 'But someone whose allegiance is easily bought must be kept in sight at all times. When – *if* – you find Solomon's people, he wishes you to dispatch her then.'

'I see the reasoning.' Khadir nodded to himself. 'Leave her with them. Make it appear as if they were allies. That will serve the Combine's ends.'

'In the end, everything does.'

Saito experienced a moment of bleak clarity, a sense that he was trapped in a tunnel with walls closing in on him, forced to move deeper and deeper into the dark. *Locked in his path.*

The nameless hamlet was little more than a cluster of tin-roofed shacks arranged in a rough grid around the eastern road, but it was the first thing approaching safe harbour any of them had seen all night, and silently they decided to take their chances there.

Under cover of darkness, they crossed into Cabo Delgado Province aboard a truck bartered for one of their assault rifles and a few magazines of ammunition. The fires from the crash lit up the sky, and burned around the tip of the low hill where the Airbus had finally come to rest after running out of roadway. Even now, the distant glow was still visible far behind them.

They stank of sweat, smoke and aviation fuel, crammed together inside a dilapidated barn on the edge of the dusty township. What they had among them was what had been carried out of the crashed jet on their backs. A few guns, some equipment, the contents of a couple of survival kits. Nothing else remained.

With each blow the Combine had scored against them, more and more had been stripped away. Now they counted one of their own in those losses.

Ari Silber had saved their lives. The veteran pilot had put the Airbus down in one piece, well enough that Marc, Lucy and the others were out of the wreck and free before they realised he wasn't coming after them.

The downed jet was already in flames as Marc tried to climb back up the emergency slide, but then the fire came over the top of the fuselage in thick orange talons and he knew it was too late for his friend.

He heard one of the FAM MiG-21s make a low pass to confirm the crash and then thunder away to the south. Marc stood there, rooted to the spot as the inferno consumed the crash site, until Malte came and pulled him away from the searing heat, and into the night.

People would come, Solomon told them, and it would not do to be here when they arrived.

Lucy took point and they formed into a ragged line, Solomon following her with Assim a few steps behind, Mark and Malte taking up the rear. Everyone had a weapon, for what it was worth, but Assim was only too happy to give up his when they made the trade down on the road.

No one spoke. There was nothing any one of them could say, nothing that wouldn't have seemed trite or pointless. A brave man was dead, and they were stranded here, in a wilderness that was unknown to all but one of them.

The truck was low on fuel when they found the hamlet, and they had only dead reckoning to guess they were heading in the right direction. They needed a map, they needed petrol and they needed rest.

When Malte slipped the truck into cover behind the shack, the five of them moved inside and found places to bed down. The Finn took the first watch, and Lucy the second. When Marc awoke for his turn before dawn, he thought he heard her swallow a faint sob.

'I'll take it from here,' he whispered, finding her in the back of the truck. 'Get some shut-eye.'

'Don't know if I want to.'

Lucy leaned into him and Marc put his arm around her, drawing her close. In their shared moment of loss, the simple act of human connection comforted them both.

She looked up at him and gave a rueful nod.

'Someone is going to have to tell his wife.'

'Vada.' Marc still felt heavy-headed from the blow he'd suffered in the cockpit. In his dazed state, he hadn't understood what Ari had been saying to him, but now he did. 'I think he knew, Lucy. He knew he was done.'

'Ari hauled us out of trouble more times than I could count,' she said softly. 'We couldn't do the same for him.'

'He was one of the good ones.'

Marc stumbled over the words and stopped. That was the truth, and there was nothing else to add to it. They had both buried enough friends to know that sometimes, no more needed to be said.

For a long while they held each other in silence, neither one wanting to break the embrace and let the moment end. This felt like *safety*, like *certainty*, even if that was an illusion.

Then at length, Lucy took a ragged breath and pulled away from him. She handed Marc the FN SCAR rifle she had strapped across her back, formally turning over guard duty.

'Sun'll be up soon,' she said, shifting back to business. 'Haven't seen any people yet, but I heard someone moving around about an hour ago, off to the west.'

Marc took the gun and checked it over.

'Could be a problem?'

'Never can tell.'

She moved to the back of the truck, but someone else was already there.

'These people will not trouble us if we do not interfere with their lives.' Solomon stood in the shadows, staring out towards the predawn glow on the horizon. He was wearing Malte's dusty combat jacket over his cotton shirt and his ruined Savile Row slacks. 'We must move on as soon as possible, for their sake as well as ours.'

'Couldn't sleep?' said Marc.

Solomon shook his head. He looked to Lucy.

'Would you join me for a walk, if you are not too tired?'

'Sure.' She stifled a yawn as she pulled out her denim shirt, concealing the Walther P99 pistol in the back of her belt. 'Where are we going?'

'We need a few items,' said Solomon, as the two of them walked off towards the centre of the township.

Marc spotted a few local children as the sun came up, a cluster of skinny young boys with a tattered football who played some half-hearted goal practice as an excuse to scope out the truck.

When they saw Marc in the back with the rifle, they decided to keep their distance, and so far no one else had come looking.

The others had not returned by the time Malte came out to take over, and despite his misgivings, Marc reluctantly returned to the abandoned barn.

Inside, the air was thick and unmoving and it smelled of animals. Assim, who had been running on adrenaline and caffeine for pretty much most of the last week, had finally lost his match with exhaustion. The Saudi hacker lay sprawled in an uncomfortable pose, all arms and legs like a scrawny, dozing cat. He snored gently, lost to the world, and Marc was unexpectedly jealous.

He instinctively knew what he would see if he closed his eyes. *Fire and dust. Darkness and smoke.*

He drank some water and made himself useful checking over the gear that had come with them after the crash landing. Marc's laptop was hooked up to a solar trickle charger wedged in between two wooden planks, and he saw that Assim had manage to jury-rig a satellite comms unit from two backup modules.

He unfolded a field antenna dish that looked like a collapsible pocket umbrella, and hooked it up, aiming it into the sky through a hole in the sheet metal roof. Within a few minutes, Marc was able to remotely access the internet via an orbiting telecommunications cluster, and he armoured his virtual self with layers of masking proxies that would hide his real-world location from any snoopers.

Marc Dane had been in this place before. Cut off from support, considered a criminal on the run.

The lessons that experience taught him had not gone unremembered. His life had become more secure after he joined the

Rubicon Group, but he knew that *security* was never as solid a concept as people believed it to be. Everything that mattered to you could be torn away in moments by disaster, by happenstance, or by malice, and that was a truth most people were too afraid to accept. Marc had learned the hard way how fragile life could be, and he had vowed to be as ready as he could the next time something went wrong.

And this was why he had assets of his own that not even Rubicon knew about: phantom servers out in the dark corners of the web stocked with bitcoin wallets, fake IDs and blacker-than-black hacking software.

Professional covert operatives like Lucy and Malte had gear caches and go-bags stowed in left luggage lockers in major cities, in case of emergency; Marc's secret stashes were the same, but digital.

He nicknamed them 'parachutes', because they were the last thing he would grab before leaping into the abyss. Each one was hidden behind walls of dead, old files, mostly ancient abandonware like forgotten 8-bit video games or office programs for computers that didn't exist any more.

He downloaded what he needed from a file called Blue Parachute, concealed on the server of a Madagascan college campus, conscious of the time he was spending online. Marc was well aware that the Combine's own hacker cadre would be out in the net, like a pack of hunter-killer subs sweeping the ocean depths for an elusive fugitive contact.

There was one other thing to do before he logged off. Marc was still processing the sudden shock of losing Ari Silber, and he couldn't help but wonder after the fate of another friend in the aftermath. His last sight of John Farrier being hustled aboard an

RAF medevac flight stuck in his mind, and Marc felt compelled to check in on his mentor's condition. In the midst of all going wrong around him, he desperately needed to hear something positive.

Hacking the outer layers of a military hospital's network was difficult but within Marc's talents, and he was soon inside. It would just be a drive-by, he told himself, a quick look to check on Farrier's status and then he would be gone.

But where John Farrier's patient notes were supposed to be, there was nothing but a blank page and a short string of digits.

Marc's throat turned dry. He recognised the digits as a contact number for Signal, an end-to-end encrypted communications app favoured by whistle-blowers and undercover agents worldwide.

Someone who knew Marc Dane had left a message in a place where he was likely to come looking.

He backed out of his hack and covered his virtual path. Marc visited Rubicon's coded email server and peeked in at his own personal data workspace, hosted on a computer back in the tower in Monaco. The same Signal code was waiting for him. Just to be sure, he visited a couple more sites that he knew had to be compromised, and each time the message was there.

Someone wants to talk to me, he thought.

It took a few minutes to prepare, to make sure that there were enough blinds in place to be certain he could not be tracked. At each stage, Marc paused, questioning whether this was worth the risk. It was clearly, unmistakably, an attempt to entrap him, but he took that as a small victory. If the Combine were reduced to using the same tactics as email spammers and social engineers trawling for credit card numbers, they had to be on the back foot.

He knew if he waited for the others to return, they would talk him out of it. Marc took a breath, and logged on.

The numbers took him to a virtual chat room where a single participant was already present. Marc's masking software made him invisible, so the lone voice was all alone there. At first it seemed to be an automated message, printing up line by line.

Mr Dane, if you are still alive.

I imagine your curiosity has gotten the better of you.

You need not worry about the health of your friend at MI6.

He is mending, but he has greater problems to deal with.

The tone was familiar. Stiff, formal, and superior. It had to be Lau.

By now you must understand the seriousness of your situation.

Nothing less than the complete disassembly of the SCD will suffice.

You and your comrades are in grave danger.

Will you speak to me?

A muscle twitched in Marc's hand as it hovered over the keyboard. It was impossible for Lau to know he was viewing the encrypted chat room, but the question still made his blood run cold.

'I don't think so,' Marc said quietly. 'You've gotta be desperate, haven't you, mate? You don't know where we are and that's making you anxious.'

After a while, Lau's messages resumed.

Do you recall what I told you in Monaco, Mr Dane?

You have had time to reflect on that and draw your own conclusions.

You are outside of the cage and you see it for what it is.

Solomon lied to you, and I know by now his guilt will have driven him to confess it.

You see, I told you the truth.

How many lives have his lies cost, Mr Dane?

You know that number far better than I.

Marc looked away, staring blankly into the middle distance. As hard as he had tried to push it away, Solomon's revelation that the allegations against him were true was as devastating a blow as Ari Silber's unexpected death.

There was so little in Marc's life he could consider as solid and unshakable, and part of that had been his faith in the man who had brought him into Rubicon. To know what they had done was built on dark money and smuggled guns, on blood and buried corpses, threatened to hollow him out.

More lines scrolled out across the screen.

Solomon chose his personal cause over his comrades.

He used the deaths of men in his own cadre to get what he wanted.

Now he tells himself he is atoning for that with his good deeds.

But that is a lie for himself and a lie for those he draws into his orbit.

Marc watched the words rise slowly upwards, his vision shrinking to the train of bright green text across the dark background, with everything else fading away.

When the moment comes, he will sacrifice you and your team for his ideal of a higher goal.

You know him.

You know this is true.

Marc hated himself for it, but he gave a vague nod as he read the words. Solomon was a man of singular will and vision, and Marc didn't doubt for one second that if it served a greater good, he was capable of making that choice.

There is still time to avoid becoming collateral damage, Mr Dane.

We will let you and the woman Keyes walk away.

Solomon is the only one who needs to fall for this to end.

Are you willing to give up your life and her life for his?

There was a sound outside near the truck, and it brought Marc racing back to the hot, stale reality of the barn. He let out a gasp of breath. He could hear Lucy's voice, quick and intent.

Mr Dane, if you are still alive, will you speak to me?

This is your last chance.

Solomon replied to whatever Lucy had said, a low and serious rumble like faraway thunder.

Marc scowled and clicked on the DISCONNECT tab, setting the laptop to flush the data caches and erase any record of the Signal communication ever having taken place.

The barn door slid open with a grinding creak that woke Assim with a start, as Lucy entered with Solomon a step behind. She was carrying a grubby laundry bag, and he had a net sack heavy with fruit and sweating cans of cola.

Lucy saw the expression on Marc's face that he tried to conceal.

'What's up?'

'Nothing.'

He covered with a yawn, suddenly finding it hard to look either of them in the eye. His own reaction surprised him. *Why aren't you telling them?*

Marc wasn't sure if he trusted Lau's offer. Anything that came from the Combine was tainted as a matter of course, but now there was a question forming in his mind, an option he might never have considered until this moment.

If it was him and Lucy – just Marc Dane and the one person in the world he still trusted without question – they *could* disappear.

And all of this, the deaths and the lies – they could leave it behind.

'What?' she repeated, coming closer, forcing him to hold her gaze.

Marc searched, but he couldn't find the words; and then Solomon was speaking.

'Gather everything,' he said. 'We are leaving.'

'Where are we going?' Assim said, blinking away sleep.

'For now, it is better that only I know our exact destination,' Solomon replied, his features unreadable.

Malte took the truck's wheel and Solomon joined him in the cab. After topping up the tank with a few gallons of gasoline from a plastic demijohn, Lucy scrambled into the back, beneath the ragged tarp that provided shade to the flatbed. Assim sat close to the front, staring out through a tear in the cloth to watch the road ahead, while Marc was low near a wheel well at the rear, taking up the shadows in one corner.

They bounced back onto the rough track and picked up speed. Lucy distributed the sodas and sweet, red-green mangoes before taking a spot opposite.

She pointed at her wrist as Marc worked his way around the fruit.

'Traded them for his watch and cufflinks,' Lucy explained, nodding in the cab's direction. 'I threw in a tactical flashlight and some euros. Along with a little local intel, it was a good deal.'

'Right.'

Marc chewed slowly, watching the sun-beaten road unfold behind them.

When the Brit turned monosyllabic, it was a bad sign. She'd known from the second she returned to the barn that something was bothering him, but if he wasn't going to open up, Lucy had little chance of prising it out. Marc's go-to was to withdraw and turn watchful, and if she pushed him, he'd slip further away. He'd come around eventually.

But she had her fill of the bleak silence that filled the truck as they drove through the night, and Lucy kept talking, hoping to hook Marc into the conversation as they sped through the savannah.

'We bartered a used cell phone from one of the villagers. A piece-of-shit burner, but it works.' He eyed her, but said nothing. 'Don't worry, we watched our info-sec. Short calls, pulled the SIM card and battery right after, just in case.'

'Why risk it at all?'

'Solomon reached out to a contact in country. His bush buddy from the bad old days. We need resources if we're gonna get through this in one piece.'

Marc tossed an inedible piece of mango into the truck's wake.

'We've not had much luck with old mates recently.'

'True enough,' she agreed. 'But Solomon's got this. I trust his judgement.'

Marc's head snapped up as she said the words, and for a second he looked like he was going to say something. Then he returned to the mango, picking off another strip to chew on.

On either side of the truck, palm trees and greenery crowded in on the sandy highway, and low plumes of ochre dust rose from the uneven road as they passed. Women balancing loads on their heads marched along the edges of the track, giving way as they raced by, and once or twice they drove around battered pickups heading in the opposite direction.

Solomon had told Lucy little more than a rough location for their target. The backup server was concealed in a building a few kilometres away, towards Mozambique's eastern coastline.

'Hidden in plain sight,' she told Marc, repeating Solomon's description.

'He say what we'll do once we find it?'

That thought had crossed her mind.

'I guess we get the hell out of Dodge.'

'And go where?'

She blew out a breath. Her patience was starting to thin.

'He didn't give me a slide show, Marc. We are doing this on the fly . . . That's S-O-P for you, you should be right at home with it.'

'Now is not the time to be working without a net,' he retorted. 'We need to be more proactive, less reactive.'

'You have something?' Lucy flipped it around on him. 'I'm listening. Seriously. I know you've been thinking up an angle, it's how you tick.'

'I . . . don't know.'

And when he said that, she knew he was lying to her.

'What—'

She was going to say *what are you not telling me?* But the truck bounced over a low hill and the brakes abruptly kicked in with a grinding crunch. Everyone lurched as the vehicle came to an unsteady halt and Lucy fell against Marc.

'Oh no,' said Assim, pressed to the rip in the tarpaulin cover. 'This looks bad.'

'Stay out of sight,' ordered Lucy

She climbed up on the top of the tailgate, peeking up over the back of the truck to look down its length.

Up ahead, a crossroads cut diagonally over the roadway, and parked nose to nose to block it were a pair of militia technicals and a big yellow Hummer H2 SUV. A handful of soldiers milled around, clearly waiting for something.

The technicals were battered Toyota pickups with heavy .50-calibre machine guns mounted on box-steel stands in the bed. Sharp-eyed men in ChiCom army surplus gear put their weight into the weapons to bring them to bear on the halted truck. If they chose to open fire, there was little chance anyone in the vehicle would survive.

'What was that you said about info-sec?'

Mark spoke in low tones from beneath her.

Lucy watched the Hummer's rear doors swing open, and a huge bull of a man climbed out. He was big enough that the vehicle rose noticeably without him in it. He started towards them, the soldiers on foot stepping back to give him room.

The big guy was clearly the top dog, as evidenced by the swagger in his walk and fact that his uniform was tailored. Like the other soldiers, the outfit had no other identifying insignia beyond a low-vis patch of the design from the Mozambique national flag – an AK-47 and a mattock tool crossed over a book, atop a pale five-point star.

That would suggest they were 'official' militia, tied to the country's leading Frelimo party, but Lucy knew well enough that appearances could be deceiving in this part of the world. Some zones down here were run more like warlords' fiefdoms, under the control of groups who made their own laws as long as they kept the ordinary folks in line and the insurgents at bay.

The big man noticed her and smiled, but it didn't reach his eyes. His hand dropped to his hip, where a large-frame revolver sat in a fast-draw holster.

With a creak of metal, the truck cab door opened and Solomon climbed out. The gunners on the .50s tracked their weapons to aim at him, but he didn't react.

The smile on the top dog's face went out like a light as he saw Solomon's face.

Not good, Lucy thought, and suddenly she wished she had a weapon of her own.

Solomon shot her a look and made a gesture with his open hand. *Stay back, be calm, don't interfere*, it said. That was fine, but Lucy didn't trust any of these men to think first and shoot second.

From beneath her in the flatbed, she heard the click of the SCAR's safety catch. Marc clearly shared her misgivings.

'Ekko,' said the big man, drawing out the name. 'It really is you.' He turned his head and spat into the dirt. 'It shows a great deal of arrogance to come back here, after what you did.'

He spoke unhurried, over-enunciated English with a smoker's growl. The look in his eye told Lucy that he wanted nothing more than to haul off right there, and crack Solomon across the chin with a right cross.

Solomon spread his open hands.

'Simbarashe, brother. Last time I saw you, we parted as friends. Or am I mistaken?'

'That was a long time ago,' said the man. 'The world has changed.'

'That's one of Solomon's soldier mates from the civil war,' said Marc, his voice filtering up to Lucy's vantage point.

'He doesn't look pleased to see him,' she said quietly.

The comment had barely left her mouth when Simbarashe lunged, cocking a fat haymaker of a fist at Solomon's head. At the last moment, Simbarashe halted the blow, and burst out laughing. For his part, Solomon never flinched, but the big man didn't notice or care.

'Ice water!' Simbarashe clapped Solomon on the shoulder and gestured to him, showing him off to his men. 'Didn't I tell you? This one has ice water in his veins!'

Given permission to do so, his men chuckled, and at length the long barrels of the .50s dropped away.

'The world may have changed but your sense of humour has not,' Solomon said dryly.

'The consistent man,' Simbarashe grinned, 'is the constant man.'

'Who said that? Marx?' Solomon eyed his old friend.

'No!' The other man made a mock-wounded face. 'It was me!' He looked Solomon up and down, then surveyed the truck, pausing to meet Lucy's gaze. 'Ekko, it seems your circumstances are in a poor state. If I ask you about the bird that fell from the sky last night, what will I learn?'

'Nothing that will benefit you.'

'Ah.' Simbarashe gave a solemn nod. 'Your plane has crashed and so have you. Did you come seeking the safety of home?'

'In a way.' Solomon paused. 'You told me you would meet us tomorrow, on the road to Pemba.'

'I couldn't wait!' he replied. 'I decided to intercept you early. If you are here, Ekko, you need my help.'

Was that jollity in his voice a little forced? Lucy couldn't be sure, and she had already decided to stay wary of the big man.

'Well,' she heard Assim say, 'he seems friendly ... more or less.'

'More or less,' repeated Marc.

The technicals moved out of their roadblock positions, making space for the truck to pass.

'You'll ride with me, brother,' insisted Simbarashe. 'Come, come!' He beckoned Solomon towards the Hummer. 'There is so much for us to discuss!'

Solomon gave a reluctant nod and shot a look back at the truck.

'Do not fall behind,' he called out.

He looked at Lucy and ran a fingertip over his cheek, beneath his eye, as if scratching an itch.

Stay alert.

She nodded and dropped back into the flatbed as Malte put the truck in gear. With another lurch it set off in the wake of the Hummer, and the technicals, now stuffed with soldiers, followed on behind.

'That seem weird to you?' Marc asked the question as he scoped out the closest pickup. 'And Solomon being up there on his own with that bloke? They could be talking about anything.'

'That Simbarashe dude had time and opportunity to smoke us back there,' Lucy noted. 'This is Solomon's old turf, Marc. We gotta let him play this out his way.'

'Do we?'

He let the question hang.

It was the middle of the day by the time they reached the site, and the sun was high and hard, bringing up mirage shimmers from the landscape.

The convoy parked in another nameless settlement, another grid of single-storey houses, with a low, squat structure crouching next to the highway that merged petrol station, general store and cafe. Further back Marc spotted a blockhouse-type construction that could have been a community hall or maybe a school. He noted that the buildings looked in better order than those of the hamlet where they had spent the previous night. Walls were sturdier, roofs were better made, and the tracks between them had been flattened out.

Simbarashe's soldiers disembarked and encouraged the cafe owner to feed and water them, and Marc watched the way the locals acted around the militia. They were cautious of them and their weapons, but it didn't look like the buttoned-down fear of a captive populace. Simbarashe didn't appear to be running a police state here, and there were even nods and smiles as the soldiers played a kickabout with some youngsters.

Malte put the truck close to their objective, a square plot of land on the edge of the little town, about half the size of a football pitch. In the centre of the square stood a ten- by ten-metre concrete cube, and emerging from its upper surface was a tall, spindly antenna tower. Rattling gently in the midday breeze, the tower was weathered metal and clusters of enclosed antennae, one of hundreds of similar masts scattered throughout the country to relay cellular telephone signals.

Civil infrastructure in this part of the world could be patchy at best, sometimes due to the remoteness of locations, sometimes because of cost, sometimes the victim of institutionalised corruption. Wired telecommunications were sparse, but the rise of cheap cell phone technology had leapt ahead of its cable and telegraph counterpart, and now the continent had one of the largest user bases for mobile phones in the world. People knew well enough to leave the cell towers alone, aware that each of the gleaming metal trees was a lifeline.

A fence of densely packed stainless steel chain-link surrounded it, rising to a height of around twenty metres, and there was only one way in or out, through a gate best described as 'substantial'.

Shouldering his daypack, Marc climbed out of the truck and peered at the lock on the gate. He expected to see a thick, industrial-grade deadbolt but instead there was a heavy-duty magnetic mechanism with no visible keypad or card slot.

Arranged in rings around the base of the tower, the black panes of solar cells captured the harsh daylight and channelled it into the cube. Marc guessed that surplus power would probably be passed over to the people in the town. The tower's base had the same kind of construction as the other buildings in the settlement.

'It was a deal they were happy to accept,' Solomon told him, walking up. 'One day, men came to this settlement and offered to build new homes for everyone, a new school . . . In return, they put up this cell tower and asked the locals to keep an eye on it. Everyone was given free smartphones when it went on line. We repeated the same trial in several places along the coast of East Africa.'

Marc took that in. A key part of Rubicon's corporate wealth came from managing telecoms subsidiaries in the developing world, and as he looked in through a gap in the fence, Marc could make out the company logo on a steel door in the side of the cube.

'So what are we doing here?'

Solomon leaned close to the hatch. He placed his heavy titanium signet ring with the onyx stone on the lock's blank face.

'We will recover the Grey Record.'

The hatch's bolts retracted with a loud thud that drew everyone's attention.

The cube beneath the antenna looked too small to house a server of the same dimensions as the one Marc had destroyed in Monaco, and he gave Solomon a questioning look.

'Can you bring that, please?' Solomon indicated an empty ammunition crate that one of Simbarashe's men had left on the ground. He looked across to Lucy. 'I am leaving you in charge.'

'Copy that,' she replied.

As Marc gathered up the crate, Simbarashe approached, smiling that alligator grin of his.

'You came out here for this place?' His manner became mocking and sly. 'Did you hide something there?' He laughed. 'I'll bet you did! It's so like him!' Simbarashe looked at Marc. 'He did this all the time when we were young, Ekko loves to play with secrets.'

There was a little bite on the last few words, but only Marc caught it.

Solomon was nodding. 'I apologise, old friend. This is your territory and I did not tell you I had buried something here. But it was necessary for everyone's protection. And I knew you could be trusted to keep these townships safe.'

Simbarashe bobbed his head. 'It is true, I am the guardian of these people. I'll forgive you . . . if you give me a cut! Ha!'

'We will talk about that when we return,' Solomon agreed. 'There is more we can do together, and you will be well compensated.'

Simbarashe made a fluttering motion near his head.

'Music to my ears!'

Solomon moved through the gate and Marc followed, picking his way around the strange metallic orchard of the solar arrays. At the steel door in the base of the cell tower, Solomon did the trick with the signet ring again, using embedded circuitry inside the ring to open a concealed lock.

They went inside, into a hot, dusty chamber no bigger than a prison cell. The air within was dry and heavy with ozone, and there was barely enough space to move. Racks of automatic routing gear and electronics crowded in.

'I don't see any backup server,' said Marc.

'We are standing on it,' Solomon explained.

He tapped the signet ring on what appeared to be a safety warning sign and the floor beneath Marc's feet twitched.

He stepped back as a seam opened in the metal panelling and a gust of cold, processed air washed upwards through the widening gap.

Lights blinked on, revealing a narrow steel stairwell extending down into the red earth.

NINETEEN

The creaking steel stairs descended into the sweating earth, and Marc found himself in a concrete chamber with a low ceiling. An anteroom, he guessed, dominated by a heavy steel hatch on slide runners. Hidden below the floor, he heard the humming of power and cooling systems.

As Solomon approached the metal door, automated lights flicked on and revealed a covered control panel, which he unlocked with a final touch of his signet ring key.

Marc put down the empty ammunition crate he was carrying and folded his arms, watching intently. Behind the panel was another voice-recognition mechanism, like the one in Monaco. Solomon whispered his *King Lear* quote once more, deactivating the first set of locks.

'Did you have a plan for opening this without Delancort?' said Marc.

'I brought you,' Solomon replied. 'You are one of the most resourceful men I have ever known—'

'Flattery will get you everywhere.' Marc cut him off and dropped his pack on the ground, rooting through it to pull out his laptop computer. He opened the device, folding it back on itself to turn it into a tablet screen, and ran his fingers over the touch-sensitive surface. 'Same code as before?'

'Correct.' Solomon frowned. 'You can circumvent the voice-print, yes?'

Instead of answering, Marc tapped out a string of text, and after a moment the computer spoke in a passable synthetic imitation of Henri Delancort's clipped French-Canadian accent.

'*Chacun voit midi à sa porte.*'

'You sampled his speech?'

Marc typed something else.

'*Correct*,' said the artificial Delancort. '*He likes the sound of his own voice so I had plenty to draw from.*'

'Henri would be unhappy if he knew.' The second set of locks retracted and Solomon took a step towards the hatch, then paused. 'Tell me, how many other patterns do you have stored on that device?'

Marc tapped in another code string, and Solomon's voice answered.

'*A few,*' said the computer.

The computer ran the same software the team had used to bypass the security of the Horizon Integral Corporation in Sydney a couple of years earlier. Marc's work on improving the code was an ongoing side project during his downtime.

'I have no recollection of authorising that,' Solomon noted, after he explained.

'Well, part of being resourceful is being prepared for any eventuality.'

'A fair point,' Solomon allowed.

He pulled a lever and the hatch slid back.

Cold air from the chamber beyond prickled over Marc's exposed skin and it was a relief from the dense heat up on the surface. He let himself enjoy it for a moment before following Solomon inside.

The backup server was smaller but functionally identical to the primary they had destroyed in the Rubicon tower. Racks of removable solid-state hard drives whirred in the air-cooled quiet, green *ready* lights blinking in unison to show they were powered and active. Marc looked up, finding a communications hub mounted on a support above his head. The device showed only crimson indicators, confirming that the backup's links to the wider world had been shut down according to plan.

He ran a hand over one of the drives. Each one was labelled with the name of a mythological figure. Marc saw *Charon*, *Athena*, *Phobos*, *Callisto*, and a dozen more.

'What's on these? Really?' he asked.

'The deeds that many men and nations would rather remain unknown,' said Solomon. 'And more than that ... Access data for black bank accounts in Switzerland and the Cayman Islands. Discretionary funds that not even the Rubicon board are aware of.'

'Parachutes,' Marc said quietly.

Solomon leaned across to take the handle of *Callisto*, and pulled it out with a smooth click, the light on the fascia fading. The drive was no larger than a paperback book, and he put it inside the ammo crate.

'We should proceed. I do not wish to remain down here any longer than we need to.'

'Right.'

Marc grabbed a drive labelled *Deimos* and did the same. The two men set to the work of detaching the modules, one after another.

After a moment, Solomon spoke again, and when he did there was something different in his voice – a vulnerability.

'I am sorry, Marc. For bringing you to this. For everything I have kept from you, and the others.'

'I understand why,' Marc told him. 'But don't ask me to excuse it.'

'What I told you and Lucy on the flight, about the shooting at the mine – I have revealed that to no one.' Solomon's gaze turned inwards. 'It is my responsibility to carry that guilt.'

Sam Green's face rose briefly in Marc's thoughts, along with those of his lost Nomad teammates.

'Yeah, I know how that goes.'

'You do,' said Solomon, with a nod. 'As do Lucy, and Malte and the others. All of us seek a way back from something we regret.'

Marc shot him a hard look. 'Yeah. But we need *trust*, Solomon. If we want to survive this, we need to believe in one another. No more secrets.'

'That is a difficult request,' said the other man. 'I have always been guarded. It is how I endured growing up under the gun.'

Marc tried to imagine what that had been like: forced to fight while still a boy, dragged through atrocities and firefights, unable to show the slightest sign of weakness for fear of being killed.

How would that shape you? What kind of man would you become?

'I've been searching for trust all my life.' Marc voiced the thought before he was even aware of it. 'When I was a kid, my dad dumped us. My mum and my sister Kate and me. Took everything, walked out of our lives and left us to fend for ourselves. We had nothing – no one to protect us from the wolves at the door. I know it doesn't compare to what you went through, but—'

'We fight the battles before us in our own way,' offered Solomon. 'There is no reward for greater suffering.'

'You'd think that after growing up like that, it would harden you. Make you doubt everyone and everything. But not me. I kept looking for what I didn't have. In the Navy, in Nomad. With Sam.' Marc paused, musing. 'I used to tell myself it was a flaw in my character. That it made me weak. But being part of Rubicon was the first time trust felt real to me in a long while. You understand that?'

The other man gave a solemn nod.

'No more secrets,' he intoned, and offered his hand.

Marc took it, but Solomon saw the flicker of doubt in his eyes. 'There is something else,' he said.

'Lau . . .' Marc saw Solomon stiffen at the mention of his nemesis. 'He reached out to me, after we escaped. Left me messages where he knew I'd find them.'

Solomon stepped away, his expression clouding.

'What did he offer you?'

'Lucy and me . . .' Marc began, 'He said he'd let us go if we gave you to the Combine.'

'Of course. I sacrificed him. He would have you sacrifice me.' Solomon returned to the drives, removing the next in line.

'Don't you want to know if I took him up on it?'

'That is not a question I need to ask.' Solomon didn't look at him. 'I trust you.'

In silence, they loaded the last of the drives into the ammo crate and Solomon deactivated the server rack for the final time. The cooling units beneath the rig stuttered to a halt and the chill in the air began a slow fade towards blood heat.

Marc shouldered his bag and grabbed one handle of the crate, while Solomon took the other.

'Now we have this, what are we going to do with it?' He jerked his head towards the crate. 'We made sure Glovkonin and his cronies don't get their paws on a ton of covert intelligence, but what next? Do we drop it in the sea? Fry it like we did back at the tower?'

'Destroy it in order to save it, you mean? Or do we use the Grey Record for the purpose it was intended?' Solomon shook his head, pulling at the sweat-stained collar of his grubby shirt. 'I confess to you, I have no good answer. I was uncertain we would even survive this long.'

'Huh. I always thought you were the man who had a plan for everything,' said Marc, as they stepped out into the bright, blazing sun.

'Yesterday, perhaps. Today I am following your example,' Solomon replied, with the hint of a smile. 'I am making this up as I go.'

But then the smile faded as they stepped past the fence line, and Marc saw what had suddenly taken Solomon's attention.

'So much . . .' grinned Simbarashe, making wide gestures with a Super Redhawk revolver in his fist. 'So much has changed, old friend.'

His militiamen were arranged in a row, their rifles raised and aimed towards Marc and Solomon. The warlord ambled back and forth in front of the soldiers, and down in the dirt before him, Lucy, Malte and Assim were on their knees with their hands on their heads.

'The problem with trust,' Solomon said quietly, 'is that one can misplace it.'

'What did you say?' Simbarashe's false grin was gone in an instant, and the swaggering belligerence that lurked beneath the surface took its place. 'Speak up, Ekko!'

He pointed his heavy-calibre gun in Solomon's direction; the weapon was a bear-killer, loaded with big bore .454 Casull rounds that would tear through an unarmoured human body.

'Do you know what saddens me most, brother?' Slowly, Solomon bent to put down the ammo crate, and Marc followed along. 'I would have expected this from Barandi, perhaps, but not you.'

Simbarashe gave a snorting laugh. 'You have become slow and complacent, with your riches and foreign friends.'

Marc locked eyes with Lucy and she looked to Malte, then back at the warlord. He knew what she was leading towards.

She'll wait until Simbarashe gets close to her, make a grab for him, and try to get him in a neck-lock before his men can shoot . . .

He shook his head. 'Don't,' he said. Marc had a sudden, horrible vision of them falling in a hail of bullets, the dry earth drinking their blood as they perished. 'You don't want to die here.'

'Dying here?' Simbarashe thought the words were directed at him, and he advanced on Marc. 'Dying is easy, *intruso*! Living, surviving here – that is hard!' He pointed at Solomon. 'That is why he ran away. Money made him weak.'

'But that is what you want, is it not? Riches?' said Solomon. 'What did they offer you?'

Simbarashe stiffened. He clearly had his own ideas about how this drama would play out, and he didn't like Solomon messing with the script.

'The Combine made me a very fine proposal, very fine indeed.' Simbarashe's crocodile grin returned.

'If money is what you desire, I will double what you were promised.' Solomon spread his hands. 'And unlike the Combine, you know I will keep my word.'

'You could do that, couldn't you?' Simbarashe spat the question back. 'You are so wealthy that it would mean nothing to pay your way out of this! The same way you got out of here and left the rest of us behind!' He spat into the dirt. 'You could pay me a hundred times what I was promised and it would not be enough, Ekko.'

Marc saw it then, the deep hate rising in the warlord's throat. It was old resentment and sour bitterness held back for decades, spewing out into the air.

'We went to war against men like the Combine.' Solomon tried again to reach his former friend, but he was wasting his breath. 'They are everything we fought to destroy. You hate me so much you would ally with them, just to humiliate me?'

'Yes!' Simbarashe roared the reply without a second's hesitation. 'A thousand times, yes!' He pulled back the Redhawk's hammer with one thumb, taking aim. 'You have no power here, Ekko Solomon. You sold it when you left us behind, Barandi and me and the rest. He was a thug but he believed in you. I knew better. I knew you abandoned us!'

Solomon's expression shifted. 'Barandi . . .'

'He is not dead, if that is what you think.' Simbarashe gave a snort. 'He lost his taste for the fight. He keeps a low profile and stays out of my way, if he knows what is good for him.'

The warlord kicked open the lid of the ammo crate and studied the hard drives piled inside it, unimpressed with what he saw.

'Brother,' Solomon began again, 'you must—'

'Do not tell me what I *must* do!' Simbarashe screamed the retort, and fired a thunderous shot from the revolver into the dirt, making everyone jump with shock. 'This is not your land any more, no matter what you paid for it! You will not be obeyed!'

'Then I surrender to you.' Solomon crouched, going down on one knee. 'I surrender, Simbarashe.'

'You give up too easily.' The other man was disgusted. 'I hardly recognise you.'

Solomon released a low sigh. 'I have already lost one of my people today. I have no wish to lose more. Promise me you will not harm them, and I will not resist.'

'Your people?' The warlord turned a callous glare towards Marc. 'You do not know the meaning of those words.' He walked away and gestured to his men. 'Put them in the trucks. I will claim their bounty.'

'Sir?'

Glovkonin looked up from the shimmering ashes in the pit of the hall's baroque fireplace and found the technician, the one called Andre, hovering nearby. The man had a satellite telephone in his hand, a light blinking on its screen.

'What do you want?'

'Contact,' said Andre. 'From the asset in Mozambique.'

Glovkonin eyed his subordinate. 'So deal with it. Give it to Saito.'

'He will only speak to you.' Andre offered the device. 'He says he has captured Ekko Solomon and he wants to discuss a . . . a reward.'

The Russian's face twisted briefly into a sneer and he snatched the handset from Andre's grip. Glovkonin dismissed the man with an angry flick of his wrist, rising from his armchair to stalk across the ornate room.

'My time is valuable and I have little tolerance for pretence,' he began. 'Speak.'

'*Do I have the pleasure of conversing with Mr Pytor Glovkonin of G-Kor?*'

The man on the other end of the line mangled his name, cutting it up into pieces with his clipped intonation.

Glovkonin drew in a hiss through his teeth. He disliked the exaggerated falsity and long-windedness of African manners, always seeing it as poor cover for baser intentions.

'Give me your name,' he demanded.

'*If you please, you are speaking with Colonel Surtur Simbarashe, military commander of the—*'

'I do not need to know your life story.'

Glovkonin nodded to himself. This was the man Saito had mentioned, the one whose name had been gleaned from the intelligence files on Solomon's past. A viable vector for influence, so he had been described, which was another way of saying he could be bought for the right price.

'*As you wish.*' Simbarashe's tone shifted, becoming curt and irritable. '*We will speak plainly.*'

'Good,' he replied. 'Tell me what you have.'

'*I am holding Ekko Solomon as my captive, along with four of his operatives. A British, an Arab, a European, an American woman. No harm has come to them, so far.*'

Glovkonin suppressed a smile. 'They may be carrying certain items—'

It was Simbarashe's turn to interrupt.

'*Yes, yes, their equipment is secure. Weapons, computers, other devices.*'

The Russian snapped his fingers at Andre, summoning him over.

'Where can I collect them? Give me co-ordinates. I have a team in the area, I will direct them to you.'

Simbarashe took a breath. '*There is the matter of recompense.*'

'What were you promised?'

'*Your man, Saito. When he contacted me, a figure of four million US dollars was discussed. However, there have been some complications.*'

'You'll be paid six million.'

Glovkonin didn't wait for Simbarashe to attempt to inflate the finder's fee, and cut off the train of conversation. The money was irrelevant. Solomon had acted as predicted, and now Glovkonin's enemy was within his grasp.

Solomon and the Grey Record would be Glovkonin's key to the inner circle of the Combine, the price of his passage to a seat at their highest table.

'*That will be sufficient,*' said Simbarashe, after a long pause.

'I want Solomon and his possessions perfectly intact, do you understand? Your fee is conditional on that fact. The other captives are of lesser importance.'

'*Of course.*'

'Do I need to tell you what will happen if you attempt to cheat us?'

'*No.*' Simbarashe bit out the word. '*The Combine's reputation is well known.*'

Glovkonin tossed the sat-phone back to Andre, who caught it awkwardly.

'Get the location co-ordinates from him and feed them to Khadir's team. I want this wrapped up.'

'Yes, sir.'

Andre nodded and walked away, pulling the handset to his ear.

The smile Glovkonin had fought against finally won the battle and it grew into a cruel slash across his face, then a muttering snarl of amusement. The sound of it echoed in the mansion's empty hall, and he caught sight of his own reflection in the towering French doors that led out to the gardens. In the grey half-light, he resembled a hawk forced into the shape of a man, a predator balanced perfectly before the moment of a killing strike.

This is how it will end, he told himself, sensing his fortunes pivoting around him, at long last aligning towards the victory he deserved.

This is how it will begin.

With rifle barrels resting between their shoulder blades, Lucy and the others were forced aboard Simbarashe's trucks and they rode in silence from the dusty township through the middle of the day. They drove north, the quality of the roads getting better with every mile, until at last the vehicles pulled into the walled grounds of a big Portuguese-style colonial mansion.

The building was shabby and faded, the sun-bleached stucco crumbling at the edges, and it reminded her of the kind of place that minor league cartel *jefes* kept down in South America. Maybe that was deliberate. Simbarashe seemed like the kind of guy who would think it was cool to emulate the *narco* style out here in East Africa.

The big man gave some orders and walked away, letting his soldier boys hustle them past the house and a few outbuildings, then down through a workshop and into a basement level. These men weren't smart enough to put hoods on their captives, so Lucy had a decent chance to scope the layout of the compound as they walked.

She saw more technicals parked out in front, armed guards patrolling the low walls, garages, a barracks block, and what looked like a vacant helipad in the back. Weapons and vehicles were everywhere, which would come in real useful, she mused.

In the basement, cages were set up with three reeking, threadbare cots in each, along with a slop bucket and nothing else. The holding cells were more like enclosures for animals, spaces where dogs would have been penned up out of sight. They weren't built for humans, but that didn't matter to the militia.

There were no partition walls, only rows of black steel bars that divided up the hot, stale space into roughly equal sections, allowing the captives to see one another. A single metal door with a window of reinforced glass looked in on them from a guardroom beyond, and light leaked into the basement through grimy pillbox slits high up the wall, level with the ground above.

Solomon had a cage to himself, and the rest of them were put into pairs, Marc and Lucy to one side, Assim and Malte to the other. The doors clanged loudly as they were shut, locked firmly by metal keys that were thick enough to look medieval.

One of the guards drew the butt of his Kalashnikov across the bars in front of them, making a rat-tat-tat noise as he laughed at them. Lucy thought about telling the fool to treat his long arm a little better, but kept her silence. Abusing his weapon would make it blow up in his face one day, and the grinning punk seemed like he deserved it.

Another of Simbarashe's militia apparently drew the short straw, glaring moodily at them when it became clear he had pulled guard duty.

'Can we get some water?' Marc made a drinking motion. 'Water? Yeah?'

The guard was in his mid-twenties, Lucy reckoned, built big but not muscular, and his uniform looked a size too small for comfort. He sucked his teeth, eyeballing Marc like the Brit had cussed out his mother, and then pulled a smartphone from his back pocket. He wandered away, fiddling with the device and pointedly ignoring them.

When the guardroom door slammed and locked, and it became obvious no water was on the way, Marc swore under his breath.

'Well, that tosser isn't going to get a tip.'

Malte was already working his way around the edges of the cage he shared with Assim, testing every bar at their welded joints, methodically searching for a weak spot.

Lucy looked closely at the lock on their cage, rapping it with a knuckle.

'Cast iron,' she pronounced. 'Like a goddamn Wild West jail.'

'They're not going to kill us,' said Assim to himself. 'They could have done that back in the township.'

Lucy saw how he was holding his hands together to stop them from shaking. The young man was a house cat, and it had never been plainer that he wasn't cut out for work in the field.

'Simbarashe will get his money,' Solomon said quietly. 'A price for one and all, no doubt.' He hung his head. 'I was a fool to think I could still believe in him.'

'Blaming yourself gets us nothing,' Lucy said, more sharply than she expected. 'We need to work on this problem.'

'They took the kit we had on us,' said Marc. 'Anyone got anything hidden away?'

'Yes.' Malte hesitated in his survey, and worked at his boot for a moment. His pale fingers came back with a stubby, skeleton-handled knife. 'Missed it.'

Lucy's lip curled. 'That's not much against an army of AK-carrying assholes.'

'Then we come up with a different exit strategy.' Marc crouched, scanning the floor. He found a bent nail and frowned at it. 'Can't pick the lock with this.'

'Could kill a guy with it,' Lucy offered.

'Hold that thought,' he replied, pulling at something half-buried in the dirt that covered the flagstone floor. A tiny length of chain glittered in his fingers, resembling the sort of toy-like bracelet one might give to a little girl.

'Give me that.'

Lucy took it from him and held it up to the light. It was a cheap trinket, the gold plating worn off along most of the length where someone had fingered it, kept it close. The edges were broken, and a chill came over her as she imagined who it had belonged to and where that person might be now.

'They've used these cells a lot,' said Marc, and she knew he was seeing the same thing she did.

'Yeah.'

Lucy didn't say any more than that.

'If we get out of here, where can we go?' Assim looked towards Solomon as he asked the question. 'We just flee . . . ?'

'Didn't come all this way to *run*.' It took a second for Lucy to realise that it was Malte who had spoken. It was rare to get more than two words out of the reticent Finn at a time, and Malte uttering complete sentences was practically unheard of. 'Cost us a good man to get to those drives.' He ran a hand through his hair, giving each of them a wary look. 'Can't leave them behind.'

'He's right,' said Marc. 'It's all or nothing.'

He moved to the corner of their shared cell, craning his neck to see into the guardroom.

Lucy did the same, and saw a sliver of the big-built guard's back. He was hunched over in a chair, backlit by a rainbow of bright colours coming off the game he was playing on his phone.

'Break the problem into bits,' said Marc, stepping back down. 'Last part first. We're out, we got the drives, we got a vehicle. Where do we go?'

All eyes turned to Solomon, and he looked up at them. At length, he gave a rueful nod.

'Barandi, perhaps. In the old days he had an airstrip close to the coastline. But we would have to get there first. It is hours away from here.'

Marc frowned. 'Would he help us?'

'Would he back-stab us?' Lucy asked, more pointedly.

Solomon sighed. 'I saved his life when we were young. He owes me that debt.'

Assim raised his hand, doing that schoolboy-in-a-classroom thing again.

'Uh ... I could work with that. I mean, there's someone I could call. To get us a plane.'

'Your black hat pal on the dark net?' Marc eyed him suspiciously.

'Don't ask, don't tell.' Assim gave a nervous chuckle. 'I need a cell phone and ten minutes.'

Lucy looked back at the door to the guardroom.

'Okay, let's start with that, and get him what he wants.'

Attracting the guard's attention was a case of Marc shouting and kicking the bars until the man couldn't ignore him any more, and with a rattle of the adjoining door's deadbolt, he came storming in with his rifle dangling from one hand. The phone he had been using was in his back pocket, the screen still aglow with his hi-scores.

'Shut up!' shouted the guard, waving the AK-47 in Marc's direction. 'I kill you if you don't shut up!'

'Do you want to be rich?'

Lucy put a seductive purr into her voice that gave everyone in the room a moment's pause. She immediately reeled in the guard, tamping down his bluster.

'What?'

'You see him?' Lucy pointed towards Solomon. 'You know who he is, right? You must've heard your boss talking about how loaded he is, right?'

The guard gave a slow nod but said nothing.

'Rich and powerful,' Lucy added.

'More wealth than you can imagine,' offered Marc. 'You let us out of here, you could be set for life.'

The guard started to snigger. 'How much?'

Solomon rose to his feet, adjusting his ragged cuffs as he stood.

'Name your price, my friend.'

The guard's snigger became a full-throated laugh, and Lucy cracked a smile along with him, enticing him a little closer.

But then the amusement turned hateful and angry.

'Fuck you!' He spat the words at them. 'The colonel told me you would try to buy me like I am a *puta*! I say fuck you and fuck your money! You will see what happens to *prositutas* here!'

The guard lifted the rifle and ordered Marc and Lucy to the back of the cage, then he unlocked the door and stepped inside, keeping the weapon trained on them.

'Easy, man,' said Marc, raising his hands.

The muzzle of the Kalashnikov pointed down at one of the soiled camp beds at the far side of the cage.

'Pick it up! Look underneath and you see!'

Marc wasn't sure what was going on here, but the guard was furious and too close to the trigger, so he did what he was told. Grabbing the side of the lightweight folding bed, Marc tilted it up to reveal the dirty stone floor beneath.

'Good grief.'

The words came from Assim, looking through the bars from the next cage.

Hidden by the shadows beneath the beds was bare stone stained rust-brown by patches of old, dried blood. The dark stains were running alive with tiny black insects feasting on the crusted fluids, and Marc felt his gorge rise. Someone had been cut here and left to bleed out.

'That is what is left of those who are bought and sold!' snarled the guard.

Marc let the bed drop back down, his breath caught in his throat.

'Okay, mate. You made your point.'

'We can still work something out.' Lucy said the words gently, taking a step towards the guard.

He whipped the gun towards her, and Marc instinctively advanced, getting into the younger man's personal space, putting a hand on his shoulder.

'Hey—!'

White fire exploded in Marc's skull as the rifle butt flew up and caught him across the side of the face. He stumbled into the guard, bouncing off him, staggering back until he tripped over his own feet and went down.

The guard shouted something at Lucy, but it was hard to understand. Marc's ears were filled with wool and he could only hear the rushing hiss of his own blood.

He held one hand to his head, clutching it as if he was afraid it would crack open.

The cage door clanged shut and the guard stormed out of the basement. Marc swallowed the pain, the hiss in his ears fading. He heard the thudding of boots on wooden stairs as the guards stomped up and out into the fading day.

Lucy helped him up. 'You break anything?'

'Just my face,' he said thickly, tasting blood.

'You never were that pretty,' she replied, in a way that made him smile a little, and that hurt, so he flinched.

Marc leaned against the bars and beckoned Assim closer. He dropped something into the Saudi's hand. The guard's phone, snatched from the man's pocket when they bumped.

'You sneaky sod,' Assim said admiringly. He tapped at the device and smiled.

'Yeah.'

Marc waved him away, probing along his jaw to make sure none of his teeth had been knocked loose.

'What exactly are you doing, Mr Kader?'

Solomon came to the door of his cage and hung onto the bars.

Assim worked at the phone, thumb-typing at a frenetic pace, pausing here and there as he replied.

'Think of it as . . . like calling for a ride-share . . . from a less than legal source . . .' He asked Solomon for the location of

Barandi's airstrip, and then typed that into his message. 'It'll cost us a bit,' he added.

'I suppose it will,' said Solomon.

'Given the day we've had . . . Shit, the *days we're having*,' Lucy said, correcting herself as she went on. 'You'll excuse me if I am having some issues right now. Assim, I didn't press you on this before, but now there's need. Who's this black hat you're talking to?'

'Someone I have confidence in,' he replied, and he wiped a film of sweat off his brow. 'Look, can we not have this conversation right now?'

Lucy's expression hardened. 'Last time you duck me on this, Assim. Last time, you get it?'

'Got it,' he replied, blowing out a breath. The hacker held out the phone at arm's length, peering at what he had written. 'Okay, I just have to—'

The heavy boots sounded on the stairs and this time they were racing down in double-time.

'He's coming back!' said Marc, as a shadow moved behind the locked door.

It slammed open and in came the guard, with two other men following quickly behind him. The guard's face was thunderous, and he swept the cages with a savage glare.

'Who took it?' he roared, bringing up his rifle. The gun turned towards Lucy and Marc. '*You?*'

'Took what?' said Marc, the lie sounding weak.

The guard spat an angry order at his comrades, and they opened the first cage, rushing inside. Marc and Lucy stood back, arms raised, as the guards tore around the makeshift cell, searching every corner of it and coming up with nothing.

Next, they pulled the two of them apart and rifled through their pockets. Lucy swore at one of the men as he pawed at her, and got a backhand slap for her troubles. Eventually, empty-handed, they stepped back out.

The guard changed targets, aiming his rifle at Assim. The Saudi was pale and shaky, and he looked as guilty as hell.

'You have it! Give me my phone!'

'I . . . I don't . . .'

Assim backed away, into the bars between his cell and Marc's.

'He doesn't have your bloody phone,' Marc snapped, stepping closer. 'Did you look in there?' He jerked his thumb at the guardroom. 'Maybe you dropped it—'

'I told you, shut up!'

The guard unlocked the second cage, and while one of the other men kept a pistol trained on Malte, he walked in and slammed Assim against the bars, hard enough to make Marc back off a few steps.

'Lying!' he snarled, his face a few centimetres from the young hacker's face. 'You will talk!'

Unseen by any of the others, Marc palmed the phone that Assim had slipped to him through the bars, but his heart was hammering in his chest. If he didn't give it up, his friend might die for it.

'It's not here!' Assim screamed the words, and he looked past the guard, right into Marc's eyes. 'It's not here,' he repeated, shaking his head. 'We d-don't have it, do we?'

'You will help me find it,' spat the guard

He dragged Assim out of the cell, hauling him away and out of the basement. The man with the pistol locked the cage and followed his comrades, leaving them alone again.

Lucy broke the grim silence that followed.

'What did we just let happen?'

Marc slipped the stolen phone from his sleeve and watched the stilted, repeating animation of an envelope winging its way from the device and into the ether. The screen spelled out *SENDING* over and over, and the process was taking forever. Then at last it gave a soft ping and the display changed to *SENT*.

'Done,' said Marc. 'He knew we had to cover until the message was gone.'

Lucy looked away. 'Assim just put his life on the line to do it.'

It was late in the day by the time they arrived at the rendezvous co-ordinates Glovkonin had provided.

The sun was vanishing below the far horizon as the gaunt Russian gunship came in low over the trees, the downwash from its rotors blasting the ground.

The Mil Mi-24 Hind D was an ugly, brutal machine, resembling a horror-show remix of a killer insect spliced to something low-slung and crocodilian. A heavy multi-barrelled cannon hung off the helicopter's chin, twitching in the air as the gunner in the forward bubble cockpit panned it back and forth over the buildings of Simbarashe's compound. Stub winglets on the Hind's flanks were heavy with rocket pods, enough that the machine could have laid waste to the central mansion with a single salvo.

Under orders from Khadir, who sat watching from behind the pilot in the secondary cockpit, the gunship made a long, slow orbit of the buildings, so that everyone within earshot would hear the menacing drone of its engines. At length, the Hind deployed a set of undercarriage and put down on the empty landing pad behind the mansion, blowing up a last wave of dust and detritus into the faces of the militiamen who had come out to meet their arrival.

The gunship had a large cabin for an aircraft of this type, with more than enough room for Khadir and the rest of the Combine's field team. The Arab disembarked first, followed by Grace and the two other men, Cord and Vine. They kept their weapons slung as they advanced, as the line of soldiers broke and one of Simbarashe's lieutenants presented himself.

'I am Dahma,' he told them, clutching at a forage cap on his head so that the gust from the idling rotors would not dislodge it. 'The colonel is expecting you. Please come this way.'

Dahma was heavyset, with a round face and small eyes, and he kept shooting wary looks at the parked Hind, like a man fearful of the reach of a chained dog.

Satisfied that the power dynamic of this relationship was already clear, Khadir inclined his head and gestured for Dahma to lead the way.

Behind him, the woman gave Vine a command.

'Stay here, keep watch. Don't let the locals get too close or talk to the chopper crew.'

'Right,' he replied, dropping his rifle into a ready position.

The militiamen dispersed in twos and threes, and Khadir frowned at their poor order. If they had officers here, they had to be few and far between. He had seen the same thing in other makeshift militaries, where those in command liked to have rank upon rank of common soldiers they could rule like serfs, and precious few men to delegate to.

Useful to know, he told himself.

If the need arose, terminating Simbarashe would likely put his forces into disarray if they had no clear line of authority beyond their self-appointed 'colonel'.

Dahma walked them through the lower floor of the house, past kitchens and living rooms with many expensive modern conveniences – huge widescreen televisions, bulky refrigerators, and so on – all of which were beyond the dreams of the common people living in Simbarashe's territory.

Khadir assumed that this man would meet them in one of these rooms, showing off his relative wealth as a way to cement his high status, but that did not happen. Instead, Dahma took them into an open vehicle garage where a large civilian SUV in bright canary yellow was parked. The vehicle was revving, and clustered around the back of it were several men in militia uniforms.

He saw Simbarashe step into view. The colonel wiped blood off his hands with a rag, and he met Khadir's gaze but did not dwell there.

'Ah, Mr Khadir. Your reputation precedes you! Welcome, welcome.' He flashed a practised smile. 'Forgive me, I have been busy with this.'

He gestured at a figure lying slumped against the back of the vehicle, then signalled to the driver to kill the engine.

Khadir moved to get a clearer look, wafting away the monoxide stink of exhaust fumes. A swarthy young man in his twenties, his face distorted by swelling, was tethered to the rear of the vehicle by cables around his wrists. Other cables led from his ankles to bolts fixed in the concrete floor, and the situation became apparent. If the vehicle inched forward, the young man would be pulled taut, his limbs distended. In ancient martial cultures, a disloyal man would be torn apart by horses in such a fashion. Here, the threat of that was being used for torture.

'Assim Kader,' said Cord, identifying the unfortunate victim. 'SCD's resident data thief.'

Glovkonin had provided the team with current intelligence on the members of Solomon's vigilante group.

'Not . . .' Kader's head jerked up at the mention of his name. 'Didn't . . . take anything.'

'Your employer did say that only Solomon was to be kept intact.' Simbarashe smiled coldly. 'This one made a fool of one of my soldiers.' He gestured vaguely in Kader's direction, indicating his handiwork. 'I have to maintain discipline, you understand. Examples must be made.'

'Of course.' Khadir's reply was a low mutter.

One of Kader's eyes was swollen shut, but he blinked up at Khadir and a slow change came over him as he recognised the towering Arab assassin.

'Oh, bollocks.'

'I will have this one cleaned up and placed with the others,' Simbarashe was saying. 'Now you are here, you may take the prizes we have captured for you.'

He said this to his men, giving them a smirk that they returned, pretending that he and they were the strong ones here, the victors.

This little game irritated Khadir down to his core. The pain inflicted on Kader – it had no real value beyond Simbarashe using it to show off how tough he was. Why else had he come in here and beaten a weaker person chained to a car? What other value could there have been to it?

Provincial, short-sighted men like Simbarashe always failed to understand that true authority came not from violence for violence's sake, but violence as a means of control. Khadir decided he would show him who was really in charge here.

'Get him on his feet,' Simbarashe was saying, and one of his men moved to detach the cables.

'No,' Khadir replied, drawing his pistol. 'I do not need this one.'

He put a single bullet through Kader's throat and the hacker's body shook, his life ending in a strangled choke as he fell forward against the restraints.

TWENTY

'What do you see?' said Lucy, shifting from foot to foot.

'No more activity at the helicopter.'

Malte was holding himself up to the slit-windows high up the wall, peering out into the gloom.

Marc sat on the edge of one of the folding beds, with the Finn's boot knife in one hand and the stolen cell phone in the other. He looked worse for wear, the new bloom of a nasty impact bruise on his face and one eye marked red with burst blood vessels.

'They're here for us,' he muttered, using the tip of the blade to lever open the phone's casing.

'Who's *they*?' she asked.

'Take a wild guess.'

Marc got into the device's guts and began poking around.

'Is that a good idea, Mr Dane?' Solomon was watching from the other cage. 'That is our only means of communication with the outside world.'

'It's our only means of escape,' Marc corrected, his attention totally focused on the innards of the phone. Lucy watched him peel off a thin sliver of microcircuitry and discard it.

Malte dropped back down to the floor with a grunt.

'Heard a gunshot,' he said quietly.

No one replied. None of them wanted to acknowledge what the sound might signify.

'Okay . . .' Marc stood and grabbed the grubby, stained blanket lying on the cot. 'Here we go.'

He held the torn-open phone up, and jabbed the tip of the knife into the battery pack inside, piercing the casing in a dozen places.

Immediately, faint wisps of white smoke began to issue out of the holes as the lithium-heavy compound inside the battery reacted with the moisture in the air.

'Get back!'

Marc jammed the sabotaged phone into the thin gap between their cage's lock mechanism and the door frame, wrapping the blanket around it.

Lucy smelled the bitter odour of a chemical reaction, and she knew what would come next. Cheap batteries in knock-off phones like the guard's handset were prone to overheat and catch alight in the wrong circumstances, a reaction that Marc was forcing in order to turn the device into a makeshift explosive.

With a fizzing, spitting jolt, the phone burst into flames as the battery went into catastrophic thermal runaway. Pinkish-blue fire flared around the cage lock, consuming the material of the blanket and burning into the metal.

Marc gave Lucy a nod, and together the pair of them aimed boot-heel kicks into the weakened lock mechanism. On the second blow, it gave and the door groaned open on its hinges.

While Marc smothered the remains of the smoking phone with another blanket, Lucy ran to the guardroom door and peered through the window.

Luck was on their side. The last man out of the basement had been so eager to leave, he had forgotten to throw the deadbolt. She slipped into the next room and searched it, quickly finding the bulky ring of keys in a desk drawer.

In moments, the other cells were open, and Solomon and Malte were free. Marc returned the Finn's knife with a nod.

'Thanks, mate.'

'We must escape and evade,' said Solomon. 'That is our priority now.'

'Copy that,' agreed Lucy. She glanced at Marc. 'I hope you brought some more bright ideas.'

'Yeah, me too,' he said.

The equipment and weapons taken from the Rubicon team were arranged on tables in one of the mansion's living rooms, guns piled on one side, hardware and portable computers on the other.

Khadir examined the inert shape of a thick-framed watch, then discarded it. Solomon and his people had been carrying little when they were captured, he reflected. At each stage of this scheme, their agency and the layers of their protection had been stripped away, paring them down again and again until all they had were the clothes on their backs.

They must have known they could not elude us forever, he thought. *Every road eventually runs out.*

'These are the real deal,' said Grace. Her peculiar, drifting-accent affectation had irritated Khadir at first, but now he no longer paid attention to it. The woman crouched over a steel ammunition crate, picking out the compact modules inside at random and comparing them to an image on a hand-held screen. 'Looks like they're intact. Your boss is gonna be pleased.'

Khadir gave a slow nod, wondering what kind of digital bounty was hidden on the consignment of hard drives.

Something worth a great deal, of course. Pytor Glovkonin would not commit so many resources to recovering them unless he believed they would enrich him still further.

A possibility flitted through Khadir's thoughts. He could take the drives for himself and vanish, use whatever was on them to rebuild his own mission. Although the Al Sayf terrorist network had been systematically dismantled by the American military, there were still sympathisers operating in the Middle East. A hard core of beleaguered jihadis and warriors with their own causes, who would take in a man like Omar Khadir on the strength of his reputation alone.

He lingered on the notion. It was true that Glovkonin had done much to protect Khadir from perishing along with Al Sayf, but that was a purely transactional relationship. The Russian had forced the Arab to become his own personal assassin, trading off safe harbour for the clandestine murders of his rivals. There was no loyalty between them, only the dynamics of power.

What would upset that relationship the most? wondered Khadir. *To steal this from him, or to use it to usurp him?*

Ekko Solomon's hoard of secret intelligence was to be Glovkonin's ticket into the heart of the Combine, that nest of moneyed power brokers who profited from the conflicts of lesser men. They were the ones who had bankrolled Al Sayf, and ultimately, the ones who had failed them.

Khadir picked up one of the drive modules and weighed it in his hand. He had never been a believer in Al Sayf's brand of bloody, fanatical Islamism. He was a nihilist, if truth be told, a man seeking a path that led to the destruction of the current world order. The thought that the Combine might be a tool towards that end amused him.

'Something funny?'

Grace was looking at him, one eyebrow arched in a quizzical expression.

'It would lose much in translation,' he offered, dropping the drive back into the crate. 'Send the Russian the picture.'

'I'm on it.'

Grace made a few keystrokes on her device, switching it to camera mode to capture images of the crate's contents. The photographs would be instantly transmitted to Glovkonin for his scrutiny.

Khadir stepped away, finding Simbarashe watching him with hooded eyes. Seated in a large leather chair on the far side of the room, the militia leader sipped from a tumbler of whisky and attempted to give an impression of disinterest. But he could not keep his attention from Khadir, Cord and Grace.

In the wake of Khadir's execution of the hacker, Simbarashe had at least shown enough awareness to understand that he was dealing with cold-blooded professionals, not the bellicose and ill-disciplined insurgents who were his usual enemies.

He cleared his throat. 'You are satisfied?'

Khadir didn't reply immediately. He waited for Grace to give him the nod that meant the Russian was content with the materials.

Her computer chimed as an incoming message arrived.

'All clear,' she said.

Khadir reached for the radio mike clipped to his tactical vest and spoke into it.

'Vine, bring the payment.'

Simbarashe downed the dregs of his drink.

'Good, good!' He jerked his chin at the plastic body bag lying in the room's far corner. 'You want that too?'

There were other bags rolled up and waiting to be used, next to the one containing the hacker's corpse. Khadir's hand dropped to his holstered pistol and he considered the best method of dispatching the remaining members of the SCD. Solomon was to be taken alive, despite his own desire for another outcome. The lives of the others, however, were less important.

Easier to kill them here, he decided.

Nothing would be gained by keeping them as live prisoners, especially given the SCD team's propensity to defy the odds. Khadir's gaze took in Grace and he considered her as well. Glovkonin's orders regarding her were clear. She was a loose end to be tied off. When the time came to execute Dane and the others, the last bullet would be for her.

It would be a clean, efficient end, and it would leave Khadir the freedom to decide what *he* wanted to do next.

The door opened and Vine entered with one of the militiamen following on behind him. He carried two steel-shell briefcases, placing them on a table. Khadir unlocked them, watching Simbarashe come closer. The man's greed was palpable.

He opened the cases to reveal dense wads of crisp US currency, stacked bundles of hundred-dollar bills.

'You've earned it,' said Khadir, but Simbarashe did not pick up on the sneer in his words.

'A pleasure doing business with you,' said the colonel, fingering the cash.

He shot a look at his men and barked out a command, and in turn, they picked up the ammunition crate and the body bag, carrying them away towards the landing pad and the waiting helicopter.

Khadir closed the lid of the nearest case with a snap, causing Simbarashe to flinch.

'Our business is not complete,' he reminded him. He patted the semi-automatic pistol at his waist. 'The other prisoners?'

'Of course!' Simbarashe was grinning widely. 'They're all yours!' He spat another order to one of his soldiers. 'Dahma, bring them here!'

'Yes, Colonel!' The other man nodded, and set off.

Khadir shifted position, seeing what had to happen next unfolding in his mind's eye. He would make the kills quickly and cleanly. There was no merit in prolonging the death of a defeated enemy.

Simbarashe gave him a sly look, nodding at the pistol as another of his men carried away his payment.

'Perhaps you would like some privacy to complete your transaction? I only ask you keep the mess to a minimum.'

He made a move to walk away, but Khadir held his arm.

'You should remain. A man should know who he is in business with, yes?'

Simbarashe's grin faltered.

'Of course.'

The darkness came quickly after sunset, and parts of the mansion compound were still thick with shadows where exterior lights had not come on.

Malte took point, with Marc and Solomon behind and Lucy at the rear. The Finn had their one weapon, the steel boot knife, keeping it poised and ready to strike as the group moved slowly from cover to cover. They stayed in the lee of the blockhouses, working their way around, avoiding the guards and the places where the lights from the house spilled out into the early evening.

Several hundred metres away, Marc caught sight of the intimidating shape of the Hind, sitting silently on the helipad.

At rest, the long rotor blades flexed gently in the breeze, and by the glow of the instrument panels, he could pick out the pilot and gunner in the cockpits.

'Can we take that from them?' Solomon said quietly.

'You get me in there, I'll fly it,' Marc replied.

Lucy dropped into a crouch next to them.

'Bad idea,' she said. 'Zero cover from here. Even if that guy with the gun pod didn't open up on us, the grounds are crawling with locals.'

She pointed up at the roof of the mansion house, and for the first time, Marc spotted shooters up there.

'Yeah, fair point.' Marc frowned. 'We don't know their numbers or weapons. There has to be a back way out of this place.'

'Company coming,' growled Malte, drawing back to the shadows. 'There.'

He pointed out three militia soldiers, one of them awkwardly carrying an ammo crate, the other two dragging a body bag between them. All of them had rifles over their shoulders, and they were talking among themselves, paying little attention to their surroundings.

'Heading towards the helo,' noted Lucy. 'Gonna pass right by us.'

'That one has the box containing the backup drives,' added Solomon. 'We cannot allow them to leave.'

'So how do you want to do this?' said Marc.

Lucy gave a shrug. 'We only need one that can talk, right?'

She stepped out of the bushes as the trio came closer, as casually as somebody out for an evening stroll.

'Can you fellas help me?' Lucy feigned confusion. 'I'm hitch-hiking to Wakanda and I got a little lost.'

The leading militia soldier dropped his end of the body bag in shock and fumbled for his weapon. In the same moment, his buddy with the ammo crate found himself in a neck-lock as Malte came out of nowhere and grabbed him in a sleeper hold. Marc and Solomon burst from their cover and ran for the third guy, who dithered over dropping his end of the bag.

The lead soldier brought his rifle up, but Lucy stepped in, getting close, and cracked him across the face with the hilt of Malte's boot knife. He recoiled and she punched him in the solar plexus. It was enough to put him on his ass, and she got an arm over his throat, following the Finn's lead to choke off the man's air and put him out for the count.

Marc tackled his man to the ground and tore his rifle off him. With Solomon's help, they had the guard face down in the dirt, holding him there with a knee in the back.

Malte and Lucy dragged their unconscious targets out of sight into the deeper shadows, securing them with their own belts and taking their AKs. The whole thing was over in less than thirty seconds.

Lucy squatted next to the captive.

'Hey. Shithead. Pay attention.'

He swore at her, the words muffled as Marc kept him pressed into the ground.

'Answer her questions and you may live,' Solomon told him.

Malte upended the dropped crate. The lid had cracked open and he peered inside.

'The drives,' he noted. 'All here.'

They exchanged a wary glance, and Lucy inclined her head towards the body bag. Malte gave a nod and moved to check it.

'Where's our friend?' she asked.

The guard gave a nervous chuckle.

'The Arab did it.'

'Yeah, he's an Arab,' said Marc. 'Where is he?'

'Not *that* Arab,' grated the captive. 'The other one, the soldier.'

'*Jumalauta!*'

Lucy didn't know the meaning of the Finnish curse, but the tone of Malte's voice told her all she needed to know. The ex-cop stood over the body bag, holding the zip half-open, and his pale face was hard as stone.

She had to see for herself. She took a step towards Malte, but he waved her off.

'Don't,' he told her. 'Assim . . .'

Malte stopped, unable to find the words, and finally he shook his head.

'You bastard!' Marc slammed the guard's head into the dirt. 'He was no threat to you!'

'Not me, not me!' bleated the guard. 'Ones from helicopter. The colonel beat him but the soldier, he kill!'

'Help me get him up,' demanded Marc, and he and Solomon pulled the guard into a kneeling position, holding his arms back. 'This Arab, he have a name?'

'The colonel call him Khadir.'

'Son of a bitch.'

Lucy's skin prickled. Four years ago, Omar Khadir and his terrorists had almost killed them, and while the rest of the world believed the man was dead or in hiding, she had always believed that they would cross paths again.

'We suspected Glovkonin had a hand in keeping him alive,' Solomon said gravely. 'He must be here as an agent of the Combine.'

'Who else?' Marc snarled the question. 'From the helicopter, who came?'

'Two white men. A woman. Like you, English.'

'Has to be Grace,' said Lucy. 'They've come to cross us off. Finish it.'

Marc wasn't listening to her. His voice turned ice-cold as he spoke into the guard's ear.

'We need a vehicle. You're going to take us to the garage, get it? You want to live, you won't fuck around.'

'Yes, yes.' The guard nodded frantically. 'I take you.'

'Move.'

Marc gave him a shove and let the man go. With Solomon, Lucy and Marc now brandishing AK-47s, the guard set off at a quick jog, throwing fearful looks over his shoulder.

Malte bent down and gathered up the body bag by himself, hoisting it over his shoulder in a fireman's carry.

'We don't leave him,' he said.

Solomon picked up the ammo crate and followed on, as Marc and Lucy went after their petrified guide.

She fell in step with Marc, who walked eyes-front, lost in his own dark thoughts.

'It's not on you,' said Lucy, her voice cracking as she spoke. 'We should have left him back in Monaco with Delancort.' She ran out of words and took a breath.

It was hitting her harder than expected and Lucy tried to get a grip on the surge of grief that churned in her chest. She'd lost friends and squad-mates before – every soldier knew that feeling – but this moment felt sombre and heavy. So soon after losing Ari Silber, so soon after being forced on the run by their enemies, in this moment Lucy felt the weight of it. A nagging, toxic thought sickened her: she'd gone into this unfit for field duty and people were dying because of it. She wanted the earth to open up and swallow her whole.

'No,' Marc was saying. 'Assim came with us because he believed in what we are. So did Ari. We didn't make them do it, Lucy, they chose to. So we push through. We keep fighting, for them.' He looked her way. 'Right?'

'Right,' she repeated, and the affirmation was what she needed to force the fear and the grief back where it belonged.

'Vehicle is here,' called the guard, from up ahead. He was looking around, trying to see in every direction at once, desperate to find some way out of his predicament. 'I help you, you let me go.'

Marc shouldered open the doors that opened into the barn-like garage. Inside, work lights illuminated the shape of the big yellow Hummer Lucy had seen out on the road that morning.

'This'll do,' said Marc, as Solomon and Malte vanished inside.

'You let me go,' repeated the guard, his voice rising. 'Now!'

'Calm down,' Lucy growled, throwing a look towards the mansion. He was going to attract attention if he didn't shut the hell up.

And then it went to shit.

The guard saw what he thought was an opportunity, with Marc distracted at the doors and only Lucy standing in his way. He threw himself at her, shoving her as hard as he could, snatching at the barrel of the AK-47 she had taken from him. He grabbed at her hands and tried to get his fingers around the assault rifle's trigger.

The weapon brayed, a wild burst going high and wide, and the guard cried out in surprise. He started shouting, and it was only a blow from the butt of Marc's rifle that silenced him, dropping the man into the dirt.

Voices called out from the roof of Simbarashe's mansion, and shadows moved up there.

'Damn it, we're blown!'

She shoved Marc into the garage and pulled the door shut behind her, leaving the semi-conscious guard where he had fallen.

'Kalashnikov,' said Cord, cocking his head like a dog, automatically parsing the sound of the weapon discharge. 'Close by.'

Khadir's pistol leapt into his hand and he spun to place the muzzle of the Beretta squarely between Simbarashe's eyes.

'What are you doing, Colonel?'

To his credit, the warlord seemed as surprised as Khadir was. 'I am doing nothing!' He recovered his composure and snarled as his second in command came rushing back into the room. 'Who is shooting?'

'Sir!' Dahma gave a sloppy, distracted salute. 'The cages are empty! Solomon is gone.'

'*What?*' Simbarashe exploded with rage. 'Find him, you idiot!'

Dahma nodded, running out into the hall, calling out to his men. Khadir glanced at Cord and Vine, and without a word, he indicated for them to follow.

'Copy,' said Cord, dropping his M4 into the ready.

As the mercenaries set off, Simbarashe retreated deeper into the room, his eyes darting around as he measured his options.

'You're not trying to fuck us over, are you, Surtur?' Grace used his first name as she picked up one of the discarded Rubicon sidearms. 'Because that would not go well for you.'

'Huh.' Simbarashe forced a sneer and took on a defiant posture. 'I am wondering if it *you* who are trying to fuck with *me*!' He waved at the air, looking towards his soldiers in the room, playing to them. 'Foreigners are all the same. Come and throw your weight around. All you are good for is talk and money, and I don't like to talk to you. You think we are fools!'

'You should be more concerned with fulfilling your part of our agreement,' Khadir told him. 'If you fail in that, I guarantee there will be nothing left to discuss.'

'Best bet is to put as much distance as we can between us and that Hind,' said Marc, searching a rack for the Hummer's ignition key. 'Once they get the gunship in the air, our odds of survival will be a lot worse.'

He found what he was looking for and ran to the driver's side door.

Behind him, Malte gently laid down the bag containing Assim's body in the rear cargo bay. Beside it, the crate of hard drives was lashed in place with webbing, and Marc found himself caught on the moment.

A box of secrets and lies, and we've already traded two good friends for it. The grim conclusion to the thought followed inexorably. *How much more is it going to cost us before this is over?*

Marc recalled Assim's eager grin and his mile-a-minute enthusiasm, and it seemed unreal, impossible to accept that the keen young hacker was gone.

He shook himself out of the reverie and climbed into the vehicle. Lucy was in the back, checking her weapons.

'You know where to go?' she said.

Marc looked to Solomon, who stood on the Hummer's running board, listening to the shouts from outside.

'What she said.'

'If you can drive, I will guide you,' he replied.

'I can drive,' Marc promised, and the Hummer rumbled into life.

The noise from beyond the garage doors grew louder, and then suddenly the wood was cracking and splintering as Simbarashe's militia blind-fired into the outbuilding.

Bullets spanked off the bonnet and the windscreen, cracking but not penetrating the toughened glass. Marc heard Lucy swear and Solomon flinched, lurching into the front passenger seat and out of the line of fire. Simbarashe had clearly spent the extra cash to pay for protective upgrades, but Marc had no desire to test the limits of its durability.

'Doors!' he shouted, throwing the Hummer into gear.

Marc held the brake for half a second and put it into a burnout, sending up a cloud of white fumes that filled the garage as the rear wheels spun and shrieked.

He let it go and stood on the accelerator pedal, the vehicle rocking forward like a charging bull. They crashed through the shredded doors, turning them to matchwood, and soldiers too slow to get out of the way thudded off the chrome-plated grille.

Gunfire sparked as Marc went into a skidding turn, pitching them over a dusty ornamental berm and down a wide track towards the compound's rear gate.

Lucy fired back, keeping low, using the door frame as cover, while Malte was standing on his seat, head and shoulders above the line of the open sunroof. Their AKs kept up a steady chatter of burst fire, directed to discourage any immediate pursuit.

Some of the militia were running towards a pair of technicals parked close by, looking to get on the heavy machine guns in their flatbeds and put .50-calibre rounds their way, but Marc had already put them in the rear-view, leaving them in a dusty backwash.

'Gate ahead!' he called out, as the Hummer's powerful headlights illuminated a five-metre tall barrier blocking off the compound from the roadway. He saw two white men in black tactical gear take up positions either side of the gate, and draw down on the oncoming vehicle. 'Contact forward!'

In the split second as they converged, Marc didn't read the faces of the mercenaries, but he knew the gear and he knew the guns.

M4 carbines and low-signature tactical rigs.

The same kit used by the Special Conditions Division, the same kit that their doppelgängers had used to double them back in Cyprus.

'See 'em!'

Behind him, Lucy switched angles to squeeze off a few more shots towards the gunmen, knocking off the aim of the one on the right.

The man on the left showed the cool hand of a professional soldier, and paced his shots. Marc realised he was aiming for the tyres.

Keeping the hammer down, Marc shoved the vehicle into a snaking motion over the track, as if he was passing through an invisible chicane. Bullets clanked off the framework and one of the headlights blew out, but then there was the shriek of tortured metal as the Hummer connected with the gate and threw it clean off its hinges.

Malte narrowly avoided decapitation, dropping back into the cabin as part of the metal barrier split and screeched up and over the top of the vehicle.

They bounded out onto the highway and the wheels bit into the asphalt.

'East,' said Solomon, panting with exertion. 'Go east!'

Khadir strode into the humid night, listening to the familiar chaos of gunshots and battle. He knew this music intimately, and if he was honest with himself, he missed it.

Striking from the gloom, killing the unwary – that was the assassin's way. As capable as he was of that, Khadir remained a soldier at heart. He had a soldier's longing for *contact*, for the moment of true conflict.

Militiamen were firing at Simbarashe's vehicle out on the road, the gaudy yellow thing hurtling past the compound walls at full throttle, disappearing into the dark. Khadir's lip curled as Cord and Vine came running back to meet him. Cord was wounded, binding up the injury on the run with a gauze bandage.

'Report,' he demanded.

'Targets are free and mobile,' said Vine, jerking his thumb in the direction of the fleeing vehicle.

'Obviously.'

Following him out, Khadir heard Grace give a derisive snort.

'Slippery buggers,' she added.

Simbarashe pushed past her, yelling to his soldiers.

'Get the trucks! Go after them, I want them dead!'

His men swarmed aboard the parked technicals, dragging boxes of ammunition up with them for the mounted guns.

'That's not your choice to make, love,' said Grace, giving the warlord an arch sniff.

Simbarashe faltered, his anger so high that for a moment he was lost for a reply.

Khadir holstered his pistol and summoned Cord, Grace and Vine with a flick of his wrist. He started towards the landing pad, pressing the radio microphone tab at his throat.

'Start it up,' he told the pilot. 'It seems we need to finish this ourselves.'

Behind the bubble canopy, the Hind's pilot gave a terse salute, and the gunship's rotors began to turn.

Once they were away from the compound, the landscape around the vehicle became a backdrop of layered shadows, the only illumination coming from a distended pool of white glow from the Hummer's one remaining headlight. The cracked asphalt of the highway was a black blur, mile markers and patches of encroaching scrub flashing past alongside them to mark the motion of the road.

Inside the vehicle, Marc smelt spent gunpowder, hot oil and human sweat. A fair amount of the latter was his, as the rush of the escape echoed through him.

'I'd kill for a pair of NVGs right now,' he muttered.

'Rocket launcher would be better,' said Lucy, reloading her rifle. 'How many rounds left?'

'Two mags remaining,' Malte replied.

Marc saw a flicker of light in his wing mirror and hissed, 'They're gaining on us.'

Lucy turned in her seat, aiming backwards. The rear window was webbed with bullet impacts and part of it hung away from the frame, flapping in the wind.

'I make two pickups, coming up fast.'

Solomon dropped the passenger-side window and shifted around.

'We cannot let them take us. My old comrade is not a forgiving man.'

'Yeah, no shit.'

The first bullets fired by their pursuers went wide, but still Marc flinched at the sound. In the bright yellow behemoth, he felt like the world's most obvious target.

The technicals were Toyota Land Cruisers, one a rusted white, the other a patchwork of salvaged panels. Both were bog-standard pickup trucks as common as anything in Third World countries, but their engines had been tweaked by militia mechanics for more horsepower. On the rough roads, the lighter vehicles could match the more powerful Hummer in short spurts, and that would be enough to put them in firing range.

Shots chewed up the dirt at their heels and then Marc heard them hit the tailgate, cutting wads out of the metal frame. Caught on the pincers of two .50-calibre guns, the Hummer wouldn't last long, and the hail of flying lead forced the others to keep their heads down, stopping them from returning fire.

'Bridge up ahead,' grunted Solomon.

In the gloom, Marc saw the outline of a short wooden pontoon affair over a dried-out river bed, where the road narrowed to a single vehicle's width. It was coming up fast, giving him little time to choose his next move.

He slipped the Hummer left and directly into the path of the rust-stained pickup, stamping on the brakes to kill some of their forward momentum. The other technical howled past at speed, the patchwork vehicle's rear gunner unable to swing his gun around fast enough to get a bead on them.

'The fuck are you doing . . . ?' Lucy yelled.

The wide rear of the Hummer struck the front of the trailing pickup, the impact shocking through both vehicles with a shuddering crash. The gunner was momentarily unseated, the long barrel of his mounted weapon flicking up to aim at the sky.

Marc didn't hesitate, riding out of the collision and accelerating away again, straight towards the patchwork technical, now ahead of them as it rumbled onto the bridge.

Rapidly running out of road width, Marc brought the Hummer up towards the other pickup's rear quarter and executed a pit block. He'd learned the manoeuvre in MI6 field training, a tried and tested police pursuit tactic where a chaser could deal with a vehicle ahead by forcing it into an uncontrolled swerve.

The heavier vehicle hit hard and put the patchwork truck off-kilter, spinning it as both vehicles bounced onto the bridge. Marc gave the Hummer more gas and kept up the momentum. He locked eyes with the technical's screaming gunner as the militiaman put his weight into the gun to bring it to bear.

The lighter pickup lost traction and rebounded off the Hummer's cracked grille. It skidded away and dived nose-first over the edge of the bridge, a ten-metre fall that sent it down into the cracked mud.

They rocketed off the bridge and back onto the highway, the road quality worsening the further they were from the compound. Marc felt the steering working against him, and the Hummer listed to the right.

Tyres, he thought.

Simbarashe had fitted his personal vehicle with run-flats, but not even those could stand up to sustained heavy weapons fire.

'Coming up!' called Lucy.

The remaining technical was close behind, and the other gunner was back in the saddle, riding the recoil of his gun as he worked it back and forth over the rear of the Hummer. A bright bolt of tracer keened through the inside of the cabin as the shots blasted away the last of the armoured window and penetrated the framework. Rifle-toting militia shooters in the flatbed added their weapons to the screaming chorus, and bullets ricocheted around inside the rear cargo space.

Lucy slammed the heel of her hand into the back of the driver's seat.

'They're chewing us up!'

Solomon tried to return fire, but it was blind shooting. If he exposed enough of himself to take aim, he would be torn apart.

The two vehicles raced over a low rise and the Hummer accelerated into the drop. Up ahead, a small hill grew out of the landscape, momentarily filling the cracked windscreen with a wall of orange-red dirt.

'Get ready!' shouted Marc. 'Solomon, your side!'

The Hummer crested the hill and caught air, the engine howling as it over-revved. They slammed down hard, and for a split second the line of sight between the two vehicles was blocked.

Marc worked the brakes, throwing the Hummer into a jackknife skid that slewed it to a stop lengthwise across the highway, presenting the passenger side of the vehicle towards the crest of the hill.

Solomon, Lucy and Malte didn't need to be told what to do next. As the technical came flying over the rise, they opened up as one, unloading their weapons into the Toyota.

A spurt of crimson painted the technical's windscreen as a bullet nicked the driver's jugular, and the vehicle veered out of control. Concentrated fire bore down on the gunner and kicked him off the .50, seconds before the rusting pickup sank into a ditch and slammed to a halt.

Lucy and Malte scrambled out and ran to the crashed truck, looting weapons and ammunition from the dead crew to augment their meagre stock. Marc brought the Hummer around, but he could feel it complaining with each turn of the wheel. The vehicle had been badly damaged, its frame soaking up hundreds of rounds. It wouldn't get them much further.

He sucked in a shuddering breath and checked himself over. Aside from the nasty shiner he'd earned in the cages, Marc's only injuries were a few cuts from flying fragments of broken glass. He looked to Solomon.

'You okay? You hit?'

'We must get off this road,' said the other man, staring out into the endless night. 'They will find us if we remain on it.' He jabbed a finger at the darkness. 'Go across country.'

Marc frowned. The Hummer was solidly built, but he doubted it would make more than a few more kilometres.

'It's your old manor. I'll follow your lead, but this thing isn't going to get us far.'

The vehicle rocked as the others climbed back in.

'Next time, Dane,' Lucy snapped, 'a little warning before you pull that kinda stunt?'

'No need to thank me.'

Marc put the Hummer back into drive, and pointed it into the wilderness.

The Hind's engine note rose to a high-pitched whine, and the gunship rocked on its undercarriage as the rotors spun up to take-off speed.

Khadir climbed into the crew compartment and found his M4 carbine where he'd left it. Force of habit made him take down the weapon and double-check its readiness, as Grace followed him on board with Cord and Vine a step behind her.

He eyed the woman.

Did she have any inkling that her death had already been ordained by her employer?

Khadir knew that when the moment came, he would have to execute her himself. She knew too much about their operations, and that knowledge in the hands of someone who served the highest bidder could not be tolerated.

'How do we play this?' called Vine, pitching his voice up to be heard over the roar of the engine above their heads.

'Quadrant sweep pattern,' said Khadir. 'This aircraft has a searchlight and forward-looking infrared scanner. We track their vehicle, disable it, secure our objective.'

'Secure,' repeated Cord. 'Just Solomon, right?'

Khadir nodded. 'The others are irrelevant. Be sure to recover all kills. Glovkonin will want proof that his orders have been followed.'

Vine reached out to pull shut the drawbridge hatch in the helicopter's flank, but at the last moment, hands grabbed the edges from outside and forced it open again.

Now equipped with a plate carrier armour vest and a Bizon sub-machine gun on a shoulder strap, Simbarashe clambered into the Hind, his eyes wide and chemically bright.

'You are going nowhere without me!' he snarled, and with him came three more militia soldiers in similar gear.

Khadir glared at the colonel with new disdain, wondering what he had taken to steel his courage.

'Your assistance is not required,' he replied. 'Stay home and count your money.'

'No!' Simbarashe dropped heavily into one of the cramped cabin's folding seats. 'I will see this to its end!'

Arguing the point would waste more time, and as much as Khadir wanted to throw the militia leader out onto the dirt, he had other considerations. He looked away, towards the flight crew.

'Get us in the air.'

'Sir.'

The pilot saluted again and pulled on the controls.

The reptilian silhouette of the Hind rose smoothly off the landing pad and rose up into the night, pivoting in the direction of its fleeing prey.

TWENTY-ONE

The Hummer started making a sound like a sack of bricks thrown into a cement mixer, and the stink of hot oil was heavy in the cabin, making Marc's breath catch.

The scrubland had not been kind to the vehicle, and they were barely lurching along now, forced to veer back to another rough highway or lose the whole thing down some unseen gulley.

'Structure ahead,' Malte called out from the open sunroof, where he lay across the top of the bullet-riddled frame.

'Yeah, I see it.'

The only illumination for miles in any direction was coming from a dilapidated petrol station, a low two-storey building with a square awning that extended out over a solitary gas pump on the dusty forecourt. Lights burned inside an office and what were probably a garage and a living room on the second floor.

The Hummer rolled to a halt short of the awning, the engine dying with a pathetic splutter, and Marc knew the thing had given up the ghost. He gave the dashboard a pat.

'Got us this far,' he told it.

The four of them decamped from the hissing, leaking vehicle and moved with weapons at the ready. Lucy and Malte took the lead, while Marc hung back. Solomon stuck close to the Hummer, pulling the black jacket tight over his shoulders.

As far as Marc could make out, the road they were on cut through the middle of a wide, shallow valley, bordered by distant ridges that formed inky walls far beyond the glow of the petrol station's lights. The dirt-track road ran west to east beneath the bowl of a starry night, vanishing into the distance.

'They will keep coming,' Solomon said quietly. 'Until they know we are dead.' He looked up to find Marc watching him. 'They are picking us off one by one, Mr Dane.'

'We need fresh horses,' Marc countered. 'We have a decent lead on them. How far is the airstrip from here?'

'Far enough.'

Marc knew where this was going.

'Look around, man. This is not a good place to dig in.'

'You fight with what you have.' Solomon took a long, exhausted breath. He looked down at the assault rifle again and a rueful smile split his face. 'This is an old friend. Fitting that I have one in my hands again.'

He reached up to his collar and pulled out the silver chain that hung around his throat, fingering the object that dangled from it – the trigger from a weapon of the same type. The one he had carried as a boy soldier.

Marc was going to say more, but then the wind down the highway brought a faint, distant sound to them, and he instinctively turned towards it.

It was the faraway rattle of rotor blades, the noise rebounding off the ridge line. Marc leaned into the Hummer, searching the glove compartment, and came back with a pair of compact binoculars.

Sweeping the horizon, he glimpsed a dot of light, moving and then gone as the rotor noise faded.

'The gunship's out there.'

'How long until they reach us?'

Marc shrugged. 'Soon as their sweep brings them this way, they'll spot this place. Could be ten minutes from now, could be an hour.'

He pocketed the binoculars and moved to the rear of the Hummer.

The tailgate was distorted and jammed in place, but with a swift kick Marc had it open and forced it clear. He grimaced to see that Assim's body bag was holed in several places, from bullets that had peppered the vehicle. The indignity of it was galling, but he forced the reaction down and out of his thoughts.

Back to the old pattern, said a voice in his head, a voice that sounded like Benjamin Harun.

The soldier-shrink had pulled that out of Marc in one of their first meetings, unpicking his tendency to shut down and go cold in the face of an emotional shock. It had happened in his naval service, when the Lynx helicopter he crewed had crashed in the South China Sea, in MI6 when Nomad and Sam Green were killed, when his mother died in hospital . . . again and again.

Marc always told himself that he would grieve later, box up the pain in the moment and keep his mind on the mission, but that was a lie. He kept those boxes sealed up, one after another.

Now is not the time, he told himself. But a part of him knew it never would be.

He put a hand on Assim's body, the closest he would get to a farewell to his young friend, and then went back to the job at hand. Marc dragged the ammo crate out from under the webbing that secured it, and frowned as he saw that it too was pockmarked with bullet holes.

'There's a vehicle in the shop,' said Lucy, jogging back to them from the garage. 'A ranger jeep from the national park up the coast. Looks like it's missing a battery, though.' She halted as she saw the state of the ammo crate. 'That seems bad.'

Marc opened the lid and tilted the crate. Broken pieces of hard drive rattled around inside.

'We've lost a few. Not all of them, though.'

'That's something.'

'You may want to hold your applause,' he replied, and told her about the gunship.

'We knew they were coming,' she said. 'What do we do about it?'

Marc took in the ramshackle building.

'I really do not like the idea of making a last stand in a location like this.'

'It's only a *last* stand if you wind up dead,' she noted. 'Look, we swap vehicles, we get on the move, that's one way to go. But that helo is going to run us down no matter what. We'd just die tired.'

'Lucy's point is well made, as ever,' Solomon said wearily. 'I have had my fill of being the prey.'

There was a commotion at the office door, and Malte emerged, pushing an older man and his younger companion out into the night. They were shouting at the Finn in loud Portuguese, and he clearly had no idea what they were saying.

Marc looked the pair over, and saw the resemblance immediately.

Father and son, he thought. *This is a family business.*

Solomon walked stiffly over to the two men and intervened, waving Malte away. Marc couldn't follow any of the conversation, but he saw Solomon switch into that same composed and collected manner he displayed in billion-dollar boardrooms. In a few moments, the dad and his son were calming down, and Marc knew Solomon was carefully talking them into walking away.

'When we were on the road, did he take a hit?' Lucy asked quietly, watching the discussion.

'Would he tell us if he had?' said Marc.

'Guess not.'

At length, the three men shook hands like old friends, and Solomon waved them off as the old guy climbed aboard a grubby trail bike, the younger man getting on the saddle behind as his passenger. The motorcycle's engine snarled and it sped away into the night.

Marc raised an eyebrow. 'What did you say?'

'I told him where to find a better life for his son and the rest of his family.'

Solomon left it at that, and wandered into the office.

'That guy could get an army of snowmen to follow him into Hell,' said Lucy.

Marc gave a humourless snort. 'What does that make us, then?'

Malte spoke before Lucy could come up with a retort.

'Found the generator,' he said, indicating a square shape at the rear of the building.

'Good,' she said. 'We can kill the power when we need to.'

'Gear in the jeep,' added the Finn.

'Oh yeah?'

Marc carried the ammo crate into the petrol station's tiny, oil-reeking garage, and found the vehicle in question, with its bonnet raised and one wheel off at the axle.

As Lucy had mentioned, the jeep's battery was missing, but the one in the Hummer had escaped major damage, so a straight exchange would be enough to get it running. Without being asked, Malte set to work replacing the wheel, while Marc circled the jeep, looking it over.

Where the Hummer had been an armoured metal box on wheels, the skeletal 4 × 4 was totally open to the elements, with nothing but a windscreen and a tubular rollbar over the bucket seats. The rear section was an enclosed cargo box, the lid dominated by the logo of the Quirimbas National Park, and Marc flipped it open.

He emptied it out, making space for the ammo crate and Assim's remains. The contents were kit used by whatever park ranger the jeep belonged to: a field medical pack, survival gear and a pair of hard cases. Marc cracked open the first and found a collection of tubes inside.

'What's this?'

'Give.'

Lucy saw something he didn't, and plucked a telescopic sight from in among the components. Beneath the tubular sections were a trigger mechanism and a smaller box containing heavy aluminium darts with colourful fibre flights.

'This is more my speed,' she said, assembling the parts into a long rifle configuration.

'It's a tranquiliser gun,' Marc realised, as it came together. 'For tigers, that kind of thing?'

'Only lions here, no tigers,' Malte offered as he worked.

Lucy racked a dart into the chamber and peered down the sight.

'Yeah, I can work with this.'

Marc opened the second case, and found a second dissembled firearm, but this one was bulkier, and instead of ending in a gun barrel, the device mounted a net projector containing a web of unbreakable nylon strands.

'Not a rocket launcher, then. Pity.'

'Can't have everything,' said Lucy.

Marc looked up as Solomon came into the barn-like space.

'If we're agreed on this, we need a plan of attack. Because making it up on the fly isn't going to work this time, and if our luck is going to run out anywhere, tonight's the night.'

They looked to Solomon, but he nodded back to Marc, tacitly ceding the decision to him.

'Mr Dane, you have a proven talent for adaptability. What do you propose?'

Marc took in the workshop, scanning the room for whatever they could use. Racks of rusty tools and grubby spares hung next to paint-stained tarpaulins and cans of engine oil.

'Okay,' he said, after a long moment. 'I've got some ideas.'

'There,' called the gunner, 'civilian structure, near the highway.' He peered into the hood over the FLIR sensor's repeater screen. 'I see the target vehicle, but no signs of movement.'

'Show me,' began Simbarashe, but Khadir stood up and pushed past him, once more making it clear who was in command aboard the helicopter. The colonel met his gaze, and decided it was better to remain in his seat.

Khadir leaned into the cockpit. The Hind was running dark, the only illumination coming from the soft glow of the pilot's instruments, and outside the bubble canopy the night was ink-black.

The gunship's pilot nodded in the direction of the target, his bulky flight helmet exaggerating the motion. The boxy cluster of buildings appeared small and toy-like from overhead, but Khadir could pick out the bulk of Simbarashe's gaudy SUV parked on the forecourt. Behind him, he heard the colonel call out, seeing the same thing through the crew cabin's portholes.

'Are they even in there?' said the pilot.

A hard-faced man in his forties, he had a gruff Afrikaans accent, and like the gunner, he was a local soldier of fortune hired on by Saito. He gave Khadir a sideways look.

'Circle around,' he ordered.

The pilot did as he was told, orbiting the Hind about the petrol station at a distance, keeping it nose-on to the building.

Without warning, the lights in the building went out, plunging the surroundings into darkness.

'That answers my question.' The pilot nodded at the gunner. 'You want he should use the gun, yah? We can strafe that place. Or the rockets. Blow it apart, easy.'

'Tempting,' noted Khadir. But he had not come this far to put an end to Rubicon's meddling by striking from a distance. 'This must be done face to face.' He pointed down. 'Put us on the ground and be ready to lift off again at a moment's notice.'

'Got it.'

The pilot nodded his assent, and pulled the Hind away from the highway, out of small arms range and down towards the only patch of open ground.

'Weapons ready,' Khadir ordered, dropping back into the cabin.

Cord, Vine and Grace double-checked their gear, and the woman pulled low-light goggle rigs from a container beneath her seat, distributing them to the team. Simbarashe held out his hand, expecting to be given a set, but she presented him a mock-sorrowful look.

'Sorry, handsome, not enough for everyone.'

The colonel scowled and said something low and sneering to his own men. The three militia soldiers wore the same wary expression, equally suspicious of the Combine operatives as they were of their shared enemy.

Simbarashe turned his glare on Khadir as the helicopter touched down and Vine kicked open the hatch.

'My men are capable fighters!' he shouted. 'You will respect them!'

Khadir indicated the hatch.

'Then by all means, proceed.'

Simbarashe gave another order, and the soldiers boiled out of the cabin. Khadir and the colonel were the last to disembark, and as his boots hit the dirt, he pulled his night vision optics down over his eyes. The landscape was revealed in shades of grey, white and black, and ahead the figures of the militiamen showed up as bright blobs of body heat.

The soldiers advanced cautiously through the patchy scrub towards the roadway, leading with their rifles, but they showed poor discipline and moved too close together.

Spreading out from under the disc of the gunship's idling rotors, Khadir and his team fell into a finger-four formation, wide enough apart that any aggressor would not easily be able to shoot more than one of them at a time.

Simbarashe lagged back, staying uncomfortably close to Khadir.

'What can you see?' he demanded.

Khadir ignored the question, and tried to put himself into the mindset of Solomon's people. If he were defending this place, how would he face an assault force? The petrol station's buildings were blank and empty-looking, the doors and windows black squares filled with shadows that his NVGs could not penetrate.

They will draw us close, he decided. *Engage only when a kill is certain.*

Solomon's people would not be well equipped, of that he was certain. They had spotted the wreck of one of Simbarashe's technicals several miles away, and Khadir noted that the guns had been looted.

Assault rifles only. A maximum of four shooters.

He smiled thinly. Simbarashe's men would be good for something after all, drawing fire from Solomon's people so that Khadir and the others could pinpoint their positions.

The first of the militiamen reached the edge of the road, and broke into a run to get across the open space. His two comrades were close behind, dithering over the same decision, when Khadir saw a flicker of motion near the south edge of the main building. A shiny object described an arc through the air, hurled by some invisible hand from behind a low wall.

It landed at the feet of the first soldier with a crash of breaking glass and a sudden whoosh of combustion. The object was a firebomb, throwing out a sphere of orange flames that caught the unlucky man along his left side, and he screamed into the night.

More of the improvised weapons came out of cover in a quick volley, landing in a rough line along the middle of the roadway between the attackers and their target. Each one hit the ground with a wet crash that birthed another patch of flames, and through Khadir's low-light gear it was like looking into the sun. The writhing, dazzling whiteout instantly rendered the NVGs useless, destroying their tactical advantage. He pulled off the goggles, seeing Grace and the others do the same.

'Clever,' Khadir said to himself.

He had used the exact same ploy against American Special Forces during attacks on their bases in the Middle East, robbing them of their ability to see in the dark. It was a good trick, but it worked both ways.

If we cannot see through the fire, neither can they.

The fallen militia soldier was on the ground, dragging himself through the dirt, trying to douse the flames. His screams were high and reedy, but they quickly faded, as did his movements.

Khadir brought his rifle up to his shoulder, anticipating what would come next, and in the next second he saw flashes of yellow muzzle flare from both ends of the main building. He dropped into a crouch, noting single shots from the defenders' weapons. Just as he thought, they were making each bullet count.

Simbarashe's remaining men had no such concerns, however, and they opened up on full automatic, peppering the crumbling concrete with wildfire bursts.

Khadir estimated two shooters engaging them: one inside the building behind the solitary petrol pump, a second firing from the cover of the low wall. He cast around, searching for where the other two might be. The fact that he could not locate them was a serious concern. He threw a look back towards the waiting gunship, considering the pilot's offer once more.

'What are you waiting for?' Simbarashe called out; the colonel was down behind a low rock. He gripped his Russian-made submachine gun tightly, kneading the grip. 'Shoot back!'

As if to underline the point, he popped up and sprayed a loud burst from his weapon, more for show than effect.

'Move in!' The second command was directed towards his own men, and one of them obeyed.

Firing from the hip, the militia soldier attempted to flank the shooter behind the wall, but he opened himself up to attack as he vaulted over a low ditch, and Khadir glimpsed a figure momentarily making themselves visible, long enough to put a snap-shot through the running man's legs. The second militiaman went tumbling out of sight into the ditch and did not reappear.

'*On the right.*'

Khadir heard Cord's voice through the radio bead in his ear, and spotted the mercenary on the run, as he jogged towards the ruined yellow vehicle standing half-off the highway.

'Understood.'

Khadir moved forward, and fired for the first time, putting paced shots towards the window in the building where rounds had been coming from. Off to his left, Vine covered his comrade, but Grace was still keeping low, seemingly reticent to give away her position.

Simbarashe burst out of cover and fired with his Bizon, so close that the noise of the spent brass from his SMG clattered in Khadir's ears.

He kept his focus on the buildings, and saw movement towards the north edge, a brief shape passing before an open doorway. Shots burst from the darkness, the muzzle flash briefly illuminating a dark face, and Khadir realised that Cord's advance had been spotted.

'Cord, you are seen—!'

His warning came too late. Before he could reach the cover of the Hummer, the mercenary's head snapped back as if pulled on an invisible line, a spurt of fluid erupting from the back of his skull. It was an instant kill, clear as day, and Cord's body dropped in a heap.

'*Lost a man,*' Vine reported, with clinical dispassion. '*Shooter on the move. Flanking left.*'

Khadir saw him advance, as Grace jogged away in a quick spurt of movement, disappearing towards the opposite end of the building.

'Wasting time . . .'

Simbarashe's gun was empty, and he threw away the Bizon's cylindrical under-barrel magazine before slotting a fresh one into place.

Khadir's patience vanished in that instant, and he stepped to the other man, grabbing him by the strap of his plate carrier.

'You have been away from the field of battle for a long time. Stay silent and let us work.'

Simbarashe spluttered an angry retort, but Khadir had no time for his bluster in the middle of an active firefight. From the corner of his eye, he saw motion once more, but not inside the building. This time, the shadow was moving above, up on the edge of the wide, square-sided awning that hung out over the fuel pump and the abandoned vehicle.

Someone up there. But how was that possible? The gunship's infrared scope had swept the rooftop and seen nothing.

He heard a chug of discharge, and a heavy dart came whistling down out of the dark, narrowly missing him. The projectile was large, and moving slow enough to see it as it blurred through the air. Up on the awning, heavy cloth crackled as it caught in the wind and he suddenly understood.

It has to be the sniper, Keyes, hiding herself up there beneath some heavy oilcloth.

'Release me!' Simbarashe shouted, pulling at Khadir's grip. He too had heard the dart speed past them and wanted to find cover.

Khadir shoved him forward, knowing that the other man's silhouette would eclipse his, as the next shot came and a second dart spun in towards them.

The projectile hit Simbarashe in the throat with enough force to bury it in the soft tissues there. He dropped his gun and clutched at his neck as bright crimson jetted from the wound, fingers scrambling uselessly at the multicoloured flight at the end of the dart.

Raising his carbine, Khadir fired bursts into the awning to discourage the sniper from attempting a third shot, as the colonel stumbled to the ground.

He gave the wounded man a passing glance. Simbarashe's armour vest, inadequate against the throat hit, was soaked with patches of blood, smeared across him as the colonel clawed at the thick dart.

With the bellicose warlord finally silenced, Khadir walked on, leaving him to bleed out into the dirt.

The hardest part was hiding there, waiting. Not moving. Not daring to lift his head. Holding down the edges of the oily tarpaulin and hoping that this would work.

When the Hind started in towards them, Marc threw himself into the gulley in the ground across from the petrol station, and pulled the heavy cloth over him. In daylight, it would have been lousy camouflage, but under full dark it could blend with the earth and keep him hidden.

That's the idea, anyway, he thought.

But as the helicopter gunship circled overhead, Marc had a sudden, horrible vision of the Hind's heavy downdraught blowing away his cover, leaving him exposed to that lethal chin turret.

He clung to the edges of the tarp, willing it to stay put, and held on tight as the aircraft seemed to come down right on top of him. He'd picked out this hiding place because of its proximity to the nearby clearing, the best landing spot other than the road itself, gambling that the Hind's pilot would choose it. Now Marc was wondering if he'd been too smart for his own good.

Former Navy helicopter crewman crushed to death by helicopter.

As manners of death went, there was an unpleasant irony in it. The ghosts of his old Fleet Air Arm crew would laugh at that.

The noise of the Hind's engine changed, downshifting from flight power to grounded idle, and the gusts from the rotors eased. Marc waited until he heard gunfire start up from the direction of the petrol station, before he dared to pull back the edge of the tarp and peek out of his dusty pit.

He found the bug-eyed, crocodilian profile of the Russian chopper squatting roughly fifty metres from his position. The helicopter was parked nose-on towards the highway and perpendicular to Marc's position, but the pilot had landed it much further back than he had anticipated. It was behind his hiding place, not in front of it.

The moment Marc left the gulley, he would be in full view of the gunship's crew, and the only cover in between were sparse, dry bushes.

'That's not optimal,' he said aloud, reaching behind him for his weapon, pulling it up into his hands by its nylon strap.

Over on the road, he saw the flicker of fires and hazy shadows moving against the orange light and black smoke. Simbarashe's precious canary-coloured Hummer had been hit by another improvised bomb and it was going up like a tinderbox.

Would that be enough to draw the attention of the men in the cockpit?

The only way to know was to go for it.

'It's only a last stand if you wind up dead.'

Marc repeated Lucy's words like they were a mantra, steeling himself for what would come next.

He put the weapon over his shoulder and cinched the strap tight, then drew into a runner's crouch, shifting his weight to push against the floor of the shallow gulley. On the road, the Hummer's fuel tank burst with a thudding concussion and that was his starting gun.

Marc vaulted out of the pit with all the speed he could manage, his boots biting into the dry earth as he surged up, out and away. Every primitive impulse for self-preservation screamed at him to go in the other direction and flee from the menacing form of the helicopter, but he went against that compulsion and sprinted across the rough ground towards it.

Inside the fishbowl bubble of the forward cockpit, the Hind's gunner reacted with a start, seeing the tarp flap away in the wind from the spinning rotors. He saw Marc immediately, and reacted with unpleasant speed.

The long Yak-B Gatling gun in the Hind's nose twitched into life and pivoted towards him, humming loudly as it spun up to firing speed.

With a droning snarl, the cannon opened up as it continued to turn. A whip of searing tracer fire cut into the dirt as the gunner depressed the weapon to aim at his bolting target, carving a semicircle of molten divots out of the ruddy-coloured earth.

Marc yelled as he felt the ground around him being churned into mud, the yowling of the rotary cannon buzzing in his bones.

Then just as suddenly he was in the clear, sprinting over the uneven valley floor towards the rear of the helicopter. The chin gun could only turn so far in its forward arc, and the angle was too obtuse to traverse after him.

He tripped over an exposed stone and fell in a half-stumble, the weapon on his back pulling at him with its extra weight. Marc shot a look back towards the nose of the Hind and saw the gunner gesturing wildly. In the next second, the gunship's engine note shifted up a gear, and he knew they were about to lift off.

Once the Hind was off the ground, the pilot could angle it in any direction, and Marc had nowhere to hide.

Battered by the helicopter's roaring exhaust and the hurricane from its whistling blades, Marc staggered back to his feet and shrugged off his weapon, bringing it up to aim at the fast-spinning blur of the Hind's tail rotor. As close as he dared to come, he pulled the buttstock of the park ranger's net projector gun into his shoulder and squeezed the trigger bar.

Four explosive charges aimed at angles to one another fired simultaneously, shooting off in different directions to pull open a weighted, heavy-duty net between them, blasting it out and forward. The weapon's restraining net was a web of nylon cored with steel wire, rated strong enough to put down a charging rhino, and Marc hoped it would be enough. His shot went straight into the hub of the stabilising rotor and immediately snarled around the axle mechanism.

The tail rotor vomited sparks and juddered alarmingly, even as the Hind's bulky airframe rose off the ground. The stabiliser oscillated so much, Marc was suddenly terrified it might fly off and cut him in half. He dropped the spent net gun and ran, hearing the engines whine as the pilot applied power.

Without the stabilising blades rotating in sync, the gunship began to turn with the spinning force of the main rotors, and the mercenary pilot made a fatal error, over-correcting as he tried to get the helicopter back under his control. The Hind lurched and tipped sideways towards the ground. Too low to recover, the Hind's main rotors thwacked into the earth, distended and cracked.

Marc threw himself back into the safety of his hiding place as the gunship flipped over and crashed, tearing off one of its winglets and spinning its rotors into twisted, broken shards. The engine howled as the stricken helicopter lay on its side, bleeding black smoke into the night.

The explosion Marc expected didn't come, so he fled the scene of his takedown, conscious that the aircrew might have survived and be in the mood for some retaliation.

He looped wide of the ongoing firefight, running as fast as he could towards the main building.

Lucy came off the gas station's awning by sliding down the access ladder on the far side, boots skipping off the rungs, gloves hissing as she let gravity take her to the ground.

As she hit the dirt, a slim shadow came out of the gloom and she narrowly missed getting a rifle butt in the stomach. One of Simbarashe's eager fighters was right there, eyes wide and teeth bared as he dived at her, swinging the gun like an oar.

She didn't dwell on why the hell he hadn't just shot her dead. The AK was probably jammed, she guessed, parsing the situation in an instant just as Delta had trained her. These Chinese copies of the classic Russian assault rifle were old and well used, and sometimes all it took was a bang on the frame to get them shooting again.

None of that helped Lucy here or now, though. The militia-man landed a glancing hit on her shoulder, and she had only the empty rhino-trank rifle to answer back.

Or not.

She parried another incoming blow with one hand and plucked the boot dagger Malte had loaned her from the loop of her belt. Metal glittered in the firelight and she jammed it into the side of his head, wrenched it free, and did it again.

The soldier crumpled against the side of the building and Lucy discarded the trank gun, snatching up her attacker's assault rifle. True to form, the slide was fouled with a spent casing, and she struck it hard, freeing it up.

Oily smoke tickled her throat and she cast around, hearing more gunfire and the droning of the Hind's chin cannon. That did not bode well.

Lucy filled her lungs and shouted one world as loudly as she could.

'*Time!*'

It was the signal they'd agreed on, the *get out of Dodge* order, the last goddamn word. She broke into a run, sprinting away from the building towards a wide gulley where they had concealed the jeep. Whoever met her there would be the ones who had made it through this.

Peering out from behind the low wall, Malte saw the man in black tactical gear emerge from cover, and knew that he was looking at a shooter of a different class from the men he had fought so far.

Combine.

There was little doubt in his mind that was who he was facing. The clandestine power brokers used Russian muscle from the

ALEPH private military contractor, usually ex-Soviet Special Forces troops with reputations for ferocity, and their own elite cadre of hired assassins and black ops specialists.

The man in black drew Malte's shots, and his agility made him hard to hit. He kept dodging around the fire smoke, using the cover to his advantage. Cursing inwardly, the Finn made a choice and flicked his rifle over to full-auto setting.

Malte sprayed the last few rounds in his magazine, gambling that he could hit something, but the risk didn't pay off. The AK-47's slide snapped open with an audible clatter as the mag emptied, and the noise rang like a gong in the Finn's head.

The man in black rose through a plume of dark haze and put two shots directly into Malte. The first round skipped over his shoulder, drawing a burning line of pain and blood, but the second punctured his bicep, ripping muscle and cracking bone. A hammer blow of raw agony sent Malte falling back, the empty AK tumbling from his twitching grip.

He swallowed down the urge to cry out in pain and failed, breaking his silence with a guttural snarl. Malte made out the shape of his assailant, carefully picking his way around the burning Hummer. Coming his way.

The Combine operative would want to confirm the kill. Malte scrambled to reach for his weapon. He still had another half-mag left, but where was it?

A grave voice spoke from behind him.

'I have you, my friend.'

Solomon grabbed the collar of Malte's shirt and dragged him back, away from the wall, towards the main building. Solomon fired as he moved, shooting one-handed to discourage the Combine gunman from his approach. Rounds sparked off the burning Hummer and the man in black retreated.

A heavy, reeking gloom enveloped Malte as Solomon pulled him inside, and he blinked, panting through the excruciating pain.

'Can you move?'

Malte managed a nod. 'But can't shoot.'

His useless arm was awash with blood.

Marc stumbled into the main building through a bullet-shredded door, finding himself in a space that was half office, half general store. Or at least, it had been that before the Rubicon team had arrived with their party crashers following close behind. Debris, shattered glass and broken wood were everywhere, and the brick structure was riddled with bullet holes.

From the shadows a gun spun in his direction, and he threw up his hands.

'Easy!'

Solomon lowered his weapon and blew out a pained breath.

'Lucy gave the call. It is time to leave.'

He gestured to Malte, who leaned painfully against one of the roof supports.

Marc nodded. 'Yeah, green for go, I heard her.' Keeping low, he moved closer to the other men. 'There's still a few out there, three or four? Saw them moving.'

'Helicopter?' said Malte, jutting his chin in the direction of the downed Hind.

'Swatted.' Marc coughed.

Malte showed his teeth in an uncharacteristic grin, and that was when Marc knew the Finn was really hurting.

'Right, we're on the move.' Marc glanced at Solomon. 'We're all set. You lead and I'll follow.'

'You have done that enough,' Solomon replied, pulling his jacket close. 'Get Malte to the jeep. I will be right behind you.'

An unpleasant tension pulled on Marc as he realised that Ekko Solomon was lying to him.

The man had kept his secrets and there were times when he had held back, but Solomon had never once looked Marc Dane in the eye and outright lied.

Until now.

He stepped forward, quick enough to do it before Solomon could react, and grabbed the edge of his jacket. The black material was damp, and it flapped back to reveal a makeshift bandage around the bullet wound that Solomon had been hiding from them. Lucy had been on the money. It was a belly shot, a bleeder, a slow killer.

'You got that on the road?'

Marc remembered Solomon jerking in shock as they had taken fire in the fleeing Hummer.

'I can shoot,' Solomon said, hefting his rifle. 'But not run.'

He beckoned Marc closer.

Marc gave Malte a look, then shook his head.

'This is not how it is going to play out. *No.* No fucking last stands. We got a—'

Solomon tugged his titanium signet off his finger and forced the ring into Marc's palm.

'Take it,' he said, then looked down at the rifle in his hand with a wry smile. 'This is all I need now. My old friend.'

Closer now, and Marc saw that beneath that wadding, Solomon's injury was a horror. It was a miracle he was still on his feet.

'We're not doing this,' Marc insisted. 'Damn it, man! Do I have to knock you down and drag you away?'

'Can you carry two people at once?'

Solomon nodded towards Malte. The Finn's colour was paler than usual, and he was on the verge of passing out.

Marc grabbed him as he slumped, shouldering Malte's weight.

'I'll come back with the jeep,' he insisted. 'Do not be a fucking hero, do you read me?'

'Loud and clear—'

Gunfire erupted outside, and a new rain of bullets screamed into the building, ripping through whatever was still standing. Solomon dodged behind cover as Marc pulled his injured teammate out of the line of fire.

'Get him out!' bellowed Solomon, shooting back across the smoke-wreathed highway. 'Hurry, Marc!'

He didn't want to move. That same sense had come over him when he left his mother in her hospital bed for the last time, when he watched John Farrier being loaded onto the medevac flight, when he saw Sam Green fade into the dark water.

But then he did turn away, and he did move, because to stay was to die.

Carrying Malte as best he could, Marc staggered back into the burning, hellish night.

TWENTY-TWO

'*What the hell was that?*'

Vine appended his question with a few random curse-words as the gunship flattened itself into the dirt a few hundred metres behind them.

Khadir bared his teeth and cast around.

'We underestimate Solomon's people at our peril,' he growled.

With the Hind neutralised, the Combine assault team had lost an advantage, but Khadir was certain his objectives could still be attained. He would do it alone, if need be.

'Grace, report,' he ordered, but the woman didn't reply. He sucked in a breath, and pressed on. 'Move in and finish it,' said Khadir, advancing in a loping run.

Vine was visible in the corner of his vision as a dark blotch against the flames and smoke. The mercenary's rifle spoke, the gunshots flattened into a heavy metallic chugging by a sound suppressor on the muzzle.

Khadir followed, putting three-round bursts through the windows of the petrol station's main building, aiming at the moving shadows inside. Their renewed attack had the reaction he expected, as a braying flash of return fire briefly lit the darkness.

Solomon.

Khadir knew it was him; he was willing it to be so.

After all this time, years since Rubicon's agents had ruined Khadir's terror strike against the United States, the two men were finally within killing distance of one another.

Ekko Solomon had cost Khadir his greatest victory, and there had to be a reckoning. He had held onto his seething resentment for just this moment.

He flanked the building as Vine broke into a run, dodging left and right to present a difficult target. His boots scuffing over another fallen tarpaulin, Khadir glimpsed shadows moving awkwardly out towards the back of the building and hesitated.

Someone wounded, he guessed, *but not the African.*

Whoever it was, they were of secondary importance to him.

Vine lurched into a full-tilt run past the petrol pump and threw himself in the direction of one of the blown-out windows. But Solomon was ready for him, and his AK-47 drew a comma of yellow heat in the air as the muzzle rose in a burst of fire.

Khadir flattened himself against the exterior wall, seeing Vine knocked out of his headlong sprint as if he had collided with an invisible wall. The mercenary's right leg twisted under him and he dropped clumsily to the ground. Vine landed on his knees and sagged into himself. Twitching, mortally wounded, but not yet fully dead.

Then, distinctly, Khadir heard the sound of an empty ammunition box clatter to the floor.

Solomon let the AK's spent sickle magazine drop, flicking the release with his thumb and ramming home his last in its place. The action was smooth and intuitive, the assault rifle no longer existing in his mind as an object, instead as a deadly extension of his will.

Your gun is your life, his teacher had told him, beating young Ekko when his thin boy's hands could not properly grip the adult-sized rifle. *It is like your arm or your leg, eyes or ears. Without it you are no better than a cripple.*

The gun was power. That was the lesson the child soldiers had learned. Death was power.

'A lie,' Solomon whispered to himself. 'Life is power, not death . . .'

He choked off the words as the wound in his side added its weight to the argument.

He glared at the Combine agent kneeling in the dirt out on the forecourt, and questioned his own convictions.

At the end, is this how it must be? Bullets and fire, in the dark and the dust?

There was an ironic kind of circularity to it, he reflected. His homeland had called him back, and now it was reaching out to reclaim him, blood, bone and all.

In his pain and his reverie, Solomon did not notice the woman in the room with him until she moved into a pool of light and spoke. She had a pistol aimed at his face.

'Lose the shooter,' she told him, in an accent that mimicked Marc Dane's.

Grimacing, he let the Kalashnikov drop and raised his hands. Solomon's breath was coming in jagged, painful gulps now. It was as if something vital inside him had broken.

'Grace,' he said, turning slightly towards the woman. 'Do you remember the name you were born with?'

A hint of irritation glittered in her eyes.

'Names are for tombstones,' she told him.

'And graves are for the lucky,' he replied.

'Where's my boyfriend and the rest of your gang, eh?' She kept up the fake Londoner drawl. 'You and yours take a lot of putting down.'

'The others are inconsequential.' A heavy, deep voice cut through the darkness, and Solomon turned towards it. 'He is all that matters.'

One of the world's most wanted men advanced out of the shadows and gave Solomon a level look. Omar Khadir appeared every inch the killer he was purported to be. A face that was granite hard and sculpted by cold fury, feral eyes and the manner of an uncaged predator.

'You should be dead,' said Solomon.

'Men and nations alike have tried,' said Khadir. 'I endure.'

'And for what?'

'For this moment.' Khadir shouldered his rifle and drew his own sidearm, considering it. 'For hate's sake.'

Solomon had often wondered about this man, knowing what he knew of Khadir's martial upbringing among an Egyptian military family, and the shared legacy of brutal violence that had moulded both of them in their youth. How many points of commonality where there between them? It was more than either would have wanted to admit.

'I have thought about this meeting on many occasions,' said Khadir. 'Of what I could ask you. What I might do to you. There is a balance, you see. Intent, action, consequence. You sent your people to interfere with my destiny, so there must be reparation.' He gestured with the pistol. 'You need to answer for what you have done.'

'Yes.' A rough, pain-laced chuckle forced its way up and out of Solomon's mouth. It was a bitter, rueful sound. 'I must. For the last twenty years, that is all my life has been. Consequences.'

As he said the last word, he tasted blood in his mouth, and wiped a droplet from his lips.

Grace saw the action and frowned.

'He's hurt bad.' She holstered her pistol and pulled a medical pack from her tactical vest. 'We need to—'

Khadir silenced the woman with a look, his pistol rising in Solomon's direction.

'Glovkonin sent me here for you,' he explained. 'He wants you alive.'

Khadir pulled back the hammer on the handgun, taking aim. 'I have something else in mind.'

'That's not the fucking deal!' Grace held up her hands. 'You kill him, we don't get paid! I didn't come out here for you to get your revenge on!'

'That is not your concern.'

Khadir pivoted his aim a few degrees, past Solomon's head and straight towards the woman.

He squeezed the trigger, but Solomon was already moving at him, going for the blocky semi-automatic. Solomon knocked Khadir's arm and the gun discharged, drawing a thin scream from Grace as she reeled back.

If the bullet hit her, it had not been a fatal wound, but Solomon had no time to focus on the woman's status. He was vaguely aware of her vanishing into the shadows, stumbling towards the far doorway and out into the night.

His attention was on Khadir, whose rage at being denied a kill blazed brightly in his eyes. The assassin tried to bring the pistol back around to Solomon's face, and the two of them locked into a violent struggle, pushing and pressing against one another.

The black maw of the gun barrel floated between them, the raw scent of spent powder mingling with the gasoline stink from the fires. Their boots crunched on the carpet of broken glass and spent shells as they went around and around. Solomon gasped as he tried to get his leg in a position to trip his opponent, while Khadir kept his strength in the push and pull with the gun.

Inexorably, he was pushing the barrel of the Beretta into line with Solomon's head, degree by degree.

Grasping the frame of the weapon, Solomon tried to put a finger behind the trigger to stop it moving, or jam his thumb into the gap between hammer and strike plate, but Khadir was uninjured and he was stronger. The killer was taking his time with this, playing out the conflict between them. He was savouring it.

That arrogance could be used against him. Solomon found the pistol's magazine release button and crushed Khadir's finger against it, earning a snarl from the other man. The ammunition magazine slipped out of the gun and tumbled away, leaving only the single round still in the pipe. Solomon ducked back and squeezed with all the force he could apply, and the gun went off. The bullet hummed past his ear, hornet-loud and searing, but the weapon's slide locked back and he let go.

Khadir cursed and hit him with the butt of the empty pistol, then jabbed him in the belly with the sharp edge of the frame. Blinded by pain, Solomon threw a wild punch and scored a lucky hit, striking Khadir in the neck at his brachial plexus.

They disengaged momentarily, and Solomon collapsed back against the wall. He grasped at the splintered bricks for support, reaching for a light switch at shoulder height. The switch box had been forced open, and jump leads salvaged from the garage repurposed to turn it into an on-off control for the gasoline-powered generator outside.

More cannibalised wiring snaked away, out to the forecourt beneath the sheets of tarpaulin. The far ends of the wires were looped inside powder-filled jars that had formerly contained nuts and bolts. Now they lay beneath a buried service hatch, which in turn led to the half-empty storage tank under the petrol station's forecourt.

Half-empty, but still filled with enough gasoline and fumes to be dangerous.

Solomon flipped the switch, and the jury-rigged circuit buzzed and spat. Marc had told him that it would take a few seconds for the improvised electric detonator to heat up enough to trigger the chemical reaction. The mix of volatiles he had brewed from the supplies in the garage would combust, and the contents of the big tank would go with it.

There's enough time to get out, Marc had told them, as they waited for the helicopter to arrive. *Whoever does it, just flick the light switch and run like hell.*

Solomon leaned back and let the wall take his weight, breathing unevenly.

'What have you done?' Khadir saw the switch, the wires, and cast around in alarm. 'Answer me!'

Solomon's face split in a smile, and although it was becoming difficult to speak, he did so.

'That . . . is not your concern.'

Malte moaned as Marc dumped him in the back of the jeep.

'Where's Solomon?' Lucy was in the driver's seat, with the engine running and her hand on the stick-shift, ready to floor it. 'He should be here!'

'Back there,' Marc gasped, twisting to point in the direction of the buildings. 'We need to go get him—'

The explosion lit up the night with searing orange colour, the contents of the buried storage tank erupting out of the ground in a ball of fire that rose high over their heads.

The roaring shock wave slammed Marc against the side of the vehicle and he saw the buildings framed by the inferno. The fire roiled and churned upwards, but the force of the blast was a hammer blow, and it flattened everything. The petrol station, the overhead awning, the garage shack, sheds and outhouse beside it – all came down in a long, rolling peal of thunder.

'No!'

Marc shouted the word into the bitter wave of dust that rose in the wake of the collapse. He pushed away from the jeep and ran into the choking cloud, as burning debris came down around him from out of the sky.

He tried to take a breath to call out, but his mouth filled with displaced soil and thick smoke. He stumbled and wheezed, squinting into the haze.

Where the building had stood, there was a great heap of fallen brickwork and rubble, slumped into a blackened crater where the fuel tank had been buried. Fires burned everywhere, the dry scrub caught alight by the explosion. Marc heard the sizzle and crack of superheated metal, and the thick carbon stink of spent petrol was lead-heavy in his lungs.

'No . . .'

The denial was all he could manage, all he could muster against the destruction. He staggered to a halt, unable to process it. Rage and sorrow and dread spun through him in a terrible surge.

Marc's legs twitched and he wanted to give in to the impulse to fall to his knees. The fire-smell engulfed him; he felt it like it was a part of him, a black shadow of loss and horror.

If he closed his eyes, he knew he would be back on that burning dockside in France, with the woman he loved dying in his arms; he would be on a hill in the savannah watching flames consume the shell of a downed airliner.

He was here now, and the fire was taking more from him. A friend, a mentor, a man he had admired and respected.

Marc felt Lucy's hand on his shoulder and turned. Caked in dust, she looked like a wraith. Her eyes were wide and childlike, tears cutting lines through the dirt on her cheeks.

He had never seen her cry before. She looked at Marc and he knew she wanted him to tell her that the worst was not so, that Solomon had escaped this destruction. They could not lose another, not after Ari and Assim.

No more. The fight could not take any more from them.

But what they wanted did not matter.

All Marc could do was give a faint shake of the head, and draw Lucy to him.

Lau looked up as Esther McFarlane entered the darkened conference room, and for a moment she lost a step. The man seemed to have aged ten years in the past few days, as if the tension and the fatigue inside him had finally broken the banks of his self-control and flooded out. At her side, Henri Delancort was uncharacteristically muted, walking through the building with her in the manner of a man attending his own funeral.

And that was closer to the truth than McFarlane wanted to admit.

Lau eyed her. 'What do you want?' Before she could reply, he fired off a second demand. 'Why are you still here?'

She stiffened. She wasn't about to answer Lau's questions, and a lifetime of being the only woman in a corporate bear-pit had taught her how to avoid being deflected from her purpose.

'I've had a report from our financial analysis team. They've tracked a series of massive stock transfers to shell companies in Eastern Europe and Russia. A suicide run on shares across Rubicon's primary and secondary divisions. We're being cut up. Butchered like a fucking ox.'

Lau looked away, out of the window and over Monaco to the morning light across the bay. He appeared as if he had slept in that suit of his, and perhaps he had. There was no sign that he had left the Rubicon tower since this whole debacle had started.

'The other board members – are they as coarse as you?'

Her lip twisted as she thought about Keller and Cruz.

'They've gone running back to their own corners. Fighting their own fires.' She stepped forward. 'You used me, you duplicitous bastard. Somehow you got to Finlay, and he smoothed the way. I was so caught up trying to handle Solomon, I wasn't seeing the bigger picture.' McFarlane jabbed a finger at him. 'Who do you really work for? It sure as shit isn't Interpol.'

'I have no idea what you are talking about,' Lau insisted. 'What has happened here is the inevitable end result of the choices Ekko Solomon made,' he told her. 'You yourself saw it coming. Do not play the victim here. You had ample time to disengage yourself. But instead you remained tied to Rubicon because you liked the profits.' He gave a low snort. 'If you had displayed the courage of your convictions, you would be long gone. But now you are being pulled under, so do not pretend you do not know why.'

'Now see here—' she began, her native burr emerging.

'*Madame* . . .'

Delancort broke in, reacting to something out of her field of view and she turned towards a doorway leading into another part of the conference space.

Standing on the threshold in an immaculate steel-grey suit was a man that McFarlane knew only too well. Pytor Glovkonin was high up on her personal list of arseholes, the consequence of his many underhanded attempts in the past to brute-force the acquisition of her oil company for absorption into his energy conglomerate. But more than that, the Russian wasn't only your garden-variety billionaire shitehawk. He was in deep with the Combine, and if the rumours were true, he was making advances up their ranks.

McFarlane was simultaneously anger-hot and sickly chilled by the man's unexpected presence in the tower. He looked around with a barely concealed smirk, exhibiting the air of a conquering king in the palace of a defeated enemy.

And that, she realised, *is exactly what he is.*

'Well, this explains a lot,' she said. 'Solomon warned us about you. I thought he was exaggerating.'

With difficulty, Lau rose from his chair and used his stick to support himself.

'Come to check in on your investment?' he said, shooting a look towards McFarlane and Delancort. 'We can discuss matters in more secure circumstances.'

'No need,' Glovkonin replied. 'I believe in clarity, Mr Lau. Everyone involved must understand the realities of the current situation.'

'You did this,' said Delancort, his gaze fixed on the Russian. 'It's your way of paying us back for the SCD's interference. To get back at Solomon.'

'Ekko Solomon is dead.'

Glovkonin tossed out the comment with a casual dismissal that seemed too smooth to be real. He let the words lie there, enjoying the reaction they stirred.

'Bullshit!' snapped Delancort.

'Anything but.' Glovkonin's eyes narrowed at the French-Canadian's profanity. 'The others too, most likely. Dane and the woman, the Jew pilot, the rest of them. I have confirmation from trusted sources. In due time, I imagine bodies will be recovered.'

The last information on Solomon had placed his private air-liner on a southerly heading towards the equator. McFarlane was momentarily at a loss for words, and to her surprise, Lau appeared equally shocked. At her side, Delancort became unnaturally still, his gaze drifting away and turning inwards.

All of them shared the same thought: *Impossible.*

'Solomon's jet is a mass of blackened wreckage on a hill somewhere,' Glovkonin added. 'A terrible accident. Shot down by some trigger-happy fighter pilot. But then Ekko had shown such poor judgement in recent times. These accusations from Interpol, the video footage from Cyprus . . .' He shook his head and made a soft tut-tut sound. 'Solomon led his people to their destruction. Them . . . and now you.'

He nodded to McFarlane and Delancort.

She pushed away a jolt of fear and forced a note of control back into her voice.

'Do you have what you wanted, Pytor? I'll take a wild stab here, because this has your stink all over it – did you have your fun manipulating us into doing your dirty work?'

Glovkonin walked further into the room, with one of his brawny bodyguards a few steps behind him.

'You allowed yourself to be manipulated, Esther. Because you thought it would bring you what you wanted. Ekko Solomon's expulsion.' He waved at the otherwise empty room. 'Your wish has been granted. He won't come back.'

She tried to find the words to snipe back at him, but the simple truth was Glovkonin was correct. Her focus had been so tightly set on ending the unchecked vigilantism of Solomon's Special Conditions Division that she had opened a door to their enemies. Even as that bleak reality settled in on her, part of McFarlane – the dispassionate, analytical businesswoman – began to calculate the choices still open to her, counting the cost that would inevitably come next.

If the Russian was to be believed, the only man who could have defied him was lost. Glovkonin must have seen the shift behind McFarlane's eyes, and he knew that he had won.

'I am disappointed Solomon was allowed to destroy vital company materials before he fled. As your new majority shareholder, I would have preferred that data intact. But no matter, I will adapt to the circumstances.' Glovkonin glanced at Lau, then away again. 'By the end of the week, the Rubicon Group as an entity will no longer exist. The structure will be broken up, absorbed or sold. It's for the best,' he added. 'With this negative news coverage, the brand has become rather soiled.'

'We won't let you do this,' Delancort insisted.

His fists were tight, and he shook with emotion.

'You don't have a say in it!' Glovkonin barked the reply in a sudden, angry shout, and McFarlane saw a brief glimpse of the real man beneath the studied mask. 'I am going to take what I want from Rubicon and you are going to let me! Because you have no other choice!'

'No . . .' Lau was shaking his head. 'No, this is not what was agreed. I made Rubicon . . . It is mine by right, I was there at the beginning—'

'And you're here at the end,' Glovkonin snapped. His manner switched back to false good humour. 'Lau, be realistic. A man like you, in control of this? Once upon a time, you could have had that life, but now?' He gave a mocking laugh. 'Tell me, truthfully, what do you really have except your need for revenge? As one man to another, admit it.' The Russian prodded him in the chest. 'In there, you are hollow. Empty and worn out. The only vigour in you came from wanting Solomon to suffer. That's gone now. So what do you have left?'

'I . . .' Lau struggled for an answer, but it was clear he could not find one. 'I did what you asked. I am *owed*.'

Suddenly, the other man seemed so old and so small. The fire in his eyes that had been there when he first met McFarlane had become cinder and ash. With effort, he recovered a measure of his strength and spat back a reply.

'After all that has been taken from me, *I am owed*!'

Glovkonin nodded towards McFarlane.

'You're just like her, my friend. You were a means to an end. But the similarity ends there. Esther is a consummate pragmatist, and she knows when a battle is over. She knows how to lose with poise and intelligence. But you?' He snorted with derision. 'You are like all soldiers. You believe that martial intellect makes you a match for men like me. But in the end, you are only a tool. Incapable of being anything more.'

Lau's face creased in a snarling grimace and he let his steel cane drop, one hand flicking into the folds of his jacket, returning with a snub-nosed revolver.

'I want my due!'

The bodyguard drew his own pistol, and McFarlane and Delancort shrank back at the sight of the guns, but Glovkonin appeared unimpressed with the threat.

'You prove my point. In the end, hate is all you have. You need more than that if you are to succeed.'

Then, before Lau could speak again, Glovkonin gave his man the slightest of nods, and the bodyguard fired twice. Both shots were deafeningly loud in the soundproofed conference room, and Lau's thin, angular body crumpled back over the wide mahogany table and spun to the floor.

McFarlane turned white, appalled by the shooting.

An execution, she told herself.

'Tragic,' said the Russian, shaking his head as more of his men came in to secure Lau's body. 'But inevitable. When a person understands that they are no longer of use, they react in extreme ways. But predictable ones.'

He turned towards McFarlane and she couldn't stop herself from backing away another step, instinctively afraid that she and Delancort would be next.

'Misha had no choice but to fire, of course,' Glovkonin was saying, gesturing at the bodyguard. 'I am sure you agree.' He took their silence as affirmation. 'Regrettably, we now need to discuss damage limitation.'

He snapped his fingers, beckoning an assistant in from the other room. A lithe young woman entered, carrying a digital tablet displaying contract documents, and she seemed completely undisturbed by either the gunshots or the dead man being gathered up by the Russian's team. The woman handed the tablet to McFarlane and she read the first block of text at the top of the page. It was the framework for a G-Kor buy-out deal that would purchase her controlling interests in the Rubicon Group, and cut her company loose from the conglomerate.

'It's a generous offer, Esther,' said Glovkonin. 'I suggest you accept it while you still can.'

Marc sat on the bonnet of the jeep and stared blankly at the rough runway, looking but not seeing, his gaze lost and unfocused.

His fingers were still cracked and seared from trying to shift the rubble from the collapsed petrol station. It had been a pointless exercise, born out of frustration, and in the end they had to flee as the sound of approaching vehicles reached them. Simbarashe's soldiers were hunting those responsible for their murdered commander, and they had called in reinforcements from every garrison of the militia.

Barandi's outpost was exactly where Solomon had told them it would be: a worn-out and tumbledown airstrip to the east, in a forgotten corner of Mozambique's coastline. His old comrade was heavyset and balding, with the stature of a fighter now gone to seed and all too aware of it. Barandi moved stiffly, revealing a crude metal prosthetic where his lower right leg should have been. The mark a landmine had left on him, he explained. Suspicious of them at first, he only changed his manner when Marc showed him the scratched and dented signet ring.

Ekko is dead?

Barandi asked the question, but he didn't need any of them to answer. The shared silence from Marc, Lucy and Malte said enough.

He spoke about unpaid debts, and gave them the shelter they needed, but Marc could not find sleep and stayed outside, listening to the buzz and whirr of insects.

Each time he tried to pull himself back to the moment, Marc's mind recoiled from the horrible reality of their situation. The grim truth sat like a stone in his chest, impossible to dislodge.

In the dilapidated tin-sheet hangar behind him, lost in the shadows, Assim Kader's body rested inside a shapeless black sack. Beside Marc's dead friend, the bullet-riddled ammunition case with the salvaged hard drives lay close to where Malte Riis was sleeping. The Finn stayed near, ready to protect what little they had recovered from this mess.

Marc dwelled on what to do with Assim. He had a family that would want his remains returned to them, but so did Ari Silber, and there was nothing of the pilot to send home.

And Solomon?

It troubled Marc deeply to imagine the man's body buried beneath that hill of rubble. It was an undeserved fate for someone who had fought so hard to do the right thing.

Shuffling footsteps approached, and presently Barandi appeared at Marc's side. He offered him a cracked mug of strong coffee, and Marc took it gratefully.

'Did he come back here to die?'

Barandi had a low, whispering voice that carried in the still morning air.

'I don't think that was his plan,' Marc offered. 'If anything, he was trying to find a way to keep us alive.'

Barandi nodded. 'That sounds like him. Carried the weight of the world, that one. Every sorrow was his burden.'

'Yeah.'

After a while, the other man spoke again.

'A long time ago, I told Ekko not to return to this place. Not because of bad blood between us, you understand? But because I knew it would only end poorly for him.' He shook his head. 'I am sad I was right.'

Bit by bit, Marc parcelled out the events that had brought them to this moment, and Barandi listened in solemn silence. It seemed the least he could do – to give this man the facts that had led to his friend's death.

When he was done, Barandi gave a slow nod.

'So now you are lost. You have paid for your escape with your dearest blood, and your home is in ruins.'

'That's about the size of it,' Marc agreed. 'Rubicon belongs to our enemies. We have nothing but the clothes on our backs and a few rounds of ammo.'

Barandi gave Marc a measuring look, the same kind of expression that Solomon had often challenged him with.

'Is that all you have? I do not think it is.'

'I'm not sure a plucky attitude and a disregard for danger will be enough this time.'

A radio clipped to Barandi's belt gave a flat crackle of static, and he reached for it.

'In the worst of days,' he replied, 'it is best to go with what you know.' He held the handset to his mouth and looked towards the shabby control tower hundreds of metres away down the length of the airstrip. 'What?'

One of Barandi's crew up in the tower waved and a rapid-fire babble of words came out of the radio, too fast and too garbled for Marc to interpret them.

Barandi seemed to understand, however.

'Let me hear.'

The radio spluttered and a new voice clicked in, speaking in lazy Portuguese.

'*Homem de ferro chamando ganso selvagem, over.*'

'What's he saying?'

As Marc spoke, he heard the sound of aero engines coming in from over the sea, and turned to look. The cloud was low, but there was no mistaking the familiar, husky form of a C-130 Hercules as it dropped out of the haze and angled towards them.

'Your ride is here,' said Barandi.

Alerted by the snarl of the cargo plane's engines, Lucy emerged from the hangar and jogged across to them, as the aircraft made a pass over the runway. The Hercules turned inbound, the glass panels of the flight deck catching the morning sun as it lined up with the rough strip, and the crew put it down with a skill that spoke of great experience in bush landings.

As the aircraft turned and rolled to a halt, Lucy leaned in and talked into Marc's ear.

'What are we expecting here?' She had one of the AKs over her shoulder, her hand on the strap and ready to pull it. 'No insignia on that thing. Who's it belong to?'

Marc shrugged. 'No idea. This was Assim's work. He called it in.'

'Pulling favours from his buddies on the dark net,' she noted. 'Black hat hackers and techno-anarchists. I know I don't need to remind you what happened the last time we met those kinda folks.'

'We're not the position to be choosy right now.' He held out a hand. 'But . . . just keep your eyes open, eh?'

'Always.'

The wide cargo ramp tucked beneath the tail of the plane dropped like a drawbridge, and the first person out was the last one Marc expected to see.

'*Mes amis,*' said Benjamin Harun, offering his hands. 'How is it going?'

'Could be better.'

Marc shook off the moment of surprise. It was surreal to see the Frenchman here, when he was so used to meeting him in the soothing pastel context of the Rubicon therapist's office. But it was equally good to see his colleague, and Marc felt a little of the gloom about him lift.

The ex-legionnaire nodded and looked to Lucy.

'I'm glad you are both okay. I came as soon as I received the message . . .' He trailed off, sensing something amiss. 'Where are the rest?'

'It's just Malte and us,' said Lucy, holding the control of her voice. 'Solomon and the others . . . They didn't make it.'

'Oh.' Benjamin stiffened and took a moment to process that. Marc watched him take in his own jolt of grief, then put it away, making himself ready to support them. 'My friends, I am so sorry.' He was still holding their hands, and he gave them a final squeeze before disengaging. 'We couldn't get here any faster—'

'It wouldn't have made any difference,' Marc told him. 'I'm just glad Assim could reach you, otherwise we'd be stranded down here.'

'It wasn't Assim who contacted me,' Benjamin corrected, as someone else emerged from the interior of the Hercules. 'She did.'

He nodded towards the new arrival, a slim East Asian woman in a red leather jacket.

The woman peeled off a pair of mirrored sunglasses and showed them an unreadable, cat-like expression.

'Hey,' she said, by way of greeting.

'You gotta be goddamn kidding me!' Lucy's tone flipped from muted to iron-hard and angry in an instant. She glared at Benjamin. 'What the hell is *she* doing here?'

'I know you two have a lot of unresolved issues,' began the Frenchman, 'but it was Kara who called me, and—'

'Kara *fucking* Wei.' Lucy ground out the name of her former friend as if she were chewing shards of glass. 'You're the dark web source Assim was keeping secret from us.' She made a spitting noise. 'Sure you are. Because the universe isn't done screwing with me yet.'

She turned and walked away a few steps, swearing under her breath, unable to look the other woman in the eye.

Kara gave Marc a questioning look.

'She's still not over what happened in Korea?'

'Well, you did lie to us about who you were, betray us to mercenary hackers, and then ghost on us when the hammer dropped.' Marc glanced in Lucy's direction. 'She trusted you, more than anyone.'

Kara Wei had been a key member of the Special Conditions Division, working alongside Marc, Lucy and the rest of the unit as their cyber-operations specialist; but she had concealed her true origins from them. When her former comrades in a radical cybercrime collective embarked on a plan to drag the nations of North and South Korea into war, Kara had ultimately put her own agenda before that of the team. She had almost got them killed in the process.

'I left a note,' Kara countered. 'I'm not good with apologies. Or people, really.'

'The Combine killed Assim,' Lucy shot back. 'And they're responsible for killing Ari and Solomon. Does that mean anything to you? Or are you too clockwork to feel it?'

Kara said nothing, her expression unchanged. Marc searched her eyes for some hint to how she was processing those harsh facts, but the woman seemed distant and removed from the moment.

'That's upsetting,' she said, after a long pause. 'Assim asked me for my help, so I'm here. I'm here to help you.'

Lucy grabbed Marc's hand and pulled him away so they could speak privately.

'We can't rely on her,' she hissed. 'Assim kept his contact with her a secret because he knew that, but he didn't want to admit it!'

Marc nodded. 'Okay, but the intel from her was solid. Like it or not, she's already helped us.'

'Yeah,' Lucy retorted, 'and Kara's good at what she does, that's not in doubt. But she left us twisting in the wind, Marc! We can't trust her motives.'

Lucy's words brought Marc up short, and in his mind's eye he saw the woman Grace, smiling Sam Green's smile at him.

'Kara's not our enemy,' he said. 'She made bad choices, but she's not on the wrong side.'

Lucy let go of him and her anger faded.

'You sure about that?'

'Not 100 per cent, no,' he admitted. 'But I don't have a better idea, do you?'

Lucy frowned, and at length, she gave a bitter shake of the head.

'I don't. And I guess this is your show now, so I'll go with what you decide.'

'You can trust me if you don't trust her,' he said, hoping that there was more conviction in the words than he felt.

'That'll have to be enough,' said Lucy.

Barandi refused to accept anything approaching payment for sheltering them.

He tapped his missing leg and told Marc that he was making amends for an old debt, and then warned him to get moving. His man in the tower had picked up radio messages on militia frequencies, and it wouldn't be long before Colonel Simbarashe's men came to the airstrip looking for answers.

Marc gathered them on the cargo plane's ramp. Lucy and Malte carried Assim's remains aboard with the martial dignity of a military burial detail, and one hard look from the Finn stopped the C-130's loadmaster dead when he offered to help. Marc had the ammo crate, and he put it down on the deck, flipping over the lid to reveal the contents.

'So what you're looking at here is a bunch of parachutes.' He beckoned them in and pointed at the damaged hard drive modules. 'This is all that is left of Rubicon's Grey Record database. We lost some of it getting here, but there's still plenty left.'

Despite herself, Kara licked her lips.

'I'd like to take a look.'

'I am sure you would,' said Marc. 'There's also money in there. Account codes for black bag funds that Solomon kept off the books. We can divide it up between us.' He looked to Lucy and Malte. 'Plus a generous share for Assim's and Ari's families. I reckon there's enough that we can each take a cut and get gone. Go dark.' He gestured out at the wilderness. 'Let's not sugar-coat it. We've lost. And when the Combine catch up to the fact that we're still breathing, they'll come gunning for us. They don't like loose ends.'

'You are suggesting that we walk.' Benjamin's broad face creased in a frown. 'Go our separate ways, buy new identities and spend the rest of our days looking over our shoulders. That's not much of a life, Marc.'

'No,' he agreed, 'but it is a life.'

'As long as it lasts,' Malte said quietly. 'The files?'

'We destroy them.' Marc nudged the crate with his boot. 'We've seen how far Glovkonin was willing to go to get this shit. Better no one has it than he does.'

'But that's not Plan A, right?' Lucy stared at him. 'You have that look in your eyes, Dane. I always see it before you do something reckless.'

He smiled thinly. 'There is another option. And if we take it, it's the biggest roll of the dice any of us will make. All the chips in, a one-shot deal. We lose, and it's the end. None of us come out of it alive.' He crouched, and pulled out one of the intact drives. 'We can take the black money, we can take what's on these, and turn it on the Combine.'

No one spoke. Marc knew what he proposed was a big ask, especially in the wake of having lost so much. But time was against them, and a choice had to be made.

He did something that Solomon used to do, looking each of them in the eye as he spoke.

'This has to be something we all agree on. There'll be no judgement here if anyone wants to take the first option.'

He came to Lucy last and she met his gaze.

A silent communication passed between them. The unspoken thought was there.

Together, we could make it work. Become ghosts, watch each other's backs. Vanish and leave this behind.

And for a moment, that was what Marc wanted to do. But then she gave the slightest shake of the head, and he knew, like him, she would not be able to live with that.

Malte spoke again. 'How do we clear our names?'

'The real, unaltered source footage from the Cyprus attack must exist somewhere,' said Kara. 'It can be found and released to the world.'

'Even if you did that, it may not matter,' Benjamin noted. 'But I sense Marc is thinking of a larger goal. Something bigger than us.'

Each of them watched Marc, waiting for him to continue. He felt the world shifting around him, a change in the air that made him feel strangely renewed. Before, it was Ekko Solomon they had looked to, but now it was him. He felt the weight of that expectation, but he also drew strength from it.

'Are we in?' Lucy, Malte, Benjamin and Kara gave him a silent nod, and he returned it. 'Then this is where we start. Whatever it takes. We don't look back. And we don't stop until we burn the Combine to the ground.'

TWENTY-THREE

The men on the screens toasted Glovkonin with their glasses, and he returned the salute with a tumbler full of Stolichnaya Elit, nodding indulgently as the light in the cabin shifted. The G-Kor Gulfstream was still a few hours from touchdown at Moscow-Sheremetyevo, and it amused him to imagine his flight home as some sort of victory lap over the heads of those who had doubted him.

The other members of the Combine's committee took their turns to congratulate him. The American was the most animated, pleased with the financial opportunity that Rubicon's disruption had provided, and he insisted on rehashing the details of the hostile takeovers he had initiated in the past week, savouring the way he had plundered the best cuts from the crippled corporation. The Swiss banker was his usual terse self, but even he had to grudgingly admit that Glovkonin's complex plan to undermine Ekko Solomon had borne fruit. In particular, he highlighted the use of Lau as the critical element in destabilising Rubicon, and that was as close to a compliment as he was capable of giving. The Italian, of course, was all smiles and comradely affability, but that was undercut by a faint air of disdain that could not be completely hidden.

Predictably, it was the Italian who had to remind them that despite his success, Glovkonin had failed in one particular area.

'It is a disappointment that you were unable to secure any of this Grey Record database,' said the other man. 'It certainly would have been a valuable asset.'

'*Do we even need that?*' snorted the American, still high on his own enrichment. '*This is a goddamn windfall. In fact, the liquidation of Rubicon's assets is gonna enable us to move up the programme with our next operation. I call that a win.*'

'*And there is the other matter,*' continued the Italian, still smiling as he pressed his point, '*confirmation of death.*'

'That is in hand,' Glovkonin assured him. 'Perhaps you'd like a physical sample as proof? I can arrange for something to be delivered.'

The Swiss banker made a snorting noise, his equivalent of a snigger.

'*There's no need for that.*'

'*No need,*' echoed the American. '*I reckon we've kept our Russian friend here hanging long enough, gentlemen. Time to make it formal, huh?*'

'*Indeed,*' said the Swiss, and he led another salute to Glovkonin. '*Welcome to the committee. You have earned your seat at our table.*'

'Thank you for this honour.' He raised his glass once more. 'I will strive to be worthy of it.'

I will destroy every one of you.

The words pushed at his lips, and Glovkonin smiled widely as he imagined saying them out loud. His life was one long struggle to gain what others had denied him, the rewards that some enjoyed and that he had always been told he was unworthy of.

It was not enough for Pytor Glovkonin to be rich and powerful. It was not enough for him to merely succeed. Others – *all the others* – had to fail for his victory to mean anything.

Walking through the debris of Ekko Solomon's empire had reminded him of that singular truth. The energy he had felt at that moment, the near-sexual thrill of knowing that he had obliterated an adversary . . . Nothing compared to it. No drug, no vice, no pleasure could come close.

And so, even as the ashes of this battle were cooling, he smiled at his new enemies as he drew his plans against them.

Henri Delancort stood at the window and watched the vehicles coming and going on the Avenue de Grande Bretagne. For the past two days, unmarked trucks had backed up to the loading bays at the base of the Rubicon tower and filled up with everything that wasn't bolted to the floor.

Who had instigated this purge and where the trucks were going was not something that Delancort was privy to. He only knew that there were entire levels of the building denuded of equipment, emptied of people. Rumours were already circling that a major corporate banking interest had made a bid to take over the property.

And where do I go then?

Delancort's contract with Rubicon had not been terminated, unlike those of countless other employees, but he had no function to fulfil in this gutted, echoing place. If he resigned, there were harsh clauses in the agreement that would ruin him.

He suspected this was some petty punishment being inflicted on him by Glovkonin, forcing him to stand as mute witness to the steady dismantling of Ekko Solomon's legacy.

On his desk, next to a laptop computer and a telephone, was the only thing he had been able to rescue from the stripping of Solomon's apartments. A small metal sculpture resembling the wings of an abstract bird about to take flight.

Sorrow welled up in him as he stared at the object and nursed his regrets. He would never forgive himself that he had parted on poor terms with Solomon, and now there was no way to make amends. Despite everything they disagreed over, Delancort's deep respect for the other man had never wavered. It saddened him that, in the end, they had found themselves on opposite sides of an ultimately losing proposition.

The telephone rang, making him jump. Delancort stared at it for a full three seconds. He was a non-person here, an object lesson left behind to warn others to behave. Why would anyone want to speak to him?

'*Oui?*'

He tapped the phone's speaker button and sat down in front of the computer.

'*How's life in the ruins, Henri?*'

Marc Dane's low Londoner snarl filled the room.

Delancort snatched up the handset in a moment of panic.

'They'll be monitoring this call—'

'*No, they won't,*' Marc replied. '*I worked there, remember? I know my way around that mainframe.*'

'Of course.' Delancort took a breath and composed himself. 'ALEPH are looking for you. I've heard resources are being diverted to an international search. If you are smart, you will run and not look back.'

'*I'm not that smart,*' Marc replied.

'Ari Silber's wife, his children . . .' Delancort changed tack. 'They have been taken care of. And Assim . . .'

'*We're dealing with that.*'

'I am sorry.'

'*We all are.*'

A moment of silence stretched between them, and Delancort could hear the metallic whispering of encryption software masking the call.

'If you want to accuse me or decry me, you are wasting your time.' He sighed. 'I made my choice because I believed in it. I would do so again.' His words rang hollow.

'*Solomon didn't blame you,*' Marc said, after a moment. '*That's why I'm calling, Henri. Because he would want you to know.*'

Delancort leaned forward, propping himself up on the desk.

'Thank you for that. I regret how this progressed.' He hesitated, summoning the will to ask the next question. 'How . . . ? How did it happen?'

'*We're alive because of him.*' The Englishman didn't elaborate any further. '*There's something else I have to say,*' he continued. '*This is not over. Not by a long shot.*'

Delancort rose and walked to the window, his voice dropping to a low hiss.

'Look what this has already cost! It is a grave mistake to go against them, Dane. Surely you can see that?'

'*What I see is a bloke who picked the wrong side, and now he has to live with it.*'

And then Delancort heard another familiar voice on the same line.

'*He looks like shit,*' said Lucy Keyes. '*Tell him to go take a shower.*'

He froze, suddenly aware that they were watching him. Delancort slammed the laptop lid shut, and glanced around, searching for monitoring devices. He turned back and stared out over the Monaco skyline. There were thousands of windows out there, and they could be behind any one of them, observing the tower through some high-powered optics.

'Are . . . ? Are you *here*?'

'*Good luck, Henri.*' There was a calm smile in Marc's reply. '*Be seeing you.*'

The armoured 4 × 4 deposited Saito outside the sun-bleached walls of the hospital building near Porto de Pemba, and stiffly, he climbed into the heat of the day, peering around to take in his surroundings.

A handful of young soldiers in FADM uniforms patrolled the perimeter, and they gave Saito and his party a sneering once-over. But the youths did nothing more than that, unwilling to test themselves against Saito's mercenary bodyguards and the militia veterans who flanked the newly minted Colonel Dahma.

Strictly speaking, Dahma was a long way outside his territory here in the city of Pemba, but every soldier in this part of Mozambique knew who he was and the battles the militia had fought, and few would dare to question him.

Saito had arrived as the late Colonel Simbarashe was being mourned, with his former second in command seamlessly stepping into the vacated role of warlord. When it became clear that the deal between Simbarashe and Glovkonin was still in effect, Dahma became a model host, providing Saito with whatever he needed.

Within a day, he pieced together the events of that night. The gunner of the Hind had perished in the helicopter crash, but the pilot had escaped unharmed and he established the narrative.

Glovkonin's orders were clear and unequivocal.

'*I want proof,*' he said, growling the command over a satellite link. '*Not some bloodstained cloth or an eyewitness account. Like the ancient tradition of your people, in the samurai fashion,*

I want Ekko Solomon's head brought to me in a box. Nothing else will suffice.'

And so for the past few days, Saito had been both figuratively and literally digging through the rubble, gathering up the truth. Dahma's men excavated the site and took what they found to Pemba, and after more money changed hands, the new colonel had agreed to show it to Saito.

First, he came to a grubby room in a far corner of the hospital, where more soldiers stood guard. The room's sole occupant sat on the threadbare bed, her legs drawn up, her knees at her chest. Dahma told him that she had been found several miles away, wandering injured and disoriented through the savannah a day after the explosion at the petrol station.

When she saw Saito she froze, and he saw a new expression form on her face. The woman did not know what to do.

He studied her. She was bandaged around the head, and covered in scratches.

'Were you there when it happened?'

Grace frowned. 'Are you here to finish it?'

'Answer my question.'

'Khadir was going to kill me,' she insisted. 'You knew that, didn't you?'

'As far as anyone else knows, he did.' Saito folded his arms over his chest. 'Tell me what you saw.'

At length, Grace unfolded her version of events, concluding with a sigh.

'Solomon actually saved my life, can you believe that? I'd have let me take the bullet.' She told him what she saw as she fled, the explosion of the gas tank and the collapse of the building. 'I hope that fucker Khadir died screaming.'

Saito glanced at the soldiers and the ALEPH bodyguard outside the room. He had his misericorde dagger in the arm sheath beneath his left sleeve, and he was sure that he could draw it, use it, and end Grace's life without interruption. That was what Glovkonin had ordered Khadir to do.

She saw him making that calculation in his thoughts.

'I can still be of use to you,' Grace insisted. 'Just give me a window, yeah? Get rid of those yokels for ten minutes and I'm gone.'

'A blonde-haired white woman would not be able to vanish easily here,' he told her.

Despite herself, she grinned.

'Try me. Your boss doesn't have to know. And I'd owe you a marker, big-time.' Her tone changed, becoming sly, and for a moment she was the woman he had met for the first time in a dingy Greek taverna. 'You think Glovkonin is going to let you run out the clock? Sooner or later, he'll have no use for you too. You planned for that, Jackie Chan?'

'I will consider it,' he said, and left her there.

Dhama had more for him to see.

'You enjoyed that,' said Lucy, as she stuffed her gear into a ballistic nylon holdall. 'Dragging poor Henri.'

'Little bit,' Marc admitted.

He ran a subroutine to erase his intrusion software, which had allowed him to hack a home security camera in an apartment block across the avenue from the Rubicon tower. The camera returned to its normal functions and there would be no evidence that it had done anything untoward, but it had been surveilling Henri Delancort's office for the past few days, feeding that data back to an anonymous server ticking over in the depths of the internet.

Lucy shifted a blind at the window and peered out into the rain falling hard on Friedrichstrasse. She watched a U-Bahn tram halt outside their hotel, disgorging passengers into the downpour before setting off in the direction of Berlin-Tempelhof.

In the belly of the Hercules, somewhere over the Indian Ocean, they had drawn lots and she had got Germany. Lucy was still sore about that, even if her company was good.

Marc glanced at his Cabot dive watch.

'Time to go.'

He had barely unpacked, and it took only a moment to toss his gear into his bag and throw it over his shoulder. On the hotel room's wide bed there were two identical cell phones, each of the cheap little burners coded with a coloured strip of insulating tape. Marc picked up the blue-labelled one, and Lucy took the one with a red marker.

They moved to separate corners of the room and made their calls. Lucy's contact answered first.

'*I'm here.*' Malte sounded tired but focused. She could hear voices in the background talking in animated Cantonese. '*On the pier at Central. All clear.*'

'Stay safe out there.'

'*You too.*'

She cut the call and set to work taking the phone apart.

'He's getting the ferry,' Lucy offered. 'He'll be in Kowloon within the hour.'

Marc acknowledged her with a nod as his contact picked up. Lucy couldn't make out the words spoken, but she recognised Benjamin Harun's voice.

'All good here,' Marc told him. 'Is she behaving herself?'

The *she* in question had to be Kara, and thinking of the hacker made Lucy scowl. Harun and the woman had the job in Istanbul, and part of Lucy wished that she could have taken that gig, if for no other reason than to keep an eye on Kara Wei.

'Okay,' Marc was saying, 'you know what to do. Let us know when it's done.'

He followed Lucy's example, ending the call and gutting his phone so nothing would be left to trace.

The dismantled handsets went into a garbage bag, and Lucy took out the FN Five-Seven pistols they'd picked up the night before in Sonnenallee, passing one to Marc and checking the other before putting it into her waistband.

'This guy we're meeting, he's ex-Stasi, right? Will he help us . . . ?' She stopped, realising that Marc was staring at her. 'What?'

'Just thinking,' he said, looking her in the eye. 'I don't want to lose anyone else I care about.'

She moved to him. 'You don't get to decide that. Life don't work that way.' Lucy reached for his hand and took it. 'We gotta play what we've been dealt.'

'All or nothing?'

She nodded. 'All or nothing.'

Marc had one of the hard drives in his other hand, and he weighed it there, a faint and wolfish smile playing on him.

'Let's go start a fire,' he said.

Dhama led Saito down to the hospital's basement mortuary, and after a roll of American dollars had changed hands, the glum, white-coated attendant presented them with a greasy body bag.

Saito's nose wrinkled at the stink of sour death and disinfectant, but he did not allow anyone else to open the zip. Pulling
open the bag revealed a body crushed and distorted by fire damage and great pressure. A flattened ribcage was split and open,
allowing organ matter to pool where it had burst through flesh
and bone. One muscular arm had been completely torn off, and
it lay there in the bag along with the rest of the remains, still
covered in a coating of pale dust. Fingerprints were visible on it
from whoever had found the limb and stowed it with the mangled corpse.

Saito rolled back the mouth of the body bag and came across
the upper torso and quarter of the dead man. Dropping his slen-
der, stiletto-like dagger into his grip, he used the tip of it to move
the rigor-stiffened head towards him.

Omar Khadir's face was slack in death, his umber skin
turned waxy and sunken. Fire had marked him, leaving raw
lesions across his throat and up to his brow. The lion of a man
whose presence had stalked the nightmares of thousands was
inanimate, decaying meat and broken bone. Saito looked
down and saw the ruins of the assassin, of someone only
fanatics and killers would mourn.

He took a series of digital photos and a DNA sample, then
withdrew and moved to the second bag the attendant presented for his consideration. In halting English, the man in the
stained lab coat explained that this body had been dug out of
the rubble in close proximity to Khadir's, but it had sustained
considerable fire damage.

Inside, Saito found a charred mass that was barely identifi-
able, the flesh bloated and blackened to such a degree that there

was no immediate way to make an identification. The corpse reeked of spent gasoline and burned meat, and once again Saito imaged and sampled it. He paused before zipping the bag closed, noting a piece of charred material that flaked away in his hand. A fragment of nylon, the same fabric that made up the tactical vests used by Khadir's strike team.

'Are you satisfied?' said Dahma.

Saito's dagger blurred through the air like an arc of mercury and suddenly the tip of it was pressing into the colonel's thick neck. The ALEPH bodyguard reacted in kind, his gun whipping out to aim into the face of the lone militiaman who had accompanied Dahma into the mortuary.

'I am not satisfied,' said Saito. 'You are beholden to the agreement made by Simbarashe. Will you follow it, or will you follow him?'

At length, Dahma gave a slight nod, careful not to cut himself on the misericorde's point.

'This way,' he said, pointing.

In the next room, a storage area had hastily been converted into a recovery space of sorts, with a bed and an outdated medical monitor for a lone occupant. A man with teak-dark flesh, half-mummified by bloody bandages, lay at the mercy of an intubated ventilator. Much of his face was lost behind more dressings, and his chest rose and fell in low stutters. Saito saw an IV line and heard the slow pulse of a regular heartbeat.

Saito shrugged off Dhama's hand as the colonel tried to stop him from moving closer.

'No one should have been able to survive that,' insisted Dahma, as if denying what was right in front of them. 'Buried under it. He should be dead. Everyone has been told he is dead.'

From behind him, Saito heard the low electronic chime of a sat-phone alert, but he ignored it, leaning in as something metallic caught his eye. Hanging on a blackened silver chain around the injured man's neck was a comma of pressed steel. The familiar shape of a rifle trigger.

Reaching for the metal object, Saito's proximity caused the man in the bed to stir, one bloodshot eye cracking open to study him.

'Saito.' The ALEPH bodyguard called out from the mortuary in his terse Ukrainian accent. 'Message from the principal. He wants an update.'

Saito met Solomon's gaze, and silently considered what he would do next.

Acknowledgements

My thanks to Robert Kirby, Kate Walsh, Zoe Ross, Jonathan Lyons, Ben Willis, Ciara Corrigan, Steve O'Gorman, Nick Stearn, Margaret Stead and Kate Parkin for their hard work in bringing this novel to the world.

As ever, any errors are mine but every attempt is made to be accurate. In the pursuit of that, my thanks go to Ben Aaronovitch, Peter J. Evans, and David and Kara Mack for both moral support and sterling advice; to Hans Zimmer, James Newton Howard and Lorne Balfe for musical inspiration, and to Tom Burgis, Marc Dubin, Jeff Goins, Naomi Klein, Jack Rhysider, Algarve Extreme, Deutsches Spionage Museum, Skater Powerboats, SOS Parachutes and SpyScape for resources and research materials.

And as always, much love to my mother and to my better half, Mandy.

This novel was written on location in London, Vilamoura, New York City, and 35,000 feet over the Atlantic.

A message from the author . . .

Hello!

Thanks for picking up ROGUE, the fifth book in my Marc Dane action thriller series. I hope you enjoyed reading it as much as I did writing and researching this story. If you are new to Marc Dane, Lucy Keyes and the Rubicon team, it's great to have you aboard and I hope you'll check out the other books in the series – and to all my returning readers out there, thanks for your ongoing support, it really means a lot!

I've always said that the Marc Dane novels scratch the itch I have to write modern, tech-savvy action-adventure thrillers, like the high-octane fiction I loved from the 80's and 90's, with an everyman hero facing off against deadly threats.

Marc is my way of inverting that old character trope of the "bloke in the van", the person always on the side-lines while others are in the thick of the action. I wanted to explore what would happen if that guy was pulled kicking and screaming out of his comfort zone and into danger . . . I love the idea of a hero who *isn't* the toughest guy in the room, but instead has to rely on his wits and his resourcefulness . . .

After Marc's journey through the events of NOMAD, searching for vengeance and racing to stop a brutal terrorist, he finds himself in dire new circumstances for EXILE, chasing down a rogue nuclear device. In GHOST he faces a betrayal in his own team, in SHADOW Marc fights to stop a bioweapon attack in the heart of Europe, and as you've just read in ROGUE, Marc and the Rubicon team finally come face to face with the forces that have been plotting their downfall from the shadows.

Where do our heroes go from here? With the ruthless power brokers known as the Combine victorious, Marc, Lucy and the surviving members of Rubicon have nothing left to lose. They're going to risk everything on one high-stakes mission, to take the battle to their enemies and bring them down once and for all. But if they fail, it will be the last thing they ever do . . .

If you would like to keep up to date about my books and be the first to know about the next novel in this series, remember to go to bit.ly/JamesSwallowClub where you can become part of the JAMES SWALLOW READERS' CLUB.

It only takes a few moments to sign up, there's no catch and no cost. New members automatically receive an exclusive article from me that features a scene cut from the original draft of NOMAD – think of it as a novel version of a "DVD extra" with a bit of author's commentary!

Zaffre keep your data private and confidential, and it will never be passed on to a third party. We won't spam you with loads of emails, just get in touch with occasional updates from me and news about my books, and you're free to unsubscribe at any time.

You can also find more information about all of my writing at my official website over at www.jswallow.com – and while you're there, you can download a free copy of ROUGH AIR, an all-new original Marc Dane eBook novella. Elsewhere on the World Wide Web, you can chat to me on Twitter at @jmswallow.

If you would like to get involved in the larger conversation about my books, please do review ROGUE on Amazon,

GoodReads, or your favourite site – or talk about it on your own blog and social media accounts, with friends, family or reader groups! Sharing your thoughts helps other readers, and I always enjoy hearing about what people experience from my writing.

Thanks again for your interest in ROGUE, and watch out for Marc Dane's next adventure in 2021!

Best regards,

James